Yours to Hold

By Darcy Burke

CONTEMPORARY ROMANCE

Ribbon Ridge

Where the Heart Is (a prequel Christmas novella)
Only In My Dreams
Yours to Hold

Coming soon

When Love Happens

HISTORICAL ROMANCE

Secrets and Scandals

Her Wicked Ways
His Wicked Heart
To Seduce a Scoundrel
To Love a Thief (a novella)
Never Love a Scoundrel
Scoundrel Ever After

Regency Treasure Hunters

The de Valery Code
Romancing the Earl
Raiders of the Lost Heart (2015)
The Legacy of an Extraordinary Gentleman (2016)

Yours to Hold

RIBBON RIDGE BOOK TWO

DARCY BURKE

AVONIMPULSE
An Imprint of HarperCollinsPublishers

This is a work of fiction. Names, characters, places, and incidents are products of the author's imagination or are used fictitiously and are not to be construed as real. Any resemblance to actual events, locales, organizations, or persons, living or dead, is entirely coincidental.

EPub Edition MARCH 2015 ISBN: 9780062389329

Print Edition ISBN: 9780062389312

AM 10 9 8 7 6 5 4 3 2 1

For my son, Zane, the storyteller.
Next time, I'll try to include Billy Bob the Shark
and his ever-present cache of dynamite.
Thank you for making me laugh
every single day. I love you!
#legit #rockstarzaniac #swagalicious

Chapter One

KYLE ARCHER WANTED answers. The elevator chimed as it hit the third floor. He stepped into the corridor, his gaze finding the list of medical offices, and more specifically, the name he sought.

PSYCHOLOGY, MAGGIE TRENT, PhD, 320

Following the arrow indicating the suite numbers, he turned left and strode down the hall with purpose. Suite 320 was on the right, about halfway down. Without pausing, he pushed open the door and took in the gurgling fountain in the corner, the instrumental music featuring what he thought was probably a lute and a sitar, and the muted lighting. He supposed it was meant to establish a calming environment, though none of it did anything to soothe the frustration that had taken root in his gut over the past week.

He went to the check-in window, which was closed. The glass slid open as he approached. A guy in his late twenties with brown, wavy hair and horn-rimmed glasses looked up at him. "May I help you?" he asked in a quiet, almost tranquilizing tone. His mouth relaxed into a pleasant, rather bland smile. He was probably trained to put people at ease, but he only set Kyle's teeth further on edge.

Kyle forced a brittle smile. "Hello, I have an appointment with Dr. Trent. I'm Cal Drogo." He tried not to smirk as he said the TV character name, but given the receptionist's lack of reaction, it was apparent he'd neither watched *Game of Thrones* nor read the books.

"Yes, Mr. Drogo." He glanced at his computer screen. "No insurance, is that right?"

"Yes."

The receptionist's lips pursed. "The scheduler explained that you'll receive a discount if you pay in full today?"

"She did. And I will." Kyle whisked out his wallet and handed over a hundred bucks. The fifty-minute appointment was ninety dollars without insurance.

Horn-rims gave him change and handed him a form on a clipboard. "You'll need to fill this out—front and back."

Kyle didn't touch the proffered item. "I explained that I didn't want to complete any paperwork before I meet the psychologist. It's part of my…paranoia." He glanced away in an effort to convince Horn-rims that he might suffer from some sort of anxiety disorder. Kyle was a lot of things, but anxious or high-strung wasn't one of them.

"I see. No problem." Another patronizing smile to accompany his sugar-sweet tone. "Have a seat, and we'll call you when it's time. Feel free to help yourself to some herbal tea." He indicated a minibar in the corner that surely lacked the accoutrements of a typical minibar. Bummer. Kyle could've used a stiff shot of something to get through the next hour. If this even took that long.

Kyle stowed his wallet in his back pocket and nodded. "Thanks, I'll check it out."

The tea station had no coffee and no tea with any caffeine. It did, however, have little bags of gluten-free crackers. How hypoallergenic.

"Cal Dr—" The feminine voice cut off. "Cal Drogo?" She sounded skeptical, and Kyle knew this one had gotten the joke.

He turned, smiling, then crossed the empty waiting room to where the young woman stood at an open door with a clipboard in her hand.

"Your name is seriously Cal Drogo? Like that massive guy on *Game of Thrones*?"

He'd needed a fake name, and it had been the first thing that had come to mind. Kyle, Cal, they sounded alike. Though he hadn't spelled it the same as the character. That would've been a dead giveaway. He'd take the little bits of humor he could find in life. "Weird, right?"

She laughed. "Totally. You're pretty tall, I'll give you that, but nowhere near dark enough. You look like a surfer dude."

"Guilty as charged." At six-three, he *was* nearly as tall as the actor on the show, but where that guy was tall, dark, and scary looking, Kyle was blond, blue-green-eyed, and in possession of a smile that said *I'm all about having a good time*. So far that had served him pretty well.

They turned a corner, and he followed her to a door at the end. Next to it was a shiny placard that read MAGGIE TRENT, PHD. Kyle's gut tightened, and just like that, his brief bout with good humor evaporated.

The young woman who'd escorted him smiled warmly. "Go on in, Mr. Drogo."

Kyle didn't spare her another glance as he moved into Dr. Trent's office. The door closed behind him as he stepped farther inside. Dr. Trent looked up from where she stood behind her desk. The smile curving her lips froze, and her eyes—dark like the TV show character whose name he'd borrowed—widened.

"Your name isn't Cal Drogo."

"What gave me away? I'm pretty sure your assistant, or whatever she is, doubted that was actually my name, but she went along with my joke. Why won't you?" Normally, his tone would be light, teasing. He could scarcely carry on a conversation without injecting some sort of humor or sarcasm. But he wasn't messing around with Maggie Trent, and so his words came out hard, clipped.

Her gaze turned wary. "I've seen your picture. You're Kyle Archer."

"Alex showed you pictures of us?" It bothered him to think his deceased brother had talked about them to a stranger, but then that's what you do in therapy, right?

Talk about your family? He wished he could ask Alex, but of course he couldn't. Not now. Not ever.

She nodded stiffly. "Yes. This," her voice squeaked, "this is highly inappropriate. I can't talk to you."

Kyle glanced around her cozy office. Besides her desk and the bookshelf behind it, there were windows, a leather couch, and a chair. He assumed the couch was for clients and the chair for her. He sat in the chair. "I figured you would say that. It's why I made the appointment under a fake name and refused to give them any of my information."

She scanned the paper on her desk and frowned. "You told them you were too paranoid to give that information over the phone."

He leaned back and put his feet up on the leather ottoman. "Yep, I did."

Straightening, she crossed her arms. She was more attractive than he'd envisioned. He'd pictured a middle-aged, dried-up hag with a pointy nose. Maybe with a little greenish tinge to her skin. He'd imagined a monster. How else would he see the woman who'd counseled his brother and failed to stop him from killing himself?

However, life was a cruel bitch, and Maggie Trent was quite pretty. She was about Kyle's age—twenty-eight—but had little pleats between her eyebrows that gave the sense she worried too much. Maybe *she* had anxiety.

She blinked—her eyes were the color of Dad's special recipe Christmas stout, dark and rich like bittersweet chocolate. A light freckle dotted her upper right cheek. He couldn't get a good sense of her hair because it was wound up on her head, though it was also dark, and little springy curls grazed the back of her neck.

"If you're done staring, you should go."

"No, I don't think so." He cracked a lazy smile, which didn't reflect the animosity roiling inside of him. "The going, I mean. I'm done staring."

She exhaled loudly and dropped her hands to her sides. "I'm not doing this. I'm really sorry about Alex. *So* sorry." Her voice broke, and she looked away toward the windows.

A pang of sorrow hit Kyle, and he hesitated. No, he was doing this for Alex.

That wasn't necessarily true. He was doing it for the entire family.

Kyle didn't want to prolong this interview, so he got right to the point. "How did my brother get the drugs he took?" He'd taken a mix of antidepressants, sleeping pills, and painkillers. A potentially lethal mix for anyone, but for someone with Alex's chronic lung disease, it was absolutely deadly.

She looked at him sharply, her gaze shrouded with anguish and regret. "I don't know." Her words carried the weight of unshed tears. "I...I cared about him a great deal."

He steeled himself against feeling sorry for her. "He was my brother. And he never should've been able to get his hands on drugs like that, not with his illness. He had to have obtained them illegally."

She shook her head. "I can't prescribe drugs. I'm not a medical doctor."

"I know that." He needed to move. He stood up and walked the length of the couch.

She backed up a step, even though her desk and several feet separated them. "Are you here to accuse me of something?"

"Like what, lethal incompetence? Yeah, I think you have to be a pretty shitty therapist if one of your clients killed himself. *You* have to live with that, though. I just want to know who contributed to my brother's death. What they're doing is illegal, and I'm going to put a stop to it."

Moisture gave her eyes a luminous sheen. "It won't bring him back."

"It'll make a lot of us feel better." He moved forward again. "There's a psychiatrist in this office. Did he give Alex the drugs?"

She shook her head, jostling the curls that grazed her neck. "No one would prescribe them to him—not with his condition. You're right that he had to have obtained them illegally. But I don't know how. He didn't discuss—" She sank down onto her chair. "I can't talk to you about this. It's unethical."

"Why? Are you telling me about his treatment? I haven't asked what you talked about, though I'm sure we'd all like to know. You do realize his suicide shocked the hell out of all of us? My family is a mess. Our parents are barely speaking to each other."

Her expression was pained, those lines between her eyes creased to full effect. "But you're back home. That's a good thing, right?"

Alex must have told her about him and that he'd moved to Florida almost four years ago. Like everyone else in his damn family, Alex believed he'd run away and had wanted him to come home. Kyle didn't think Alex had killed himself to provoke that, though he couldn't help but think it had made it onto his list of pros. As if Alex had sat down and made out a list of reasons to off himself and reasons to live. Even if he had, why hadn't the latter been long enough?

Kyle's chest tightened. "I don't think that's any of your business." He had enough trouble dealing with his family members regarding his return. He didn't need some shrink nosing in, too.

"You blame me," she said softly, her hand rising to her chest, where it fluttered briefly before dropping to her lap once more. "I'd blame me too, I think."

Damn, she was making it hard to be pissed at her. With those sad eyes and lips that were an inch from quivering—or so he imagined. He could also imagine kissing them. Now, *that* pissed him off.

He gritted his teeth. "So what are you going to do to make it right?"

She blinked at him and her eyes darkened, which he hadn't thought possible. The emotion around her mouth shifted into something harder. "If you think anyone can make this right, you're fooling yourself. Even if you find out how he got the drugs, it won't bring him back. It won't change the fact that he chose death over life." Now her lip did quiver. Exhaling roughly, she looked away again.

"It's the only thing I can do." Kyle shoved his remorse aside. It sounded like she might blame herself, but so did he. Hell, every person in their family carried a hefty piece of guilt. If he'd been here, maybe he would've seen something to indicate his state of mind. His sister Sara, who *had* been here, insisted that wouldn't have been possible.

"I don't think that's true. I think you honor Alex by coming back here, by rejoining your family." She glanced at him nervously. "*If* that's what you're doing. I don't mean to presume."

"Keep your therapy to yourself. It didn't help Alex, and I don't want what you're selling, *doctor*." He set his hands on his hips, his forefingers dipping into the pockets of his jeans. "I want those drug dealers, whoever they are, to pay."

She stood and crossed her arms across her chest again, as if they could provide some sort of defense against his anger. "I told you already that I can't help you with that."

"Did he talk to the psychiatrist here?"

She shook her head. "I didn't even work here then. I had my own practice in Ribbon Ridge."

"Which you conveniently shut down after Alex died."

"There was nothing convenient about it," she snapped. "I was devastated." She flicked him an uneasy glance and edged closer to her desk. "I think you should go."

"I'm not finished."

Her gaze turned stoic. "I'll call security if I have to."

"Security? Do you feel threatened?"

She tightened her arms around herself. "I don't feel comfortable."

"Then welcome to our hell." He pulled out the business card he'd stashed in his front pocket. He dropped the creased rectangle on her desk. The Archer logo with its *A* shaped into a bow and arrow stared up from the face. "Call me when you have information to share—and don't tell me you don't have anything. You talked to my brother—what, every week for nearly a year? I'm sure you'll think of something that can help me." He speared her with an icy glare. "It's the least you can do."

Her look of remorse did nothing to ease his frustration at walking away empty-handed, but he hoped she'd come around. She had to have something that could help him track down the person—or people—who'd provided Alex with the means to kill himself. If she didn't…He refused to go down that path.

He turned and strode from her office, leaving the door ajar as he went. Her assistant was in the corridor. "Finished already?" she asked.

"For now," he said darkly, not bothering to adjust his tone.

A half hour later, he walked into the headquarters of Archer Enterprises on the southwestern edge of Ribbon Ridge. Home to nearly fifty employees, it oversaw operations of nine brewpubs and countless real estate endeavors. The two-story building, designed to Dad's specifications about eight years prior, sprawled at the edge of wine country with epic views. Yet, stepping inside never failed to jolt Kyle with uneasiness. He was filling in for his younger brother Hayden while he was on a year-long leave of absence making wine in France. And Kyle was, as everyone liked to point out, no Hayden.

Nodding at the receptionist as he passed, he took the central curving staircase up to the second floor.

Hayden's—rather, Kyle's—office was toward the southeast corner, situated between his dad and Derek Sumner, the two people who currently despised him most. Altogether, the work environment was *awesome*.

The executive assistant he shared with Derek looked up at him as he approached. "Hey, Kyle. How was your lunch?"

Natalie Frobish was young, attractive, and worked like a fiend. She was the first person there in the morning and the last one who left at night. She'd only been with Archer two years—since graduating from nearby Williver College—but both Dad and Derek constantly remarked how Archer would be lost without her. Kyle was pretty sure Dad wanted to promote her to his assistant when his retired next year. But it didn't take a rocket scientist to see Natalie had ambition, and Kyle thought her upward mobility at Archer would move her out of the executive assistant category before that could happen.

"It was fine." He hadn't told anyone he'd planned to ambush Dr. Trent. Better to keep his plans to himself until he had something important to share. He *hoped* he'd have something important to share—and soon.

Natalie gestured for him to come around to her desk. It was tucked behind a counter at which she greeted those who visited the executive wing.

Since she was being a bit secretive, Kyle glanced around, but the office was quiet. Dad's assistant, Paula, was out to lunch, and Dad's office door was closed. Derek, who was CFO, didn't seem to be about either. Kyle stepped around to where Natalie was sitting. "What's up?" he asked quietly.

Her dark eyes—maybe a shade lighter than Dr. Trent's—found his, and she pointed at her computer screen, which showed a large bouquet of flowers. "Paula and I were thinking of sending these to Emily from Rob."

Too bad Dad hadn't thought to send flowers to his wife on his own. Things between them had been strained since Alex's death, and then Mom had gone to France with Hayden almost two months ago. Kyle and his siblings hoped this separation would help both of them heal.

He'd spoken to Mom several times, and she sounded better, more relaxed. Dad, however, was as tense and short-tempered as ever. It was like he just didn't want to deal with the grief at all, so he shoved it away. Since he was already pissed at Kyle from four years ago, their relationship was as uneasy as ever. Kyle's desire to help his father find some closure following Alex's death had prompted Kyle to track down how Alex had obtained the drugs he'd used to kill himself. And scoring some points in the meantime wouldn't be a bad thing.

Kyle put his hand on her desk as he leaned down to look at the flower arrangement. "It's a nice sentiment, but I wouldn't do it. I'm not sure how things are between them." They'd find out when Mom came home in a few weeks for Derek's wedding.

"Okay, it was just a thought." Natalie touched Kyle's hand, catching him a bit off guard with the gesture. "I really care about your dad—about all of you. Paula does, too." She smiled brightly.

Kyle withdrew his hand from beneath hers and moved back around to the other side of her desk. "It was a good idea. Just maybe not right now." Dad was so uptight all of the time—Kyle and his siblings were all worried about him.

Dad's office door opened. His slate-gray eyes landed on Kyle. "I thought I heard you."

"Hey, Dad." Though they had yet to discuss Kyle's departure four years ago, Kyle knew it was coming at some point. Dad was still pissed that Kyle hadn't accepted the job he'd offered, and Kyle was still frustrated with how Dad had meddled in his life. And if he were truly honest with himself, he was ashamed, too. A conversation would happen someday, preferably when Dad was in a more positive mental state.

"Come in here for a minute." Dad turned from the door and went back behind his desk. When Kyle came in, he said, "Shut the door." *Uh-oh.* Dad sat down.

Kyle didn't want to sit, so he stood in the center of the office and folded his arms over his chest. "What's up?"

Dad glanced at the chair, registered that Kyle wasn't going to get comfortable, and briefly pressed his lips together. "Have you and Derek nailed down the details for our booth at the Ribbon Ridge Festival?"

"Nearly." Though it was taking forever, as they were communicating almost entirely by e-mail.

"You know, things might happen faster if you and Derek actually talked."

Probably, but the rift between Kyle and his former best friend was deep. He imagined they would've lost touch entirely if Derek hadn't moved in with the Archers during their senior year of high school when his mother died and he'd subsequently become the de facto eighth Archer sibling. Now Derek was as much a part of their family as Kyle. And, like the situation with Dad, Kyle didn't think they could ignore the past forever. But he was fine doing it for now. Better than fine. "Hey, don't blame me."

Dad leaned back in his chair, his gaze cool with skepticism. "So if Derek came to you tomorrow and said, 'Let's start over, forget what happened four years ago,' you'd drop whatever grudge you're holding and move on?"

Derek had betrayed him. He owed Kyle an apology, and it was *never* going to come. Fuck it. "We'll take care of it." Kyle's response was clipped. He itched to turn and leave.

"How? I want to know how you're going to improve your working relationship at least. When I agreed to let you fill in for Hayden, I expected you to behave professionally."

Kyle dropped his arms to his sides. "Haven't I? If you have an issue with how I've performed, I'd like to hear it." Kyle hadn't really known the first thing about being a chief operating officer, but Hayden had been very helpful, even from France. Kyle had worked harder than he'd ever worked in his life to try to prove himself, and he was sick of taking the brunt of Dad's grief and anger. "When are you going to cut me some slack?"

"When you're ready to talk about what happened before you ran off." Dad set his forearms on his desk, which had become far more cluttered than Kyle ever remembered it being. "You never even thanked me."

The familiar resentment gathered in Kyle's chest, made him grit his teeth. "Because I didn't ask for your help. I had things under control."

Dad's eyes narrowed. "You didn't, and the fact that you still don't realize that is why I don't cut you any slack."

Kyle threw up his hands. "I guess my coming back and participating in Alex's project and taking over for Hayden didn't earn me any points at all." He turned to go.

"Is that why you're doing all of this, to earn points?"

Not precisely. He'd wanted to see if he could make something of himself in the face of everyone's doubt—Alex had given him a perfect opportunity. "I wanted to come home."

"For how long?" Dad asked quietly. "You need to regain my trust, Kyle. You need to regain everyone's trust. And you're not going to do that if you don't actually engage and really come *back*."

What more could he do? He was afraid he knew the answer—patch things up with Derek—but he wasn't ready for that. Not yet. "I am back, Dad, and I'm doing the best I can. Too bad it's never been enough."

MAGGIE PRESSED THE button on her iPhone and watched the screen light up, but instead of punching in her password, she pushed the top button to darken the screen again. Over and over, her fingers moved around the device—screen on, screen off.

Finally, Amy's door opened, and the friendly face of her therapist gave Maggie a much-needed wave of relief.

She got to her feet in the tiny waiting room and made her way to Amy's office.

"Maggie, come in." Amy's fifty-something face creased with concern. "I'm so glad I had a cancellation and could fit you in this morning. Your message yesterday afternoon was so frantic, and now, looking at you…I can see you're stressed."

Stressed was probably an understatement. Freaking out was a much better description. "Kyle Archer came to see me yesterday," she blurted.

Amy closed the door behind Maggie. "I see." As always, her response was calm and mellow. There was never any drama with Amy, but then, wasn't that a therapist's job? Maggie was able to treat her own patients with drama-free composure even while her own life was a complete disaster.

Okay, that wasn't precisely accurate. For a while there, she'd hadn't even been able to *see* patients because she'd barely been able to get out of bed.

Maggie sat on Amy's cozy suede couch, which was situated next to a bank of four windows that looked out over some of the northern Willamette Valley's most beautiful wine country. Grapevines marched in neat lines up the hillside, giving a sense of order to nature's utter randomness. But then that's what they, as people, did. They tried to make sense of the chaos. In the end, however, it didn't matter. Disorder and unpredictability would always win out. Someday those tidy rows would be overgrown, and the grapes would go wild.

"Maggie?" Amy said softly. "Have you been meditating like we discussed?"

"Yes." Until yesterday. "But last night I was too upset. I pruned a rosebush to within an inch of its life and then drowned myself in a book and a glass of pinot."

Amy's answering smile was understanding. "That's all right. You don't need my permission or approval. I just wanted to make sure you're taking care of yourself."

"I am." Anxiety bunched through her shoulders, and she tried to push them back in protest. *This would not control her.* "Yesterday just threw me for a loop. I wasn't expecting to see another Archer, let alone Kyle."

"Why not Kyle?" Amy picked up a notepad from her desk on the other side of the office and sat in her oversized chair facing the couch.

"Because he lives in Florida. *Lived.* I don't know. I guess he came home after...." Why couldn't she say the words? She'd worked so hard over the past five months to get to a place where she could think of what had happened without losing her breath. But after seeing Kyle—and the familiar angle of his nose that reminded her so much of Alex—she was lost again.

"You can say it." Amy's tone was comforting, but firm.

"Alex's death." Maggie felt like she'd run a mile. "After Alex's death."

Amy's lips curved into a warm smile as she scratched notes across the paper in her lap.

Maggie could imagine what she was writing. *Clearly anxious. Emotional trauma. Potential relapse.*

No, she wouldn't go back to those weeks when she'd relied on a steady dose of Xanax and could barely bother to shower, let alone eat. Just being here in Amy's office meant that she was well enough to take care of herself, that she was able to get help when she needed it. How many times had she told her own patients that this was half the battle?

"Where are you?" Amy asked, with a hint of a smile. "I can see you're either working yourself into a fine lather over this man's visit yesterday or effectively talking yourself down from the ledge."

The brief pang of relief Maggie had felt in the waiting room crested over her again, this time with a more lasting sensation. "Currently working on the latter."

"Excellent. You're doing well. Do you want to tell me about the visit, or is just being here enough?"

Amy was a great therapist. She got to know each patient, learned their strengths and weaknesses, and read their moods. She knew that on some occasions, just coming to her office was enough to jump-start a patient on the right path. Though Maggie was still trying to find where her path led...Acceptance? Exoneration? Forgiveness?

All of those things and probably much more. They'd only just begun to dig past the trauma of Alex's suicide to get to the heart of Maggie's issues. Her mom. Her ex. It was astonishing how one could provide therapy for other people and yet inhabit a life that was a complete and utter mess.

"I think..." Maggie's mind turned over itself, and her thumb ran across the screen of her phone. Realizing this, she tossed the device onto the coffee table in front of her.

"He wanted to know how Alex had gotten the drugs to kill himself."

Amy's nostrils flared. They'd discussed this many times. Maggie had also wanted to know how he'd gotten the drugs—a sleeping pill, an antidepressant, and a painkiller—that he'd used to kill himself. He'd obtained prescription-level narcotics from somewhere, and it hadn't been from her.

"We'd all like to know that." Amy shook her head ruefully.

"Kyle asked if Dr. Innes had prescribed them."

Amy looked as horrified as Maggie had felt. "No psychiatrist would have, not with his medical history."

Talking felt good. Some of the tension left Maggie's body. "I told him that. And that I didn't know where Alex had gotten the drugs and couldn't help him. But I don't think he's going to leave it alone."

"You think he'll bother you? If he starts to harass you—"

"Oh, I won't let that happen." Maggie had experience with restraining orders after her ex-boyfriend had taken issue with her breaking up with him.

Amy nodded. "I know. You're very capable. But Kyle Archer isn't Mark Fielding."

Thank God. "No, he's not."

Amy jotted a note on her pad and then cocked her head to the side. "How was Mr. Archer with you? Was he intimidating?"

Maggie went back over their encounter, which was easy to do since she'd replayed it a thousand times since yesterday afternoon. "He was...angry, but I never felt afraid." Uncomfortable? Yes. But she recognized now that her discomfort came from his grief and her feeling responsible for it. "To get rid of him, I threatened to call security." And that seemed to have worked, which told her he was far more reasonable than her ex.

"Did you recognize his anger came from a sympathetic place?"

Of course—the man was grieving his brother's death. As devastating as Alex's suicide had been to Maggie, she knew her pain paled to that of his family's. His sister Tori had left several messages in the weeks following Alex's death. She'd asked if Maggie had known he was suicidal and why he had done it. Maggie hadn't returned the calls. What could she have said?

Compassion eased her anguish, and she let the emotion seep into her bones. She closed her eyes for a moment, and when she opened them, knew she appeared sheepish. "Perhaps I'm overreacting."

"Not at all. This was a traumatic event. Don't discount your own feelings and reactions because you think they aren't somehow worthy or earned. There is no finite amount of grief to go around here—you feel what you feel, and you're entitled to it."

Intellectually, Maggie knew this, but emotionally? Gah, she was such a disaster. She dropped her forehead into her hands. "Maybe I shouldn't have gone back to work. Maybe I should be teaching or something. What's that saying? *If you can't do it, coach*?"

Amy laughed. "The very tenet of our profession. We're all messed up, Maggie. It's why we help others not to be. *Do as I say, not as I do*—there's another saying for you."

Maggie thought about why she'd chosen to become a therapist in the first place. She liked problem-solving and helping others. That this career path was a disappointment to her parents—they'd really hoped that Maggie and her brother would pursue their artistic sides—had been an added bonus. She'd been eager to separate herself from them as much as possible. And maybe, no probably, she'd hoped that counseling others would give her the ability to work through her own issues. She was still waiting for that part to kick in, which made Amy's comment truer than ever. "You're right."

Amy went back to nodding—a default action for any therapist—and wrote on her pad. Her gun-metal gray bob swung against her jawbone as she looked up once more. "Do you think you'll see Kyle again?"

"I hope not." In another life, she might've liked to. Whenever Alex had shared pictures of his family, her eye had always been drawn to the tall, blond god whose megawatt grin surely lit up every room he entered. But the man she'd met yesterday, though still attractive, hadn't looked a thing like the Kyle who'd always intrigued her, the brother who'd disappointed everyone and who Alex had said was his hero.

Because he was fearless.

Yes, he'd made mistakes, which Alex hadn't delved too deeply into, but Kyle did everything with gusto and a love for life that most people never had. The envy in Alex's voice when he'd spoken of his brother had always pierced Maggie's heart. Probably because she had no idea what living one's life with that sort of joy felt like.

"Where's your mind at right now?" Amy interrupted Maggie's total rathole train of thought.

Maggie shook her head. "Sorry. I was thinking about Alex and Kyle's relationship. Kyle left Ribbon Ridge rather abruptly a few years back. The family took it hard, and from what Alex said, they pretty much treat him like a massive disappointment."

"Ah." Amy made a note. "He's looking for some approval and acceptance then."

"Should I have tried to help him? I'd actually like to know how Alex got those drugs, too." Maybe solving that mystery would appease some of her guilt. The person inside of her wanted to cling to that even while the therapist told her it didn't work that way.

"If you do, you'll need to do it for the right reasons."

Maggie finished what Amy didn't say in her head: *Don't expect it to alleviate the pain. It might push it away for a while, but only one thing will ease your grief: time.* How she hated telling patients that, even though she knew it was true. She was particularly glad Amy hadn't said it out loud to her.

"I'm not saying I'm going to help him." But she was thinking it. Geez, the more she thought about it, the more she was *interested* in helping him. "Would it be bad if I did?"

Amy shrugged. "That depends. If you're doing it to find some healing and comfort for yourself and for him and his family, then probably not. But, Maggie, I have to wonder if any association with the Archer family is a good idea. You closed your practice in Ribbon Ridge and moved out of that bungalow you loved because you said you couldn't face the Archers."

Right. And they owned over half of Ribbon Ridge. Hell, they owned a good part of the entire county and had for over a century. "I did love that bungalow." Especially the garden—the English daisies would be in full bloom right now. "You're right. The Archers have every reason to despise me." The animosity in Kyle's tone yesterday pinged in her memory. "I don't want to cause them any more pain."

He'd told her she'd think of something to help him. Was he waiting for her to call him with information? She didn't know anything.

"So you're going to leave it alone?" Amy asked.

"Yes." There was nothing she could do anyway, even if she wanted to. And she sort of did. *Careful, Maggie...*

They spent the rest of the fifty-minute appointment discussing Maggie's transition to the new practice and whether some of her former clients had followed her. They had—which had surprised Maggie. One of her patients had killed himself. She would've thought people would steer clear of her brand of treatment. However, Amy and a handful of friends from grad school had persuaded Maggie to not only start again, but to stay in the same area. They'd been right—the patients who had followed her needed her, and they didn't blame her. What's more, the consistency of staying with them had done wonders for her own sense of self-worth.

By the time she left, she was feeling much better and had convinced herself that things were never as bad as they seemed.

Then her phone buzzed in her purse. She'd left it on silent after the appointment. Sliding it from the front pocket as she used her key fob to unlock her ten-year-old Jetta, she glanced at the caller ID on the screen only briefly before sliding her thumb across it. Damn, was it too late to simply hang up and pretend the call had dropped?

No, she'd just call back.

Maggie forced a smile into her voice. If she didn't, there would be an inquisition. "Hi, Mom."

"Hello, my little flower bud. Haven't heard from you since dinner last week. We haven't had a chance to discuss Rowan's new girlfriend. She's a little uptight, don't you think?"

Maggie slid into the car and closed the door. "Mom, you think everyone we've ever dated is uptight." Though in this case, Maggie agreed that her younger brother's latest was at least high maintenance. Designer purse? Check. Immaculate hair and nails? Double check. Name dropping, need to impress, and overly touchy with Rowan? Triple check. But it was natural that he'd go for either someone just like his mother or the polar opposite. Rowan was definitely a polar opposite guy. Not that Maggie hadn't done the exact same thing with Mark.

"Well, that's probably true." Mom made some sort of noise away from the phone—it sounded like she was talking to one of her two dogs. "At least he's dating someone," she said with a hint of accusation that was impossible to ignore.

Maggie stuck her key in the ignition but didn't turn it. "Hey, you're the one who encouraged me to put myself and my goals first. That's what I'm doing."

"And I will always encourage you to do that. But I know you, dear. Better than you know yourself." Nothing she said grated Maggie's nerves more than that. "You need someone in your life. Someone you can take care of." *Because then maybe you'll take better care of yourself.* The words, spoken so many times before, hung on the phone line between them.

"Mom, can I call you later? I was just getting into my car, and I need to get to an appointment."

"Oh! I didn't mean to keep you. I always forget to ask if it's a good time to talk. Just cut me off in the future, will you?"

Hadn't she just done that? "I'll try. Talk to you later."

Maggie ended the call and started her car. She didn't really have an appointment—it was Wednesday, and she didn't see patients on Wednesdays. She did have some work she could do, but instead of driving to the clinic or home to work in her office, she found herself at the local nursery.

Twenty-five bucks and two flats of premium annuals later, she went home and did the only thing that would absolutely soothe her—she got herself nice and dirty.

Chapter Two

KYLE PULLED INTO the large dirt lot that served as the parking area of The Alex. He still smiled when he thought of Sara coming up with the idea to name their brother's dying wish after him. It only made sense.

The hundred-plus-year-old monastery rose in front of him, its church spire stretching two hundred feet into the vivid blue summer sky. The sounds of construction came from the west end of the property. A dirt lane led to what had once been a small house occupied by the head monk or whoever had been in charge at the monastery before it had been abandoned twenty-odd years ago. Phase one of the project Alex had conceived—renovating the property into a premier hotel and event destination—was underway. It would be the newest space and the first of its kind under the Archer name, which included nine brewpubs across the northern valley and into Portland.

Alex had purchased the property using the trust fund left to each of them by their grandfather, then set up a trust for each sibling to inherit an equal share of the project. He'd planned for everyone to participate in the renovation, assigning key roles to every sibling. And he'd made his attorney, Aubrey Tallinger, the trustee.

She'd endured copious amounts of anger and blame immediately following Alex's suicide, because to all of them, it had seemed unlikely that she'd established the trust without knowing what Alex had planned. But she insisted she hadn't known, that Alex had told her he was simply preparing in the event that he died young, something he'd convinced her was likely with his chronic lung disease.

However, things hadn't quite worked out the way Alex had envisioned. Not everyone had been eager to return to Ribbon Ridge, least of all Kyle. He'd declined to come at first, as had Liam and Evan, but Kyle had come home a few months later. Alex's project had given him a purpose, but it wasn't the sole reason he'd fled Florida.

A sharp prick of regret pierced his chest. He shook the discomfort away. He'd fucked up. A lot. And he was trying to fix it. He owed it to Alex.

While Alex had been tethered at home with his oxygen tank and debilitating illness, the rest of them had gone off and pursued their dreams. Well, all but Hayden. As the youngest, he'd sort of gotten stuck staying in Ribbon Ridge and working for the family company. His participation in the project should've been a given, but then his dream had finally knocked down his door, and he was currently in France for a yearlong internship at a winery.

Kyle stepped out of Hayden's black Honda Pilot. He'd completely taken over his brother's life while Hayden was off making wine—his car, his job, his house. Too bad Kyle couldn't also borrow the respect and appreciation Hayden received.

He slammed the car door. It wasn't going to be that easy, and he didn't deserve it to be. He should be driving his own goddamned car, but he'd had to sell it before leaving Florida so the same shit that had driven him from Ribbon Ridge wouldn't also drive him from Miami.

But hadn't it? *No.* Things hadn't gotten as bad as they had four years ago. No one had bailed his ass out this time. He'd learned. He wasn't the same man.

His sister Tori stepped out of the trailer that served as the site office. She slid a pair of dark glasses on and fidgeted with her long, straight hair, now sporting some light streaks. He swore she changed something about her hair color every couple of weeks.

"Hey, sis," he said, striding over to her.

"Hey. Did we have a meeting?" She looked up at him, though he couldn't see her eyes behind the sunglasses.

"No." And it wasn't like her to even ask a question like that. She was the most organized, the most managerial, the most *anal* of all of them. "Just here checking on the progress. What's up with the cabinetry?"

The wrong color had been delivered a few days prior. Kyle had almost felt sorry for the sales rep when not one,

but two Archer women ripped him a new one. After
Tori had chewed him out, Sara had called him back and
demanded a discount for the fuckup. Reticent in their
youth, Sara had blossomed into a capable and formidable
force of nature. Kyle couldn't have been prouder of his
youngest sister.

"They're delivering the right color on Monday. Dylan
also worked a deal to get the cabinetry for the restaurant
at a reduced rate."

Even the contractor had taken a piece out of them?
Now Kyle did feel sorry for the cabinet guy. Dylan was
ex-military and could be a total hard-ass. He was also
Sara's boyfriend, and he was as committed to this project as the rest of them. Maybe even more, since he'd
worked his butt off to land the entire construction
project.

"What does that do to the schedule?" Kyle asked. The
renovation of the house into a midsized entertainment
space was being managed by Sara, who was an event
planner, and was due to be finished by early August. They
had to make the date because Derek and Chloe were getting married here.

"Dylan says he's working around it. It's going to be
tight, but we knew it would be."

"I'll offer to help out again this weekend." Kyle had
worked onsite with Dylan and his crew the past couple
of Saturdays. He'd become quite accomplished at grout-
ing tile.

Tori offered a rare but fleeting smile. "Careful, or
you'll make yourself indispensable, and when you run

back to Florida, everyone will be even more pissed than last time."

He knew she was kidding. Wasn't she? She and Sara had gone easier on him since he and Sara had patched things up last month. Of all his siblings, he shared the closest bond with Sara, and his leaving four years ago had impacted her the most. He'd apologized but still hadn't come completely clean about why he'd left. And he wasn't sure he ever would. There was only so much disappointment one could endure.

He decided to ignore the comment altogether. "Are your latest restaurant drawings in the trailer?"

She nodded. "I'm ready to submit them for permits if you are."

"I think so." He'd been over them a million times, ensuring everything was perfect, but he was petrified he was missing something. Seems like if you heard that you were a screw-up enough times, you began to believe it. "I'll let you know later if I have any final changes."

"Okay," she said, a tinge of admonishment in her voice, "but don't add any more refrigerators or stoves or anything. I'll have to redraw the entire power grid."

He grinned, knowing he'd made some changes that had likely driven her nuts. "Gotcha, sis."

"Does that mean I'll see you for dinner tonight?"

Kyle often went and cooked dinner for Tori at the Archer family house, which is where she stayed when she was in town. Sara and Dylan joined them from time to time, and it was always a fun evening. "Will Dad be there?" Kyle had been avoiding him since their confrontation the other day.

"Probably. Why does it matter? You've come and cooked for him before." Tori slid her purse strap over her shoulder. "You should talk to him."

He should. And he would. When he had something good to say—when he could tell Dad who had supplied Alex with the drugs. Then maybe Dad could move on. Or grieve. Or whatever he needed to do. "It's not just me, you know."

"I do. Alex's death devastated him. I think he's even worse off than Mom was—not that you were here for that."

He glared at her. "Thanks for the dig. At least I came home later, which is more than I can say for some of our siblings."

"Sorry." But the flash in her gaze said she wasn't really. "It was a really shitty time."

"I know, and if I could go back, I would've stayed." Would he have? Yes, and not just because it would've avoided the problems he'd spiraled into in Miami.

She pushed her sunglasses up into her hair. Her blue-green eyes, the same color as his, clouded with concern. "I want to believe that, Kyle, but it's so hard when there seems to be this thing…I don't know. I just don't understand why you disappeared like that, why you rarely came home. It's like you just forgot you had a family for four years."

"I didn't forget. Why is it that Liam can leave Ribbon Ridge without anyone accusing him of turning his back on the family? For that matter, why can *you*?" She lived in San Francisco and was only here temporarily for the renovation.

She pursed her lips. "You know it's not the same."

"That's right. The rules aren't the same for everyone in this family, and I'm tired of it. No, I won't see you for dinner." He stalked off toward the job site without looking back at her. The sound of her car firing up and pulling out of the lot drained the tension from his shoulder blades.

This was why he hadn't come home sooner. He couldn't stand the scrutiny, the meddling. Growing up, people always commented on how great it must be to live in such a big, loving family. In reality, it was a major pain in the ass.

After talking with Dylan and arranging to help out on Saturday, he went to the trailer and reviewed the drawings. Still annoyed by his conversation with Tori, he decided to take the drawings and leave before she got back from lunch.

His mind went back to Dad and trying to find a way to demonstrate that he was worthy of respect and trust and…love. Kyle was doing his best at Archer and here on The Alex. Add that to discovering the identity of Alex's drug dealer, and Dad would see how much Kyle had changed, that he could be proud of him.

Kyle turned the Bluetooth on in the car and dialed the number of Maggie Trent's office. The ultra-mellow receptionist dude answered, "Mental Health Services."

Christ, that guy's voice would sedate a sleepwalker.

"Yeah, hi. May I speak with Dr. Trent?" Kyle looked at the clock—it was 1:23. He knew from scheduling his appointment that her lunch ran from twelve thirty to two. Hopefully she was in the office. "She should be free right now," he added, in case the guy wanted to send him to voicemail.

"May I say who's calling?"

"Cal Drogo."

"Thank you, Mr. Drogo. Hold on, please."

Kyle fought the urge to take a nap as a result of the receptionist's droning voice and the hypnotic lute hold music.

"Mr. Drogo?"

Kyle couldn't be sure, but he didn't think that was Maggie Trent's sultry voice.

Sultry? What the hell?

"Yes?"

"This is Dr. Trent's assistant, Stacy. Listen, I know who you are, Mr. Archer. She asked me to tell you that she doesn't have any information for you and wishes you luck in your endeavor."

"I need to speak with her, please."

"No, you don't."

The annoyance he'd felt toward his sister earlier came back with a vengeance. "Actually I do."

"She's not coming to the phone, okay? Sorry, but have a nice day."

Click.

He growled in frustration as he redialed the number.

Again, Monotone Man answered. This time, Kyle altered his voice, pitching it lower. "Hello, my name is Ned Stark. Dr. Trent is expecting my call at one thirty." Kyle glanced at the clock. *Close enough.* "She told me to ask you to put me straight through to her office."

"Will do."

More fucking lute music. This time with a dash of sitar thrown in. *Awesome.*

Coming off the hill on which the monastery was perched, he pulled onto the main road that went through Ribbon Ridge and, after a few blocks, turned right toward Archer Enterprises.

"Ned Stark? Really?" The assistant's voice again. "You do realize I watch *Game of Thrones*? That I said as much the other day?"

Of course he knew that. "I wasn't expecting to have to talk to you again."

"Clearly. Your attempt to get straight to Dr. Trent, while amusing, was a complete fail. Do yourself a favor and think twice before calling back as Jon Snow."

She hung up again.

Goddamn it.

Kyle gave up trying to get the woman on the phone. What the hell was her problem? He'd been clear about wanting—no, needing—her help. She'd spent hours and hours with his brother. She might know something about where Alex had gotten his drugs. Something she didn't even realize was *something.*

Why wouldn't she help him? Kyle had the impression she'd held Alex in high regard. Her reaction had been that of someone who'd cared about Alex, but then she likely cared for all of her patients. Enough to close up her practice in Ribbon Ridge and start over someplace else? No. There had to be something more going on. Her dark eyes had been full of emotion—anxiety, concern, trepidation—and he meant to find out why.

He had a vague idea of her overall schedule from when he'd set his appointment. Monotone Man had asked him if he'd needed an evening appointment, which was available on Thursdays. Today was Thursday, and her last appointment would be over at eight o'clock.

Gripping his steering wheel with grim determination, he made plans to be there waiting for her.

MAGGIE LOCKED THE main door of the office and took the elevator down to the lobby. It was almost dark outside, but the remnants of the sun cast a pale glow on the partially cloudy sky. The automatic doors slid open, and she stepped into the summer night, inhaling the scent of grass and juniper.

She turned to the right, toward her car, and jumped as a figure moved into her path from the shadow of the building.

She shrieked and threw her purse and keys, the former landing at her feet and the latter ending up who-knew-where.

Kyle Archer's face came into the light of the parking lot lamp. His expression was one of surprise, which really pissed her off, as he'd been the one to scare her.

"God, you're an asshole!" she yelled, her hands shaking and her stomach twisting in knots. Mark had done this to her four or five times before she'd gone to get the restraining order. He'd wait for her to leave the library or finish up her intern shift at the hospital, then jump out at her from the shadows in an effort to convince her that he loved her and she should come back to him. Except sane men didn't menace the women they loved or make them feel unsafe.

"Let me get that." Kyle bent and tried to retrieve her purse.

She slapped his hand away. "Don't touch it. Just leave me alone."

"Hey, I'm sorry." He sounded genuinely concerned.

She glanced at him and saw that he also looked genuinely concerned.

"I didn't mean to spook you. I just wanted to talk. Lurking in the dark was maybe not my best move. I've been waiting like forty minutes, so I sat over there." He gestured to a bench tucked against the side of the building, completely out of range of the light. Perfect place for a stalker to lie in wait.

"I need to point that out to security," she muttered, picking up her purse and slinging it over her shoulder.

"What?" he asked.

"You're lucky I didn't bring my laptop tonight. If I'd dropped that and it had broken, you'd be buying me a new one."

"I absolutely would. Is there a chance you broke anything in your purse that I ought to replace? A tube of lipstick perhaps? Or a bottle of hand sanitizer?"

She looked at him quizzically, not sure what to make of his questions. "Aren't those usually plastic?"

"Plastic can break." His eyes narrowed slightly again—with concern, like before. "Are you sure you're all right? I feel really terrible about scaring you."

"I'm fine." Her hands were still a little quivery, but she wasn't going to tell him that.

He gave her a long, assessing look. "Okay. So can I buy you a drink or something?"

"Hell no!" He had the nerve to ask her out after scaring the shit out of her?

His eyes narrowed once more, but this time with some other emotion. Irritation maybe. "Not on a date or anything...social. I want to talk to you about my brother. I told you I wanted your help."

"And I told you—via Stacy—that I have nothing to tell you."

"Maybe you think that, but if you could just spend fifteen minutes answering some questions. We can sit in your car, if you like."

Like she'd invite him into her car as if they were on some teenage make-out date? She envisioned sitting in the backseat with him, the windows steamed, their lips locked, his hand creeping up her thigh...

Damn, where had that come from?

Her overactive, undersexed imagination that found him totally hot; wasn't it obvious?

"I'm not sitting in my car with you." She turned to go and realized she didn't have her keys. She bent over and scanned the pavement. "I dropped my keys."

"Let me help you find them."

She cast him a dubious glance. "I don't think I want any of your 'help.'"

He joined her in searching anyway. "Hey, I already apologized. A lot. I'm really, really sorry."

She widened her search area. "Do you stalk lots of women?"

"Nope, you're my first. Usually it's the other way around."

She nearly laughed but reminded herself she couldn't get cozy with this guy.

"I don't see them," he said.

"Me neither."

"Maybe they're in your purse?"

Maybe. She'd thought they were in her hand, but it was possible she'd dropped them into her purse, which was a bottomless pit. She could dump it out, but then he'd see what a mess it was—five million receipts, twelve pens, three tubes of lip balm, perhaps even Jimmy Hoffa.

She went to the light and opened her purse as wide as she could. "You keep looking on the ground," she said as she rifled through the pockets of the abyss of her handbag. After a few minutes, she gave up. She couldn't see, feel, or hear them anywhere. "They have to be on the ground somewhere."

"Did you leave them upstairs?" he asked.

"No, I had them in my hand." Her finger had already been poised on the unlock button on the fob.

He stopped his search, setting his hands low on his hips. "Are you sure?"

"You're going to second-guess me after scaring me senseless? You really are a class-A jerk." She pulled her phone from the front pocket of her purse and punched in her password.

"What are you doing?"

She glared at him. "Calling a cab. I'm tired. I want to go home. And thanks to you, I have no way to get there."

"What about finding your keys? Maybe they fell into the bushes." He gestured to the thick junipers next to the walkway.

"Unless you have a flashlight, don't bother. I'll get them in the morning when I can be sure I'm not sticking my hand into a hobo spider's hideaway." Although the idea of *him* putting his hand within reach of a nasty spider with a poisonous bite maybe wasn't a bad idea…

He took a step toward her. "Let me drive you home."

She glanced up at him before continuing her search for a cab company. "No."

"It's the least I can do. I'm trying to do the right thing here. You could at least acknowledge that."

"No, *thank you*."

He moved closer and peered at her phone. "You can't take a cab. That'll take forever, and you'll spend at least seventy-five bucks. Please let me drive you home?"

As much as she wanted to refuse him, she recognized that waiting for a cab all the way out here would probably take an hour, and it would cost a fortune.

"Fine—since it's your fault I'm even in this mess."

"So it is." He turned toward the parking lot and gestured toward a black SUV, one of only a handful of cars remaining at this hour. "Honda Pilot, over there at two o'clock."

She stepped off the curb, and he walked beside her.

"Now that I have your attention, why don't you help me figure out where Alex got his drugs?"

She glanced at him, the parking lot lights illuminating the rugged planes of his face in profile. "I already told you, *several times*, that I don't know anything that would help you."

"Who did he talk about besides the family? Any friends or people he saw?"

"That's all confidential information."

They'd arrived at his car, and he remotely unlocked the doors. "You mean to tell me that you really don't care to bring the person who sold him these drugs to justice?"

"Of course I care." The desire to help him, to do something positive, was overwhelming, but Amy's words of caution sounded in her head.

Kyle opened her door for her, and she stared at him blankly for a moment. "Who opens car doors anymore?"

"My mother insisted that my brothers and I behave like gentlemen."

She scowled at him. "I guess you forgot about that when you jumped out at me from the shadows."

He rolled his eyes. "I already apologized. I should've realized from the other day that you're oversensitive."

Overemotional is what her mother would say, but that was beside the point—which was that he'd really scared her. Continuing to harass him about it covered up just how much. Ignoring his comment, she climbed into the car. He shut the door and circled around to the driver's side.

He slid into the seat and started the engine, then turned to look at her. "Where to?"

His face was shadowed, but the light closest to the car filtered through the windshield and made his eyes glimmer like the ocean in Hawaii. She'd gone for a college graduation trip and now felt the heat of the sun—or maybe it was his presence. Despite the fact that he was Alex's brother, probably hated her guts, and had just scared the daylights out of her, she found him incredibly attractive.

"Dr. Trent?"

"Call me Maggie." Damn, why had she said that? Because she'd been distracted by his hotness. *Pull yourself together, Maggie!* "I live over on Adams. Do you know where that is?"

"Sure. I'll just shoot up Third Street."

He knew his way around Newberg, which wasn't surprising. If you lived in one of the small towns dotting the northern valley, you could likely navigate them all.

He backed out of the spot and drove through the parking lot to the highway. "Is there anything from your sessions with Alex that you'd consider sharing? I don't need to know what he said about me or the family."

"Good, because I couldn't tell you that." Part of her wanted to let him know that Alex had admired him and looked up to him, even when everyone else had seemed to write him off. She looked at him askance and wondered how he dealt with his family. He didn't seem depressed or maladjusted. Maybe their opinion didn't matter to him. Families were a tricky business—something she knew better than most.

"You had no inkling he was going to kill himself?"

She'd been asked this question by a variety of people— colleagues, friends, her mother, his sister—but hearing it never got any easier. "No. He was depressed, and we constantly worked through it, but there was always an underlying sense of acceptance in him that I interpreted as hope." *Mis*interpreted. She now believed the acceptance came from him deciding that his life was going to be short and that by choosing his own death, he would finally have some control. "I was wrong," she said softly. "I should have known."

Kyle didn't say anything, and she didn't blame him for his silence. No one could blame her more than she did.

"Have you looked through his phone or his laptop?" she asked, surrendering to the need to help. She shoved Amy's warning to the recesses of her mind.

"That's how I found you," he said, turning left onto Third Street.

"Are there any names you don't recognize?"

"Loads." He cast her a quick glance. "Maybe you should look at them with me."

She couldn't. She *shouldn't*. "I could maybe do that." The words came out slow and uncertain.

"You don't sound very convincing. Are you going to brush me off again?"

Like that had worked the first time. "Would you let me?"

He chuckled as he took a right onto Adams. "Where's your house?"

"Next block. Second on the right."

"Nice neighborhood," he said.

The street was lined with early twentieth-century homes, most of which had been thoroughly remodeled within the last ten years.

He drove through the intersection with Fourth Street and then slowed as he approached her driveway. The streetlight illuminated the two-story craftsman.

"That's a big house for just you," he said, throwing his SUV into park.

Was he trying to determine if she lived alone? "If you're digging for information, you're not helping to convince me that you aren't a stalker."

He gave her a bemused look. "I assumed you lived alone because you were going to call a cab instead of someone to come pick you up."

Okay, maybe he wasn't actually a stalker. *Of course he wasn't.* He was just a grieving man who was desperate for something that would make sense of his brother's death. Someone she ought to stay far away from.

She opened the door. "Thanks for the ride."

He got out and followed her to the walkway that led to her front door. "Your yard is really nice." He gestured toward the riot of purple and pink petunias she'd put in the ground the day before.

She turned, waiting for him to leave before going to fetch her spare key from the magnetic container stuck to the back of the drain spout on the corner of the house. "I like to garden."

"Looks like it." He shoved his hand in his jeans pocket. "Listen, do you need a ride to work in the morning?"

She was a little surprised he was being so nice. Wasn't he supposed to despise her? *She* would. "No, I'll call a colleague. Or I'll walk. It's not that far, and it'll be daylight."

He nodded. "Let me know if you need help finding your keys in those bushes."

"I'll have security help me. I have a spare car key anyway." Not that she didn't plan on finding her keychain.

His eyes widened. "Shit! Do you have a key to get into your house? If not, I can probably help you break in."

She couldn't help the shot of derisive laughter that escaped her. "First you scare the hell out of me, then you make me lose my car keys, and now you want to vandalize the house I'm renting? You're a piece of work."

"Yeah, well I'm trying to be helpful." There was an acidity to his tone that made her feel instantly contrite. Knowing what she knew about him, she regretted making him out to be a total clusterfuck. "At least I'm not the world's shittiest therapist," he said.

She couldn't stop her sharp intake of breath, which was stupid. She *was* the world's shittiest therapist. That didn't mean she wanted to hear it from him. Maybe he wasn't so nice after all. "If your opinion of me is so low, why do you keep asking for my help?"

"Because you knew my brother, and the way I see it, you owe me and my family." He took a step toward her and leaned in close enough that she caught a whiff of his aftershave or cologne or whatever it was that smelled like spice and sandalwood. "And I mean to collect."

He turned and headed back toward his car. When he got to the driver's door, he looked at her. "I'll call you about the names in the laptop. Pick an evening when I can take you out for a drink."

No invitation, no polite query, just an expectation that she'd jump to do his bidding. Yeah, *nice* was not how she'd describe Kyle Archer. Nice-looking, for sure…

A minute passed, and he didn't leave. She stood there and watched him, waiting for him to go so that she could get her key and go inside. And pour a giant glass of pinot.

She finally strode to the passenger side and rapped on the window.

He rolled it down and arched a brow at her. God, he was sexy. That really sucked.

"Aren't you going to leave?" she asked.

"I was waiting until after you went inside."

"Let me guess, another lesson in gentlemanliness from your mother?"

His mouth tried to smile, but he suppressed it. "You don't have to sound so annoyed by it. Any other woman would be impressed."

Her purse strap slipped down her arm. "Is that what you're trying to do, impress me?" Was she flirting with him? Why in the hell was she flirting with him?

"Hell no."

Stung, she swung her purse over her shoulder and backed away from the car. "There's no way I'm getting my key out in front of you so that you can let yourself into my house and search it for clues that don't exist." Wow, paranoid much? Yes, ever since she'd come home after breaking up with Mark and found her entire bedroom covered in red rose petals. She hadn't been able to move out of that apartment fast enough.

Kyle leaned over the console and glared at her. "I think I already established that I could break in if I wanted to, but I also thought I'd proven myself to be a gentleman. Since that's gotten me absolutely nowhere, I give up trying to be nice." He started the car. "Don't forget to call me."

She watched him back out of the driveway and take off down the quiet street. Exhaling the tension that had bottled up during their bickering, she retrieved her spare key and let herself into the house. She quickly locked the deadbolt, not because she was scared, but because it was an ingrained habit. No, Kyle Archer didn't scare her. At least not the way that Mark had. The fear she felt about Kyle had nothing to do with her safety and everything to do with her emotional well-being. In any other circumstance, she could see herself liking him, maybe even wanting to date him.

She blew air through her teeth as she went into the kitchen and set her purse on the built-in desk. Pouring a glass of her favorite Oregon pinot noir, she took a fortifying sip and tried to think of how she could avoid seeing him again.

Unfortunately, she was certain he wouldn't give up. And she was just as certain that she didn't want him to.

Chapter Three

HOLED UP IN his office Friday morning, Kyle scrutinized the names in Alex's laptop for the hundredth time. He knew a lot of them—family, friends, Ribbon Ridge business associates and acquaintances. He didn't know others, however, and those taunted him from the screen. Maybe it was time he included the family in this quest.

Not Dad because he wanted to give Dad satisfaction, not frustration, which was all Kyle felt at this point. He didn't want to involve Sara. She was too busy with the renovation project, Derek and Chloe's wedding, and Dylan. Kyle had never seen her so happy—a burst of warmth nudged through his dissatisfaction.

He also didn't want to include Tori. She was the likeliest candidate, but she'd seemed distracted the past couple of weeks, and he wondered if she needed to get back to her job in San Francisco. He made a note to talk to her about it. He'd missed his siblings while he'd been in self-induced exile. Being here with them made him realize just how much, and he was eager to make up for lost time.

Except with Derek.

He heard his former friend-slash-current almost-brother moving around in his office next door. He was truly the heart and soul of Archer Enterprises. Dad was a good CEO, but he was a brewer at heart. Derek, on the other hand, loved all aspects of the business, and Kyle fully expected him to be the one to take over some day. The irony that his last name wasn't Archer would've made Kyle smile in years past, but now it made him feel unsettled. Like Derek was more an Archer than he was. And that it was Kyle's fault.

He shook the unpleasant thought away and stared at the names again. Why wouldn't Maggie help him? Even the smallest thing could point him in the right direction. Hell, *any* direction. Maybe he should call her again.

No, he didn't want to be a stalker. Especially after scaring her last night. He still felt really bad about that. And about calling her a shitty therapist. He winced. How did he expect her to help him when he came off all creepy and rude? He thought of the flowers Natalie had wanted to send his mom. Maybe he should send some to Maggie as an apology—she clearly liked flowers.

What the hell was he thinking? Send flowers to his dead brother's therapist? *Pull your head out, Kyle.*

Not for the first time, he thought about meeting her in different circumstances. Asking her out for real. Working to make her smile and laugh—he sensed she needed to do more of that.

A knock on his door interrupted his thoughts. It was a good thing because he couldn't actually contemplate dating Maggie. Taking out Alex's therapist would guarantee he didn't earn anyone's forgiveness. "Come in," he answered, closing Alex's laptop and setting it to the side of his desk.

Natalie poked her head inside and smiled. "Hey." Her long, dark hair hung past her shoulders, and she tucked a strand behind her ear. "You have a visitor. Shane Dawkins?"

What the hell was his bookie doing here? Had anyone seen him? Would Derek or Dad even remember what he looked like? They'd only met him the one time.

Wanting to get Shane out of the office as soon as possible, Kyle shot to his feet. "Thanks."

Natalie opened the door wider and moved out of the way.

Kyle glanced at Derek's and Dad's doors. Both closed. With a jolt of relief, Kyle turned to his one-time friend and bookie. Shane was a gym rat with close-cropped dark hair. His arms and chest were as beefy as ever and filled out his fitted black tee. He grinned as he sized up Kyle. "Damn, brother. Florida agreed with you."

"Hey, Shane. Let's get a cup of coffee downstairs and take a walk." Archer Enterprises boasted a small café on the ground floor, and there were walking paths around the building. They'd stick to the one that circled the parking lot so that they wouldn't be in view of Dad's or Derek's offices.

Kyle led Shane down the wide, open staircase and over to the café bar, where he asked for a black iced coffee while Shane ordered a caramel latte. Shane reached for his wallet, but Kyle swiped his card first. "I got this."

Shane laughed. "You've changed, man."

Kyle's shoulders bunched with tension. "What brings you all the way to Ribbon Ridge?" Shane lived in Northeast Portland, a good hour and forty-five minutes away.

"Heard you were back in town. I'm headed to the beach for the weekend, and I wanted to stop in and say hi. It's been a long time—what, four years?"

"Something like that, yeah." As if Kyle could forget. That night almost four years ago was crystallized in his brain. He'd been out of time. Owed Shane and his boss thirty grand. Was in danger of being thrashed to within an inch of his life if he couldn't sell them on his repayment plan. Cold sweat dappled the back of his neck as the barista handed him his coffee.

Shane picked up his latte, and Kyle led him out the front doors into the bright summer day. "What brings you back home?"

Kyle looked at him askance, squinting against the sunlight. Sensitivity had never been Shane's forte. "My brother committed suicide."

Shane waved his arm like he was going to smack himself in the head, but didn't. "Oh shit! Sorry, dude. I forgot about that. I did hear about it, though. Really sorry that happened."

"Thanks." Kyle tried to think of something else to say, but he didn't want to continue a friendship—or whatever their relationship had been, because really, "friends" didn't threaten to break your fingers so you couldn't cook—with him. "Listen, Shane, I'm not gambling any-more, so if you're here to solicit…"

Shane slapped him on the back. "God no. Dude, really, I just wanted to check up on you. Say hi. Catch up. How was Florida?"

Good for a while. Kyle had gone cold turkey and hadn't gambled once in three and a half years. Until Alex had died. Then in a matter of weeks, Kyle had burned through the savings he'd accumulated in Florida and found himself in over his head again, forcing him to sell his car to pay his bookie and dash out of town as fast as he could.

"It was fine. Beautiful beaches, laid-back lifestyle."

Shane's mouth split into a wide grin. "Gorgeous babes, I'm sure."

Kyle let his lips curve into a smile. "Yeah, lots of those." And not one had kept his attention long enough for him to want to form a relationship, but then Kyle wondered if anyone could. He'd had a girlfriend one year in high school and an on-and-off girlfriend who'd really been more of a fuck buddy in his early twenties, but long-term girlfriends had never been his thing. And marriage? Forget it. Not interested. He'd been shocked when he'd heard Derek was engaged. They'd made a pact in high school to stay single at least through their twenties so they could be young and free and enjoy life. Would they have done that if their friendship hadn't crashed and burned?

Kyle forced himself to pay attention to Shane, though he longed to escort him directly to his car. "What've you been up to?"

"Oh, you know, same old, same old." *Still booking, if you're interested.*

Kyle heard the invitation loud and clear but ignored it. "Still training at the gym?"

"Yep. I'm thinking of opening my own place in the next year or two. Business has been good." He looked askance at Kyle. "Real good."

Kyle stopped on the path and turned toward Shane. "Look, I don't want to be a dick here, but you're sort of from a part of my life I'd rather forget."

Shane sipped his latte. "Sure, sure, I get it. And I'm not here to pressure you or whatever. You were young then. But look at you now..." He gestured toward the high-end office building with the Archer logo stamped on the outside. "You're part of the family now. I bet you're rolling in dough with your trust fund. I won't let you get in over your head again."

Kyle gripped his coffee cup. Dad had taken control of his trust fund and ensured Kyle didn't inherit it when he turned twenty-five, like every other one of his siblings had. And he'd likely never get it. "I'm actually not rolling in anything except family upheaval. I'm here on a temporary gig while my brother's doing an internship. Then I'm going back to cooking." At The Alex, where he'd oversee a world-class restaurant. It was the first time in his adult life he'd felt energized by something other than a game of chance.

Shane snorted. "Eh, I don't see it. You're a great chef and all, but you were bored."

At his last job in Portland. The upscale Northeast Portland eatery he'd helped put on the map—and that had fired him when his gambling addiction had over-taken his life. "I wasn't bored. I was unfocused." He'd been floundering, feeling like a failure because he'd dropped out of college, and even though he'd graduated at the top of his culinary school class, he'd had to work crap kitchen jobs because of the lousy economy. "Shane, it's great to see you," *not really*, "but I hope you don't take this wrong when I say I think I'd rather call it quits here."

Shane looked up at the hills where the monastery was situated. "That's a bummer, but I get it. You still have my number?"

He did, but he resolved to delete it from his contacts as soon as he got back to his office. Would that matter? Though it was programmed into his phone, Kyle had memorized his number so that he could call him from anywhere, and the digits were still emblazoned in his mind.

"Take care of yourself, Shane."

Shane nodded. "You too, bro. Really." He slipped a pair of sunglasses from his pocket and slid them on. With a wave, he walked to his car and got inside. A woman sat in the passenger seat and leaned over to kiss him.

Kyle turned and stalked back to the building. He jogged back up the stairs and passed Natalie without saying a word. When he got to his office, he stopped short. Both Dad and Derek were standing there waiting for him. Anger, scalding and brisk, assaulted him as he moved past them. "We don't have a meeting scheduled. I'm busy."

Derek closed the door. "What was Shane Dawkins doing here?"

Shit, they'd seen him after all. Kyle went behind the desk, using it as a sort of shield.

Dad's brow was creased. "I wanted to talk to you about something, and Natalie said you'd stepped out with someone—Shane."

Damn it.

Kyle shrugged. "So? He just stopped in to say hi on his way to the beach."

Dad stepped toward the desk. "If you're gambling again, I need to know. I can't let you work here if—"

"I'm not." Kyle set his coffee down on his desk and ran his hand through his hair. "Jesus, Dad, I wouldn't do that."

"Okay, I had to ask," Dad said, but Kyle couldn't tell if he believed him or not.

"You actually didn't. You could try trusting me instead."

"In time."

"How much time?" Kyle snapped.

Derek moved forward, his dark blue eyes cool. "As long as it takes. You don't get to waltz in here and act like everything is okay. Did you even deal with your addiction? How do we really know you're not gambling? The last four years of your life are a complete mystery."

Kyle stared him down. "I don't owe you anything."

Derek's lip curled. "I don't owe you anything either— even though you think I do. I'm never going to apologize for bringing in Rob to save your ass. Family looks out for its own, and there's no shame in asking for help."

Kyle hated Derek's superior attitude. "I get that your parents died and for you, this family—*my family*—is all you ever wanted, but you never fail to understand that my perspective, and hell, that of all my siblings', isn't the same as yours. Stop trying to make us all feel like loser assholes because we don't cling to the mother ship."

Dad set his hand on Derek's shoulder and gave him an encouraging look before turning his sharp gaze on Kyle. "You're right that your perspectives are different, but that doesn't make Derek's any less valid. It might be nice if you tried to step outside yourself for five minutes and realize you aren't the center of the universe."

"Oh, that's just great. All I need is another 'why can't you be more like Derek' speech. Too bad Liam isn't here so you could compare me to him, too." Liam was Alex's identical twin—in looks only. Whereas Alex had been small and ill, Liam had come out of the womb fighting. He was the oldest, the smartest, the most successful, and also the biggest jerk—or so he'd become in the last five years as he'd grown his Denver real estate empire. "Is it any wonder why I left, Dad? How the hell am I supposed to compete with these brothers of mine? I will *never* be what they are. I'm a college dropout. A chef whose entire future is based on a project that fell into his lap because his brother killed himself."

Dad and Derek both stared at him, and the weight of their judgment was more than Kyle could bear. He pulled his keys from his top drawer and stalked past them.

"Where are you going?" Dad asked.

Kyle opened the door but turned to throw them a glare. "Out. Maybe the racetrack or the Indian casino. Why don't you guys bet each other on which one?"

Without a backward glance or telling Natalie where he was going, he left. In the parking lot, he realized he'd left his coffee upstairs, but there was no way he was going back. Not today.

Climbing into the car, he pulled his phone from his back pocket and texted Natalie.

Heading to The Alex for the rest of the day.

He put on his sunglasses, then started the engine and drove through the lot, stopping at the driveway as Natalie's response chimed.

I don't know what happened, but I'm here if you ever need to talk. Sorry.

Kyle set the phone down between the seats and pulled out of the lot. As he drove up toward the monastery, his phone rang. Swearing, he glanced at the display, not intending to talk to Dad or Derek, though he never expected the latter to call him. He was shocked to see that it was Maggie Trent.

Turning on the Bluetooth, he answered the call. "Hey!"

"Kyle?" Her voice—and yeah, it was sultry all right—washed over him, soothing his ire.

"Yeah. I'm...surprised you called."

"Me, too." She laughed, but the sound was jangly, like she was nervous. "Um, I would be happy to meet you and look at Alex's laptop. Okay, maybe not happy, but I'm willing to help."

He liked happy, but he'd take willing. "That's great. When?" *How about right now? As it turns out, my day got blown to hell.*

"Tonight? I'll meet you somewhere. Not Ribbon Ridge, though."

She'd closed her practice here and was avoiding the town. Why? "Okay. How about Hazel?" It was the best restaurant in Newberg—great menu, but casual—and was owned by a friend of his from culinary school. They could camp out at a table in the corner and hang as long as they wanted.

"Sounds good," she said. "Six?"

"Great. Hey, I've been wondering if you found your keys. I still feel really bad about that."

"My keys...yeah, they were in the juniper bushes."

"I'm glad you found them. Spider-free, I hope."

She laughed softly. "Someone from maintenance fished them out for me, but yeah, no spiders." There was a beat of silence. "I need to run. See you tonight."

Suddenly his day had a decidedly better outlook. He shrugged away the irritation of Dad and Derek's ambush and thought of spending the evening getting to know Maggie Trent. He hoped she'd maybe spill some information about Alex. Yeah, it might be unethical, but something told him she wanted to share. Perhaps he could ply her with wine. Hazel had a killer cellar.

At the very least, he'd get a second pair of eyes on Alex's contacts. Hopefully together they'd find something.

Kyle smacked the steering wheel. Hell, he'd have to go back and get Alex's laptop from his office. No way was he doing that now—he'd stop by later, on his way to the restaurant. Everyone would be gone by five.

Unless Dad and Derek were leaving now, trying to head him off before he did something stupid at the race-track or the casino. Kyle shook his head, irritated with himself for baiting them. He *was* a gambling addict, and their concerns were valid. Why, then, did they piss him off so much?

MAGGIE DECIDED TO walk the four blocks to Hazel. It was located on the main highway through town, and parking would be dicey on a Friday night since it was so popular. The walk also gave her a chance to meditate—or at least practice her version of inner soul-seeking.

Tonight that meant thinking over her last appoint-ment of the day. Doris was a sixty-year-old woman try-ing to work through her fear of flying so that she could take a trip to Europe. Maggie had only seen her a handful of times, and they'd made great progress. She imagined Doris might be ready to "graduate" after a couple more sessions. The issue, however, lay in Maggie's engagement. Twice during their fifty minutes, she'd lost track of what Doris had been saying. First, she'd contemplated how to lay out her mother's flowerbed tomorrow. Then later, she'd thought about tonight's meeting—it wasn't a date—with Kyle Archer.

Doris hadn't picked up on Maggie's lapses, but that didn't make it acceptable. Maggie was horrified and had spent the last couple of hours mentally berating herself. What kind of therapist was she?

The shittiest one in the world, according to her din-ner date.

No, he was *not* a date.

Her phone rang in her purse, blasting the latest Maroon 5 song. She dug it out of the front pocket, sighed upon seeing her mother's number, and answered the call. "Hi, Mom."

"Hello, my little flower bud. Are you still coming tomorrow?"

"Yes, ten, right?"

"Sure, whenever." Mom prided herself on flexibility. She might show up early, she might be late. She was, however, universally unapologetic. "I think you need to look at my roses, too."

"What's wrong with them?"

"That black spot thing."

Maggie frowned. "You're not using the spray I gave you, are you?"

"Oh, honey, you know I'm not good at that sort of thing."

Yes, routine is almost impossible for you. Maggie exhaled. "Should I show Dad how to do it?"

"I don't know if he has time, but you can ask. Why don't you text him?"

"I'll do that. Listen, Mom, I need to go. I'm meeting someone for dinner." As soon as she said it, she wished she could take it back. How stupid was she, opening herself up to twenty questions?

"Do you have a date?" Mom sounded hopeful.

"No. Just meeting a…friend."

"Does this friend have a penis?"

"Mom!"

Mom laughed. She always enjoyed provoking a response, which meant choosing shock-value words, regardless of her audience. After twenty-eight years, Maggie ought to be somewhat immune, but Mom knew exactly which buttons to push to get a rise out of her. "Don't be a prude."

"I'm not a prude."

"Bullshit. You've always been a prude."

If she only knew the kinky stuff Mark had demanded she try…Maggie's flesh started to crawl. Not from those particular memories, but from who Mark really was and how she'd totally missed the warning signs that he was a controlling bastard.

"Mom, I really do need to go."

"Oh fine, run off with your tail between your legs like you always do." Mom exhaled in frustration. "Sometimes I'm amazed you actually sprang from my loins."

"Why, because I speak appropriately in polite company? Or because I think open sexual relationships are a bad idea?" Her parents had a completely open marriage, and by the time Maggie had started middle school, they'd moved into a duplex so that each could inhabit their own private dwelling. It suited them just fine, but for two teenage kids, it had been a nightmare. They'd been careful not to expose Maggie and Rowan to their activities or partners, but Maggie and her brother weren't stupid. They were also eternally mortified.

"See, you *are* a prude. It's okay, honey. I love you just the way you are. And some man will, too." There she went—like Maggie was some charity case.

"I gotta go. See you tomorrow." Maggie hung up before Mom could say anything else and further batter her self-worth. She stopped on the sidewalk and slipped the phone back into the front of her purse, then dove her fingers into a small inner pocket for her pillbox.

The oval tin was old and had an image of a lily on the top—her grandmother's favorite flower. It had been a gift when Maggie had started high school. For when she might need to take something for "those inconvenient times of the month." How she missed Gran, the only sane voice in her upbringing. She'd also possessed a green thumb, which she'd passed on to Maggie. Summers in Gran's garden were her favorite childhood memories.

Thinking of her paternal grandmother relaxed her whirling nerves. She opened the lid and stared at the Xanax inside. She had been taking it less and less since losing Alex and closing her practice, but talking to her mom was one of the few times that still drove her to pop one. She closed her eyes and inhaled the summer air, catching scents of roses, honeysuckle, and fresh-cut grass.

Did she really want to go over there tomorrow and listen to Mom badger her about her choices?

Why are you a therapist? You're so much happier in the garden getting your hands dirty.

If you'd dumped Mark when I told you to, you'd be in a much better place now emotionally. You're so closed off.

Maggie picked up one of the pills, ready to swallow it down to calm the tumult inside. The worst part of it was that Mom had been right about Mark and maybe was even right about Maggie's career choice.

Damn it all to hell.

Just then a car pulled onto the street and parked right next to her. Belatedly, she recognized Kyle's black SUV. She dropped the pill back into the box and stowed it in her purse.

He opened the door and stepped out, his long, tan legs exposed beneath the hem of his khaki shorts. He wore brown leather flip-flops and a white V-neck tee that only accentuated his tan. He looked like he'd stepped out of an ad for Bacardi Rum or maybe a Caribbean cruise. Or out of the pages of *GQ* or *People*. He flashed a smile, which only served to intensify his celebrity good looks. "Hey there."

Her chest actually constricted because he was so damn attractive. She should've taken the stupid Xanax. "Hey yourself."

"Walking to the restaurant?"

"It isn't far." She gestured a block ahead at the highway. Hazel was just to the right.

"And it's a great summer night." He pulled a laptop case from the car and tucked it under his arm. "Ready?" He locked the car and turned toward the highway. "I'd offer you my arm, but that's a little old school, right?"

She couldn't resist smiling. "Another recommendation from your mom?"

"Yep. Parents are funny, right?" She half choked, half laughed. He looked sideways at her. "You all right?"

"Yes. I was just talking to my mom, in fact. *Funny* isn't the word I'd use to describe her."

"What would you use?"

The word came out before she could censor herself: "Strange."

He laughed, the sound deep and delicious, sliding over her skin like the softest T-shirt after a relaxing hot bath. "That's a new one. Why is she strange?"

"Oh geez, you wouldn't believe me if I told you." And she didn't want to tell him. There was a reason Mom had only met Mark five times in three years. As a general rule, Maggie kept Mom sequestered from the rest of her life. It was why she lived over an hour away.

He stopped at the corner, waiting for the crosswalk light to turn. "Come on, you can do better than that."

"Okay. Have you ever seen the show *Portlandia*?"

"Of course. I'm from here. It's the perfect lampooning of Portland's hipster subculture. I tried to explain to people in Florida that while it's satire, it isn't really that far off the mark. They thought I was full of it." He chuckled.

She nodded in agreement. "Totally. And my mother is living proof that it *is* true. She actually pickles things, shops at a feminist bookstore, and, yes, has even 'put a bird on it.'"

He laughed harder and then stopped when he saw her face. "Oh my God, you're serious."

"Serious as hipsters insisting on locally sourced produce."

He grinned. "That's sort of awesome. I bet she's a hoot."

Maggie couldn't resist smiling. "Ha, not quite."

"Maybe I'll meet her sometime and judge for myself."

Not even if this actually *was* a date. But it wasn't, she reminded herself.

The light turned, and his hand grazed her lower back as they stepped into the crosswalk. For just a moment, she imagined what a date with him might be like. They passed a woman who looked him up and down then shot Maggie an envious glance. Oh yes, going on a date with Kyle Archer would be ridiculously fantastic.

He was a complete gentleman. When he wasn't leaping out of the shadows and scaring her half to death.

He was thoughtful. Even when he was offering to break into her rental house.

He was also dedicated. As evidenced by his commitment to finding out who'd sold his brother drugs.

Yes, Kyle Archer was far too attractive for his own good. Perhaps she ought to focus on the negative things Alex had told her—that he was a bit self-centered, rash, and stubborn as all hell. She supposed the stubborn and the dedicated probably went hand in hand.

They reached the other side of the street, and he guided her to the path that led to the stairs up to the restaurant. When they stepped into the entryway of the old, renovated house, the hostess met them. "Good evening."

"Hi, Kyle Archer for two."

She glanced at the iPad mini in her hand. "Welcome. This way." She led them to a table in the back corner next to a window. "You requested this table, right?"

"Yep, thank you." He held out one of the chairs and looked at Maggie. *Total gentleman.*

She sat, and he pushed her gently in before taking his chair across the table. He placed his laptop next to his setting.

The hostess set the menus before them. "All the specials are there—we print the menus every day. Can I have your server bring you a cocktail? A glass of wine?"

"How about a bottle of the two thousand eight WillaKenzie Triple Black Slopes?" He looked at Maggie, his brow raised in question. She nodded.

"Excellent choice," the hostess said. She left them alone, and Maggie perused the menu.

"What's good?" She looked up at him. "You're the chef."

"You're asking my professional opinion?"

"Of course."

He looked over the menu. "I haven't actually eaten here yet, but since I know the chef from culinary school, I have a good idea of what he'll make. I'm sure the beet salad is amazing, but maybe you don't like pickled things given your disdain for *Portlandia*."

She laughed. "I actually love that show, but it's sometimes a little too close to home for my comfort."

"The hand-cut potato chips are also fantastic, and the onion dip that comes with it is about as close to a sex-free orgasm as you can get."

His words heated her in places she didn't want to think about when she was on a not-date with him. "I'm not sure I've ever had one of those."

He winked at her. "Then we'll definitely need the onion dip."

Their server arrived with the wine. "Hi, I'm Whitney. Andy said this bottle's on the house." She cut the foil and pierced the cork with the corkscrew.

Maggie looked at Kyle as Whitney opened the wine. "Is Andy your friend?"

Kyle nodded. "This is his restaurant."

Maggie glanced around at the rustic décor and the cabinet stocked with what was probably only a portion of the wine collection. "It's great." She'd eaten here a few times but only for lunch.

Whitney splashed a few swallows of pinot noir into a balloon glass in front of Kyle. He picked it up and swirled it, inspecting it as it moved around the glass. Then he inhaled the scent, and finally, he took a sip. "Perfect."

Whitney smiled, then filled Maggie's glass and added to Kyle's. "Can I get anything started for you?"

"The onion dip, please," Kyle said.

"Great choice." The server left again.

Maggie looked down at her menu. "What about dinner? I can't decide. It all looks good."

"I'd go with the scallops. Or the duck." He looked over at her. "Or maybe the risotto if you're vegetarian."

"Not a vegetarian, despite my mother's best efforts. She's full vegan, of course." Maggie sipped her wine. "Oh, this is really good."

They discussed the menu for another minute before Maggie noticed a couple across the room glancing over at Kyle and then talking, as if they were discussing him. "Do you know those people over there?" she asked.

He turned his head briefly. "No. Should I?"

"They keep looking over here at you, like they know you."

His lips spread in a lazy smile. "That happens sometimes. I used to be on a TV show."

"Oh my gosh, that's right. What was it called again, *Seven Is Enough*?"

"That's it." He leaned forward, his blue-green eyes spearing her with a humorously intense gaze. "Quick, how old were we when it ran?"

She knew he was kidding, so she played along. "Ten, twelve?"

He looked to the side. "You don't know?" He laughed. "That's about right."

"I admit I didn't watch it very much. Mom didn't allow us a lot of television." Which had totally sucked when all of her friends were glued to *Buffy the Vampire Slayer* and she'd had to wait to watch it at Dad's, provided he remembered to record it for her.

"I'm sure we have copies of it, if you'd like to educate yourself."

She took another sip of wine. "How'd you guys end up on TV anyway?"

"A friend of my parents. His uncle was a producer, I think, and they were looking for a 'feel-good' show."

"That was before reality shows were really big."

"Yeah, and I think we were actually ahead of the trend. The idea sort of came from MTV's *The Real World* and early reality shows like that. But people weren't as into feeding off of others' drama back then."

She chuckled, thinking of the volume and variety of reality shows available now and how ridiculous most of them were. Dance moms and duck hunters. Crazy. "True. It sounds like maybe you didn't like it?"

"Actually, I loved it. My siblings, not so much. Tori didn't mind it, but Liam hated it, and Sara and Evan just sort of clung to the background. Hayden didn't love it either, but that's because he was the 'oops' kid and consequently not one of the focal points of the show." She noticed he didn't mention Alex but didn't want to question him about it. Alex hadn't talked to her about the show very much, but she had the sense that he'd enjoyed it.

Instead, she thought back to the few episodes that she'd seen and recalled that Kyle, Tori, and Liam had seemed to be the stars, with the emphasis on Kyle, who she remembered as funny. "You were the ham."

He cracked a half smile. "Totally. I'll admit it, I loved the spotlight. I cried when they canceled it."

She felt a tinge of remorse for him. "I'm sorry. That must've been hard, given how young you were."

"I guess. But because we were young, we bounced back." He took a drink of wine.

The couple was still sneaking glances at Kyle. "And you still have your celebrity," she said, thinking that her assessment of his Hollywood looks was dead accurate and she hadn't even realized it.

Whitney brought the dip and took their dinner order. Maggie decided on the scallops and Kyle got the duck, both on the condition that they would share bites. This was feeling more and more like a date. She needed to remember that it wasn't. "Do you want to show me the laptop now?"

He looked a little surprised. "Before dinner? Okay, sure. But first, you have to try the orgasm-inducing dip."

Picking up a chip, she swiped it into the thick, creamy dip and took a taste. "Oh. My. God. You weren't kidding."

His gaze was fixed on her mouth, heightening the pull she felt toward him. "Delicious, right?"

She had the discomfiting—and arousing—sense that he wasn't talking about the dip. Or maybe that was her prudish imagination. Ha, as if. The images that were pinging around in her mind at present were anything but sedate. She tried not to think of his muscular thighs or his long chef's fingers or the breadth of his shoulders. And she sure as hell tried not to think of how much she liked him, despite wanting to keep her distance. Oh crap, this not-date was not going the way it should. "The laptop?" she reminded him.

"Right." He pulled it from the sleeve and opened it. He ran his finger over the track pad and turned it so they could both view the screen. He'd pulled the contacts up. The *A*s stared back at her. Most of them were Archers. "Can you just scroll through and see if any names jump out at you?" he asked.

"Sure." She helped herself to another chip and the fabulous dip, then wiped her fingertips on her napkin before turning to the computer. She scrolled down through the *B*s, the *C*s, and onward. Nothing looked familiar. Her gaze landed on a phone number at the end of the *G*s that looked like her brother's but wasn't.

Kyle must've noticed she'd paused. "What is it?" His tone carried a hint of excitement.

She shot him an apologetic glance, hating disappointing him. "Nothing. Just a number that looked familiar, but it's not."

He stared at the screen, his hand frozen halfway to his mouth with a chip. "Shit."

"What?" she asked, her neck prickling for some reason.

"You're looking at the numbers as well as the names. God, I'm so stupid." He set the chip on his plate and clicked on the name: Dane Hawkins.

Maggie dipped another chip. "Why are you stupid? Did you miss that person before?"

"Yes, but I know him. As Shane Dawkins—I recognize the number now. I hadn't been looking at numbers before, just names." He sent her a grateful glance. "See, I knew you'd be helpful."

A flush of pride washed over her as she swallowed the chip. "You're welcome. Who is he?"

His mouth formed a grim line, and his dazzling blue-green eyes dimmed. "My bookie."

Chapter Four

"YOUR BOOKIE?" SHE stared at him a long moment. "You gamble?"

"Not if I can help it. I'm an addict." He couldn't believe he was telling her this, exposing his most closely held secret. He'd never discussed the depths of his problem with his family, with Derek, or with any of the friends he'd made in Florida. So why her?

She twirled her wine glass. "Wow. So...you're surprised that Alex had this guy's number?"

"Yeah, particularly since he went to the trouble of disguising his name. That seems to scream concealment."

"It does," she said slowly. "You think this guy—Shane— had something to do with the drugs?"

Kyle couldn't think of any other reason that Alex would have his number. God, if Shane was somehow involved...Kyle's shoulders bunched, and anger curled through him.

She reached out and touched his hand near the laptop. The light contact of her fingers rocked through him, tossing his already overworked senses into overdrive. "Just take a breath." Her voice caressed him, but instead of relaxing, his body coiled with frustration. "Kyle, breathe. Maybe Alex just wanted to place a bet."

Kyle blew out a breath. "Maybe." He still had to have gotten the number from Kyle, but shit, how in the world had that happened? He thought back to four years ago. "I don't know how Alex would've gotten Shane's number."

"Okay, we'll work on that. Do you want me to keep looking through the numbers?"

Kyle shook himself, but the sick feeling in his gut persisted. If Shane had provided the drugs and Kyle had somehow led Alex to him...God, how would he rebound from that? He'd made a shit-ton of mistakes and was trying to do better, but if he'd brought opportunity to Alex's door...with a shaking hand, he took a long drink of wine.

"Kyle, are you still with me?" Maggie's soothing voiced pulled him back to the here and now. "Talk to me."

Hopelessness choked him. "I don't know what to say. What if this is my fault?"

"It's not. No matter what. Your brother killed himself— you are not responsible, no one is."

The passion in her tone grounded him, gave him something to cling to. "That includes you, right?"

"That includes me." Her dark gaze bored into his. "And believe me, there are days when I still have to convince myself of that fact."

"Yeah, I bet." He winced. "Poor choice of words."

She laughed, further calming him. "I think you did that on purpose. I'm beginning to understand that you like things to be easy and fun. That makes life more palatable for you, especially now, doesn't it?"

He thought about that for a minute. "If you're asking me whether I avoid tough situations, the answer is sometimes. I just think life's short—now more than ever."

"Sure, I get that. But a gambling addiction is pretty heavy. If I were you, I think I'd want people to look at anything but me, lest they see things I don't want them to."

Hell, she was headshrinking him. He wanted to hate that, but damn it, he didn't. "You're therapizing me, Dr. Trent."

She arched a brow at him. "That's not a word."

"But you know exactly what I mean," he challenged.

"I do. And yes." Her gaze turned sheepish. "Sorry, it's what I do. Even before I was a therapist, I tried to solve people's problems. I had a teacher once who called me a busybody."

He suddenly remembered how he'd come to be here with her in the first place. She'd treated his brother. Unsuccessfully. But was that really her fault? No, like she'd said, it wasn't. Any lingering anger or resentment he felt toward her began to dissipate.

Whitney brought their entrees, and for a few minutes, they dug into their food.

"These scallops are amazing."

Kyle checked out her plate. "Great sear." Andy was a good chef. Seeing his friend's work gave him an itch. He cooked at home, had done some restaurant work in Florida the past few years, but nothing permanent. The thought of designing a menu, creating something from scratch at The Alex, filled him with excitement and reminded him of why he'd decided to go to culinary school in the first place. That and the fact that he'd dropped out of college and his parents had pushed him to find something else to do. He'd always liked to cook and decided to try it to get them off his back. He'd been surprised to find he actually had a passion for it.

"Here." She forked a bit of scallop and held it up to him.

He took the proffered bite and closed his eyes. Now he *really* hated Andy—for his successful restaurant and his amazing scallops. "Your dinner is better than mine," he said, opening his eyes. He offered her some duck.

She sampled the succulent bird and smiled. "I don't know, that's pretty freaking good."

"I heard that!" Andy came to the table with a wide grin. He liked to eat his food as much as craft it, and he looked like he'd gained a good fifteen or twenty pounds in the years since Kyle had seen him last.

Kyle stood and hugged his old friend. "Great to see you. You look good."

Andy clapped him on the back as they drew apart. "No, *you* look good. I look doughy." He smiled to take the sting out of his self-deprecation.

"You also look happy and accomplished." Kyle gestured toward Maggie. "This is Maggie. Maggie, this is Andy."

"Nice to meet you," she said.

"Ditto. Watch out for this jerk," Andy said, jabbing his thumb toward Kyle. "He's a smooth talker."

She smiled, her eyes lighting with mirth. "So I'm learning."

Kyle reluctantly pulled his gaze from her sexy stout-colored eyes and lush, peach-hued lips. He could just sit and stare at her for a long time, he realized. *And that wasn't weird.* Mentally shaking himself, he looked at Andy. "This place is fantastic. You should be really proud."

"I am, but it's a ton of work. I hear you're opening a place in Ribbon Ridge—your family's renovating that monastery?"

"It was my brother's plan."

Andy grabbed his shoulder. "I'm such a douche. I was really sorry to hear about Alex. You okay?"

Kyle glanced at Maggie, who'd stopped eating and was watching their conversation. "Yeah, I'm okay. It's been a little rough, but we're working through it. The project helps—gives us something positive to focus on."

"That's great. Keep me posted, okay? I'd love to come up and take a look some time."

"Sure thing. We haven't started construction on the restaurant yet, just finishing up the plans and waiting on permits now."

"Sounds awesome. I can't wait to see what you cook up." He winked at Kyle. "Gotta get back to the kitchen. Don't be a stranger. Maybe you can be my guest chef some night."

Kyle smiled at his old friend, a little surprised at how satisfying it felt to see someone he hadn't spoken to in years—Facebook notwithstanding. He'd done such a thorough job of closing off his life here when he'd gone to Florida that he'd all but forgotten the good things he'd left behind. "That'd be fun."

"Pleasure to have met you, Maggie—see you later." Andy retreated to the kitchen, and Kyle retook his seat.

"Nice guy. Seems like you were maybe close?" she asked as Kyle poured more wine.

"Once. Before I…" He shrugged. "Before."

"Before the gambling became a problem." She cocked her head to the side, drawing his gaze to her dark hair, which he was seeing down for the first time. It was long, reaching to just past her shoulders, and curly, which he loved. He had an urge to thread his fingers through the locks and relish the texture. "You can tell me to mind my own business, but is that why you left Oregon? The gambling?"

"Yeah. I'm surprised Alex didn't tell you that." Since he'd obviously known about Kyle's gambling, which was news to Kyle.

"Most of what he said about you was quite complimentary. He never mentioned your gambling."

Because no one knew about it, save Dad and Derek. Kyle yearned to ask for details but didn't want to push, particularly given the ethics of it, and he knew she held her responsibility to her patients in high regard. He liked that, even if it had pissed him off at first. "Thanks for sharing that. Alex wrote each of us a letter, but we don't get them until some predetermined time."

Her eyes widened. "Really? That must be hard, having to wait."

He shrugged. "I'm not as bothered by it as some, namely Tori." Mom, Dad, Derek, and Sara had already received theirs. "I appreciate hearing that he had good things to say about me."

"He had a lot of nice things to say about all of you. Okay, except one person." She looked down at her plate and scooped a bite of quinoa. "Never mind."

His curiosity was piqued, but he didn't pursue the issue. Maybe she'd tell him in time. Did that mean he planned to see her again? He hoped so—regardless of how the drug investigation panned out. He liked her. She was smart, funny, and damn if she didn't turn him on like crazy.

"You never actually answered my question," she said. "About why you left."

No, he hadn't. And for once, he hadn't intentionally deflected. He'd just gotten caught up in her talking about Alex. "Yes, that's why I left." He didn't want to get into the specifics. He'd already shared far more than he ever had. "There was a…problem, and I thought it best if I was on my own for a while."

Her eyes widened briefly. "A problem? Are you safe? I mean, you had a bookie and you left town…"

He laughed. "I wasn't about to get whacked or anything." The shit kicked out of him, sure, everything he owned seized by Shane's boss, definitely. But then Derek had told Dad about the debt Kyle owed, and Dad had shown up and paid it.

The day had been saved, and Kyle had fulfilled everyone's expectation that he'd be a complete fuckup. Dad had offered him a job to help him get on his feet, but Kyle hadn't wanted a handout. He hadn't even wanted Dad to bail him out with Shane's boss. In fact, Kyle had planned to pay him back every dime, but he'd blown the savings he'd accumulated in Florida after Alex's death, and now he had to start over. The familiar shame and anger swelled over him, darkening his mood.

"You're doing it again," she said, startling him from his lousy thoughts. The little worry lines she wore from time to time formed over the bridge of her nose. "When you feel like that—upset or overwhelmed—try breathing. Just focus on taking slow and steady breaths. Fill your lungs with air, expel it, do it again. Think of something calming. Something beautiful that makes you feel good."

A vision of her smiling, those rich eyes of hers gleaming with pleasure, crowded his mind. He took a deep breath, let it out. Better. "Thanks," he said. "Can I offer you a little advice in return?"

Her gaze turned skeptical. "Should I be afraid?"

He chuckled. "No. But I think you should laugh more. Ease those little creases." He reached over and lightly touched the space between her eyebrows. "Here. You're so pretty. I'd hate for them to stamp your face with permanent worry."

"The old 'don't make that face or it'll freeze like that' wives' tale?"

"Something like that. But I mean it. You're gorgeous when you smile. You should do it more often."

Swathes of pink highlighted her cheeks—also adorable. She looked down at her plate. "Thanks. I'll do that."

They ate for a few more minutes, discussing the preparation of the food. When they slowed down and had nearly emptied their wineglasses again, he remembered the laptop. "Do you mind looking at the rest of the names? When you're done."

She moved her plate over. "I'm finished. There's a bite of scallop left if you want it."

"Hit me."

She scooped it up and held up the fork. He took the bite, keeping his gaze locked with hers. "So good," he said around the food.

She blushed again, more lightly this time, but he caught it. This flirtation could be dangerous. He might not be angry with her or blame her for Alex's death, but she was still *that person*, and he was still the guy who didn't stick around.

She turned her attention to the laptop and scrolled through the rest of the list of contacts.

"Anything?" he asked, scooting his plate to the side.

She closed the lid. "No, sorry. I barely recognized any names—your family, some people he mentioned from work."

"Like who?"

"Paula, Natalie, Jeff, Aaron."

All people Alex knew well and had plenty of reason to interact with regularly. Kyle felt a stab of disappointment but reasoned that he wasn't empty-handed. He had Shane, and he sure as hell meant to get to the bottom of that connection.

She took a sip of her wine. "So, what are you doing here now that you're back? You're working on the restaurant?"

"And filling in for Hayden while he's doing an internship in France. He's always wanted to make wine."

"Wow, good for him. You're working for Archer?" She sounded nearly as incredulous as his family. Alex had apparently told her plenty about him if she had that sort of skepticism. He wished she didn't, that she wasn't predisposed to think less of him.

"Yeah, it's not exactly in my wheelhouse, but I'm learning. I don't *completely* suck at it."

"I'm sure you don't." She said that with enough conviction that he almost believed it—and had to reassess his earlier reaction. Maybe she hadn't cast him in a predetermined role after all.

Whitney returned and poured out the rest of the wine, then picked up their plates. "Can I get you dessert? We have a delicious marionberry tart. Or maybe the lemon curd cheesecake?"

"I'm stuffed," Maggie said. "Though the tart is tempting."

Kyle looked up at the server. "I think we're good. Thanks."

Maggie sipped her wine. "What are you going to do next?"

"Try to find out why Alex had Shane's number. I'll look through his room at home and his office."

"You haven't done that before?"

"Not his office. And when I looked through his room, I wasn't looking for anything specific—now I have a name to search for." He slid the laptop back into its sleeve, and they finished their wine. Whitney brought the check, and the evening came to a close far more quickly than Kyle would have liked.

They left the restaurant and walked back to Kyle's car. Once there, he offered to walk her the few blocks home.

"That's okay," she said. "It's not far."

"I don't mind." He wanted to, in fact.

"Really, it's fine." She resettled her purse strap on her shoulder. "I had a nice time tonight."

"You sound surprised."

She blinked at him. "Aren't you?"

He laughed softly. "Okay, yes. I might even like to do it again."

She exhaled. "That's not a good idea. I mean, unless it's about finding the drug dealer. I'm on board with that. Totally."

"I'll take that." He moved closer to her, wondering how the wine would taste on her lips, in her mouth. His body tightened with desire. "I had a great time with you."

She thrust her hand out. Slowly, he did the same and tried not to smile when she shook it. But then smiling was the last thing on his mind as electricity shot between them. He wanted to kiss her, touch her, feel her.

"Good night," she said, withdrawing her hand rather quickly. "Let me know what you find out."

She turned and stalked away, her stride devouring the sidewalk as she hurried away from him into the twilight. He watched her go and wondered how bad it would really be to take her on a real date. One that would end in kissing and touching and feeling.

It wouldn't be bad at all, he decided.

THE DIRT FELT good in Maggie's gloved hands, the rich, earthy scent comforting her, soothing her nerves, which tended to unravel when she went to her mother's house. She worked the fertilizer into the ground, sifting it through her fingers.

The gate separating her mother's backyard from her father's opened. Dad stepped through and let the wood clap shut. "Hello, my little magpie."

She smiled up at him. "Hi, Dad." With his long, dark, graying hair and full-sleeve tattoos, he was every bit as hippie-dippie as Mom, but he respected one's choice to *not* be hippie-dippie. "How're classes?"

Dad ran an art school at the local community center in southeast Portland. "Super. And my private lessons are at full capacity." He'd offered them in his garage studio for as long as Maggie could remember. "Stop in before you go, and I'll show you what I'm working on."

Maggie nodded, hoping he'd forget. She didn't mind most of his art, but some of his "experimental" stuff could be a tad unsettling. He argued that it was supposed to be, that the best art pushed you outside your comfort zone. It definitely did that.

He pushed at the bridge of his small, round wire-rimmed glasses. "What's new with you, magpie?"

"Not much." She finished working in the fertilizer and stood. A flat of plants—a mix of perennials and annuals—sat on the lawn beside her. She grabbed the shovel and dug holes where she planned to put the ornamental grasses.

"The new job's going well?" he asked. "You're feeling good?"

Dad had been incredibly supportive after Alex had died and Maggie had suffered her breakdown. He'd brought her dinner a handful of times and checked in on her regularly. "Yep, thanks." She finished the first hole.

"Taking the herbal supplements I recommended?"

That would be Dad's code for, *Are you smoking the pot I gave you?* Dad was a great believer in the healing and soothing powers of marijuana. She shook her head but smiled. "I'm good, Dad, really."

"It's better for you than those prescription drugs," he said, his voice turning stern.

As she worked on the second hole, she threw him an exasperated glance.

He held up a hand. "I'll stop. Badgering is your mother's job."

Yes, it was. Thankfully, she was embroiled in a Skype conversation with a friend on the East Coast. Maggie moved on to the third hole and contemplated whether to broach a topic with Dad. She typically kept her nose out of her parents' lives—it was better for her peace of mind if she didn't know what was going on—but she rarely got Dad alone, and sometimes he gave her a bit of insight into why they lived the life they did.

"How're you and Mom? Spending a lot of time together, or is this one of your 'off' periods?" Because they lived apart, they pretty much led separate lives. Yet they still felt a connection and responsibility to each other. When Dad broke his foot two years ago, Mom had taken care of him.

"Bit of an off period," Dad said, leaning against the fence and watching her work. "I think she's been seeing someone the last few months."

Maggie strained to hear a clue as to how Dad felt about that, but she couldn't tell. She set the shovel aside and knelt to put the grass in the first hole. Knocking it out of the pot, she glanced up at him, deciding to be bold. "Does that bother you? I admit, I still don't understand your open marriage concept. I always thought it was just physical, but then it seems like you and Mom actually date people from time to time." So weird. She knew they loved each other and couldn't imagine just turning the other cheek when your soul mate stepped out.

"It's sort of like that. We're very up front with our partners. Some of them are just sex buddies." His lips curved up. "Sorry, I know that's probably not what you want to imagine your parents doing." No, it wasn't, and if this conversation had been with her mother, Maggie would've been called a prude several times by now.

"It's okay, you're people, too." She set the grass into the ground and patted the dirt around it. Then she moved on to the next pot. "But a few months…that's longer than Mom usually spends with someone."

Dad shrugged. "Maybe. I was with someone for about eighteen months once."

Maggie nearly dropped the plant. "You were?"

He nodded, folding his arms over his chest. "Long time ago. You were nine or ten."

"Wow." She couldn't even grasp that. How did you have a relationship like that in addition to the one with your wife? And that had been before they'd moved into the duplex. They'd lived in a small house, and now that she'd thought about it, Dad had spent a lot of time at his off-site studio. Now that she *really* thought about it, that studio had included a loft, a small kitchenette, and a bathroom. Like so many things she'd learned in her life about her parents, she wished he hadn't told her.

He squatted down beside her. "Hey there, little magpie, I didn't mean to upset you." He brushed a strand of her hair that had escaped her ponytail behind her ear. "I was always very careful to insulate you." He was, but that didn't make it better.

She exaggerated her motions so that his hand fell away. She didn't want him to touch her. She loved her parents—she did—but their odd lifestyle made her uncomfortable. No, it made her feel somewhat insignificant. Her anxiety started to amp up, and she chastised herself for not taking her Xanax. Real dumb move, but after her great evening with Kyle the night before, she'd woken up this morning feeling better than she had in a long time. A morning at her mom's hadn't seemed overwhelming, but now that she was here, the familiar stress was rifling through her.

Dad stood, sighing. "I shouldn't have said anything. I know better than to trouble my sensitive little magpie."

She looked up at him as she patted dirt around the grass. "It's okay, Dad. It's not like this is surprising." Just unsettling. How many other things was she unaware of? Probably dozens, and she hoped it stayed that way. Mom kept a diary and always said she'd leave it to Maggie when she died, but Maggie planned to burn it without reading.

Dad turned the conversation to a safer topic and asked her about what she was planting. Maggie launched into an animated discussion of the grasses, the Russian sage, and the variety of annuals.

"It's going to be quite the colorful little patch when you're finished," Dad said. "I think you missed your calling, magpie. It warms my heart to see your passion for something artistic." Instead of medical. Both Mom and Dad counted Maggie's and Rowan's careers to be failures, where other parents—normal parents—would be proud of having a daughter with a PhD and a son with a juris doctorate. But for an artist and a yoga instructor, a therapist and a lawyer were apparently disappointing career goals.

"Thanks, Dad. I do enjoy it." She'd considered going into landscape design, had actually taken a couple of classes as an undergrad, but she'd enjoyed her psychology courses, and when she realized she could make more money and enjoy more stability as a therapist, she'd taken that path instead. Growing up poor was a good incentive to follow your head rather than your heart.

Mom swept out of the house like a whirlwind. "Oh, Jer! You look scrumptious." Smiling, she went to Dad and kissed him. She slid her arm around his waist and turned to survey Maggie's work. "Looks fabulous, darling. What are you two talking about out here?"

"Just the plants," Maggie said.

There was something exciting about Mom's energy, something that always made a space brighter or the atmosphere more charged. When Maggie had been younger, before she'd understood the weirdness of her upbringing and her parents' marriage, she'd loved that spark. Regardless of the strain in their adult relationship, she still envied her mom's ability to live in the moment and even her absolute honesty, despite its occasion to cause harm. Mom lived without regret, without worry. And without filters.

"Isn't it lovely, Jer?" Mom said, setting her free hand on his chest so that her stance was one of absolute possession. Or so it looked to Maggie. She imagined touching Kyle like that, claiming him for her own. The woman's jealous look in the crosswalk the night before rose in Maggie's memory, eliciting a small smile.

"What's that about?" Mom asked, demonstrating her uncanny capacity to detect even the smallest things. "That's a provocative little grin."

"Nothing, Mom. You guys look cute together, that's all." Maggie picked up a trowel and dug holes for the rest of the plants.

"We do." She patted Dad's chest and moved away. "You look so comfortable in the garden, my flower bud. I still say you should be doing this full time."

"I was just telling her that," Dad said.

Maggie dropped a marigold into the ground. "If you guys are going to harass me about my job, I'm leaving and you can finish this yourselves."

Mom laughed. "You're always so sensitive!"

Maggie patted dirt around the gold flower and threw her mother an irritated glance. Her phone vibrated in her back pocket. She pulled her right glove off and pulled it out. A 911 text from her service. Taking off her other glove, she stood. "I have to return this call."

Thankful for the reprieve, she went into the house and was immediately assaulted by Mom's little Yorkshire-Maltese mixes, Sonny and Cher. They ran around her feet barking until she leaned over to pet them both. Appeased, they flopped on the floor and stared up at her as she called the service back. "This is Maggie Trent."

"Dr. Trent, we got a call from Ryan Dillinger. He says he's feeling pretty bad and would like to see you today, if possible."

Ryan was a relatively new patient. He'd lost his job several months ago and had recently broken up with his girlfriend. He was suffering from depression, and Dr. Innes had prescribed an antidepressant, but Maggie was providing the therapy. "Sure." She looked at the clock on her mother's microwave. "Have him meet me at the clinic at one."

"Will do. He sounded pretty rough."

A thread of anxiety wound down Maggie's spine. In the two months since she'd returned to work, she hadn't had to deal with anything too depressing. But she knew it was coming. Maybe it wouldn't turn out as badly as it had with Alex—God, she hoped not—but helping people wasn't all sunshine and rainbows. While she'd known what she was getting into with this career, she hadn't anticipated that other people's problems would affect her so much. Mom had warned her they would, but as with most things, Maggie hadn't listened.

"Thanks for letting me know." She ended the call and turned to go back outside. Her eye caught her purse, and she paused at the threshold. She looked into the yard, saw her parents making out, and turned away from the slider. The tumult inside her grew until she heard a buzzing in her ears. She dug into her purse for her pillbox and pulled out a Xanax. Without overthinking, she popped it into her mouth and took a swig from the water bottle next to her purse to wash it down.

She closed her eyes and counted to three before making as much noise as possible opening the door. By the time she got to the yard, her parents had stopped kissing—how did they do that when Mom was supposedly seeing someone? Maggie shook her head and worked to clear her thoughts before she started to therapize her parents. Therapize? Kyle's word. She liked that word. She liked him. Yes, think about Kyle.

She went back to work on the flowerbed and mostly tuned out her parents, who'd moved on to discussing Rowan's girlfriend. Soon, Maggie felt relaxed, good, happy almost.

It was probably the Xanax, but she thought—no, she hoped—it was maybe because of Kyle, too.

Chapter Five

KYLE WAITED TO search Alex's office until just about
everyone was at lunch on Monday, save Natalie, who
typically went later so that she and Paula weren't gone
at the same time. Alex's office was on the other side of
Dad's. It was smaller than the others but had the best
view of the valley. They hadn't hired anyone to fill his
position as director of communications—right now
they were hiring freelancers to take care of any writing projects. Kyle suspected Dad just couldn't replace
him yet.

He pressed his lips together. He was going to find out
how Alex had gotten those drugs, and prosecuting the
person who'd sold them to him was going to help Dad
move on.

A search of Alex's room at home yesterday had yielded
nothing about Shane, so Kyle hoped he'd find something
today. He sat down behind the desk and methodically

went through each drawer. Nothing. Frustration mounting, he turned to the credenza behind the desk and looked through the hanging files.

"What're you doing?"

Kyle jumped, nearly closing his fingers in the drawer. "Shit! Natalie, you scared me."

She moved into the office, her mouth forming an O. "Sorry! I didn't mean to. My bad."

He blew air out and took a deep breath to regulate his suddenly racing heart. He didn't want his family to know what he was doing, but maybe Natalie could help him. "I'm looking for something, actually."

"Can I help?" She walked around the desk. "You know I can probably find anything."

"That's true, but this isn't work-related. Can you keep a secret? And I mean a real secret—this is important. This isn't gossip-type stuff."

She tipped her head to the side, her dark eyes narrowing slightly. "Have you ever known me to engage in office gossip? I respect your family too much, and I value my job more than anything."

"I know. I just wanted to be clear. I completely trust that you won't say anything, which is why I'm going to confide in you. But I had to say it, okay?"

She exhaled. "I get you." She crossed her fingers over her heart. "Your secret is safe with me."

He smiled. "Excellent. I'm trying to find out who sold Alex the drugs he used to kill himself."

Her eyes widened. "Oh my. Why do you think he bought them from someone?"

"No one would've prescribed them to him with his medical history. He had to have gotten them illegally." He went back to the file drawer and continued, but everything in there was a work-related project.

Natalie perched on the edge of the desk. The position hiked her skirt a little and exposed a length of very toned, very tan legs. "What are you looking for?"

"Anything really, but I'm particularly searching for the name Dane Hawkins or Shane Dawkins."

"Wait, isn't Shane the guy who visited you Friday?"

He glanced up at her. "Yeah. He's an old friend, and he has some shady contacts." Kyle had no plans to divulge his gambling background to Natalie. One secret was more than enough to share. "I think it's possible he could've hooked Alex up."

Her dark brows drew together. "Now that you mention it, I'm pretty sure I've seen that guy before."

Kyle turned sharply, letting the drawer close. "You have?"

She chewed her lip. "Yeah, I think he's been here before."

Adrenalin pumped through him. "Do you remember when?"

"Maybe late last year? Right around the holidays, I think. Yeah, the office was decorated."

The timing sounded right, as Alex had killed himself in early February. Fury burned Kyle's insides. He longed to beat answers out of Shane, but that wouldn't help anything. He breathed like Maggie had told him to. Slowly, he calmed down, but determination gripped him. He'd get to the bottom of this with Shane. Hopefully with Maggie's help.

He'd thought of her a lot over the weekend. Friday's dinner had been fun, flirty even. He'd wanted to kiss her at the end but realized that probably wasn't smart. He wasn't even sure she wanted him to. She'd flirted back, but flirting wasn't following through.

"Is that helpful at all?" Natalie asked, interrupting his thoughts and reminding him she was still there.

"Yeah, sorry. Got wrapped up in what I want to do next. Thanks for your help, really."

"What are you going to do?"

He stood up from the chair. "Crucify Shane."

She cringed as she got up from the desk. She touched his arm and looked at him intently. "Be careful. He looked like a pretty tough guy."

"I will be, thanks." He moved around the desk and paused at the threshold of the office. "Will you close the door behind you? And remember, this is between us. I don't want Dad to know what I'm doing. If this goes nowhere, he'll be disappointed, and I'm trying to give him some closure, not make him feel worse."

She nodded. "Got it. I'm happy to help you any way that I can." She crossed the office and met him at the door. Her gaze locked on his, conveying her commitment. "Really, Kyle, I'm here if you need me."

"Thanks." He smiled at her and went back to his office and closed the door. Once inside, he called Maggie's office and Monotone Man answered. Geez, he really needed her cell phone number. Kyle used his real name this time and got right through to her since she was at lunch.

"No fake *Game of Thrones* names today? How disappointing."

He smiled at the warmth in her tone. "I can call back as Jaime Lannister if you like."

She laughed. "This is fine."

"Actually, it'd be better if you gave me your cell phone number so I can bypass that snore of a receptionist."

She laughed again. "Baylor is a nice guy."

"Baylor? That's a college, not a name."

More laughter. "Stop, please. Why did you call?"

"I have news. Someone in my office remembers Shane coming here to see Alex last winter."

"Oh my God. What are you going to do?"

He was thrilled by the shock and excitement in her voice. "Confront him. Do you want to go with me?"

"Kyle, is that safe? I don't know…"

"We'll go to the gym where he works. Very public. It's just a conversation. You're free on Wednesday afternoon, right?"

"Your knowledge of my schedule is a bit frightening, you know that?"

He chuckled. "Don't worry, I'll forget at some point. I'm a guy; we don't remember that kind of stuff."

"If you say so. It's still unsettling."

He spun his chair and looked out the window. "Is it? I thought we'd established I'm not a stalker or anything else creepy. Didn't you have a good time Friday?"

She sighed. "I did. And you aren't creepy."

He smiled. "So Wednesday. I'll pick you up at two? The gym's in Northeast Portland, so we'll be gone all afternoon, probably have to pick up dinner in town to avoid rush hour before we head back."

"I don't know. You don't really need me, right?"

He heard the hesitation in her voice and sat forward in his chair, wanting to convince her. But did he need her there? "I'd *like* you there. We're in this together." Or so he hoped. He liked having a partner. It kept this endeavor from being too dark.

Silence answered him, and his muscles tightened. "You're good at talking me off the ledge too," he said. "You will undoubtedly come in handy in case I try to do something stupid."

She made a sound, a small breath, not quite the sigh she'd made before. "Okay, sure. Pick me up at two."

He smiled into the phone. "You got it."

"Bye."

"See you." He ended the call, glad that she'd be with him. Though he'd used the excuse to convince her, she might *actually* need to talk him down. Because if Shane had supplied Alex with the drugs, Kyle didn't know what he would do.

At FIVE MINUTES to two, Maggie went outside to wait for Kyle on her porch. There was no way she was giving him even a glimpse of her house. That would ignite too many questions, none of which she wanted to answer—even to herself. At one minute till, he pulled into her driveway, and she strode toward the car.

He jumped out and raced around to open her door. He smiled at her, making her stomach do a little flip. "Eager beaver today, eh?"

"Just ready to do this."

He nodded and shut the door after she climbed inside. When he was back in the driver seat, he looked over at her. "Music or no music? I tend to like music in the background."

She set her purse on the floor by her feet. "Music's fine."

"Pop, rock, jazz?"

She laughed. "Okay, your gentlemanly thoughtfulness is going a little overboard, don't you think? It doesn't matter. Whatever you have is fine."

"I'll let the radio decide." He turned it on, and a Bruno Mars song filtered through the speakers. He adjusted the volume to where they could hear the music but still talk over it and be heard. "Good?"

"Fine." She smiled at him, surprised at how thoughtful he was and how great his mom must be to have instilled that in him. "Your mom must be pretty special."

He backed out into the street. "What?" He glanced at her. "Oh, the gentlemanly thing. Actually, the music stems from my siblings. With so many of us, there were tons of arguments growing up. And background noise bothers one of my brothers and used to bother one of my sisters, so I just got in the habit of asking."

"That's still really sweet." She looked at him as he drove. "Is that your brother with Asperger's—Evan?"

Kyle flicked her a curious glance. "Alex told you about that? Yeah, I imagine he would. Evan's auditory processing isn't the best. Background noise makes it hard for him to engage."

"And your sister has sensory processing disorder, right?" She felt comfortable discussing this since it seemed to be information that Kyle had planned to share.

He nodded. "Sara. She and I are pretty close. When she was younger, loud noise gave her trouble, but she worked through it. My parents did a lot of different therapies with her and Evan." He shot her an inquisitive look. "Alex probably told you that, too."

He had, but hearing it from Kyle in this setting, outside of therapy, was different. "That's great that your family is so supportive and proactive." She looked out the window as they drove through Newberg. "So, what's the plan for today?"

"What do you mean?"

"How are you going to address the drugs with Shane?"

He glanced at her, appearing a bit perplexed. "I'm going to ask him."

She shook her head. "No, no, you'll immediately put him on the defensive. I think you should ask him if he can get you drugs. Tell him I want them—that's why I'm there."

He stopped at a light and looked at her more fully, his gaze appreciative. "Aren't you a little conniver?" A roguish smile curved his lips. "I like that. Very smooth idea. Much better than my scorched earth method. I should have come up with that to begin with—see, it's good that I have you along."

She understood why he perhaps hadn't thought ahead. "I get it," she said. "You're coming from an emotional place. It makes sense that you want to go in there with guns blazing."

He refocused on the road as the light turned green. "But I won't. Thanks to you."

She wanted to understand exactly what sort of emotional place he was coming from. Was it just the gambling? Alex's death? Or had this Shane person maybe meant more to him at some point—a friendship gone bad? "How did you meet Shane?"

"The gym. I lived over in Northeast back then. Fresh out of culinary school. I worked at a couple of different restaurants."

"How did he become your bookie?"

He cast her a sidelong glance. "I don't know. We hung out. We went to the racetrack a few times. Things just sort of developed. He liked my ribs."

An image of his cut abs—and she was sure they were cut—rose in her mind, sending a spike of desire straight through her belly. She turned in the seat to look at him. "He what?"

In profile, his grin was every bit as sexy as it was full-on. "My pork ribs—the seasoning, really. I made them for a neighborhood barbecue once, and I couldn't get rid of Shane after that. You know, I haven't made those ribs in a really long time. Do you like ribs?"

She was pretty sure he was deflecting. He didn't want to talk about his past with Shane, or more importantly, how he'd become a gambling addict. Although she was curious, she wouldn't press him. For now.

She resituated herself to face forward. "Yeah, I like ribs. Are you offering to make them for me some time?" Yikes, she hadn't meant to flirt with him today. She'd had a conscious conversation with herself—and no, that didn't make her nuts—to keep their field trip strictly platonic.

"I will absolutely make them for you some time." He turned off the highway and cut over to the freeway that would take them into Portland. "I've been contemplating what to put on the menu at The Alex, and I think I have my first contender."

It warmed Maggie's heart to know that Alex had left a lasting legacy. "I think it's so great that you guys named the place after him."

"It was Sara's idea. The restaurant will be The Arch and Fox."

"All of the Archer brewpubs have Arch in the title, don't they?" she asked.

"Yep, and we all have animals associated with us. Alex's was a fox. I think it was because he was sly. Or maybe it was just the X in his name."

She was fascinated to hear more about this family she almost felt like she knew through Alex's therapy sessions. "What's your animal?"

"A horse. I loved them when I was a kid."

"Really?" She'd been obsessed with horses, but they'd never been able to afford lessons or anything. She'd only ridden one a couple of times with Girl Scouts. "Me, too."

He smiled at her. "What about now?"

She shrugged. "I don't know. I haven't thought about it. They're beautiful animals."

"Smart, too. I rode until I started playing sports. That took up too much time."

"Do you miss riding?"

"Sometimes." He changed the radio station, presumably because a commercial had come on. "If you wanted to ride, I could probably arrange something. A friend of mine from high school owns a riding facility."

There he went talking about the future. Ribs, horseback riding. They weren't dating. They weren't even really friends. Were they? "You need to stop planning things with me."

"Why?" He pulled onto the freeway.

"Because we're going to get to the bottom of this drug thing, and then we'll be done."

"Why?"

"Because..." *I can't be in a relationship with the brother of the guy who died on my watch.* "Because we just need to be."

He cast her a sly glance, and she thought maybe *he* should've been the fox. "What are you afraid of, Maggie? That we might like each other a little too much?"

Yes, exactly that. "Maybe I'm dating someone."

"Are you?"

"No. But I might want to." Him, probably.

No, no, no.

"I'm a little shocked you're available," he said. "Must be by choice. I imagine plenty of guys ask you out."

Ha. "Not as much as you might think." It was kind of hard when you only frequented your place of employment, the nursery, the grocery store, and the gas station. "And anyway, I'm content to focus on my career right now."

"Hmm, that sounds like you're actively choosing not to date. Why? Bad relationship?"

Now who was therapizing whom? "Yes." And why had she admitted that?

The look he sent her was one of surprise, as if he'd asked himself the same question she had. "What did the prick do?"

Her insides melted at his immediate support. "Things just ended badly."

"Were you together a long time?"

"Nearly three years—most of grad school."

"Why did it end badly?"

"You know, I think I'm going to take a card from your deck and change the subject."

He laughed. "Fair enough. But I can't promise I won't ask you again someday."

She was shocked to realize she wanted him to. The rest of the ride passed quickly as they talked about food and plants, which were clearly their primary passions. When they arrived at the gym, she was sorry the trip was over.

Kyle shut the car off and looked over at her. "Ready?"

"Yes, are you?"

"As ever." He got out and came around, but she was already stepping out of the car. He closed the door after her and led her through the small parking lot into the gym. Again, his hand lightly touched her lower back, and she craved a longer connection.

An arctic blast of air conditioning met them as they moved inside. They stepped toward a wide front desk manned by a perky young woman. "Can I help you?" she asked.

"We're here to see Shane Dawkins," Kyle answered.

Perky Girl smiled. "Sure thing. I'll buzz him."

She punched something into an iPad, then looked up at them. "If you want to wait over there, he'll be right up." She pointed to a small waiting area with a handful of chairs.

Kyle walked over but didn't sit. Maggie followed him, holding her purse over her shoulder. She could sense the tension in him and considered touching his hand but advised herself against it.

A minute later, Shane came to the front. He was a beefy guy with massive biceps and tree-trunk legs, though he was a few inches shorter than Kyle. His face lit up when he saw Kyle. "Bro! I didn't think I'd see you." His gaze drifted to Maggie, but he didn't comment on her presence.

Kyle moved close to him. "Can we talk somewhere private?"

Shane's expression sobered. "Sure, sure. This way." He led them into a nearby office. It was gray and nondescript, probably where they signed up new memberships. "Have a seat." He indicated a pair of chairs on one side of the desk as he closed the door.

Maggie sat, then looked up at Kyle's clenched jaw. Throwing her own advice to keep him at arm's length out the window, she clutched his fingers and pulled him to sit beside her.

His hand came around hers, holding her fast. She didn't mind. On the contrary, her body thrilled to his touch.

Shane went to the other side of the desk. "What's up?"

Kyle wiped his free hand over his mouth. "I don't know how to segue into this casually," he said, glancing at Maggie. "We're looking for something, and I thought you could help us."

Shane's dark brows pitched low over his eyes. "You know I'll help you if I can. Haven't I always been there for you?"

Kyle's hand tightened around hers, and she gave him a comforting squeeze, willing him to breathe through his anger. Why was she so good at monitoring and managing other people's stress while she completely sucked at doing the same for her own? Amy's words came back to her: "Do as I say, not as I do." *Totally.*

"Yeah." Kyle's voice sounded strained. "This is my... friend, Maggie." Shane's gaze dipped to their joined hands and reflected his disbelief. He judged them to be more than friends. So much the better for their ruse. Kyle continued, "She's recovering from an injury and needs some oxycodone, but her prescription is out and she can't get any until next week. Do you know where she can get some?" His words came out fast to her ears, but she felt very attuned to his anxiety. Probably because she felt it too, though not at the same level. Or maybe she just cared about him.

Shane looked at Maggie, his eyes sympathetic. "I wish I could help, but I'm not into that sort of thing."

Kyle sat forward, dropping Maggie's hand so that he could put both on the desk in front of him. "Come on, Shane. You know everybody. If you can't get it, you know someone who can."

"Probably, but I don't get involved in that sort of thing." He gave Kyle a stern look. "I know you think I'm a demon or something, but I'm not."

The muscles in Kyle's jaw worked, and Maggie could see the tension rioting through the pronounced veins in his arms and legs. "What about your boss? He's gotta be into that stuff."

Shane backed his chair up from the desk and stood. "Listen, bro, I need to get back to work."

Kyle leapt up and circled around the desk toward Shane. "Don't 'bro' me. I know Alex called you. Your number was in his contacts under a pseudonym. Tell me how you got him the drugs." His voice was pitched low, and she could practically feel his fury resonating in the small room.

Shane held up his hands. "Dude, I have no idea what you're talking about. I didn't give him any drugs."

"Bullshit!" Kyle pushed him in the chest, sending him back against the wall with a thud. "My brother is dead because some asshole sold him drugs that would kill him."

Maggie jumped out of her chair and went around the desk. She clutched at Kyle's arm. "Kyle, stop. Step back."

He didn't move, just stood there glaring at Shane.

Shane's eyes narrowed, and he straightened his T-shirt. "Listen to your girlfriend and step off, bro."

"You're a lying sack of shit," Kyle spat.

"Look, I didn't have anything to do with whatever drugs you're talking about. I placed some bets for him, that's all."

Holding Kyle's arm, she felt some of the anger seep out of his frame. "What?"

Shane shrugged. "He called me up and placed some bets from time to time. Nothing big. He wasn't a major player like you. I think it gave him some excitement since he couldn't get out much."

Maggie saw the change in Kyle's expression—it was as if she was watching a flower wilt and die before her eyes.

Kyle's shoulders sagged, the fight leaching out of him. "That's all you did?"

"That's it, bro, I swear." Shane clapped Kyle's shoulder, but he flinched away, moving back around the desk. "Kyle, I wouldn't do that to you. Not after everything we've been through."

Without looking back, Kyle strode from the office and left the gym.

Maggie had to jog to catch up to him. When they got to the car, he went directly to the driver's side. "Hey, aren't you going to open the door for me?" she asked, trying to defuse his frustration.

He came around, pinning her to the car. "I have nothing now."

About the drugs. They were back to square one. "You don't have nothing," she said quietly, hating the agony in his voice. "You have me." *What the hell, Maggie?* She wanted to bite the words back, but looking at him, seeing the vulnerability hiding just beneath his confident exterior, she felt a pull that wouldn't let her.

He stared down at her, his blue-green eyes thunderous. "Do I?" He inched closer, his body pressing her back against the car. Thank goodness it wasn't an excessively hot day, or the metal would've burned her. Or maybe not. As it was, she was far too aware of the heat in front of her to care what was behind her.

Knowing she was going to regret it, she ran her hand up his shirt and wrapped her palm around the base of his neck. Her fingers had barely met his flesh when his mouth came down over hers. She hadn't really known what hot was before. A scalding, burning desire raced through her as his tongue edged around her lips, opening her. She tilted her head and pressed her hand against him, urging him deeper.

He ground his hips into hers, and God, she didn't know if she'd ever felt a hunger like this. He was totally wrong for her with his past string of casual girlfriends, off-limits because of who he was and the way his family would judge her, the very embodiment of something she couldn't have and shouldn't want. And that only made it sweeter.

She brought her other hand up and tangled it in the hair on the back of his head as she kissed him back, thrusting her tongue against his.

His hands settled on her waist, digging into her through the thin T-shirt she wore. He pulled her against him, then drove her back, showing her exactly how he would make love to her, if she'd let him. Right now, she would've permitted him anything. Right now, she wanted to give him everything.

A catcall drew her back to reality—that, and the fact that they were making out in a parking lot in the middle of the afternoon.

She slid her hands from his neck and pulled away. His fingers still curled into her hips as he looked down at her, his eyes gleaming with their intensity.

"Sorry," she mumbled, scooting to the side.

He stepped back and let her go. "I'm not. You hungry?" He opened the door for her.

She stood there and gaped, her entire body aquiver. He'd seemed as impacted by the kiss as her, but now… now he was hungry?

Her stomach growled in response. "Apparently so." She climbed into the car and wondered how things had turned so quickly—not now, but before. When they'd come out to the car. That…kiss. That…passion.

He'd been upset. Because of Alex. And maybe because of Shane. What had he said? *I wouldn't do that to you. Not after everything we've been through*.

Kyle started the engine, but Maggie put her hand on his forearm, needing to understand just what she was dealing with here. With him. "You need to tell me what's up with you and Shane. Or you can take me home. What's it going to be?"

Chapter Six

KYLE LOOKED OVER at Maggie, her dark curls caressing her face the way he longed to do. When she'd pulled away from their kiss, he felt as though he were being deprived of air, like when he held his breath waiting to see if he'd won the wager and then he lost…

He fought now to reclaim his equilibrium and not succumb to the dark thoughts swirling in his head. Part of him wanted to go back inside and place a bet with Shane. But most of him wanted to drag Maggie into the backseat and lose himself in her.

She'd asked him a question—given him an ultimatum really. Spill his guts about Shane or take her home. Either way, they had an hour-plus drive ahead of them. Did he want it to be chilly or flirty, the way the ride in had been?

He started the car. "Do you like tacos? There's a food cart not far from here with the best Asian fusion street tacos."

"Does that mean you're going to talk?"

He threw her a gimlet eye. "Do I have a choice?"

"Of course you do. I'm not forcing you to talk to me, but I'd like to be here for you. If you'll let me."

He backed out and drove out of the lot. "Are you going to bill me?"

"I meant as your friend."

"Is that what we are?" He glanced at her, saw that her lips were pursed.

She looked over at him. "Yes, I think so. Don't you?"

He was sort of hoping that kiss meant they were more than friends, but was that such a good idea? Hanging out and working together were one thing. Anything more than that would be counterproductive to what he was trying to do. He couldn't very well prove to his father that he'd changed while dating the one woman Dad would never be able to look at without thinking of his dead son.

Kyle ran his hand through his hair as he turned a corner and headed for the food cart. "I already told you how I met Shane."

"Yes, but you didn't tell me why he feels as though you have some sort of bond. Your addiction drove you out of town. Why? What happened?"

"I got in over my head, and I needed a change." Growing antsy from the topic of conversation, he pulled over and threw the car into park. "You're supposed to ask me about Shane, not about my addiction."

She speared him with an unwavering stare. "Aren't they irrevocably intertwined?"

He pulled the keys from the ignition and huffed out a breath. "Yes."

"Have you ever dealt with your addiction? I mean, talked to someone?"

He kept his gaze fixed on the food cart on the next block, only sparing her a brief glance. "Therapy? No. I quit cold turkey when I moved to Florida, and that worked just fine."

She was quiet for a moment, then her fingers touched his hand. "Did it?"

He opened the door. "Let's eat."

She jumped out and met him on the curb. "Not yet. What was Shane talking about when he mentioned what you'd been through together? What aren't you telling me?"

He wanted to avoid the frank concern in her gaze. It reminded him of his family and their judgment. "Maybe I should just take you home."

She stepped closer. "What are you so afraid of?"

"That you won't like me very much." He scowled. Why had he said that? Because it was true.

"I don't think that's it." Her stare was unrelenting. "I think it's because *you* don't like you very much."

"Oh for Christ's sake, can you stop already?" He brushed past her and started walking toward the food cart. When they got there, he went immediately to the window and ordered. Irritation prickling through him, he turned to look at her. "What do you want?"

He'd expected her to look annoyed, but her face was serene. And that only frustrated him more. "Whatever you're having," she said.

He ordered and paid for the food and picked up their drinks. When he turned around, he saw that she'd snagged one of the few tables set off the sidewalk. Wondering why in the hell he hadn't gotten back in the car and driven her home, he sat down beside her.

He knew why he hadn't. He wanted to be here with her. He liked her. Far too much.

"You're nosy," he said at last.

"Yep." She smiled, and her eyes crinkled in the sexiest way. "But I'll stop. I don't want to piss you off. I do think you should talk to someone about your addiction. It's not something you overcome once. The temptation is always there."

"Don't you think I know that?" Hell, he thought about placing a bet every damn day. It was amazing how little things could be turned into a game of chance—how many gallons would fill his gas tank, whether the coffee pot would be full when he got to work, the number of times he'd think of kissing Maggie before he fell asleep tonight.

"Yes, I do. I really will shut up now." She sipped her iced tea. "Okay, one more question. Sorry. Are you really still friends with Shane? He made it seem like you were close."

"No. I'm sure he'd like to be." He snorted. "He'd like to bleed me dry again."

She scoffed. "Some friend."

"My sentiments exactly." He didn't want to be mad at her. He wanted to figure out what the hell he was going to do now that he'd hit a dead end. "We're still right back where we started with these stupid drugs."

She exhaled. "I know. Do you have any ideas?"

"Not one." He took a drink of iced tea, wishing he'd gotten a beer instead. Damn, today was a disappointment—kissing Maggie notwithstanding. "I guess I'll just go back to the beginning. Pore over every phone number, e-mail address—"

She jerked her head up. "E-mail. Have you read his e-mails?"

"Some." There were thousands on Alex's laptop. Kyle had skimmed through them, reading ones from people he didn't know, but he hadn't found anything to do with drugs. Plus, he'd done a search for certain words, including the names of the drugs. "I can go back through them. Scratch that, I *will* go back through them."

"What about hiring a computer forensics specialist? Aren't there people who can look for data on computers that might be hidden?" She shook her head. "I have no idea how that works, and maybe it's a Hollywood trick that doesn't actually exist."

Excitement pulsed in his chest. "No, I think it does. I know what you're talking about." And he couldn't believe he hadn't thought of it sooner. "I'll look into it."

The vendor called Kyle's name, so he got up and collected their food. They ate in relative silence. Kyle's mind was working fast and furiously as he contemplated this new angle. All of his frustration and angst from earlier twisted into anticipation and enthusiasm.

"These are really good," Maggie said, finishing her last taco. "Thanks for bringing me."

"My pleasure."

Her gaze caught his, and he sensed a thread of heat stretching between them. "Seems like I should get to interrogate you now that you've had your fun with me."

Her eyes widened slightly. "Oh, you think so?"

He shrugged. "Only seems fair."

"Okay, one question."

"One? Didn't you ask me at least three? Maybe four? And really, one of them was an ultimatum."

The little lines appeared between her brows.

He reached over and smoothed them away. "Stop that. I don't want to cause you concern."

She relaxed her features and folded her hands on the edge of the table. "Okay. Two questions."

Two questions. He had to make these good. Immediately, he knew what he had to ask and turned the tables on her. "Your bad relationship. What happened?"

She said something almost inaudible, but he was pretty sure it was "motherfucker." He suppressed a grin.

She looked at him dubiously. "I have to answer that?"

"Uh-huh."

With a loud exhalation, she got up and took her empty paper tray to the garbage. He leapt up and followed her as she started toward the car.

"He was controlling. Things got...weird."

He snagged her elbow and drew her to a stop. A primitive urge to find this asshole and beat him to within an inch of his life pulsed through him. "What do you mean?"

"He demanded too much of my time, wanted to decide who our friends were, where we would work—together." She shook him off and walked quickly back to the car.

Kyle rushed to open her door, waited until she was situated, then closed it and went to his side. He started the car and pulled into traffic. "That's it? You're going to leave me hanging?"

"There's not much more to tell. I didn't think we were doing specifics here." Her tone had gone cool.

"Hey, you started this, Nosey Parker."

She threw him a quizzical look. "What's a Nosey Parker?"

"You!" He laughed. "Okay, look, we've clearly entered a new stage of our relationship here. We're friends, I guess. Friends get to know each other, and that's what we're doing. I'll be here for you when you want to talk about Assclown."

She chuckled. "Good name for him."

For some reason he thought about the night he'd been waiting for her outside of her office. "I get one more question. That night that I scared you, had that happened to you before?" He tightened his grip on the steering wheel. If she said yes, he really might hunt this bastard down.

She was quiet a long time. Too long. "Yes. He…stalked me. But I got a restraining order, and I haven't heard from him in well over a year."

Oh yeah, if he ever saw that guy, he was totally punching him in the face. "What's his name?"

She shook her head. "Uh-uh. Two questions. And it's in the past. There's no need for you to go all *Gladiator* on him for me."

"I completely disagree, but I won't debate you." Time to get back to the easier conversation they'd enjoyed earlier. He needed to lighten things up if he was going to snag another kiss when he took her home. "*Gladiator*? Why *Gladiator*?"

She rolled her gorgeous brown eyes. "Because it's an awesome movie, duh. Russell Crowe kicks major ass."

"You're comparing me to Russell Crowe in *Gladiator*. Damn, that's about the best compliment I've had all week."

She punched him in the arm, reminding him sweetly of his sister Sara. "All week? You're pretty full of yourself, you know that?"

"Look at me, baby; wouldn't you be too?"

Her peals of laughter filled the car, and their conversation for the next hour centered around movie star comparisons and the benefits of a healthy ego.

When he pulled into her driveway, he was sorry to see their date come to an end. Date? Yeah, that had felt like a date.

This time when he got out of the car, she waited for him to open her door. He took her hand and helped her out, awareness tingling along every one of his nerve endings. Disappointingly, she withdrew her hand as he walked her to her front door.

She turned and looked up at him—the distance between them not very great since she was a good five foot eight. "Thanks for a fun afternoon. I'm sorry it didn't quite turn out the way you wanted it to, but I'm hopeful you'll find something in Alex's laptop."

"Yeah, me, too." He edged closer, inhaling her floral, citrusy scent. "I'm pretty happy with the way today turned out. And today's not technically over."

Her eyes narrowed slightly. "I...uh, I have plans tonight."

"Do you?" He moved even closer, and she backed against the door.

"Yes." She pursed her lips.

"When you do that, I just want to kiss you, and it looks as though your mouth wants me to, too. Does it?"

She blinked up at him. Her tongue darted out and glossed her lower lip.

"I'll take that as a yes," he murmured before claiming her mouth. He laid his palms flat against her door as he leaned in and angled his head to deepen the kiss.

Her mouth opened beneath his. He drove his tongue inside, sweeping against her moist heat. She tasted like sun and summer and everything he loved about life. *Delicious*.

Her hands came up and grasped the front of his T-shirt, holding him fast and steady while she rose up to meet him. It wasn't enough; he wanted to feel her flush against him, breast to chest, hip to thigh, groin to pelvis, like in the parking lot earlier. God, that had been amazing. He'd wanted her right then and there, public indecency be damned. And now here he was contemplating picking her up and spreading her thighs...

He pulled his head up. "Let's go inside," he rasped.

"No." She pushed him away—gently, but still away from her.

He frowned down at her. "What's the matter? You were totally into that." Yikes, if he wasn't careful, he might venture into ex-boyfriend assclown territory. "I mean, am I reading this wrong?"

She closed her eyes briefly, and when she opened them again, there was a certainty in her gaze. "You're not, but I'm not ready to invite you in."

He brushed her hair back from her face, his fingertips lingering on a soft, springy curl. "I'm not a vampire. It's not like I'll take advantage if you do."

She smiled. "I know. Just not today."

He exhaled, disappointed but hopeful since she hadn't said never. "Fair enough." He dipped his head and caught her lips once more. The kiss was brief but hot, and when he drew back, he tugged her bottom lip with his teeth and then grinned. "Next time, Maggie."

Pivoting, he walked back to Hayden's car, whistling. He knew when he turned around, she'd still be outside her door watching him. He wasn't wrong. She waved as he backed out.

No, today hadn't worked out the way he'd imagined at all. It had turned out far better.

KYLE SIPPED HIS iced coffee, tapped his foot to the song on Pandora, and smiled to himself as he looked over the final plans for the Ribbon Ridge Festival booth. He didn't remember the last time he'd been in such a good mood. Yesterday had been amazing, despite the dead end with Shane. After leaving Maggie's, he'd spent the evening scouring Alex's computer, and this morning, he'd scheduled an appointment with a computer forensics specialist for early next week.

Things were good. Now if he could only figure out a way to take Maggie to the Ribbon Ridge Festival. Maybe

he could pass her off as someone other than Alex's therapist. No one else in the family had met her, as far as he
knew. Perhaps he ought to verify that.

But would she come? She seemed to avoid Ribbon
Ridge like the plague.

A knock on his door interrupted his groove. He
paused the music. "Come in."

Dad stepped inside and closed the door behind him.
"Got a minute?"

They hadn't spoken much since their confrontation
the other day. And when they had, they'd steered clear of
personal topics, sticking only to work issues.

Kyle sat back in his chair. "Sure, what's up?"

Dad looked at one of the chairs but didn't take it.
Instead, he walked over to the windows and looked out
at the rolling hills. Kyle turned and watched him warily.

"I hope you won't fly off the handle," Dad started,
almost making Kyle laugh, as Dad's temper since Alex's
death was the shortest Kyle could ever remember, "but we
need to talk about your problem."

"My 'problem.'" *How condescending.* "My gambling
addiction, you mean? Let's just call it what it is, okay?"

Dad turned to look at him, his gray eyes piercing.
"Yes, let's. Did you get help in Florida?"

Christ, had he and Maggie compared notes since
yesterday? Her questions had made him uncomfortable,
but Dad's query positively rankled. "I managed things
just fine."

"How were things when you left to come home? I
know Mom paid for your plane ticket…"

Which means you must've been broke.

Gooseflesh broke out on the back of Kyle's neck. "She offered." That was true, but so was the broke part. He did *not* want Dad to know that. His disappointment was already so palpable and so disheartening.

"I'm sure she did." Dad was quiet a moment, as if he were carefully choosing his words. He probably was. "I noticed you brought nothing home with you, save clothing. You were gone nearly four years. What were you doing? What do you have to show for it?"

Kyle stared at him. What could he say? "I'm not gambling now, Dad."

"But you were." Dad cut his hand through the air. "Goddamn it, Kyle. I won't bail you out again."

Kyle clutched the arm of his chair, fighting the urge to run, to escape his father's censure. "I haven't asked you to. In fact, I've *never* asked you to."

Dad's brows angled over his ice-gray eyes. "You would've let those men break your legs or whatever they'd threatened to do before asking for help. Your pride is that important to you?"

"Your approval and respect are."

Dad's eyes widened. "This isn't about that."

"Isn't it?" Kyle gritted his teeth, hating how weak and desperate he felt. How the realization that he would never be good enough in his father's eyes cut into his very soul. "Do you approve of the choices I made? Do you respect them?"

Dad looked out the window again, and Kyle's chest tightened. "You're my son, and I love you." He turned back to Kyle. "This isn't about respect. This is about honesty and trust and accountability."

A part of Kyle wanted to tell him everything. How devastated he'd been after Alex's death. How he'd gone back to Florida thinking he'd feel better far away, since that had seemed to work before. But he hadn't. He'd felt even worse being away from everyone and anyone who had known Alex. So he'd gambled. Just a bit at first, but for someone like him, it never stayed small. He'd been on a roll. At one point, he'd won enough money that he could've opened a restaurant, but he hadn't stopped. The pain had receded, and he was the king of the world. Then he'd started losing. And soon he was in that spiral where the next bet was going to turn it around. Only it never did. Until the losses had piled up and obliterated his bank account. He'd sold everything he owned to pay it all off so that when he came back home, he wouldn't be absolutely flat broke. Close, but not quite.

But the words stuttered in his throat and died before they could reach his tongue. Instead, he said, "I'm trying really hard to be accountable, to contribute, to earn your respect. Can you let me do that? Will you give me that chance?"

"I'm trying to."

Kyle considered saying something about Dad's apparent inability to grieve the loss of Alex. He couldn't help but wonder if Dad was focusing even more on Kyle's shortcomings in an effort to ignore his own pain. But in the end, he couldn't do it. He just wasn't ready to open wounds, or maybe he just didn't want to give Dad another reason to find fault with him.

Dad came forward and clapped him on the knee. "All right then, what's going on for tomorrow? Everything all set for the booth?" He moved around to the front of the desk.

Kyle swung his chair back and looked down at the plan they'd laid out, pushing the bitter conversation to the back of his mind. "Yep. We've got everything ready. The booth is going up at eight tomorrow morning. I'll be there overseeing it. We've got all the beer, snacks, merchandise, and the staffing schedule is complete."

"You'll be there tomorrow evening too? I know you haven't gone in years, but typically the whole family's there—well, whoever's here." He looked a little unsettled.

"Are you thinking about Mom?" Kyle didn't know if things were still tense between them.

Dad nodded. "And Hayden. It's very strange not having him here. And that's no dig against you."

"None taken. I know Sara and Dylan will be there."

"Right, and Tori. I wish Evan and Liam were coming. Liam usually does, but not this year."

Liam had been a real prick since Alex had died. He'd refused any involvement in the renovation project whatsoever. Granted, Kyle had done the same at the beginning, but partly because Liam had been such a jerk about presuming that Kyle had no life in Florida and could simply drop everything and move home to work on the project. It turned out that Kyle's anger had come from the fact that Liam had been right. Which still made Liam an asshole.

"Of course Derek and Chloe too," Dad said.

Of course.

Kyle could handle that. He liked Chloe, not that they'd spent much time getting to know each other considering he and Derek could barely stand being in the same room together. Tomorrow could be awkward since it would be a more social setting than the office, but with so many people around to act as buffers, especially Sara, Kyle shelved his apprehension to the back of his mind.

With a nod, Dad left.

Kyle thought again about bringing Maggie, but the prospect of Dad finding out that he was dating—*dating?*—the therapist who'd failed to see suicidal signs in Alex's behavior was enough to prevent him from actually inviting her. Crap, what was he doing with her anyway? What sort of future could they have given who she was and how much his family would despise him for being with her? If he was trying to earn respect and approval, getting into a relationship with Maggie Trent was the last thing he should do.

Why was he even thinking about this? He wasn't a relationship guy. Twenty-eight years old and not one long relationship. Maybe he was also addicted to being alone.

And just like that, his good mood went right down the toilet.

Chapter Seven

WITH A FINAL snip, Maggie concluded her rose bush trimming. The rental house had a nice little rose garden with five plants in the backyard, but they'd been woefully ignored. Instead of coming right in and whacking them to bits, she'd carefully trimmed over the past several weeks to coax new growth and encourage blooms. That and some fertilizer had already transformed them from sad, spindly shrubs to glowing, happy bushes.

With this success, a bit of her anxiety faded. It had been a rough afternoon with Ryan—her toughest patient at present. After last Saturday's emergency appointment, today had been his regular session, and it had run long since the one after had canceled. They'd been alone in the clinic by the time they'd finished, and she was surprised to find it had made her a little uncomfortable. She wasn't afraid of Ryan—the poor man was an emotional mess—but there was something about him that reminded her of Mark. His neediness, maybe?

She shook her head, stowing her clippers in the pocket of her apron and picking up the basket of rose clippings. She was a therapist, for crying out loud. Dealing with needy people was part of the job. A *huge* part of it. Plus, it had never bothered her before, so why now? Because Alex's death had made her doubt her abilities.

Walking to the large debris bin she'd wheeled from the front, she dumped the clippings and moved on to her next project: the vegetable garden.

She'd gotten a late start since she hadn't moved into the house until the first of June, but the tomatoes, cucumbers, and squash were coming along nicely. And the lettuce bed was already ripe for harvest and would continue to be for some time. She smiled at her happy little plants before turning to get the hose.

The hose bib was at the corner of the house, near the path from the front. As she bent to pick up the hose, a shadow darkened the path, but it wasn't the outline of a shrub or tree from the setting sun. It was a person. Holding the spray nozzle like a gun, her heart picked up speed.

"Maggie?"

Kyle's voice immediately calmed the sudden wild pounding of her pulse, but she decided to spray him as he rounded the corner. He sucked in air as his T-shirt became plastered to his chest.

Whoa, that had been a bad idea; now his abs were perfectly delineated beneath the wet cotton. And she'd been right—totally cut.

"Kyle, you scared me again. Knock it off!"

He plucked at his shirt. "Good thing it's still warm out." Summer nights in northwestern Oregon ranged from hot to chilly, but at this point in July, hot often won out.

"Sorry." She actually wasn't. He'd deserved it, and now she got to enjoy the view. Averting her gaze before she full-on stared, she put the fertilizer canister onto the end of the hose. "What are you doing here?"

"Hi there, nice to see you, too. I had a terrific day, how about you?"

She suppressed a smile at his teasing tone—it wouldn't do to encourage him. "Did you find something on Alex's computer?"

"Not yet, but I have an appointment with a computer forensics specialist on Monday." He trailed her as she went to the vegetable garden to water the plants. "Do we have to use the drug investigation as the only reason to talk? I thought we were friends."

She glanced at him, wondering what he was up to tonight. Yesterday had been amazing—the conversation, the revelations, the kisses. She hadn't been that amped up in a very long time. It had felt good. So why not let it continue? Because he was Kyle freaking Archer, that's why.

"We *are* friends, but friends don't usually drop by unannounced." She started spraying the veggies.

"I did text, but it looks like you were maybe busy out here. You have a real talent in the garden. Those tomato plants are going to be amazing. I'll have to make you some of my salsa."

Now she wished she'd planted peppers. Damn. "Promise?"

He nodded, grinning. "Is that an heirloom plant?"

"Yes, those are my favorites."

"Mine, too. I make a mean heirloom tomato salad. Guess I'm going to be feeding you all summer. How's the kitchen in there?" He nodded toward the house.

"Fine." She barely knew. Cooking was not her thing, unless you counted heating frozen meals or ordering takeout. About the only thing she made was salad, hence the vegetable garden she'd planted. "It's a little outdated, but it has all the essentials." Not that she planned on showing him anytime soon. Or ever.

"Can I go check it out?"

She shook her head. "Nope. Still not inviting you inside. I didn't even invite you *over*." She gave him a scolding look.

He held up his hands. "Sheesh, tough crowd tonight. You sure your day was fine?"

No, but she didn't want to get into it. Listening to Ryan talk to her about contemplating suicide had been enough to drive her directly to the Xanax as soon as she'd gotten into her car.

"It was fine. Look, when I've restocked my garlic and collection of cross-shaped mirrors, I'll invite you in, okay?"

He laughed. "Fair enough. I won't push it, since I didn't give you warning. I did want to ask you something."

She looked over at him, sensing a thread of nervousness that was sort of cute. Was he about to ask her on a real date? Her blood heated just as her neck iced—such a damn conundrum.

"Why do you avoid Ribbon Ridge?"

After soaking the tomatoes, she moved on to the cukes. "I don't avoid it." The hell she didn't. "I just don't have any reason to go there."

"The Ribbon Ridge Festival is this weekend. It's really fun. Great food, Archer beer of course, arts and crafts, fireworks."

Yeah, she'd gone last year. She'd loved it. She'd loved Ribbon Ridge. It was just far enough from the big city to be a cozy half-country town, but close enough to feel civilized. And she loved the wine country views and the denizens' charm. But after Alex had died, it had completely lost its luster. The Archers were the first family of Ribbon Ridge, and she'd utterly failed one of them.

"Mmmm," was all she said.

"I though you might like to go."

Her finger came off the trigger of the hose nozzle, and she snapped her head around to look at him. Was he crazy? Being in Ribbon Ridge would be disquieting enough, but being in Ribbon Ridge with Kyle Archer would invite a whole world of criticism she wasn't remotely ready to endure and might never be.

"Thanks, but no."

When he looked genuinely disappointed, she felt a moment's regret. However, just the thought of being in Ribbon Ridge was taking the edge off her Xanax.

"Are you going to tell me why you left?"

She pressed the trigger on the hose again and shot water all over the cucumbers and zucchini. "Isn't it obvious?"

"You had a practice there and a home, right? You threw all of that away because Alex killed himself?" There was a note of concern in the questions, but his phrasing pushed her over the edge.

She swung around, and he jumped back before the spray hit him. She lifted her finger from the nozzle, cutting off the stream of water. "I didn't throw anything away. I had to leave. I couldn't...I'm not talking about this." She pulsed a bit more water on the zucchinis.

He stepped closer. She could see him from the corner of her eye but didn't turn to look at him. "Hey, I'm sorry. I didn't mean to push. I figured his death must have been hard for you, but I guess I didn't realize just how bad it was."

"I'd never lost a patient before." But then she'd only been practicing for about a year and a half. After breaking up with Mark and looking to start over somewhere completely new, she'd bought a retiring therapist's practice in Ribbon Ridge. She'd been so excited for the future, for the changes she'd made. Things had started slow, but by the time Alex had killed himself, she'd established a decent little practice. And just like that, her dreams had collapsed. "I felt like a complete failure." She still did, but she couldn't tell him that. She wouldn't.

He touched her arm, tugged her elbow to get her to turn around. "Maggie."

She shut the hose off and let herself be pulled. His blue-green eyes were full of compassion, and she nearly spilled everything—Mark, her breakdown...

"Helloooooo? Magnolia?" Mom's voice cut off Maggie's train of thought and shrouded her in dread. The questions she'd have to suffer once Mom caught sight of Kyle in all his wet T-shirt glory...

Mom stopped short as she stepped into the backyard. "Oh! You have company. I didn't realize."

No, because you just dropped in. Like Kyle. What happened to respecting a person's privacy?

Kyle had also turned at the sound of Mom's voice, and now he looked between them, probably guessing they were related. The curly hair, though Mom's was almost entirely silver, was a dead giveaway.

Mom strode forward with purpose. "Hi, I'm Magnolia's mom, Val." She offered her hand.

Kyle shook it, looking perhaps a tad bemused. But most people were when they took in the henna tattoos covering Mom's hands, the long batik skirt that grazed her Birkenstocks, and the amalgamation of jewelry cluttering her neck and arms. At least she was wearing a bra.

"Hi, I'm Kyle Archer."

Mom's brow curved up, and she shot Maggie a questioning glance. Mom knew all about Alex, of course, and Maggie only prayed she wouldn't taunt the elephant in the room, er, yard.

Mom shook his hand. "Are you, now? Well, it's a pleasure to meet you. I'm so sorry to have interrupted." She darted a suggestive look between them, and it was all Maggie could stand.

"Kyle just stopped in to return something he thought I might like to have. A totem I gave Alex during therapy."

She was rather impressed with herself for coming up with such a good lie so easily.

Kyle looked at her in question, clearly wanting to ask if the totem part was true. She averted her gaze, wanting nothing more than for one of them to leave. Or both, preferably. Why wasn't her Xanax working better?

"Is that all?" Mom asked, sounding dismayed. "I was hoping Kyle was the guy you had dinner with last week." She glanced between them again, her hazel eyes dancing. "Oops, did I just let the cat out of the bag? Maybe my little flower bud has a few boys trailing after her." She patted Maggie on the shoulder. "That's my girl."

Maggie wanted to melt into the ground in mortification. She chanced a look at Kyle, who didn't look the least bit upset. No, he looked amused, the jerk. Nothing about her mother was funny.

"All righty, then," Maggie said, dragging the hose back to the house and winding it up. "Thanks for stopping by, Kyle."

Thankfully, he took the hint. "Nice to meet you, Val." He waved at Mom and then came over to Maggie. He dipped his head toward hers and spoke next to her ear. "Magnolia? Your name is Magnolia?"

She gritted her teeth. "Can it."

A low chuckle rumbled in his chest. He kissed her cheek. "Next time I come over, you're going to invite me in and tell me all about this situation." When he backed away from her, his eyes glowed with mirth, and she resisted the urge to kick him in the shin.

Instead, she forced a smile. "Bye."

He turned and waved at Mom again before disappearing around the side of the house.

"Oooh, he's yummy!" Mom brought her hands together, jangling the bracelets encircling both wrists. "You've been holding out on me."

"I haven't. He's no one. What are you doing here, Mom? It's not like I live down the street, for crying out loud."

"Oh I know, dear, but I wanted to bring you something. It's in the car. I couldn't carry it on my own. My neighbor is downsizing, and he wanted you to have his night-blooming cereus."

"Really?" Maggie stalked past her mom and followed the path around the house to the front. She heard Kyle drive away and was glad that he was gone and away from her mother. She also heard Mom following her.

"I know how much you've always liked it."

No, she loved it. Coveted it. Had wanted one of her very own since the first time she'd watched it bloom. Harv—their neighbor—held parties to watch the flower because each bud opened for just one night. Maggie had seen it for the first time when she was twelve, and she'd been entranced with plants ever since.

It sat in the back of Harv's truck, which Mom had clearly borrowed to transport it. Over six feet tall and in a large box-like planter, it was an incredibly ugly plant from the cactus family, with spindly branches and stems. Its flat, uninteresting leaves were sparse, almost making the plant look as if it were dead or dying half the time. You'd never guess the massive flowers, which bloomed just once and only at night, were so delicate and beautiful.

"I brought a little wheeled cart to get it inside," Mom said.

Sure enough, there was a flat cart, sort of like the scooter Maggie had zoomed around on in gym class as a kid.

"We should've had Kyle stay and help us," Mom said beside her. "Call him and have him come back."

That would mean letting him inside—no way. "No, we'll manage." But now she had to let Mom inside. There was no help for it. Thank God Maggie had taken the Xanax, or she'd probably insist on wrestling the thing inside by herself. Or settle for just leaving it in the garage.

Mom lowered the gate to the truck and pulled out the cart, setting it on the driveway. She climbed up into the back, incredibly agile for a woman in her late fifties, but then she'd done yoga every day for the last thirty-plus years. She unhooked the bungee cords holding the plant against the side of the truck while Maggie circled around to the side to help her scoot it to the edge of the bed.

"You like it?" Mom's tone was hopeful, like a child asking his parents if they liked the macaroni necklace he'd made them.

But Maggie didn't have to pretend to like anything about it. Her mother's lifestyle drove her crazy, but Maggie couldn't deny her thoughtfulness or find fault with the depth of her love. Despite their differences, she was grateful to have someone who cared for her that much. "I love it, Mom. Really. Thank you."

Mom smiled. "I knew you'd love it. How many nights did you go over to Harv's to watch this thing bloom?"

"As many as I was around for." It could bloom several times in a summer, sometimes multiple flowers going at once. The most she remembered was four…and the stench! The fragrance was sweet and somewhat pretty with one flower, but with so many it had become cloying and oppressive. Harv had opened every window and even run some fans to move the air. Maggie smiled at the memory. Sometimes it was good to remember that her youth wasn't all awkwardness.

With Mom in the back of the truck and Maggie walking alongside it, they worked together to slide the planter to the edge of the bed and lower it to the cart. Maggie wheeled it into the garage, which was open; then they had to take it off the cart to get it up the step and into the laundry room. She transferred the cart inside, and they hefted the planter up onto it.

Maggie's gaze flicked to the basket of clean clothes on the dryer and the stack of recyclable bags on the washer. This room wasn't bad, but the rest…She turned to Mom. "I can take it from here. Thanks."

Mom glanced down at the cart. "I'll need to take that back to Harv."

Duh, right. "Okay, wait here, and I'll just bring it right back." She started pushing it through the laundry room into the kitchen.

"Can't I come see where you're going to put it?"

No. "Um…I don't know where. You know, I'll just set it here for now." She pushed it through the kitchen to the eating nook. Stacks of mail and some work papers cluttered the table, and a few boxes she had yet to unpack formed a short tower in the corner.

"You're acting strange—" Mom's jaw dropped as she turned and looked into the large living room. She inhaled sharply. "Holy mother. Haven't you moved in?"

Not really. Several stacks of boxes sat at intervals throughout the space. Pictures leaned against the wall. The television was perched on its media cabinet facing away from the couch, its wires hanging to the ground in a mess. The couch was covered with a pile of clothes, mostly coats.

Mom swung around and looked at Maggie. "I don't understand. What's wrong with you?"

"Nothing. I only moved in at the beginning of last month." Her defenses kicked into high gear. "Thanks for bringing the plant, Mom. You should probably head back into town before it gets too late." Maggie bent and guided the planter off the cart.

"Oh, no. You aren't getting rid of me yet, Magnolia." God, how that name grated on Maggie's nerves. Who named their kid after a flowering tree? A hippie who thought sticking out was far better than fitting in, that's who. "Why does your house look like this? It never used to—not when you lived with Mark anyway."

No, because he'd required everything to be perfect. When she'd moved to Ribbon Ridge, she'd done what he'd trained her to do—adhered to strict order and tidiness. But over time, she'd realized she didn't have to do that anymore. With each item of clothing she didn't hang up and every book she left sitting on a table instead of on a bookshelf, she felt a little more of her freedom returning. Perhaps she'd gone a little too far…

No, she knew she'd gone more than a little too far. But now it was overwhelming. She'd accumulated so much stuff, things that Mark insisted she take, things she hated and ought to get rid of but simply couldn't face.

"Maggie, are you going to answer me?"

Jarred back to the present, Maggie refocused on Mom. "I've been putting all my energy into the yard because it's summer and the weather's good. I'll take care of the house later. It's not like I have company."

Mom shook her head. "That's another problem entirely. How can you invite that attractive man over when your place looks like you've become a hoarder?" She flicked a glance at the television. "Though I wholeheartedly approve of you forgoing the TV."

Never mind that Mom had become quite the Internet whore over the past few years. What was the difference really? Maggie couldn't resist saying, "I have a TV in my bedroom that I watch."

"Ah." She touched Maggie's arm. "Maybe you should see a therapist."

I am. But Maggie didn't tell her that. "I'll think about it. Listen, Mom, I need to finish up outside before it gets dark. Thanks again for the plant, really." She smiled, and it wasn't forced. She was genuinely happy about the cactus. "That was really thoughtful, and I appreciate it." She leaned over and kissed Mom's soft cheek, catching the faint scent of patchouli.

Maggie could tell Mom wanted to stay and say more, but she wasn't completely clueless. She said good night, then Maggie walked her back out to the truck and watched her drive away.

Boy, her next appointment with Amy was going to be busy. Mom, Kyle, her almost-suicidal patient, her house...

After finishing up in the yard and closing up the garage, Maggie trudged back inside and looked at her new acquisition. Shit, did accepting the plant prove that she was a hoarder? No, she wasn't. She just needed time to go through everything and decide what to do with it.

A tingle of unease crept up her spine. Perhaps she ought to do it soon. There was no telling when Kyle would come back and try again to come inside. She could continue to refuse him, but she was growing weak. And everyone knew the third time was the charm.

KYLE WAS IN his element. Manning the Archer booth at the Ribbon Ridge Festival reminded him of tending bar in Florida. His family might look down on how he'd spent the last few years, but he'd had a great time and grown comfortable in his skin.

Mostly.

It was good to be back home though. A steady stream of Ribbon Ridgers had stopped by all afternoon and chatted him up, happy to see him. And he felt the same.

But as it drew close to six, when all the Archers were supposed to congregate at the booth for photos and general rah-rah family shit, Kyle's nerves started to fray. He did Maggie's breathing exercises and told himself it would be fine—he'd avoid Derek like he always did.

Maggie. Had he really tried to invite her to the festival? What kind of bonehead move was that? Dating her was out of the question—at least until he regained Dad's approval. And even then, he wasn't sure he could do it. Being with Maggie could very well undo all of the work he was doing to show his family that he wasn't as selfish as they thought.

Sara and Dylan walked toward the booth early, which is what Dylan preferred to be. As the general contractor for the monastery renovation, he was punctual, tireless, and committed. He was also head-over-ass crazy about Kyle's sister.

Kyle raised a hand as they approached. "Hey there. Sorry, we don't have any cider, Sara-cat."

"I know," Sara said, tucking a strand of blonde hair behind her ear. "Any fruity beer? I forget what you brought."

"Yes, we have Will Scarlett." A raspberry ale that he knew wasn't her favorite, but then drinking beer was usually a stretch for her.

"I'll have that. Can't be an Archer at the Archer booth without an Archer beer in my hand."

Kyle flashed her a smile as he drew the beer into a cup and slid it across the narrow counter. "Dylan? Longbow, Arrowhead, or Popinjay?"

Dylan pondered a moment. "Popinjay, I think. Been awhile since I had a Belgian-style."

"Excellent choice on this fine summer evening." Kyle filled his cup and handed it to him. "I'm surprised you're here instead of at the site."

He lifted his cup. "Are you inferring I *should* be there?"

"God no, you work enough. I'm glad you knocked off early. I hope you let the crew go, too."

"I gave them the option. Some would rather work later tonight and come to the festival tomorrow with their families." Likely so they could play the carnival games and ride the rides.

Kyle nodded. "You're a good boss."

Sara slid her arm around Dylan's waist. "The best."

Kyle rolled his eyes. "Knock it off. You two are enough to make a man nauseated."

"You're just jealous—you'll find someone," Sara said, smiling.

"Ha!" Dylan chuckled. "He has to actually look first."

Actually, he'd found someone when he'd least been looking for her…not that he could compare what he felt about Maggie to the deep bond that had formed between Sara and Dylan. He was pretty sure a marriage proposal wasn't too far off.

Speaking of marriage, Derek and Chloe were striding toward the booth hand in hand. Another couple who could induce vomiting with their cuteness and general in-love-ness. Thankfully, Tori and Dad arrived at the same time with a photographer from the local paper in tow.

Kyle and the other four people manning the booth doled out beer to everyone, including the photographer and the other festival attendees who had started to arrive in droves now that they were home from work. The photographer snapped photos of the activity and asked the Archers to pose for a picture.

Derek lingered in the background—never quite sure if he ought to be included. Most people only cared about the kids who'd been on the TV show, and that didn't include him, though as Kyle's best friend, he'd appeared on it several times.

"Derek, get up here," Dad barked jovially. "And bring Chloe. You know this is my adoptive son, Derek Sumner," he said to the photographer, "and this is his fiancée, Chloe English."

They exchanged pleasantries with the photographer, who asked, "When's the big day?"

"In just a couple of weeks," Chloe answered. "Up at the monastery we're renovating."

After a few formal shots in which they held up their cups of beer, they broke up again. Kyle noticed that Dylan had stood off to the side for the pictures. "Don't want to be associated with us?" he asked, kidding.

"You know me, families give me hives." Dylan was the product of parents who'd divorced when he was very young, ensuring that he'd grown up with a foot in two households. He'd talked a little bit to Kyle about feeling more comfortable on his own, but since falling for Sara, he was becoming indoctrinated into the big, crazy Archer family, whether he liked it or not. And Kyle understood Dylan's reticence better than anyone. Sometimes the family situation was simply more than he could bear.

Natalie came rushing up to the booth. "Sorry I'm late!"

"Nah, you're fine," said Royce, the booth worker she was taking over for. He wiped his hands on a towel and gave a salute. "See you around, Archers, it's been real."

Kyle clapped him on the back. "Thanks, Royce."

"Yeah, thanks man," Derek chimed in. He was Royce's boss.

Natalie moved behind the counter. "So what do we do?"

"Just pour the beer and sell the merchandise, if someone wants a T-shirt or pint glass or whatever. We have a Square to take credit or debit cards." He indicated the iPad one of the other workers was using to charge someone's order. "And the cash box is down there." He gestured under the counter.

"Got it."

"In fact, I should count out what we made this afternoon so there isn't too much in the till." He grabbed the box and took it to the back of the booth, where there was a small work area. He counted out the starting cash and handed the box to Natalie. "Go ahead and put that back on the shelf."

The counting didn't take long, which was puzzling. They should've made more than that. He recounted, going more slowly. He got the same amount. After the third time, he decided there must've been more credit card use than he'd realized. He documented the bills on a deposit slip and stuffed all of it into a zippered bank bag, which he then locked. He tucked the bag beneath the back work area and figured he ought to give the key to Derek, who was taking over at the booth for the rest of the evening.

Natalie glanced at the work schedule on the back counter and made a duck face. "Well, that sucks."

Kyle went and stood next to her. "What?"

"I thought you were working tonight. That's why I signed up for this shift."

"I was, but Derek asked to switch because Chloe had a meeting this afternoon." Chloe was the art director for Archer Enterprises. She designed all of the decoration for the Archer spaces, which included murals and other custom paintings. The art, along with the beer, was a signature aspect of an Archer brewpub. She was also a sometimes waitress at The Arch and Vine, filling in when needed, as they all did. Kyle hadn't yet been asked to supply his cooking skills, but he'd made it known that he was available and interested.

Natalie turned and looked up at him. "That's a total bummer." She smoothed her dark hair back behind her ears and caught the mass, bringing it forward over one shoulder. "I was really looking forward to working with you. Now it'll be boring."

He laughed. "No, it won't. Dave's here. Dave's hilarious." He was a bartender at one of their pubs outside Ribbon Ridge.

She touched his arm briefly, lightly, but it was enough to convey her flirtatious intent. "Dave's not you." Her voice held a little pout.

Kyle glanced down at where she'd brushed her fingers against him.

"Sorry!" She clapped her hand over her mouth. "I might've had a large glass of pinot over at the A.F. Nichols booth."

He suppressed a laugh, not wanting to make her any more uncomfortable. "Was it good?"

Her eyes narrowed slightly with pleasure. "Delicious. You should go get a glass."

"Maybe I will." He smiled down at her. "Thanks."

He headed out of the booth, and Sara stepped into his path. "When I said you should look for someone, I didn't mean right now." Her gaze drifted to Natalie, who was pouring a beer for a customer.

"What? Natalie?" Kyle shook his head. "That's just work stuff."

Sara kept her voice low. "Didn't look like work stuff to me. Looked like flirty, cutesy stuff. She was devouring you like a menopausal woman at a chocolate buffet."

He laughed, couldn't help it. "She wasn't either." Sara's gaze turned sharp, and he relented. "Okay, she was flirting a little."

"So were you."

Was he? He hadn't meant to. He liked Natalie, but they were coworkers—hell, he was technically her boss—and that was it. "Unintentional."

"Are you sure? She's your type."

"I have a type? Sara, I barely see someone more than a few months. How can I have a type?"

"Dark hair, dark eyes." Like Maggie. "Natalie's a perfect match." Kyle glanced back at the booth. Natalie laughed at something one of the customers said. Yeah, she was a knockout, but no, not perfect...

He looked down at his sister. "Absolutely unintentional, really. I'm not interested in her."

Sara poked him lightly in the chest. "Make sure she knows that."

He winked at her, then turned to find Derek. He was over to the side of the booth, talking to Dad. Taking a deep, cleansing Maggie-breath, he strode toward them. *Smile, Kyle.*

"Hey, Derek, here's the key to the cash bag. I counted out the day's receipts, but I haven't matched them up against the totals." He dropped the key into Derek's upturned palm.

Derek closed his hand and pocketed the key. "Thanks."

Awkward silence ensued for a good thirty seconds before Kyle said, "See you later."

Tori gestured for him to come over to where she and Dylan were talking. "Kyle, I wanted to tell you that the permits are in the approval process. We'll be ready to move ahead with the restaurant and brewpub as soon as the wedding space is done."

"Great." Kyle couldn't wait to get started. He jabbed his thumb toward Dylan. "We should give this guy and his crew a few days off at least."

She looked over at Dylan. "Yeah, we should."

Dylan shook his head. "Not necessary."

Tori frowned at him. "Hey, just because you're a work-aholic doesn't mean your employees should be."

"It's cool. My guys are taking time as they need it."

"Are *you*?" Tori asked. "If you don't take at least one day off, my sister's going to have a fit."

Sara was over chatting with Chloe. As if she knew she was being mentioned, she waved at them. Dylan's eyes lit up. "Yeah, okay. I'll take a couple."

Kyle slapped him on the back. "Smart man."

They talked for a while longer about the project before Kyle asked if they wanted to join him over at the A.F. Nichols booth for a glass of pinot. Before they could be on their way, Derek came toward them. Kyle was surprised when he didn't immediately tense. Maybe Maggie's breathing exercises really were helping.

"Kyle, can I talk to you?" Derek's tone was stern, provoking Kyle's muscles to bunch up.

"Sure."

They moved away from Tori and Dylan.

Derek glanced away. He seemed uncomfortable. *Great.* "I just checked the receipts, and they don't match up with the cash bag. Are you sure you counted correctly?"

Ice pricked Kyle's spine. "Yeah, I counted it three times. I suppose I could've miscounted what I left in the box."

Derek shook his head, his dark blue eyes growing even darker. "No, I counted that, too. And I had Scott double-check it. There's money missing."

"There can't be. I was at the booth all afternoon." Except for when he'd gone to get lunch. "It has to be there somewhere."

Kyle stalked toward the booth. Derek was right behind him, and together they searched the small space.

"What're you guys looking for?" Natalie asked.

"There's some money missing—almost a hundred bucks," Derek muttered.

She glanced between them. "Can I help?"

Derek stopped and looked at Kyle. "It's not here."

They'd exhausted every nook and cranny. "I don't know what happened."

Derek inclined his head for Kyle to follow him out of the booth. When they were out of earshot of the others, he lowered his voice. "Did you take it?"

Kyle glared at him. "Are you fucking kidding me right now?"

"Unfortunately, no."

"You're a real dick, you know that? Of course I didn't take it."

"You wouldn't lie, would you?"

Kyle couldn't tell if Derek wanted to believe him or not. And he didn't care. His head was swimming. It was one thing to feel betrayed by your best friend and another to realize he'd lost all faith in you. "No, and I'll tell you this," he said, leaning forward and sneering at the man who'd once been closer to him than any of his blood brothers, "if I'd wanted to take some money to gamble, a lousy hundred bucks wouldn't cut it."

Derek's jaw tightened, but he didn't say anything.

Dad came up to them. Kyle cringed. He was just what this situation needed. "What's going on?"

"The till's missing close to a hundred dollars," Derek said, never taking his gaze from Kyle's.

Kyle's blood pounded through his veins as his heart rate sped up. "Derek thinks I took it."

Dad blinked at him. "Did you?" At least *he* looked disbelieving.

"No, Dad. I didn't. But thanks for giving me the benefit of the doubt. I gotta go." He started to turn, but Derek grabbed his bicep.

"You can't just leave."

"Why not? What're you going to do? Call the cops? Notify everyone that I'm a thief and a gambler and an utter wastrel?" He laughed bitterly. "Go ahead, but I'm not sticking around for it." He wished he had a hundred dollars on him to throw in their faces, but that would only make him look guilty. In fact…He pulled out his front pockets, showing them to be empty and took his wallet from his back pocket. Opening the slot where he kept his bills, he showed them the interior. "Here." He counted it out. "Thirty-three bucks. All yours." He shoved it at Derek. "Dock my pay for the rest." He threw Dad a glare. "Or are you going to fire me on the spot for larceny?"

Derek hadn't caught all the money. He bent to retrieve it.

"Derek, maybe you owe Kyle an apology," Dad said.

Derek shot up, his blue eyes blazing. That had been the wrong thing to say. Kyle had been waiting for an apology from him for almost four years, and according to Derek, he'd wait until hell froze over.

Kyle stood his ground and held his breath.

"I'll apologize when we find the money," Derek said. Then he turned and stalked off.

Fury twisted through Kyle, making him want to do… something.

"I know you're mad," Dad said. "I'll talk to him. You really have no idea what happened to the money?" There was a sadness to the question that indicated Dad wasn't completely sure he believed what Kyle had said. And that sent him over the edge.

"Don't bother." He spun around and took off for his car, which was across the street from the park where the festival was being held.

Sara caught up to him before he got to the edge of the park. "Kyle, wait up. I thought we were getting a glass of wine. What's wrong?"

He slowed but didn't stop. "Nothing."

She touched his back. "Can I do something?"

He looked at her over his shoulder and was surprised to find that the only person he wanted to talk to right now was Maggie. That the only person who could really help him was her.

"Thanks, Sara-cat, but I need to get out of here."

She dropped her hand. "Okay. Call me if you need anything?"

He nodded, then crossed the street to his car. He waited until he was a few blocks away before he called Maggie. Her phone went directly to voicemail.

Shit.

He circled the block and tried her again. Still voicemail.

Frustration curdled through him. He needed to talk to her, damn it. He drove to the edge of town, saw the signs for the highway, and realized he could be at the Indian casino in less than twenty minutes.

Hell, if everyone was so dead set on believing the worst of him, who was he to disappoint?

Chapter Eight

MAGGIE SPENT THE first part of her appointment with
Amy talking about her patient, Ryan. More specifically,
they'd focused on Maggie's discomfort stemming from
his suicidal thoughts.

Amy scribbled on her notepad. "I sense your anxiety
isn't entirely due to this patient—though I recognize this
is a considerable stressor for you."

Maybe an understatement. Maggie had actually worried that she was going to have a full-on panic attack that
morning when Baylor had asked if she could take a new
patient who was recovering from a suicide attempt.

She shook the recollection away and—reluctantly—
addressed Amy's unspoken question. "There's more," she
said slowly. "I decided to help Kyle Archer track down
who sold Alex the drugs he used."

Amy's brows pitched up as she made a note. "How's
that going?"

"Fine."

Amy gave her a direct look and smiled softly. "Do you really think I'm going to accept that kind of answer?"

As a therapist Maggie knew better. She exhaled and uncrossed her legs, planting her feet flat on the floor in front of the couch. "No. We've been spending a little bit of time together. I guess I've been sort of counseling him."

"Really?" Amy's surprise was evident in her tone, and her pen scratched furiously over the paper. "You were reticent at our meeting last week."

Maggie shrugged, feeling defensive, though she knew she shouldn't. "I wanted to help him." Plus, he's funny, caring, and completely gorgeous. And a magnificent kisser. "We had a lead, but it didn't pan out."

"I see. Are your interactions entirely about the drug issue, or is there more to it?"

Sometimes Amy was too clever for her own good. "There's a little more to it, I guess."

"How do you feel about that?" A therapist's favorite question.

Maggie couldn't suppress a small smile. "Fine." She laughed as she realized she'd done it again. "It makes me feel good but a little anxious. There's no future there."

"Why not?"

"Because he's Kyle Archer. I can't become romantically involved with my dead client's brother." She sat back against the couch and crossed her legs again. "And I'm a mess."

"You're not as messy as you think, and I don't see how Alex is a permanent barrier to a relationship with Kyle.

Yes, there are things you'll need to work through, but if he's also interested…"

Was he? In kissing, for sure, but more than that? She really didn't know, and she didn't want to. The "things" they'd need to work through were insurmountable in her eyes. It was one thing to work through her guilt and find a place of peace, but if she were with Kyle, his brother would always be there in the background. A grim reminder of how badly she'd failed him.

"I appreciate your vote of confidence, but I don't think I have it in me to work through this. Which is fine. I like Kyle, and I'm glad I'm helping him, but when we get to the bottom of that, we'll go our separate ways."

"I see. That sounds like a good plan. For now." Amy sounded skeptical, like she suspected Maggie would change her mind. "What else is going on?"

Maggie thought about her house and her mother's reaction and the fact that she was hiding the situation from pretty much everyone. But bringing it up now felt like an admission that there was a problem, and if she did that, she'd have to accept that she was in worse shape than she realized. If that were true, she'd have to reassess so many things, first and foremost her job. "My mom came by last night. Kyle was there."

Amy chuckled. "I can imagine how that went."

Maggie rolled her eyes. "Horrific. However, she did bring me a plant I'd always wanted."

Amy's eyes softened with understanding. "That must've been a nice moment for you. Tell me, did she embarrass you with Kyle? Did you feel anxious afterward?"

"It wasn't totally humiliating, but she assumed—verbally—that Kyle and I were together, which Kyle found amusing. I was less anxious than I would've been if I hadn't already taken a Xanax after my appointment with Ryan. I admit I did have a glass of wine after she left."

Amy scrunched her lips together in disapproval. "I'm going to pretend I didn't hear you say you mixed alcohol with antidepressants."

"I drank it hours after the Xanax, and it was a small glass." She felt like she'd been caught sneaking her mom's vodka in high school. If her mom had been the type to care about that sort of thing. "Small*ish*. Not huge."

Amy nodded, writing. Probably: *Poor decision-making. Impulse-control problems.* She looked up. "I didn't realize you were still taking Xanax. That was a short-term medication while you were taking your leave of absence, right? I thought you stopped taking it."

She'd mostly cut it out, reserving it for when Mom made her especially tense. Or when Kyle Archer had shown up in her office.

"It's important you take care of yourself, Maggie." Amy's tone was stern but kind. "It's one thing for us to joke about you being a therapist who's in therapy and another for you to lose sight of what you need to do to be truly healthy."

This wasn't soothing Maggie's angst. She considered popping another Xanax when she left, but Amy was right. She needed to learn to cope without the medication. The way she used to before Alex had killed himself. She uncrossed her legs and leaned down to pick up her purse off the floor. Retrieving her pill box, she opened it and sorted out the Xanax from the Tylenol. She held all nine pills out to Amy. "Here."

Amy stretched out her palm. "Are you sure?"

"Yes." Maggie dropped them into Amy's hand.

"Do you have more at home?"

"Yes, but I'll flush them."

"Only if you're comfortable, Maggie. This is a process, and you're doing well. I want you to know that. To own that. You don't ever give yourself enough credit. One of these days I hope you'll let me explore with you why that is."

Because Mark had robbed her of her self-worth and she'd just managed to find it again when Alex had gone and stolen it once more. She resisted the urge to snatch one of the pills back and take it.

Breathe, Maggie.

She inhaled deeply and let it out. "I know what I need to do." Just maybe not necessarily how to do it...She didn't care what Amy said—she was a mess.

"Our time's up," Amy said. "Unless you want to stay?"

No, she wanted air. She practically jumped up, grabbing her purse as she stood. "I'm good. Thanks, Amy, really."

She confirmed her next appointment, and they said good-bye. As Maggie walked out to her car, she dug her keys out of her purse. Her hand nudged the pocket with her pillbox, now devoid of Xanax. That's okay, she had more at home.

No, she said she'd throw them out. She could do this. She could think of Mark and Alex without feeling panicked.

She got into her car and tossed her purse on the passenger seat. Her phone half fell out, and she saw two
missed call notifications on the screen.

Kyle.

He'd called thirty minutes ago. Twice. But he hadn't
left a voicemail. Was he okay? The urge to focus her
energy on someone else's problem drove her to call him
back.

He picked up immediately. "Maggie?" His voice was
thin, tense.

Her angst fell away, replaced by a shock of concern for
him. "What's wrong?"

"I'm at the casino."

Shit.

"I can be there in thirty minutes." Thankfully Amy's
little office was halfway to Ribbon Ridge. Maggie started
the engine. "What are you doing?" Hopefully he hadn't
already gambled and she wasn't too late.

"Sitting in my car."

She exhaled softly as she pulled out onto the street.
"You haven't gone inside?" She ought to put in her head-
set, but she was too intent on keeping him with her.

"Not yet."

"Do you want me to stay on the phone with you?"

A beat of silence. Her neck prickled with anticipation.

He breathed. "No, just get here."

She drove toward the highway, eager to floor the gas
pedal. "I will. Don't go inside."

"I'll try not to. Just hurry."

"I'll see you soon." Reluctantly, she ended the call and drove west. She didn't turn on the radio as thoughts of what had prompted Kyle to go there swirled in her mind.

When she turned into the casino parking lot, she called him back. "I'm here. Where are you?"

"Three rows from the front on the left—between the casino and the hotel."

She drove toward his location, scanning the area for his black SUV. Catching sight of it, she found an empty spot nearby and parked. She grabbed her purse and jumped out of her car. Belatedly she realized she hadn't ended the call and did so as she strode up to his open driver's window.

From the set of his jaw, she could see he was on edge. "Kyle?"

He turned his head. She'd never seen him look so agitated. The casual beach bum with the golden smile and the sparkling oceanic eyes was nowhere to be found.

"Do you want to walk with me?" she asked, sliding her purse strap over her shoulder and wondering why in the hell she'd brought it in the first place. Habit. She hated leaving it in the car.

He turned the key in his ignition, and her breath caught. Was he going to bail?

Then his window went up, and he pulled the key out. She let the air out of her lungs and waited as he got out of the car. Instead of walking, he leaned back against the door.

Apparently they were standing here for now.

"Do you want to talk about this or something else?" It was better to let him guide the discussion. Pushing him could backfire, and she was here to help him.

"I was at the festival. At the booth. There was a… problem."

She cocked her head to the side, listening.

"Some money went missing—not much, just under a hundred dollars. Derek accused me of taking it."

Anger coiled through her. She'd never met Derek, had only heard about him through Alex and knew that he and Kyle were former best friends who were now estranged. Nevertheless, she wanted to rail at him for his faithlessness. But it wouldn't help Kyle for her to get upset. She needed to pull him back from the ledge, so she tamped down her own emotions.

"What happened after that?" She hoped that his sister or someone had stood up for him.

"Dad wasn't exactly supportive." He tipped his head back and looked up at the sky. The sun was sinking toward the horizon, but it wasn't yet dusk.

"He agreed with Derek?" she asked, also wanting to give Rob Archer a piece of her mind.

"Not exactly." Kyle lowered his head, and the look in his eyes provoked a longing she'd never felt before. An eagerness—no, a need—to reach out to him.

She stepped forward and took his hand, expecting to provide comfort but instead feeling a jolt of desire. *Cool it, Maggie.* "What did your Dad say?"

"That he'd talk to Derek. But he asked me again if I took the money, and while I think he wants to believe me when I say I didn't, I'm not sure he did."

She began to see why he might have left town and not looked back. "Was it always like this? Growing up, did it always feel like you were held to another standard?"

He gazed down at her in wonder, as if she were the first person to understand. As a therapist, she got that a lot, and she was glad for the patient when it happened. But from Kyle, she felt something far deeper—an awareness she didn't share with her patients. "Somewhat, yes. There was always competition, particularly with Liam. I was great at sports, but not much else. Liam is good at everything."

From what she knew of Liam from Alex, she knew that wasn't true. When it came to family relationships, he pretty much sucked. Of everyone in the family, Alex had spoken of him the most.

"Is this about Liam or Derek?"

Kyle raked his hand through his hair, mussing the blond strands. "It's about all of them. I just…It doesn't matter what I do."

She stroked his hand. "Yes, it does. I know it feels like you aren't making progress, but I think you are." She couldn't say that for sure since she didn't know how he was being received. But if his being here, filling in for his brother at Archer and participating in the monastery renovation didn't change their opinions, they were close-minded, judgmental assholes.

"How can you say that?" he asked, echoing her thoughts.

"Because I can't believe you came from a family of self-absorbed jerks."

The intensity of his stare would've burned her if it had been a tangible thing. "Why not? Most people think I'm the most self-absorbed jerk of them all."

"Then you aren't showing them who you really are." She moved her hand up his arm, skimming over his muscled flesh until she reached his bicep. "You aren't showing them what you show me."

He reached out, grasped a curl beside her cheek, and brushed it back, his fingertips grazing her scalp. "What do you see when you look at me?"

"A thoughtful, caring gentleman who wants to do right by his brother, by his family. Who wants to find a way back home."

"I know this is therapy, that you're saying this as a professional, but I don't care." He bent his head toward her. "Thank God you're here." His lips brushed over hers. The contact was gentle but soared through her like a bird taking flight. Triumphant, joyous.

"I'm not saying that as your therapist," she said against his mouth. "I'm not your therapist. I'm...*hell*, I don't know what I am." She curled her hands around his neck and pulled him down to kiss him more deeply. Opening her mouth, she slid her tongue into his.

With a groan, he clasped her head between his hands, angling and holding her for the onslaught of his kiss. She cast her head back and invited him to feast, just as she was taking what she wanted of him. He pressed into her, bringing his hips against hers.

She glided her hands down his chest, skidding over his muscles. God, how she wanted to feel him flesh to flesh. She wrapped her hands around his back and drew him against her. Better, but still not good enough.

Following her lead, he moved his hands down her back. One clutched her waist while the other went further and splayed over her hips, his fingertips digging deliciously into her ass.

She pushed her pelvis into him, and with the motion, her head went farther back. He left her mouth to press hot, wet kisses over her neck. The distant sound of a car starting reminded her of their location.

She opened her eyes, loving the sight of his head bent toward her chest, his mouth trailing downward into the V of her neckline. "Kyle," she said, barely recognizing the rasp of her own lust-filled voice. "We're doing it again. In the middle of a parking lot."

The unmistakable sensation of him smiling against her skin drew a soft laugh from her. His head came up swiftly, his eyes more blue than green as he looked at her with the same desire pooling in her core. "Shall we move this inside?"

"The casino?" She tried to think of how that could possibly be more private. But maybe they could find a nook or commandeer a bathroom…

His lips curved into a grin. "The hotel, silly."

More like stupid. She'd forgotten about the hotel. The suggestion was unambiguous. Hotel rooms had beds. Was she ready to go there with him? Was she ready to go there with *anyone*? She hadn't been after Mark.

"I don't think they rent by the hour," she said, her heart racing from the kissing and the prospect of more.

He lowered his head until his lips were a breath from hers. "Good. I don't want just an hour."

A delicious shiver ran down her spine. How could she refuse him? No man had ever looked at her like that, and her body had never responded with such heat and need.

"Okay." She almost giggled with anticipation. Rational thoughts tried to crowd her brain—was this a good idea? Would she regret it? How would she deal with the aftermath?

Screw it, she told herself. *You deserve this. You need this. Stop overanalyzing everything. Turn the therapist brain off.*

She took his hand and started toward the hotel. "Let's hurry."

A SEXUAL HAZE clouded Kyle's mind, shielding it from thoughts like *What are you doing? Don't you remember who she is? Are you a moron?* The glass doors parted as they approached, and they entered the lobby under a blast of air conditioning. Hand in hand, they walked to the front desk.

Kyle smiled at the woman behind the counter. "We don't have a reservation. Spontaneous trip."

The employee, a woman in her late forties, peered at them curiously, her gaze searching for...probably their luggage. Oops.

"*Really* spontaneous," he said.

"That's fun," she said with a smile. "We have toothbrushes if you need them."

Kyle shot a glance at Maggie, who was staring off somewhere into the middle distance, trying vainly not to look embarrassed. He squeezed her hand.

After providing his information, ID, and the only credit card he allowed himself—one with only a five-hundred-dollar limit—they were checked in.

"Do you need two keys?" she asked.

"One will do," Kyle said.

With a nod, she slid over a little envelope with the single key card. "You're in four twelve. Go down the hall and take the elevator."

"Thanks." Kyle snatched up the key, and they turned to go down the hall. "Hang on." He left Maggie and returned to the front desk. He lowered his voice. "Can you send up champagne later—say nine o'clock?"

"Actually, there's already a bottle in the room," she said as softly as he did. "It's one of our romance suites." She gave him a knowing look and winked.

He flashed her a grin. "You are the best front desk clerk in the history of front desks. Thank you." He spun around and practically ran back to Maggie. Taking her hand, he started toward the hallway leading to the elevator.

Once they got out of sight of the front desk, she slowed. "Maybe this wasn't such a great idea."

He stopped a few feet from the elevator. "The parking lot is better?"

"No." She blushed and looked down. "This…I came here to talk to you, to help—"

He pulled her to his chest and kissed her. Hard and fast and then lingering and soft. She melted against him.

Moving quickly, he punched the up arrow and tugged her to the elevator. "Ride up with me, and if you're still feeling uncertain, we can forget it." God, he hoped that wouldn't happen.

The elevator chimed, and the doors opened. A couple stepped out, and Kyle moved out of their way. Then he walked into the elevator and looked at Maggie. "You coming?" He held his breath.

The doors started to close. She leapt forward, causing the doors to jerk open again. With the force of her momentum, she lost her balance and crashed into him. He snaked his arms around her waist, holding her steady. Her gaze connected with his, and all he saw was heat and want—a reflection of his desire.

With a low sound coming from somewhere primitive, he dragged her up against him. She twined her arms around his neck and pulled him into her kiss. Her mouth opened beneath his, their tongues met and clashed. Her fingers curled into his flesh and tugged at his hair.

He clutched her waist and brought her hips flush to his. She pulled away, leaving him cold and surprised. She jabbed a button on the elevator panel, and ice slithered over his skin as he realized she meant to stop this.

The elevator stopped, and she came back, grabbing his head and bringing him down to her open mouth. She kissed him hungrily, like a starving woman, and he returned in kind.

"You stopped the elevator," he managed between kisses. "So hot."

"I've always wanted to do that." She ran her palm over the front of his shorts, brushing his erection and driving him to the edge.

"I need you now." He held her tight as he rotated and then restarted the elevator. He renewed the kiss and lifted her. "Put your legs around my waist."

She did as he commanded. "Aren't I too heavy?"

"You're perfect."

The elevator chimed again, and the doors opened. If anyone was waiting in the hallway, he didn't notice. He didn't even look. He carried her across to the wall, where he pinned her, his hips between her legs.

"Kyle," she gasped into his mouth. "How is the hall-way better than the parking lot?"

He looked around then. "No one here."

She pulled her legs from his waist and slid to the floor. She grabbed his hand. "Room."

Turning, she looked at the sign with the room numbers and their directions, then pulled him to the right. They traveled halfway down the corridor before she stopped in front of the door. "Four twelve."

He pulled the keycard from his pocket and slid it into the reader. The light showed red. Goddamn it, why did those things never work the first time? He tried again, and it failed again.

"Let me." She snatched the card from him and pushed it into the slot. Green.

She turned her head and flashed him the sexiest smile he'd ever seen on her. "Magic touch."

YOURS TO HOLD 163

"Show me." He pushed the door open and drove her inside, stopping in the entryway to kick off his flip-flops and devour her mouth once more.

She kissed him with open abandon, her nails digging into his shoulders as excited little sounds emerged from her throat. He was so turned on, he could barely stand it.

The door slammed closed, and she backed into the room. Then her hands shoved at his chest, and again he wondered if she was about to call a halt.

"Holy crap." Her expletive drew his attention, and he looked at their surroundings for the first time.

There was a king-sized bed splashed with several dozen red rose petals, a bar area with a sink, fridge, and champagne chilling on the counter, and a massive flat-screen TV, but the focal point of the room was the Jacuzzi tub in front of the bay windows that looked out over the rolling hillside behind the hotel.

"It's the romance suite," he said.

"You shouldn't have." She sounded awestruck.

"It was entirely the clerk's doing." He went to her, and she looked up at him, her eyes dark and lush, a thin band of gold lining the inner edge of the brown. He tipped her chin up and pulled on her lower lip with his thumb. Then he ran the pad straight down in a direct path, gliding over her neck as she cast her head slightly back. Down he went until he reached the V in her shirt, where three little buttons were sewn as some sort of taunting decoration because they didn't open. He arced his hand to the right, cupping her breast.

She gasped and brought her head up, locking her gaze with his.

"I'd rip your clothes off, but since they're all you have, I'll be gentle."

"I appreciate you not ripping them, but please, don't be gentle."

Her words stoked the heat swirling in the pit of his belly. His cock was already hard, but now it turned to stone.

He found the hem of her shirt and drew it up, exposing the smooth plane of her stomach. She lifted her arms as she swept the garment over her head and tossed it aside.

Her bra was pale green, bereft of any feminine adornment such as lace or bows, but her breasts filled it perfectly, their soft curves arching up from the cups. He leaned down and kissed the top of one, sweeping his tongue over her warm flesh. He felt her shiver.

He looked down at her shorts—khaki Bermudas. Her long, slender legs stretched out below them, and her feet were encased in brown wedge sandals. It was a hot, sassy look—the heels with the shorts. It surprised him a little, since she was such a good little doctor, always trying to keep him at arm's length. Or so he'd thought. *Please, don't be gentle.*

He swallowed as anticipation spiked his lust.

"Kyle." Her sultry voice—God, it did things to him he didn't understand—broke through the cloud of passion that had overtaken his brain. "Do you have a condom?"

"Yes." Thank God. At least two, he was sure. Not carrying a spare almost ensured a disaster. He pulled his wallet from his back pocket and withdrew one, then tossed it on the bed. "Do you want champagne now or later?"

She unbuttoned her shorts and slid the zipper down. "Later." She shimmied out of the garment and kicked it from her foot.

His mouth watered at the sight of her in bra and panties and sexy shoes.

"You like the shoes on?"

He jerked his head up, having been caught staring at them. "You have really sexy feet."

She laughed, a dark provocative sound that fed his need. "I'm not sure I believe that, but whatever turns you on."

He slipped his forefingers under her bra straps and slid them from her shoulders. "You." He pushed the undergarment down, stripping it from her breasts until they spilled forth. "Turn." Moving his hands to her back, he unclasped the bra. "Me." He dropped it to the floor and lowered his head to her breast. "On."

He closed his mouth over the tip, his hand cupping the underside and holding her captive to his tongue. She moaned as her fingers tangled in his hair and gripped his head. He fed on her, licking and teasing her flesh before moving to the other and performing the same. He used both hands to cup her, loving the size and feel of her— so soft and so smooth—and squeezed one nipple as he tongued the other.

Her legs quivered, and she clutched at his shoulders. She picked at his shirt, managing to pull it up his back. He let go of her long enough to tear it over his head and thrust it aside. Then her fingers dug into his shoulder blades.

He scooped her up and laid her back across the bed. She was breathtaking with her dark hair, hooded eyes, dusky-tipped breasts, and slender legs spread over the white bed and its shock of red rose petals.

Nearly ripping his button from his shorts, he shucked them but paused with his hands on the waistband of his boxer briefs.

"Take them off," she said, her voice husky and commanding.

He peeled them away slowly, enjoying the way her eyes followed his every movement. But then her gaze locked on his erection, and he wondered if he'd make it to the bed. She was seriously fucking with his self-control.

He climbed over her and straddled her hips. Her gaze was still glued to his cock as she licked her lips. He considered continuing upward and giving her what she clearly wanted, but he was too far gone and knew that if she put her mouth on him, he'd never get to where he wanted.

"You're still wearing panties," he said, running his fingertip along the upper edge.

She looked up at him finally, and he'd never seen her eyes darker. "You haven't taken them off."

"And that's my job?" he asked playfully, running his finger inside the soft cotton and teasing her flesh. She arched up, urging him lower, but he didn't comply. "You look so fucking beautiful like this. With the white and the roses." He scooped up a handful of petals and spread them over her breasts and stomach. The crimson against her skin tantalized him. He plucked up a single petal and lightly grazed it over her lips. She sucked in a breath, and he dragged the petal over her chin and down her neck, sweeping lower to her chest and encircling first one nipple and then the other. He skimmed it lower, gliding over her abdomen, then leaving it over the cleft of her belly button.

With quick, fluid movements, he swung his legs over her until he knelt beside her, then raked her underwear down her legs.

She gasped with the swiftness of his act, her hips jerking up with surprise. With quick flicks of his fingers, he unbuckled her shoes and tossed them to the floor.

He moved over her again, kneeling between her thighs. She pulled his head down to hers for a wet kiss.

He groped on the bed for the condom, rejecting several rose petals before his fingers closed around the wrapper. He tore the package open between them and rolled the rubber over his cock.

"I'm on the pill too, if you care."

"I care." He finished with the condom and touched her, his finger gliding along her folds. He pressed in, finding her wet and ready. "I care about everything to do with you, Maggie." He found her clit with his thumb and massaged lightly. She sucked in air and closed her eyes. "Right now, I care very much that you enjoy this. Are you enjoying this?"

He increased his pressure, attending to her clit and stroking her cleft. She moaned the word "yes," and her pelvis rotated, urging him on.

"Good. I wanted to be sure. This is happening faster than I would've normally preferred, but thanks to your brilliance, we have all night. And champagne. And a hot tub." He thrust his finger inside and drove deep.

She rose up off the bed. "Yes. Yes."

He pressed harder on her clit and added a second finger, opening her slick channel. Her legs came up and spread wider. He kissed her mouth hungrily, his tongue mimicking the stroke of his fingers. She moved her hips, fucking him, her body begging him for release. He worked his thumb faster and plunged hard and deep. She cried out as her muscles tensed around him.

Withdrawing his hand, he immediately grasped his cock and pushed inside of her while her orgasm still wracked her body. Her thighs clenched around him, and he lost any semblance of control.

Her fingers dug into the flesh of his ass, urging him deeper. He pumped into her, moving fast and frenzied. There was no gradual build, just hot pleasure sweeping over him as his balls tightened. He moved within her, clasping her hip and cradling the side of her head. Her eyes were closed, her mouth open as incoherent sounds left her lips.

Her thighs gripped his waist, and her inner muscles clenched his cock as another orgasm claimed her. It was all he needed to plummet right over the edge. He had no reason, no restraint, no mercy. He drove into her again and again. *Please, don't be gentle.*

He reached down and clasped the back of her knee, lifting her leg and opening her even wider. She made a sound like a growl and raked her nails across his lower back. His blood roared in his ears as he came. There was a sound, a low cry that he realized came from him, but he didn't care.

Her hand covered his behind her knee, holding him there until their pace slowed. Until sense began to return. He let go, and she did too, both of them slumping with a wave of satisfied exhaustion. At least, he hoped she was satisfied.

If her intense reactions and eager participation were any indication, then yeah, she was satisfied. He smiled, adjusting his weight so he was only half-lying on her. He laid his hand over her breast, claiming but not arousing her. *Later.*

She pressed a kiss to his shoulder. "Definitely later."

Apparently he'd said that out loud. It seemed as though he had no control over himself in her presence. No, that wasn't exactly true. He'd avoided going to the casino. She'd saved him from himself.

Chapter Nine

MAGGIE POLISHED OFF her second glass of champagne after finishing the delicious room service dinner they'd ordered. They sat at the small table—Kyle wearing his shorts and nothing else, and Maggie garbed in her underwear and Kyle's shirt. Her hair was an unbelievable rat's nest, but Kyle had insisted she leave it down. He said he liked the wild way it tumbled around her shoulders and that it reminded him of how thorough and pleasurable the sex had been.

She squirmed in her chair, just about ready for the "later" he'd promised. She'd almost forgotten what sex had felt like, and now that she remembered, she was desperate to do it again. With him.

"That was a great steak," he said, finishing his dinner and leaning back in his chair. He noted her empty glass. "More champagne? There's a little left."

She held out her glass. "Sure, why not? We're not going anywhere."

He grinned. "No, we are not." He poured out the rest of the bottle—half in her glass and half in his. He took a drink and then set the glass down, sitting back in his chair.

After sipping from her glass, she lifted her foot and set it in his lap. He arched a brow as she massaged his thigh with her toes. His warm palm covered the top of her foot. "You *are* a temptress, do you know that?"

She shrugged, but she knew the answer. No, she wasn't. Or at least hadn't been until now. Mark hadn't liked her to take the initiative in the bedroom. He'd wanted a submissive—not like with a true domination type of relationship, but close enough that it had made her uneasy, and she'd grown more and more uncomfortable over time.

Thinking about that doused her ardor, and she pulled her foot away.

"Hey." He reached for her, but she turned in her chair, moving her legs out of his range. "Maggie?"

She took another drink of champagne and got up. "Ready for the hot tub?"

"Sure."

She heard the uncertainty in his voice but chose to ignore it. Pulling his shirt over her head, she tossed it at the foot of the bed and then stripped her underwear away.

They'd filled the tub while they'd eaten. She turned the water off and tested it. Delightfully hot.

She climbed in and settled herself on one of the narrow benches. It was a small tub—larger than a jetted tub in a bathroom but smaller than a hot tub you'd find on someone's deck.

He got in on the other side, having divested himself of his shorts. She noted he was already half-stiff and suppressed a smile. The controls were on his side. He pressed a button, and the jets started, sending a whirlwind of bubbles around them.

She closed her eyes and sank deeper, resting her head on the side. The sound of the jets and the heat of the water lulled her, relaxing her after her mind had taken that unfortunate detour.

A pinch on her nipple drew a gasp from her throat, and her eyes shot open.

Kyle was directly in front of her, his fingers teasing her breast. "They were taunting me. Just bobbing here." He caressed her flesh as he stared into her eyes.

The subtle pain he'd just inflicted reminded her of Mark. And that pissed her off. She wanted to enjoy this. God, had he ruined her forever?

Kyle's eyes narrowed slightly before he dipped his head and drew her nipple into his mouth. His lips and tongue moved over her so softly, so reverently, all of her tension melted away. She clasped his head, running her fingers through his hair, which was growing damp from the steam.

His hand moved between her thighs, his fingers finding her center. He'd touched her so expertly earlier, and her body responded, hoping for an encore. She opened her legs wider and pushed into his hand. He drew her breast more deeply into his mouth, suckling her flesh while his finger stroked into her heat.

She laid her head back on the edge of the tub and closed her eyes, giving herself up to the sensations. His head came up, and he palmed the back of her neck, bringing her up to meet his mouth for a blistering kiss. He rose higher, driving his tongue into her mouth as his fingers copied the intrusion between her legs. He picked up speed, and she met his thrusts, desperate for the orgasm she sensed within reach.

But then he withdrew his fingers and pulled his head back. She looked up into his eyes, which had turned dark and fierce.

"Please," she breathed. "Don't stop."

"I have to. Move up." He clasped her hips and lifted her off the seat.

She followed his lead, rising until her thighs emerged from the water.

He guided her back to sit on the edge and parted her legs. "Much better."

He picked up where he left off, stroking her clit and brushing her folds, but he didn't enter her again. She squirmed on the tile, wanting—no, needing—more.

He splayed his palms on her inner thighs and licked along her slit. His thumbs opened her wide, and he plunged his tongue in deep.

Her head fell back as ecstasy rushed over her. She was so close she could taste it, but she wanted to prolong this joy, this exquisite sensation. Mark hadn't liked doing this to her and had convinced her she wasn't missing much. Now she knew how wrong she'd been, and she wanted to string Mark up by his testicles.

Kyle suckled her clit, and she came up off the tile with a sharp gasp. His finger pumped into her, fucking her while he pulled on her flesh with his lips and teeth. Her thighs quivered as her muscles clenched, heralding her orgasm.

He pushed her over the edge into shocking bliss, his mouth and fingers doing things she never imagined. She came hard and fast, the world crashing around her, leaving her in warm, euphoric darkness. But he didn't stop, and the sensations were too much. She was going to die.

She tried to pull back, just for a second, but he held her fast. His mouth gentled, but he continued his assault. Rapture streamed over her, wringing every bit of pleasure from her body, leaving her weak and sated. And full of wonder.

Kyle pulled her from the edge of the tub, sliding her back into the water. She opened her eyes and blushed at the knowing, almost arrogant look he gave her.

"You tried to get away from me," he said, his tone almost scolding. "Next time I'll tie you to the bed so you can't move."

She couldn't stop her reaction and knew the color must have drained from her face.

His expression darkened, and now he was the ones with lines on his forehead. He touched her shoulder. "Maggie, what's wrong?"

She considered evading the question, but they shared an openness she hadn't experienced with anyone in a long time, maybe ever. "My ex liked to do that."

"What, tie you up?"

"Yes."

"And you didn't like it?"

"I didn't mind it at first. But he used it as a means to control our relationship." Her pulse sped, and cold sweat broke out on her neck despite the heat of the water. "He liked me to feel helpless and weak so that he could 'save' me."

Kyle's eyes darkened. "Did he hurt you?" His voice was deceptively soft, but she heard the edge in his tone.

"Not physically, though I was afraid it might come to that. It's one of the reasons I broke things off."

"If I ever meet this guy…"

Flattered by his defense of her, she pushed over to him and grazed her breasts against his chest. "You won't. He's gone for good. Like I told you, I haven't heard from him in over a year."

"He might be gone from your life, but he's still here." He pointed to her head. "Is there any chance he's here too?" He lightly touched her chest, just over her heart.

She laid her hand over his, pressing it flat against her breast. "No chance at all." She exhaled, wishing her champagne buzz were a little stronger. "I haven't been with anyone since him, so doing this, being here with you…it's hard not to think of before."

He brushed her damp hair back from her face and kissed her lightly. "I will do whatever it takes to help you forget. Even if it's nothing at all."

Was he saying that he'd end their spontaneous romantic getaway? She didn't want that. She wanted to banish Mark forever. And she wanted Kyle to be the one she remembered. When they went their separate ways, she wanted to think of this night and smile.

She slipped her hands around his neck, loving the feel of his corded muscles. "You've done a pretty good job of putting me in the here and now. What you just did—my ex almost never did that. So congratulations on creating a singular memory that is one hundred percent Kyle Archer."

His lips spread into a lazy grin. "I'd say my work here is done, but I think I'm only just getting started, from the sounds of it."

"Undoubtedly." She reached down and grasped his cock. It was hard and hot and, of course, wet from the water. She slowly stroked him from base to tip.

He clutched the back of her neck and kissed her, spearing his tongue into her mouth. She increased her pressure on his cock and picked up speed. He massaged her back and moved lower to her ass, palming one cheek and bringing her closer so that she could barely continue her handjob.

"I can't wait, and I can't use a condom in here." He stood up quickly, sloshing water out of the tub with his movement. He climbed out onto the narrow tile floor surrounding the tub and helped her do the same.

He snagged her against him, their bodies hot and slick. He slid his hand along her neck and drew her mouth to his, ravishing her with a wild hunger that was answered in her core and spread through her, bringing her to the edge of orgasm.

She snatched a towel from the hook on the wall and moved away from him to spread it on the couch. He followed, his gaze dark and intense. She pointed for him to sit. He arched a brow but complied. When he was seated, his cock jutted up, eager and impressive.

"Condom?" She remembered him saying he had a couple more in his wallet and that he'd taken them out, but she didn't know where he'd put them.

"On the nightstand."

She found one and opened the wrapper as she returned to him. Bending over him, she stroked him like she'd done in the hot tub. He answered by fondling both of her breasts as they swayed against his chest. He tweaked her nipples, sending streaks of desire through her body.

With increasingly clumsy fingers, she rolled the condom over him, taking far longer than she wanted to. When he was finally cloaked, she straddled his hips and put the head of him at her slit. She tried to go slow, but once she felt him inside of her, she couldn't help herself and pushed down until he was seated to the hilt.

His clasped her hips, his fingers digging into her ass. "Maggie." He came up, initiating movement, but she wanted to control this. He said he'd wanted to give her new memories, and this was one she'd never had: her in the driver's seat.

"Don't move," she commanded, pushing against his shoulders. She lifted herself until he was barely inside of her, then she sank down again. He groaned, his legs twitched, his mouth latched onto her neck.

Emboldened, she did it again. And again. Each thrust of his cock was liberating and empowering. As she rose up, he captured her breast in his mouth and sucked on her hard. The orgasm that had been threatening since the hot tub cascaded over her, robbing her breath and her sanity. The control she'd exerted with her movements completely vanished as she gave herself over to ecstasy. He took over, slamming up into her with vicious, marvelous strokes. His cries matched hers, and she could only imagine what the neighboring rooms must think, but she didn't care. This moment was for her.

He pulled her down on him one last time and shouted her name as he came, his body shuddering in release. She combed her fingers through his hair and snagged his earlobe with her teeth. Their movements slowed, and she slumped against him, completely spent.

"You were incredible," he breathed. He brushed her hair back and kissed her collarbone.

She smiled as a little bit of the darkness that had taken up residence in her head broke apart and fell away. "Thank you." She climbed off him and fell onto the couch.

He stood and went toward the bathroom. "At this rate, I might have to hit the market over at the gas station and get more condoms."

She got up and dried herself, then met him in the bed a few minutes later. "We should sleep." She yawned, as if to punctuate the sentence, and closed her eyes. She'd never felt so blissfully tired in her entire life.

He rolled to his side, facing her, and kissed her temple. "Good night, Magnolia."

Her eyes flew open and stared into his. "Don't call me that." She gave him a playful swat.

He laughed. "I've been dying to ask you about that. Why on earth is your name Magnolia?"

She looked at him like he'd gone daft. "You saw my mother, right?"

"I did. She's very...eclectic."

She rolled her eyes. "Nice word choice. Like I told you before, she's a total hippie. My brother's name is Rowan."

He traced his finger along her arm and shoulder. "She likes trees, I gather. Is that where you got your green thumb?"

"No, that was my grandmother. Mom likes green things, but she doesn't know the first thing about growing them."

"She's lucky she has you then," he said, stroking her neck.

"I guess."

"What does that mean? You aren't close?"

Maggie set her hand on his chest. "We have next to nothing in common. You should know better than anyone that you can't choose your family."

He pulled her close and rolled to his back so that she snuggled against his side. "Isn't that the truth? I'm sorry you don't have a better relationship. I missed my mom when I was in Florida. I finally come home, and she leaves."

Maggie traced her finger over his chest, making invisible ovals. "I'm sorry about that. She'll be back soon, right? Didn't you tell me she was coming home for Derek's wedding?"

"Yeah, she'll be here next Friday."

She sensed he was thinking about things he shouldn't—Derek and whatnot. To distract him, she said the first thing that popped into her head: "My parents have an open marriage. They took up separate residences when I was in middle school, and I spent every summer of my life at crazy free-love communes until I was fifteen and refused to go anymore. It was the weirdest upbringing you can imagine. And yeah, I still have serious issues with it."

He turned his head to look at her. "You're kidding."

"I wish I was."

"Like, they have boyfriends and girlfriends and they're still married?"

She almost laughed at the incredulity in his tone. "Apparently Mom has a boyfriend now. But yeah, they're still married. She and Dad were making out last weekend like it was no big deal. They're so *odd*. I don't get it."

"That's…different. But I guess that's their choice, and as long as it doesn't hurt anything…"

"That's a good theory, but when your parents are so wrapped up in their own lives that they barely have time to, you know, *parent*, you grow up wondering why they had you in the first place."

"Ouch." He massaged her shoulder and pressed a kiss against the top of her head. "I'm sorry, Maggie. My experience is the total opposite. My parents couldn't have children, and they underwent a series of fertility treatments until an in vitro attempt was finally successful. When they had six viable fetuses, Mom wanted to keep them all. She went on bed rest at sixteen weeks and did everything possible to bring us into the world safe and healthy. And she only continued that commitment after we were born. Managing six kids at once, some with medical challenges, was no mean feat."

Her heart swelled at the love he described—both his mother's and his, which was evident in his voice as he spoke of her. "I can imagine. You're incredibly lucky."

"Yeah, I suppose I am."

"So your brother Hayden, he really was a major oops?"

Kyle's chest rumbled as he laughed. "Completely. They'd worked so hard to have us, and then four or five months later, boom, Mom's pregnant again without even trying." He glanced down at her, smiling. "Well, without medical intervention."

"Amazing."

"She had her tubes tied after that—seven was definitely enough."

"Hence the name of your show." She pushed up and leaned over him, looking down at his insanely handsome face. "And here I am sleeping with a celebrity."

He barked out a laugh. "I haven't noticed any sleeping going on."

She reached down and brushed his hip on her way to his cock. "Nope. Probably not yet either. I'm suddenly feeling very awake."

He curled his hand up her neck and brought her head down to kiss her. "Sleep is overrated."

WAKING UP IN Maggie's arms was about the best way Kyle had ever started a morning. He wished he could've made her a gourmet breakfast instead of the lukewarm room service they'd had. Next time.

Next time?

Hell yes, next time. In fact, they had a whole weekend staring at them.

She emerged from the bathroom dressed, unfortunately, her hair wound up on top of her head. "Ready?"

She looked and smelled so fresh, he was more than tempted to say no. He got up from the couch and strode toward her. "We don't have to check out for another hour..."

"Yes, but we're out of condoms, sadly." She flashed him a smile.

"I can think of plenty of things to do that won't require a condom." He leaned down and kissed her. She tasted like minty toothpaste, which he'd never thought of as particularly tasty, but right now he wanted to devour her whole.

She pushed away from him with a contented sigh. "You're insatiable."

"When it comes to you, yes."

She turned away and picked up her purse. "Compulsive, even."

Compulsive. Like his gambling. He'd all but forgotten they were next to a casino and that he'd come here with the intent of playing poker, maybe booking some sports action, and pretty much losing himself in the game. It still called to him like a naughty siren, but the lure of Maggie was even stronger.

He snagged her hand and drew her to face him. "Hey, are you trying to therapize me again?"

The little pleats formed between her eyes, and he had to admit they were incredibly adorable. "Isn't that why you called me out here last night?"

Yes, but about the gambling. Did she know that his track record with women wasn't much better? "What did Alex tell you about my romantic life?"

Her eyes narrowed slightly. "I shouldn't talk to you about that."

"Come on, it's about me, not him." He could tell from her reaction that she knew something. "He said I'm a lothario, right?"

"I believe he said something like 'not going to settle down anytime soon.'"

That wasn't so bad.

"But since you mentioned it, *are* you a lothario? You're certainly good-looking enough to be."

He laughed, but her question sparked an underlying discomfort, because yeah, he sort of was. Or had been. Or was in remission or something. "I haven't found a reason to settle down." He raked her with a seductive stare, imagining her full breasts filling his hands and her lush legs encircling his waist.

"Knock. It. Off." She snatched her hand away. "I need to go home and water my plants."

Reluctantly, he followed her to the door. "Any chance I can persuade you to come over tonight? After your tomatoes are good and hydrated."

She turned as she reached the threshold. "Maybe."

He trailed her into the hall and to the elevator. Once they were inside, she touched his arm. "I just had a thought. You got me thinking about something Alex said once. We talked about whether he wanted a girlfriend. And there *was* someone he liked, someone he maybe had a crush on. I think it might've been a coworker."

"Really?" Emotion socked Kyle in the gut—the familiar pain of loss coupled with the frustration about what would never be. "Do you know if he was seeing her?"

"I don't think so, but we only talked about it once or twice." She shook her head. "I shouldn't be telling you this, but maybe it will help with the drug investigation. If he was close to someone at work, maybe she could help?"

"Yeah, maybe." He got caught up in his brother for a moment. "He wanted a girlfriend?"

"I think so, yes."

"I never knew him to have one. A friend of ours went to prom with him in high school—we all went in a big group. And in college, I thought he might've been seeing someone, but he never talked about it." It was just another way in which he'd felt inadequate, probably. Kyle wished he could go back, wished he would've done more to help Alex. Maybe then he wouldn't have chosen death over life.

"Kyle?" Maggie's soft voice startled him. She was standing in the door of the elevator, holding it open. He hadn't even felt them stop or heard the chime.

"Yeah." He walked out, and she took his hand.

"Don't go there," she said. "You are not responsible for Alex's problems or the way he felt. Whether he had a girlfriend or didn't."

"I could've been a better brother. I never should've left."

"I told you not to go there." She stood on her toes and pressed a kiss to his lips. "Come on, let's get out of here."

"Wait, you mentioned a totem the other night. What did you give him? Maybe I can find it and give it back to you."

Her eyes lit for a moment and then darkened. "There isn't really a totem. I made that up to explain your being at my house."

He felt a surge of disappointment, and he wasn't sure if it was because of the fact that there wasn't really a totem or that she'd had to come up with an excuse for them being together.

They got to the lobby and checked out, then he walked her to her car. The sun was already hot. It was going to be a scorcher.

She laid her hand over his chest. "What, no parking lot shenanigans? This is the first time we've been in one without groping each other."

He knew she was trying to lighten his mood and appreciated the hell out of her for it. "If you promise to come over later, I'll keep my hands to myself."

Her eyes sparkled as she laughed softly. "Okay. Text me your address. I'm curious to see where you live."

"It's Hayden's address—his house, remember? I'm just occupying his life." It sounded so impermanent—kind of sad, really. Christ, what the hell was wrong with him? He'd just spent an incredible night with an amazing woman. He cupped her face and kissed her long and deep.

When he let her go, she was breathless. He smiled. "See you later, Magnolia."

She smacked him in the butt as he turned to go. "Don't make me change my mind."

He threw her a scalding look and held his arms out. "You won't say no to this, baby."

She grinned, shaking her head. Then she got in her car and drove away.

Feeling a bit better, Kyle worked to keep his mind from antagonizing thoughts like Alex and his own deficiency. His phone buzzed, and he turned on the Bluetooth as he glanced at the display.

"Hi, Dad." The tension he'd just managed to stow away surged anew.

"Kyle, I wanted you to know that we found the money."

He should've felt vindicated, but he only felt angry. "I knew you would."

"Royce pocketed a hundred-dollar bill because he was nervous about leaving it in the till, and then he forgot about it until this morning."

"Is that it?"

"No, it isn't," Dad said, exhaling. "I'm sorry about what happened. Derek is, too."

"I doubt that."

"You make it damned hard to apologize."

And he wasn't interested in making it easier. Why should he be when they'd been so quick to accuse him?

"Kyle?"

"Still here."

Dad exhaled. "I really am sorry. Maybe if we could talk—really talk about what happened…"

"The way you talk about Alex?"

Dad's intake of breath was sharp. "I don't need to talk about him."

"You need to do *something*."

"Stop deflecting. You can't keep doing that."

Kyle was beginning to think he'd learned the art of deflection from a master. "Why not? What's the point in rehashing history? You know what happened, I know what happened. I left, got my shit together," *somewhat*, he thought, "and now I'm back. Why can't you just accept me as I am?"

"I…I'm trying. I just still don't understand how things got that bad."

And he never would. Addiction wasn't something that was easily understood by people who didn't have one. "I gotta run, Dad."

"Kyle, are you…are you okay?"

He hoped he meant about what had happened and wasn't continuing to harp on whether he was gambling. The fact that he was currently driving away from a casino wasn't something he planned to share. "I'm fine, Dad. Really. Talk to you later."

He ended the call feeling frustrated. He summoned thoughts of Maggie and their night together to try to dispel the uneasiness pricking his insides. Gradually, his mood improved enough that he relaxed. Maggie was a balm for his soul, it seemed.

But what did that mean? He'd been fixated on plenty of women for a few weeks or a few months, but that was it. Maggie could be just another one in the parade. Or could she be more? He'd never confessed his gambling addiction to anyone the way he had to her. Did that mean she was different? That this could be something lasting?

Except, if he were honest with himself, he'd only scratched the surface with her about his gambling. She didn't know how bad things had gotten before Dad had bailed him out or how he'd spiraled in Florida—that he had to be constantly vigilant so that he didn't hit rock bottom again.

But maybe she knew. She was a therapist after all. It was her job to see beneath people's exterior. Was that really what he wanted? A girlfriend who could some-how interpret his problems without him having to share them? A girlfriend who would be better able to under-stand and cope with his faults? Put like that, it didn't sound too healthy.

For now, being with her felt good. For now, he wanted that to be enough. No, he needed it to be.

Chapter Ten

MAGGIE LEANED HER head back against the seat in
Kyle's SUV as they drove up the final hill to the monastery. She'd never been up here and was looking forward
to what had to be an amazing view. She glanced over at
Kyle, recalling their incredible night—the second in a
row. He'd made her a delicious breakfast that morning
that had included the best poached eggs she'd ever had.

And now he was showing her his family's project—
Alex's project. She felt a little apprehensive knowing that
he'd been planning this—and his suicide—for months.
Maybe even the entire time he'd come to see her for treatment. She shoved the thought away. If she didn't, it could
consume her.

Kyle pulled into the dirt parking lot, and the monastery rose before them. The monks' quarters, three stories tall, arced out to the left, while the church with its
two-hundred-foot spire dominated the landscape. It was

beautiful but overgrown, and she wished she could come back with a pair of pruners.

He parked the car and jumped out, coming around to meet her as she did the same. "This is The Alex," he said. "Or it will be anyway."

"This is a massive undertaking. I'm in awe."

"It's all Alex's vision. Well, except the wedding cottage. That was entirely Sara's doing. Come on, I'll show you." He took her hand, and they passed a trailer that likely served as the office on their way to a wide dirt and gravel path.

Like the main parking area, the path was overgrown. Shrubs and grasses crowded each other, and the scent of ripening blackberries overwhelmed her senses. "Someone needs to cut those berry bushes back," she said, pointing at a particularly nasty tangle.

"We have a landscaper due to start later this week."

"They're going to be working overtime," she said, thinking about Derek and Chloe's wedding that would be happening in less than two weeks.

"Definitely getting a late start. Dylan's pretty pissed about that, but he hasn't been able to find anyone else, so we're sticking it out."

She flashed him a smile. "Maybe I'll come up here with my pruners one night this week."

"I could see you doing that—let me know if you do, and I'll meet you."

She slid him a provocative look. "Don't tempt me."

"It's what I live for." He brought her hand up and pressed a kiss to the back.

The cottage came into view, and she was instantly impressed. It was a gorgeous, two-story craftsman-style building with wide windows, stonework, and a massive arched entry. "This is spectacular."

"You should've seen it before. It was a small, mid-twentieth-century ranch. I'll show you some pictures."

"Wow, and Dylan transformed it completely. You say this was all Sara's idea?"

"Sara's idea, Tori's design, Dylan's implementation. A team effort, really, but yeah, it's technically Sara's baby. She'll be managing all the events here. She's pretty excited about it."

"I would be, too."

"Let me show you inside." He pulled his keys out and unlocked the door, then led her into a huge space.

A wall of windows showed an expansive view of the valley. "This is magnificent. I think *I* want to get married here."

He laughed. "It's pretty spectacular. This view is exactly what Sara wanted. That entire wall opens so that this space can flow out into the outdoor area." Part of it was covered, providing shelter from sun or rain, but there was a large green space, too.

She envisioned the bride and groom standing before the panorama amid a setting of flowers and greenery, which it wasn't at present. It was a lackluster patch of half-dead, clover-infested grass. "Will the ceremony be out there, overlooking the valley?"

He nodded.

"I have to tell you, there's a ton of work to be done out there. I hope your landscaper comes through."

"You and me both. I'll follow up with Dylan again to make sure." He turned and tugged her toward the back of the building. "Wait until you see the kitchen."

"Spoken with the excitement of a chef," she said, grinning. Whereas the outside needed a lot of work, the interior looked completely done. There were little pieces of blue tape here and there to indicate things that needed fixing, but overall it was beautiful. And the kitchen was no exception. It was commercial but attractive, with stainless appliances and granite counters. There were plenty of work spaces, and she could see Kyle working his magic in here. "Do you get to test this place out?"

He shook his head. "Nope. I don't have anything to do with Derek's wedding."

She wanted to ask why they hadn't made up but figured he would talk about it when he was ready. He'd revealed so much to her, and she believed he would continue to open up.

He ran his hand over the granite and tested the water faucet in the large sink.

So he wasn't going to open up about that today. That was okay.

"What's upstairs?" she asked.

His answering look held a bit of smolder. "A wedding suite complete with a hot tub that would put the one in our hotel room to shame."

"Really?" Lust flared in her belly and spread lower, heating her core.

"Don't look at me like that." He came toward her with a growl and swept her into a kiss. His mouth was hot and demanding, his hands hard and fast against her as he lifted her onto the counter and situated himself between her legs.

When they came up for air a moment later, they were both breathing hard. She slid off the counter, her body gliding against his. "I suppose we should go before we do something we shouldn't."

"I wish the bed had been delivered." His voice was dark and sexy, and it raked along her nerve endings like a rough caress she couldn't get enough of.

She forced herself to walk away. "You're a bad influence. Come on, I want to see where your restaurant will be."

He held his hand out. "If I wasn't so excited to show you, I'd toss you back on that counter."

She shivered as she took his hand again, and he led her from the cottage. He locked the door behind them, and they retraced their steps to the parking lot.

"After the wedding, the construction will move to the other buildings?" she asked. Maybe if they kept the conversation focused on the project, she wouldn't be so tempted to jump his bones.

"Yeah, the church will be my restaurant." The pride and excitement in his voice when he said that was evident. "And the brewhouse will be added on—adapted from an outbuilding over on the other side of the church."

"Sounds great. I can't wait to see how it comes together." Yikes, saying things like that implied she would be around when it did. And she had no idea what the future held.

They walked by the monks' quarters, and he explained the plan for phase three—converting that into the hotel, which he'd earlier explained wouldn't happen until sometime after the first of the year. "When do you expect the restaurant to open?" she asked as they neared the church.

He opened one of the heavy doors and held it for her as she went into the cool, dim interior. "I'm actually hoping we can do a soft open in December and then a gala New Year's dinner."

"That sounds great."

He slid his hand around her waist and let his hand skim down to caress her backside through the thin cotton of her tank dress. "There'll be plenty of champagne," he whispered.

Again, heat flooded her core, and she wondered if she'd been too quick to scoot off the counter back at the cottage. Good lord, they weren't college kids; they could keep their hands off each other for a little while. She drifted away and looked around the cavernous expanse. She could easily see how this had been a church, though the pews and altar were long gone. High, arched windows, some with stained glass, let light in and kept it from feeling like a gloomy, abandoned house of worship. "Tell me about your vision for the space."

"We're keeping the stained glass. I love the character it provides. We'll draw that into the interior design and try to stick with a craftsman feel. Since this is an Archer property, we'll have art that matches the pubs—Chloe's taking care of that."

"I've always loved the art in the Archer pubs. My dad's an artist."

Kyle glanced toward her. "Really? What kind of art?"

"Everything—paintings, sculptures, things you would never think were art." She laughed. "Like the headdress he once made using repurposed sex toys."

Kyle froze in his tracks and turned to face her. "What?"

"I told you my parents were strange."

He burst out laughing, his blue-green eyes sparkling in the filtered light. "Oh my God, that's hilarious. How do you respond to that?"

Relieved by his reaction—he could just as easily have been horrified, which is what she had been at seventeen—she smiled. "With a nod and a 'very nice, Dad.' It's best not to engage too much, or he'll talk endlessly about the symbolism and how if we all wore our sexuality out in the open, the world would be a more peaceful place."

Kyle regained his composure and wiped a hand over his cheek. "That's probably true, but man, I don't think I'd want to wear a dildo on my head. Does he still have this thing?"

"I have no idea, and you can be sure I'm not asking."

"I don't blame you." He shook his head. "So this will be the main dining area. Lots of tables and cozy booths. We're putting a huge fireplace in over there." He pointed to the rear wall, where the altar must have once been. "And if you follow me, you can see where the kitchen will go. There are some offices back here and a small kitchen." He took her through an archway to a corridor that led to the offices and the kitchen at the back.

All the rooms were dingy and collectively contained a ramshackle assortment of furniture—odd chairs, a desk, a bookcase. The kitchen was very old—the counters had ribbed metal around the edges that held the Formica, or whatever it was, down.

She walked to the window and looked out at more overgrown bushes behind the building. "Not quite the extravagant chef's dream like in the cottage." She turned and found him staring at her, his gaze shadowed. "What?"

"I'm looking at a chef's dream right now."

Her butt was flush against the counter, a wide, discolored white sink to her right. Oh! It took her a moment to realize he meant her. But only a moment because he stalked toward her with purpose.

He thrust his hand into her hair and clasped her hip as his mouth came down hard on hers. He angled in deep, thrusting his tongue and claiming her with a fierce passion that stole her breath and her ability to think. His hand massaged her waist and hip as he pressed into her. Then he lifted her to the counter as he'd done in the cottage and spread her legs, shoving her dress up to the tops of her thighs. He splayed his hands over her flesh, his fingers kneading and stroking.

She pulled at his hair and returned his kisses, desire curling through her. Place and time fell away so that she was only aware of the scent of the body wash she'd scrubbed into him that morning, the feel of his hair against her fingertips, and the taste of his mouth—fire and need and Kyle.

He ran his hands up under the skirt of her dress and found the top of her underwear. She scooted closer to the edge as he worked the garment down over her ass. Using him as leverage, she came up off the counter so he could get the panties out from under her and strip them down her legs. He shoved them in one pocket while pulling a condom from the other.

She laughed softly. "You came prepared."

His answering look gleamed with intensity. "Always with you."

She flicked the button of his shorts open and pulled down his zipper, then slipped her hand inside his boxer briefs to stroke his eager cock. "So prepared," she murmured, licking her lips as she relived the blowjob she'd given him that morning in the shower. She'd never gotten turned on by performing oral sex before, but with him, she'd practically orgasmed. She wanted to do it again to see if she could get there…

"You're a naughty girl," he breathed, accurately tracing her thoughts. "We should be quick."

"I don't think I can wait."

"You are so fucking perfect." He pulled his cock free, and she helped him roll the condom over his length.

Then he was kissing her again, ravaging her mouth while he parted her legs and put himself at her opening. His tongue thrust at the exact moment his cock surged forward, spearing into her, filling her. She groaned into his mouth and wrapped her legs around his waist.

The kiss intensified as he slammed into her. There was nothing slow or sensuous about this—not like the marathon session they'd engaged in the night before at his house. This was fast and necessary, primitive. Like running for your life.

He wound his hand in her hair and pulled her head back, breaking the kiss with an almost violent tug. She gasped as his mouth latched onto her neck and sucked. Vaguely, she worried he might leave a mark, but she didn't care. In fact, something about that excited her. This was rough and wonderful—so far from the unyielding control she'd been forced to endure before.

She reveled in the delicious feel of his body pounding into hers and let out a series of incredibly indelicate sounds as her pleasure mounted. Clasping her legs around him, she gripped his back and dug her nails into his T-shirt. "Kyle," she moaned, so close.

He licked her neck and moved his hand down to cup her breast, squeezing her as he cried out his release. She came at the same time. Blackness veiled her brain as she lost herself to the moment. When she found her bearings again, he was heaving like he'd just run up the hill leading to the monastery—or was that her? Both of them, she realized.

He leaned his forehead against hers. "God, Maggie. That was…wow." He pressed a kiss to her lips, and she stroked the back of his neck.

"Kyle?" The call came from the old sanctuary.

Kyle straightened, his eyes widening. "Dylan," he mouthed. He ripped off the condom, careful to keep it from spilling, and looked around for a place to ditch it.

"Give me my underwear," she hissed.

He pulled them from his pocket and thrust them into her hand while he disposed of the condom in a random drawer and then readjusted his shorts.

She was just sliding from the counter and smoothing her dress over her legs when Dylan walked into the kitchen. He stopped short upon seeing them.

"Hey, Dylan, I was just showing…uh…" He looked at her in question, clearly not wanting to introduce her as Maggie Trent in case Dylan knew who that was.

She doubted he did, but since he was Sara's boyfriend, they had no idea what he knew. "Magnolia." She waved at him across the kitchen. "Nice to meet you."

"This is Dylan," Kyle said, looking relieved. "He's the contractor I told you about."

"You've done an amazing job on the cottage," she said. "Really, it's breathtaking."

"Thanks." Dylan looked between them, appearing a little confused or surprised or…something else. Did he realize he'd almost interrupted them having sex on the counter? Had he heard the noises she'd made? Maggie hoped to God she didn't look guilty.

Dylan turned to Kyle. "I came up to do a little finish work. I saw your car, but then I didn't find you at the cottage. Just wanted to make sure you weren't trapped underground or anything."

Maggie looked at Kyle in question.

"There's an underground tunnel between the cottage and the monks' quarters. There's also a large room where they used to store wine that they made. Dylan's converting it into a sweet underground pub with a hobbit door built into the ground. In his spare time." He threw Dylan a grin.

"Yeah, right. I have loads of that. Almost done with the cottage though. Ahead of schedule, if you can believe that." He shook his head as if he couldn't.

"Speaking of that," Kyle said, "what's going on with the landscaper?"

Dylan rolled his eyes. "Asshole. For the record, I'm not including that in my schedule comment because yes, he's behind, and I'm pissed. I've actually been trying to find someone else, but everyone's booked up. It's the high season, for Christ's sake." He pulled his phone from his back pocket. "That reminds me, I need to return a phone call about that. Fingers crossed this person pans out. Catch you guys later." He nodded and then left.

Maggie sagged back against the counter. "You don't think he knows who I am?"

"God no. I doubt he would've recognized your name, but I didn't want to take any chances."

"Good call. So, uh…" It was past time to address the elephant in the room. "We haven't discussed this. Whatever we have going here is great, but I'm not ready to meet your family or anything." And she might never be.

"I guess that means you never met anyone besides Alex? I'd wondered if maybe you'd met my mom or Sara, if they'd come to any of his appointments."

"If they did, they didn't come in." She'd recognize any one of them though—from pictures Alex had shown her and from the funeral. She'd snuck in late to the back of the church and had left before the service finished.

She'd watched Hayden deliver the eulogy and Tori get up and speak. Talking about this brought all of the emotions back to the surface, and she struggled against an onslaught of despair and frustration.

He broke into her troubled thoughts. "I think we're on the same page—you aren't ready to meet them, and I'm not remotely ready to introduce you. They'd never understand me seeing you. Especially my dad." He raked his hand through his hair, something he did with frequency, she realized, particularly when he was maybe feeling overwhelmed. "He'd completely lose it."

While she understood, it still hurt to hear that his family blamed her. Why wouldn't they? She blamed herself. "Well, it's a good thing it wasn't one of them. Coming up here wasn't such a good idea. Let's go before someone else shows up."

"Yeah." He gestured for her to precede him, and she noticed he didn't take her hand like he'd done before.

"Hold on, let me dispose of—"

"The condom," she finished for him. She left the church, and he came out a moment later.

When they got to his car, she paused on the passenger side while he rounded to the driver side. "Maybe we should cool it a little. Like I said, this is great, but I need to get my head back and focus."

He looked at her over the hood of the car. "Probably a good idea."

She nodded and got into the car.

All of the joy and contentment she'd felt earlier evaporated like it had been a dream. Maybe that's all this was—a beautiful dream that was destined to end. If that's what it was, she'd remember it fondly and just be grateful she'd had it at all.

MONDAYS WERE UNIVERSALLY reviled as the worst day of the week, and there was a reason. Weekends were awesome, life-affirming, and Mondays just threw you back into the rat race. Or, in Kyle's case, into the orbit of his dad and Derek, both of whom he was avoiding more than usual.

He massaged his forehead as he tried to focus on the reports he was staring at. God, he was glad this job was temporary, and he really hoped he'd be able to cut back soon so he could focus on launching his restaurant. He ought to have a conversation with Dad about it, but he hadn't yet. He added it to the growing pile of shit they should discuss but that he was avoiding.

He'd been thinking a lot about Alex, too. Both because of his conversation with Maggie yesterday and because of what she'd said on Saturday—that he'd had a crush at work. Who had it been?

His phone rang, startling him. The number was from The Arch and Vine, their Ribbon Ridge pub. "This is Kyle."

"Hey, Kyle, it's Tommy. Any chance you can cook for me later? I'm down a body, and I've got no one else to call with decent experience. You did say you were interested in helping out some time, right?"

"Absolutely." Kyle's blood surged with excitement, and his mood did a complete one-eighty. "What time?"

"Five, if you can swing it."

"No problem." Kyle could hardly wait. "One question, do I need to adhere to the menu?"

Tommy laughed. "Within reason, please. Feel free to do whatever specials you want, but you can't mess with the signature stuff."

"Dude, I would never screw with the nachos." That was like rewriting the Declaration of Independence or remaking *Raiders of the Lost Ark*. There were just some things you did *not* do.

More laughter. "See you at five."

"See you then." Kyle ended the call, then pulled up his calendar to make sure he was clear. *Shit*. He'd forgotten about his seven o'clock appointment with the computer forensics guy. How had he forgotten that? Finding who'd sold Alex those drugs had been his primary focus.

Until Maggie had taken over. Rather, his feelings for Maggie.

Feelings for Maggie?

Yesterday's close call with Dylan had rattled him a bit. He was sure Dylan had no idea who she was, but what if he had? What if that had been Tori or Sara or, God forbid, Derek?

They likely wouldn't have put it together, particularly when he'd introduced her as Magnolia. She hadn't met any of them, so they wouldn't recognize her on sight, and did any of them remember the name of Alex's therapist? He hadn't even known it until he'd looked her up in Alex's contacts on his laptop. But then he hadn't been living here. Sara had. And Derek. It was possible they knew

Maggie's name, so he was doubly glad she'd introduced herself as Magnolia.

The encounter with Dylan had put a damper on the day, effectively ending it. After they'd driven back to Hayden's house, she'd gone home almost immediately, pleading the need to water her garden. While that had been a legitimate excuse, he knew the primary reason for her departure was because of their encounter with Dylan. Or more importantly, because of the conversation that had followed.

Now that they'd discussed the need to keep their fling secret from his family, it was like they'd categorized whatever they were doing. A casual, fun hookup had become something more. Something they needed to hide. She seemed to be okay with that, but he still felt unsettled. Was it because she'd suggested they dial things back?

He was overthinking this. She'd been right. They'd had a great weekend, but it was time to reconnect with reality, with why they'd come together in the first place. The drugs.

He stared at the appointment on his screen, hating to reschedule. Maybe she could take Alex's laptop to the guy? This was a side business he ran out of his house in Newberg, not terribly far from where she lived. But Kyle didn't have time to take it to her before he had to be at The Arch and Vine. Would she come pick it up?

Glancing at the clock, he wondered if he could catch her between appointments. He dialed her cell phone and immediately got voicemail. Bummer. He texted her instead.

Can you call me when you get a sec? I have a favor to ask…Alex's laptop and the computer forensics specialist…

A few minutes later, his phone rang, and it was Maggie. "Hi, you got my message," he said.

"Yeah, I only have a second before my next patient. What do you need?"

You. Would her phone voice ever *not* arouse him? *Get a grip, Archer.* "I have an appointment with the computer forensics specialist at seven tonight. Just dropping off Alex's laptop for him to investigate. But The Arch and Vine needs me to cook. Any chance—"

"Where?"

Kyle felt a surge of relief. "He's maybe half a mile from your house—I'll text you the address. You'll have to come get the laptop though. I can't make it out to Newberg before I have to be at the pub. I know this is an imposition, but I hate to reschedule."

"It's okay. I can't come until after five though."

"I'll be at the pub then. Just drop by, and I'll give it to you. You're a lifesaver."

"You want me to come to The Arch and Vine?" Her question came with a strong undercurrent of disbelief. "After what happened yesterday, I'd rather steer clear of anywhere I might run into an Archer."

Damn, he hadn't really thought about that, but it wasn't like they lived at the pub. "It'll be fine."

"How do you know?"

He didn't. For all he knew, Chloe was working a shift or Derek was bartending—everyone pitched in as needed from time to time. "There's a small employee parking lot in back with a door to the kitchen that's usually cracked open. I'll leave my car keys on a hook by the door—just inside. You can grab them, get the laptop out of my car, and be out of there before anyone sees you." *Probably me included*, which kind of sucked, but he didn't say that. They were taking a breather, after all.

"Okay, I can do that." She still sounded a bit uncertain, but before he could further allay her concern, she said, "I gotta go. See you later."

He hoped so. They might have agreed to cool things off, but his body hadn't gotten the memo. It heated just thinking about glimpsing her gorgeous eyes, the wild mass of her dark hair, the dip of her waist as it curved into her hip...

He shook his head and forced himself to get back to the report.

By quarter after five, Kyle had to reassess his opinion about Mondays. Or at least this Monday. He'd missed being in a commercial kitchen—the camaraderie, the craft, even the impossible juggling. It was like a well-choreographed dance, and while he hadn't cooked in this kitchen in years, it was as though he'd never left.

"Are you offering different specials or what?" Tommy asked. He was on his way out to take his kid to an appointment.

Kyle surveyed the spice shelf. "Not sure yet. I might do a barbecue chicken wrap."

"Sounds great, we do those from time to time."

Kyle smiled at him as he pulled ingredients down to make his own sauce. "Not like this, you haven't."

"If customers love it, you'll have to show us how to duplicate it," he warned. "Have fun." He left through the back door, next to which dangled Kyle's keys. He was keeping half an eye on the door, but he really didn't know what time Maggie would show up. He just knew it would be some time before six thirty.

After mixing up a batch of his signature barbecue sauce, he prepped some chicken and fired up the grill top. There was an assistant on tonight, but he was back and forth helping with bussing, running to the basement for supplies, and scrubbing his hands in between so he could help Kyle as needed. Mondays weren't terribly busy, which was too bad. Kyle was in his element, and he'd missed it.

"Hey there!" A feminine voice drew him to look up from turning the chicken. Natalie stood in the doorway that led from the dining room, her dark hair pulled back in a high ponytail. She wore a fitted workout outfit—cropped pants and a bright orange shirt. "I wanted to stop in before my run and check you out in the kitchen. How's it going?" She came inside, letting the door swing shut behind her.

"Loving it."

She moved closer, looking down at the grill. "What are you making?"

"Barbecue chicken wrap." He slapped a whole wheat tortilla on the griddle and then sliced tomato and avocado on a large cutting board.

"Looks good."

He grabbed some romaine and cut it into slender strips, making a chiffonade for the wrap.

"You are amazing with that knife."

He flashed her a smile. "Don't piss me off."

She laughed. "I won't! I might have to come back after my run and order one of those."

He pulled the chicken off the grill and sliced it thin, then assembled the wrap. "Let me test it first." He cut it in half and took a small bite. "Mmmm, not bad. It's my signature sauce."

"I bet it's great. Here." She reached up and wiped the side of his mouth where a dab of sauce had escaped the side of the wrap. Then she sucked the tip of her finger. "Delicious."

Okay, that was *definitely* flirting. Outrageous, I'm-totally-interested-in-you flirting. Sara's admonition from the other day came back to him.

"Natalie, I'm flattered that you, uh, like me. Or whatever." What the fuck was he supposed to say? He wasn't typically in the habit of turning advances down. Had he *ever* done that? But she was his employee, for crying out loud. Plus, there was Maggie. Maggie, who he shouldn't be seeing but couldn't stop thinking about.

Natalie's eyes lit up, and she slid her hands around his neck, pulling him down for a kiss. For a moment, he simply stood there, shocked.

But the second her lips touched his, he jerked back. At the same moment, he heard the jingle of keys. He snapped his head around to the back door, which had swung against the doorstop that kept it cracked open. His keys were gone.

Fuck and fuck.

He took Natalie's arms from around his neck and backed away. "That was inappropriate," he said, knowing there were better ways to defuse this situation but not wanting to take the time. "You're my employee. I like you, but not romantically. Take the wrap if you want it."

He dashed out of the kitchen and into the back parking lot just as Maggie was putting the laptop in her passenger seat. He rushed toward her, trapping her between her car and his SUV. Maybe there was a chance she hadn't seen that…"I was hoping I'd see you."

"Really? You looked pretty busy." Nope, she'd seen it.

"I wasn't. Natalie's a flirt. I can't do anything about that."

"I guess not. You're a babe magnet, right? I knew that about you, but seeing it firsthand is a real eye-opener." As she turned to walk around her car, he grabbed her elbow and pressed her back against the driver door of the SUV.

Her anger pricked his ire. "You *knew* that about me? I guess Alex said more than you let on. *Now* you're going to share information from his therapy? That's convenient."

She scowled at him. "Never mind. I need to get this laptop to the specialist." She tried to squeeze past him, but he laid his palms against the window on either side of her head and pressed his body flush against hers.

"I appreciate you doing that." He didn't want her to be mad at him, especially about something that wasn't even his fault. "Natalie's just a coworker. A flirty coworker who barely registers on my radar."

She blinked up at him, looking completely uninterested all of a sudden. "You don't owe me an explanation, and I don't have a right to be pissed. We aren't a *thing*. We had a fun weekend, a great moment in time, and that moment's over."

Chapter Eleven

MAGGIE SMILED PLACIDLY up at him, hoping he'd buy it and she could get to her car and leave before she had a full-blown anxiety attack. *No.* She didn't want to do that. She'd fooled around with him because it had made her feel good, and she refused to let it turn bad. They *weren't* a thing.

She rushed to say, "I'll let you know what the guy says when I drop the laptop off. I can't pick it up for you though. Busy week." She glanced at his arms, which were blocking her in. "Are you going to let me pass?"

His gaze darkened, and his hands inched closer to her head. "You say the moment has passed. I say this is another moment."

She was too aware of the rise and fall of her chest as her heart rate accelerated. But other than that staccato rhythm, she didn't move.

He tucked a curl behind her ear. "Another glorious parking lot moment." He bent his head to whisper, "I don't think I can let another one pass me by."

His teeth snagged her earlobe, and he tugged gently before skimming light kisses along her neck and the underside of her jaw. She held perfectly still, not wanting to encourage him and yet unable to ask him to stop.

His head came up, and he brought his mouth an inch from hers. "The only woman I'm interested in right now is you."

She expected the kiss but not the searing passion that came with it. She was mad at him. He'd just said "right now" in reference to his desire for her, as if he might change his mind in an hour. But like he said, this was another moment, and in this moment she was his and he was hers, and she'd cling to that like crazy.

Clasping his hips, she anchored herself between him and the car, loving the pressure of his body against hers. The parking lot was small and secluded, with the pub on one side and a fence on two others. They could actually consummate this parking lot thing they had going if it weren't for the capri pants she was wearing—not very conducive to spontaneous sex. Why hadn't she worn the maxi dress she'd pulled out of her closet first that morning?

He pulled away but surged forward again for another quick kiss. "I need to get back inside before someone comes looking for me."

Crap. Someone like another Archer?

She pulled her hands from his waist and pushed on his shoulders. "Yes, go. The last thing I want is for someone to catch us together again."

He winced just before he turned his head to look at the door. When he faced her again, he said, "It's fine. There's no one here. No Archers anyway. Besides me."

"I'm not sure it matters, Kyle." She'd thought about it endlessly since yesterday. Alex would always be between them. "Alex is here."

Kyle looked at her quizzically. "Obviously he's not."

She exhaled. "You know what I mean. I'll always be the therapist who failed to recognize his suicidal thoughts and save him. You'll never be able to forget that—and neither will I."

His sensuous lips, so delicious a moment before, turned down in a distasteful smile. "I'm not thinking about him at all."

"Maybe not right this second, but you were yesterday when Dylan came in."

He pulled his hand through his hair, and she knew she was right. "I'm fine with it. I don't blame you," he said.

Maybe not in the way he used to blame her—with anger or vengeance—but he held her accountable. How could he not?

"Your family will, and you know that," she said.

His jaw worked for a moment, the muscles clenching and releasing. "They might not."

He didn't sound as if he believed that. So how could she? "It doesn't matter anyway. I think this moment is over, too." This time when she tried to squeeze by him, he let her go. She paused before she climbed into the car. "I'll let you know what the computer guy says."

MAGGIE TOSSED HER half-eaten frozen lunch into the garbage. Her gaze landed on her phone, which was sitting at the edge of her desk blotter. For the hundredth time that week, she thought about calling Kyle.

No. She had zero reason to. She'd texted him that the computer forensics specialist would let them know when he was finished with his review of the laptop and that they probably wouldn't hear anything until early next week.

She turned her chair away from the taunting phone.

Yesterday had been the worst because it was Wednesday, and she'd had no appointments to keep herself busy. She'd occupied the morning doing work at home—writing reports and returning a few phone calls. In the afternoon, she'd tried to tackle the boxes she'd stowed in her walk-in closet but had ended up outside in the yard instead. Typical.

Snap out of it, she told herself.

She prepared for her next appointment—Ryan Dillinger. He made her a little nervous, but she couldn't quite put her finger on why. She'd actually been thinking about how she might transfer him to a different therapist in the clinic. There were only four of them, including Dr. Innes, but maybe John or Paige could take him.

Stacy knocked lightly before opening the door. "Mr. Dillinger is here. You ready?"

Maggie nodded. "Thanks." She stood from her desk as Stacy went to get him. Taking a deep breath, Maggie picked up her notepad and went to her chair angled beside the couch.

Stacy opened the door wider to let Ryan in and then closed it behind her when she left.

"Hi, Ryan," Maggie said. Right away she could tell something was wrong. He leaned back against the closed door; he was white as a sheet, and a bead of perspiration slid down his temple.

"Are you okay?" she asked tentatively as apprehension and adrenaline spiked through her. Slowly she stood, careful not to make any quick movements.

His gaze was fixed out the windows, but he didn't seem to be actually seeing anything. "I'm...overwhelmed. I didn't get either one of those jobs I interviewed for last week."

Her chest constricted with genuine pity, an emotion she knew he'd hate—most people did, herself included. It was the absolute worst thing, a sort of validation that you were as pathetic and worthless as you imagined yourself to be. It was the world saying, "Yes, your life does in fact suck."

"You still have another one you're waiting to hear on, right?"

He shook his head. "No, I got a form letter on that one last week. I told you about that." He kicked his foot flat against the door, making her jump. "Don't you listen to me?"

The prickles of unease that had formed as soon as he'd walked in iced into genuine fear. She worked to keep her tone even, calming. "Yes, but I don't always recall every detail for every patient." She used to. Before Alex. It was just another way she'd become the world's shittiest therapist.

Ryan nodded slightly, and she allowed herself to relax. Big mistake.

He pulled a gun from the back of his waistband. Instinctively, she circled around her desk and ducked down.

"Stand up," he said, sounding weary instead of furious like he had a moment before. "I'm not going to shoot you."

She peered at him over the edge of her desk, still cowering behind the corner farthest from him. "Why do you have a gun?" She reached for the panic button installed on the underside of her center drawer. Finding the hard, round button, she pressed it until her finger hurt.

"I told you to stand up." His tone became harsh again, though not quite as angry as it had been.

She slowly rose, silently counting how long it would take for someone to come. Or would they wait for security to come over from the hospital? If she could keep him talking, maybe she could prevent him from doing something awful. "If you aren't here to shoot me, why did you bring a gun?"

He looked at her as if she were the one in the middle of a mental health crisis. "So I could kill myself."

Oh, God. No. Nooooo. Her vision blurred, and nausea swirled in her gut. Without thinking, she moved around her desk. "Ryan, don't, please. Give me the gun. There are so many reasons for you not to do that. You're bright, young, and one of the most caring people I've met." Everything she said was true, though she knew he couldn't see it now.

His answering smile was sad. "Forty-seven isn't young, I'm not that bright since I lost my job and my girlfriend dumped me, and I'm way past caring." He lifted the gun toward his temple.

"Nooooo!" She ran toward him just as the door burst open, sending Ryan flying forward. The gun went off, and she hit the floor, her hands covering her head.

Footsteps sounded, but she kept her eyes squeezed shut. She didn't want to see what had happened, whether Ryan had been successful…

She swallowed bile as she began to shake. Commotion and noise went on around her, but she stayed flat on the floor with her eyes closed.

Finally, voices broke into her panicked mind. "Dr. Trent?" Gentle hands clasped her arms, helped her to her feet. "Are you all right?"

"Is he…?" She couldn't say the word.

The security guard who'd helped her up let go of her. "He's fine. We've taken him into custody."

She carefully opened her eyes and blinked to accustom herself to the light. Her assistant, pale and frightened, stood over by the couch, talking to another security guard.

Other people from the office stood outside the door in the hallway, and she heard a collection of voices—more than just those of people who worked in the clinic.

"The police will be here in just a minute, and you can talk to them about what happened," the guard said.

Stacy rushed over to her. "I'm so sorry!"

Maggie barely registered what she was saying. She was too shaky, too upset. "Excuse me." She calmly went to her desk, pulled the garbage can from beneath it, and threw up the lasagna she'd just eaten.

Stacy came over and put her arm around Maggie's shoulders. "Come on, let's sit on the couch and wait for the police." She guided Maggie to the sofa, pulled the decorative throw blanket from the back, and wrapped it around Maggie. "Do you want some water?"

"Yes, please. And a mint if you have it." Her mouth tasted awful. Even before she'd vomited, it had tasted as though she'd sucked on a penny.

Stacy brought her a tall glass of cool water and sprinkled a few Tic Tacs into her palm. A few moments later, the police arrived and took Maggie's statement. They informed her that Ryan had been admitted to the psych ward.

Exhaustion crept over her as her body finally relaxed from the adrenaline dump. She looked up to see her assistant still lingering near her desk. "Stacy, I don't think I can see any more patients today."

She came back over as Maggie stood and folded the blanket. "We've already canceled all of the clinic's appointments."

Maggie placed the blanket back over the couch, her movements robotic and disjointed—like they belonged to someone else. "I'm not sure I'll be in tomorrow, either," she said. Just the thought of seeing a patient was tightening her stomach muscles again and making her wonder if the garbage can was close.

"I'll take care of it," Stacy said.

"Thanks, I appreciate it."

With a determination born of a sheer necessity to get away from her office, Maggie collected her things and left. All she wanted was a swimming-pool-sized glass of wine and a nice, long sit in her yard.

Chapter Twelve

IT WAS NEARLY eight o'clock when Kyle stepped out of his car, flowers in hand, and made his way to the doors of the medical building. When they didn't automatically open, he rechecked the time on his phone: only 7:56. But maybe their clock was off and they'd already locked the doors.

A security guard appeared and opened the door. "Can I help you?"

"Yeah, I'm here to meet Maggie Trent."

The guard's brow furrowed. "She's one of the therapists on three, right?"

Something about the guard's reaction and demeanor pricked Kyle's neck with dread. "Yes. Can I go up and meet her?"

He shook his head. "Everyone's gone. Left early. There was a rogue patient there this afternoon. Jerk fired a gun."

Kyle's gut clenched and then promptly dropped through his feet. He squeezed the stems of the flowers in his fist, practically snapping them in half. "Is she okay? Is everyone okay?"

"Yeah. He was trying to off himself but missed. He's in the psych ward now."

Kyle practically ran from the building. He had to get to Maggie. "Thanks." He turned and rushed back to his car, then ignored every speed limit on the way to her house.

After parking in the driveway, he leapt out of the car and sprinted toward the front door. He knocked briskly and fidgeted while he waited for her to answer. When there was no response, he rang the bell. His apprehension climbing, he pounded on the wood. "Maggie? Open up, it's me."

Still nothing. Swearing, he retraced his steps to the driveway and went around the garage to the gate leading to the backyard, where he'd found her the last time he'd stopped by. Releasing the latch, he followed the path to the back and froze when he saw her sitting at a little table on her patio, a giant glass of red wine in front of her. She was wrapped in a sweater despite the fact that it was probably seventy-five degrees outside. And she was so still as to be a painting, especially with the setting sun casting a golden patina over the entire scene.

He walked toward her. "Maggie?"

She still didn't move.

He sank down in the other chair at the table and silently willed her to look at him. "I heard about what happened. What can I do?"

"Nothing. I'm fine." She lifted the glass and took a sip of the wine.

Okay, that was total bullshit, but he didn't say so. "I don't know how you can be—was this guy one of your patients?" He assumed it was, given her state. She was too detached, too distressed.

"Yes."

The fact that she didn't say more told him she didn't want to talk about it. He wanted to help her, but he also didn't want to push.

The sound of a phone ringing from inside the house interrupted the quiet. When she didn't seem to register the noise, he got up and moved toward the door. "Should I get that? It might be someone checking up on you."

She finally turned to look at him. "No, it's fine."

It wasn't fine. Her coworkers were probably worried about her and justifiably so. He'd let them know she wasn't alone. "I'll just get it." He opened the screen door and had one foot inside before he felt her hand on his arm.

Her gaze was wide, panicked almost. "No! Don't go in there."

His eyes adjusted to the dimmer interior, and he tried to conceal his shock. The door opened into the kitchen and eating area, both of which were...to say cluttered might be an understatement. The counters were covered with papers, dishes—mostly clean—and boxes and cans of food, like she was using the space as storage. Moving boxes were stacked in the corner, and the table held a similar array of random items—a DVD player, a laptop, a package of paper towels, a mishmash of papers and envelopes, as if her mail was just mixed in with everything.

He never would've imagined her house would look like this. He'd seen her office—it was impeccably clean and organized. He'd spent plenty of time with her—she was beautiful, put-together, clever. How did someone like her live in a place like this?

He stepped further inside before turning.

She slumped against the doorframe, her gaze downcast. "Now you know my secret. I'm a total disaster."

His heart twisted, and he reached out for her, pulling her into his embrace. "You are not. You're talking to a gambling addict who had to move across the country to flee his demons, remember?"

She sniffed into his shoulder, her head bent. "Don't lie to me and say you aren't shocked. Now you see why I never asked you in."

He infused his tone with a generous dash of levity. "Damn, and I could've gotten lucky that first time if not for you worrying what I might think..."

"Ha." She made the sound, but he couldn't tell if she'd smiled or if he'd lightened her mood at all. When she pulled away and looked at him with eyes that were nearly as dark as midnight, he had his answer. "You should go. There's nothing for you to do here except watch me spiral into a puddle of self-loathing."

"Maggie, don't." Her words made him a little angry. She didn't deserve that—even from herself. "Talk to me. Why does your house look like this? On the outside you seem collected and together."

"Why shouldn't I be? It's much easier to be the person who doesn't draw attention, the person everyone thinks is absolutely normal."

"What the hell is normal? If you know what that is, please enlighten me, because growing up as an Archer, I learned that normal isn't real."

She blinked at him. "Don't say that," she said softly. So softly, he had to strain to hear. "I worked so hard to be the normal girl despite my crazy parents and the crazy clothes they bought me and the crazy things they made me do, like read poetry aloud every night before I went to bed."

"We all have crazy families. In fact, I'm pretty sure those two words together are redundant." He hoped for at least the hint of a smile, but she gave him nothing but that hollow, tortured look.

"In trying to escape that, I chose the worst possible boyfriend—a guy who looked utterly normal. Intelligent, ambitious, super motivated, attractive, funny…perfect. But he was a controlling asshole. He chose my clothes, my friends, my activities. He was just a different version of my parents—always someone else making my decisions for me, telling me what I needed to do."

Watching her ache and struggle, he was robbed of thought and speech. At last he simply said, "What can I do?"

She took a deep breath that sounded a bit like a shudder. "I don't know. I'm still trying to figure this out. I left Mark—at least I was smart enough to realize things were only going to get worse. I moved to Ribbon Ridge, took over a small practice from a retiring therapist, and began to reclaim my life. No, *claim* it, because I'd never really lived it for myself before."

Admiration swelled in his chest. "You're incredibly brave."

"I try to be, but it's hard when life kicks you in the teeth, isn't it? Things actually did seem to be going well. Until Alex killed himself."

He hadn't been expecting her to say that. Alex's actions had devastated their entire family, but Kyle was only now beginning to see what it had done to her. "That pushed you over the edge," he said quietly.

"In helpless, careening somersaults." She pulled her sweater off and threw it over one of the chairs. She paced around aimlessly. "I was a mess, Kyle. I couldn't work, I could barely get out of bed. I was taking Xanax, which I still take from time to time and shouldn't." She stopped to look at him, but he wasn't sure she was actually seeing him, lost as she was in her turmoil. "What kind of therapist has to medicate herself? A shitty one—you said so yourself." She resumed her movement, her hands twisting together. "After I broke up with Mark, I started over in Ribbon Ridge and had just begun to find myself. Maybe. I don't know. I don't know who I am. I'm not a very good daughter. I completely suck at relationships."

God, he knew what this felt like. The idea that you weren't worth anything. That you had nothing of value to offer to anyone. "You are not a bad therapist."

"No, you were right." She spoke with absolute conviction. "I really hate doing it. Trying to fix other people only reminds me how unfixable I am."

He crossed to her and cupped her face. "You aren't broken. You had a really bad day. Hell, a bad year, I guess. But it's not the totality of who you are—who you can be. I'm here. I'm with you, and that's not awful, is it?"

She shook her head, blinking. He saw the glimmer of tears in her eyes and wiped his thumbs over her lids. "Don't cry, Maggie. I'm here. We'll fix this." He glanced around at the clutter. "We'll fix all of this together."

She stared at him and said nothing. He worried he'd overstepped. He grew uncomfortable as the silence stretched, finally saying, "Do you want me to go?"

She shook her head and twined her arms around his neck. "Stay."

Standing on her toes, she kissed him. Warmth spread through his body, igniting the passion that always seemed to be lying under the surface when he was with her. She tasted of wine and sadness, and he wanted to banish the darkness—at least for tonight.

He scooped her into his arms, and she clung to his neck. "Bedroom?" he asked.

She gestured with her head toward the stairs. "And it's the cleanest room in the house."

He grinned. "I don't care, but that certainly saves us time."

He took the stairs as fast as he dared while holding her and followed the hallway to the left. Her room was in the back corner of the house. It wasn't terribly large, but it had a wrought-iron bed that was immaculately made with a fluffy comforter and a stack of pillows. Like she'd said, the room was tidy.

"Just don't go in the closet." She indicated a door in the corner.

He set her on the bed. "You got it."

Instead of lying back, she knelt at the edge and unbuttoned his shorts. He could read her intent and wanted to stop her—he'd brought her upstairs to make love to her, to help her forget. But he couldn't form the words, and when her mouth and palm touched his heated flesh, he was lost.

She pushed his shorts and boxer briefs off, and he kicked them and his shoes to the side. Her hand curled around the base of his shaft as her tongue licked around the head. She teased him, lightly moving her fingers over him but never quite taking him into her mouth.

He wound his hands in her hair, loving the sight of her bent over him. He wanted to plunge into her, but he held himself back, content—for now—to let her take the lead.

At last, she closed her lips over him and sucked. Gently and just the tip, but it was enough to send a rush of blood straight to his cock. She raked her thumb over his balls and then scooped them in her hand, holding them as she encircled her fingers around the base once more. She took him deeper, her tongue gliding along the underside. The heat and wetness and feel of her tight mouth ravaged his senses. He closed his eyes and let himself just feel.

She let go of his balls and began to pump his shaft with her hand, bringing it up to meet her mouth as she withdrew, then sliding it back down as she devoured him again. Up and down she worked him, driving him toward release. She moved faster, and the sounds of her mouth and tongue filled the room. His balls tightened. He was so close.

"Maggie," he groaned, opening his eyes. "I'm going to come."

She looked up at him, her pupils dilated with her desire. "Is that what you want?"

"I'd prefer to do it with you."

She pulled her tank top over her head and threw it at the wall, then shimmied out of her shorts and underwear, leaving her naked—she'd ditched her shoes at some point, or maybe she hadn't been wearing any. She definitely hadn't been wearing a bra—a fact he'd tried not to focus on when she'd taken her sweater off downstairs. That hadn't been the time for lascivious thoughts. Now, however, was definitely the time as she scooted back against her pillows so that she was only partially reclined. She parted her legs and held her breasts, as if she were offering herself to him. And he supposed she was.

With a growl, he tore off his shirt and fell on her. Her legs parted wider to accommodate him as he nestled between them and bent his head to her breast. She held herself for him while he tongued her. He reached for her other breast and found that she was tweaking the nipple, which only heightened his lust. He raked his teeth across her and sucked her deeply, his fingers taking over from hers. Her low moans skated over him, exciting him further.

"Let's go, Kyle," she said, lifting her legs and planting her feet flat on the bed.

God, he loved a woman who knew what she wanted. He moved his mouth to her other breast, consuming it the way he'd done the other while he moved his hand between her legs. She was so wet, beyond ready. But shit, his condom was wherever his shorts were.

He leaned up to go find them, but she pulled his head back down. "Where are you going?"

"Condom."

"In the nightstand drawer."

He also loved a woman who was prepared. Dropping a quick kiss on her mouth, he reached for the drawer and found a small box of condoms. He withdrew one and quickly tore it open. "Can I hope you were planning to invite me in?"

Her lips finally curved into the smile that could light up his entire day. "Maybe."

He slipped the condom on and narrowed his eyes down at her playfully. "You're mean."

"You're taking too long."

He barely got the condom over himself before she pulled at his hips with one hand and guided him into her heat with the other. He thrust forward and grabbed the wrought iron above her head to brace himself. "God forbid I take too long, so this is going to be hard and fast."

She wrapped her legs around his waist and squeezed his ass. "*Yes.* Come on, Kyle. *Bring it.*"

He clasped the headboard and let himself go, driving into her with long, savage strokes. She latched her mouth onto his neck and kissed him, licking and biting as her nails raked across his back.

Their moans and cries punctuated the incessant sound of their bodies' slapping together. It was like a musical piece—rough and unpracticed but so sweet and arousing to his ears. His orgasm was within reach, about to crash over him like a crescendo of cymbals. He reached between them and stroked her clit, needing to have her come with him. "Come with me, Maggie. *Come.*"

Her muscles clenched around him, squeezing his cock. He tightened as his orgasm burst upon him. He'd seen it coming, but he hadn't been prepared for the intensity. He gripped the headboard and buried his other hand in her hair, pulling at her soft curls as if they could keep him from flying away into blackness.

Her fingers dug into his backside as she rotated her pelvis against him. When they finally stilled, he let go of the bed and sank down beside her on the pillows, withdrawing from her.

She curled onto her side to face him and threw her leg over his hip. "Don't go."

"I'm not going anywhere." He kissed her forehead. "I'm going to find something to cook in your kitchen, and we're going to tidy it up so I can make you dinner."

"Okay."

He'd almost expected an argument, but he realized she didn't necessarily want her house this way. Maybe she just didn't know where to begin.

She kissed him on the mouth, her tongue meeting his for a soft, subtle dance that rekindled his desire.

"Careful," he said against her lips, "or you're going to have to let me spend the night so we can have a repeat performance."

She deepened the kiss and caressed his chest. "Don't go," she said again, looking into his eyes.

There was trust here, he realized. A foundation for something he'd never had before, something he'd never wanted. What *did* he want? Her. This *belonging*. This feeling of being needed. He'd never fallen in love but imagined it might feel like this. He really didn't know, and right now he didn't want to overanalyze it. He just wanted to enjoy it.

He brushed her wild hair back from her face. "I won't go until you tell me to."

MAGGIE LOOKED AROUND her somewhat tidy kitchen. Kyle had just left, but his imprint was everywhere. They'd worked past midnight to put everything away and get the counters and table completely empty of clutter. Then they'd gone back upstairs, where he'd made love to her again, more slowly and thoroughly—if that were possible. She felt utterly satisfied and content.

Because they'd been up so late, he'd had to leave in a bit of a hurry this morning so he could get to work, but not before he'd come back inside with the flowers he'd forgotten to give her last night.

She smiled at them, the only thing on her now-clean kitchen table. They were in a pitcher because she had no idea which box in the garage held the cheap vases that had come with all of the apology flowers Mark had sent her. Even the thought of her ex didn't dampen her mood.

What did that mean? Was she falling for Kyle? Yeah, probably. It felt a little like when she'd fallen for Mark, but not quite. There was something deeper that came from how Kyle had reacted last night. He'd shown up and simply taken charge—not in a controlling way like Mark would have done, but in a way that made them partners. He didn't do things for her or instruct her; he asked her, helped her, followed her lead.

Whatever was going on, she had to think they were past being friends with benefits. She'd shared things with him she'd never told anyone, and he'd opened himself up to her about his gambling—something she was certain he'd never done with anyone else. Rather than guess about all of this, she wanted to talk to him. They'd demonstrated their ability to be honest and open with each other, and they could do the same with regard to this burgeoning relationship.

Still, Alex hovered at the back of her mind. When she'd mentioned him last night, Kyle's expression had flattened. He'd been completely engaged in her, and then for a moment, he'd engaged in his own grief or whatever he'd been feeling. She didn't fault him for it, as she understood that Alex was a part of who they were as a couple—*if* they were a couple. He'd brought them together, and if they couldn't find a way for the Archers to forgive her, he'd drive them apart, too.

She glanced at the clock and vaguely remembered that she should've been with a patient right now but that they'd canceled today's appointments. Pouring a cup of coffee, she exhaled in relief. What about Monday? And Tuesday? The calm she'd felt all night and all morning began to unravel as she thought about work.

Her Xanax was still upstairs in the bathroom. She hadn't taken any since she'd seen Amy, but she also hadn't disposed of it like she said she would.

She ought to see if Amy could fit her in sooner. She didn't know if she wanted to return to work without talking to her therapist first. The irony of that wasn't lost on her—she needed therapy in order to provide therapy.

She called Amy's office and moved her appointment up to next week. The receptionist had heard about what happened—it was such a small community—and offered her apologies. Maggie ended the call and then padded to the downstairs bedroom she used as an office. In reality, it was a box-filled area with a desk. They'd put her laptop in there for now, but she took it back to the kitchen with her since the desk was still unusable at this point. Kyle would be back this weekend to help her attack the other rooms, and for the first time, the notion didn't fill her with anxiety.

When she was situated at the kitchen table, she pulled up her e-mail and sent a note to her boss asking for the next week off. Her finger hovered over the track pad for a moment before she clicked send. She didn't think he would have a problem with it, but what was she going to do when it came time to go back? She might've overcome her anxiety about cleaning her house, but now her angst seemed to be centered around returning to work.

Don't think about that right now, Maggie. You don't have to deal with it today.

Her e-mail alert sounded, and she glanced down at the screen. It was from the computer forensics specialist. She read through it quickly. He apologized for contacting her instead of Kyle, but he'd misplaced Kyle's information. Maggie wasn't surprised—the guy was young and definitely what you'd call a computer geek. Organization didn't seem to be his strong suit, but he'd been incredibly knowledgeable about his field.

Her stomach clenched as she read further. He'd attached deleted e-mails that he'd found in the computer's cache. E-mails that contained the names of the drugs. E-mails from someone named Natalie Frobish.

Dread curled through her. She opened the attachments, and as she read through them, her horror magnified. *Natalie.*

Alex had bought the drugs from the woman Maggie had seen kissing Kyle the other night. And from the tone of the e-mails, she'd been the one he'd had a crush on. She couldn't tell if they'd had an actual relationship of any kind, but she was certainly flirty in her responses.

Maggie stared at the screen. Not only had this woman provided Alex with the drugs he'd used to kill himself, she'd profited from it. There were no amounts listed, but the wording was such that it was clear he was compensating her.

How would Kyle take this? To have the culprit be not only someone he knew, but someone his entire family trusted would be devastating.

Maggie would be there for him, just like he'd been there for her. They'd figure it out together.

Chapter Thirteen

"THERE SHE IS!" Sara dashed toward Mom as she and Dad walked toward them down the dirt track. Dad had just picked her up from the airport and brought her directly to The Alex, where Kyle, Sara, Derek, and Dylan had convened for a meeting minus Tori, who was in San Francisco.

Kyle couldn't keep from smiling as he watched Sara give Mom a giant hug. They walked the rest of the way hand in hand, their blonde heads bent together. Sara hadn't gone more than a week without seeing Mom in their entire lives, so the past few months without her had been an adjustment, especially since Sara's sensory processing disorder sort of depended on Mom's support and regulation—or at least it had. Sara had matured into a very capable and independent woman. That didn't make their reunion any less sweet to watch.

"Hi, Mom." Kyle moved forward and wrapped her into a tight hug, sweeping her feet just off the ground.

Mom laughed. "Kyle, put me down!" Her blue eyes sparkled as he set her down.

He didn't remember the last time he'd seen her look so happy, or at least not look sad or pensive. But then, he hadn't spent much time with her the past few years before Alex had died. Regret spiraled through him and threatened to darken the moment. He shrugged it away. "Welcome home."

Derek came up to hug her next, which drove Kyle to separate himself from them. He purposefully tuned out whatever they said.

When he looked back a few moments later, Mom had moved on to Dylan, who'd been lurking in the background. "And here's the young man who's stolen my Sara's heart," Mom said with a wide grin. "Well done."

Dylan nodded his head, looking somewhat mortified. Families were not his forte, but Kyle smiled at his discomfort. If he was going to marry Sara—and Kyle was pretty certain he would—he was going to have to get used to this and more.

"Come on and give me a hug!" Mom demanded, prompting Sara to laugh.

Dylan had no choice but to hug their mother, and Kyle caught the hint of a smile teasing his mouth.

"How was your trip?" Sara asked as they broke apart.

"Great. I'm tired, of course, but it was good."

Kyle tried to get a sense of how things were between Mom and Dad, but it was impossible to tell. Dad was over studying the cottage with interest. He hadn't been up here in a while, and it looked completely different from his last visit.

Mom turned and surveyed the cottage. "I can't believe how wonderful this looks! Except for the landscaping." Her nose scrunched up. "What's going on? Why hasn't anything been started?"

"Long story," Derek said. "We're working on it—that's why we're meeting here."

"Don't suppose someone will give me a tour?" Dad asked from over near the open door. He appeared to be going inside regardless.

"Sure," Dylan said, jogging over to join him. His phone rang at that moment, prompting him to pull it from his back pocket and glance at the screen. "I have to take this—it's about the plants." He glanced back at Kyle and the others. "Can one of you take him?"

Derek started toward the door. "I will."

Alone with Sara and Mom, Kyle turned to their mother. "You look fantastic, Mom. France agrees with you."

"Thank you. I feel good."

"How was your ride back from the airport with Dad?" Sara asked the question with casual nonchalance, but Kyle knew she was as worried about them as he was—more so, probably.

"It was good." Absolutely worthless answer, but Kyle wouldn't press. Mom touched their cheeks simultaneously. "I've missed you. Kyle, I'm so glad you're here. And you both look so happy. I understand why she does." She winked at Sara. "But what's your excuse, Kyle? Things are going well here?"

"Well enough." He looked happy? He didn't think he looked any different. "Same old, same old."

"Meaning he still hasn't made up with Dad or Derek," Sara said.

Mom's eyes narrowed slightly as she looked up at him. "That makes the spark in your eye extra curious."

The spark in his eye? Shit. He blinked as if he could somehow make it go away.

Sara leaned closer to Mom and stage-whispered, "He has a secret girlfriend."

Holy fucking hell. What had Dylan told her?

Kyle speared her with a what-the-fuck glare. "Who told you that?"

Sara lifted her chin. "Not you, clearly. Dylan met her the other day. Come on, it's no big deal."

"I beg to differ with you, dear," Mom said, her gaze softening as she looked at Kyle. "I don't know that your brother has ever had a girlfriend, secret or otherwise."

Kyle wanted to shoot Dylan. Right after he disemboweled him. "Sure I have."

"That must've been in Florida then and couldn't have been too serious if you didn't mention her."

"Okay, no serious girlfriends." But Maggie wasn't a serious girlfriend. Hell, she wasn't even a *girlfriend.* Was she?

"Who is she?" Sara asked.

Couldn't this conversation just *die?* Or maybe a small asteroid could drop into the valley below—something, *anything* to divert attention from him. "Just a friend."

Dylan came back over to join them after finishing his call, and Kyle threw him the nastiest thanks-a-lot-bro stare he could manage. In response, Dylan just blinked at him before saying, "So the plants and sod are arriving Monday morning. Too bad we have no plan for them."

"Why not?" Mom asked.

Relief at the change in topic drove the tension from Kyle's shoulders. "The landscaper we hired flaked. Won't return calls."

"Can't you just show up at their place of business?"

"He doesn't have one," Sara said. "He works out of his house, and it's in Salem. He came highly recommended, but for some reason he fell off the planet."

"Had you paid him?"

"Just a deposit, but I'm working on getting it back." Dylan's eyes had turned a glacial green-gray. This topic pissed him off like no other. "In the meantime, we have to figure things out. We need to till the ground and take out the blackberries and other bushes this weekend. You still up for that, Kyle?"

"Definitely." And he'd begun to think he just might have an answer to their landscaping problem…

Dad and Derek emerged from the cottage. "This looks terrific," Dad said. "Really, I'm so impressed, especially that this all came from you, Kitten." Dad smiled at Sara.

She blushed. "Not all from me. Just my idea. Without Tori's design and Dylan and his crew, this would still be a boring ranch."

Dad put his arm around her shoulders and gave her a squeeze. "The idea is everything. Without that, none of the rest happens."

"Sounds like a quote for the bottom of my e-mail signature," Derek cracked.

Dad chuckled, and Kyle wished he could make jokes like that and get the same response. Would the tension between them ever dissipate? His neck prickled—he knew what he needed to do to make that happen. The question was could he do it?

Maybe.

Wow. That was the first time his answer hadn't been *absolutely fucking not.*

It seemed as though Maggie's therapy was working. He inwardly cringed. Is that how he thought of her? As his therapist? Hadn't he just been considering whether she might be his girlfriend?

"Ready to go?" Dad asked Mom. Had his tone wearied, or was that Kyle's imagination?

"Yes," Mom replied, also sounding a bit strained. "As much as I'd like to hear how you're going to resolve the landscaping issue, I'm too tired. See you all later?"

"How about tomorrow?" Sara asked. "I bet you're going to sleep the rest of the day."

Mom smiled before pressing a kiss to her cheek. "You're probably right. Tomorrow then."

Mom and Dad took off down the track toward the parking lot. If anyone noticed that there was plenty of space between them as they walked, no one said anything. It was, in fact, eerily quiet for a long moment as they all watched them depart.

"So," Dylan said, breaking the silence. "About this landscaping problem...Derek, I just got a call from the nursery. The order the shithead placed a few weeks back is going to be delivered Monday."

"We couldn't cancel it?" Derek asked.

"Why would we do that?" Sara stared at him as if he'd grown two heads. "We need the plants and grass—look at this place. It's horrible."

Derek crossed his arms over his chest, exhaling. "True. What are we going to do with all of it? Do we know what's coming?"

"They e-mailed me a list, so we at least know that much. And I have equipment rented for the weekend so we can till, remove shrubs, etcetera. We're going to need all hands on deck though."

Kyle spoke before he really thought things through. "I think I have a solution to our design and implementation problem."

Three gazes swung toward him, two curious, one very skeptical.

Kyle ignored the skeptical one—Derek. "I recently made the acquaintance of a landscape designer." That title was stretching things, but if Maggie's yard was any indication of her skill, she'd be able to transform this place into a gorgeous setting by next Saturday. Plus, he'd seen the light in her eyes when she'd talked about the space last weekend. She'd love to do this—provided she had time. Shit, she had a job, for Christ's sake. But no, all they needed was her design. Dylan and his crew—hell, even Kyle and whomever else they could find—would do the grunt work.

"You just happened to meet a landscape designer recently?" Derek sounded as dubious as he looked.

"It's more of a hobby for her, but she'll do a great job. Just trust me on this."

Derek narrowed his eyes at him and opened his mouth, but then snapped it shut. "Fine."

Kyle gave in to the anger that Derek's doubt had sparked. "If you have something to say, say it."

Derek's expression changed so that he looked less pissed and more...resolute. "Don't screw it up." He turned and stalked off.

"Thanks for the vote of confidence!" Kyle called after him before muttering, "Jerk."

Sara's soft touch on his arm soothed him. "You could go after him."

"Not now, Sara." His voice sounded sharper than he'd intended.

"Hey, don't be a dick," Dylan said.

"That's nice coming from the dick who told my sister I had a secret girlfriend. What the hell, dude?"

Dylan didn't back down. "I didn't say that. I said I'd met a friend of yours who happened to be a girl. If Sara decided she was a secret girlfriend, that's her interpretation."

She socked Dylan in the arm. "Hey, you said they looked like they might've been messing around."

This was not a conversation he wanted to have in front of his sister. Kyle scrubbed at his scalp as if he could rid his brain of this entire topic. "Never mind. You guys trust me to fix this landscape thing, right?"

"Of course," Sara said. "Who is this person?" A light fired behind her eyes. "Wait, is it the same woman? The secret-not-girlfriend?"

"For heaven's sake, she's not secret or a girlfriend. She's a friend I met recently, and her thumb's the greenest I've seen."

Sara fidgeted with the bracelet she was wearing—one of her favorite sensory items. "Are you going to tell us how you met her and how you know what color her thumb is?"

"No." He knew he was coming off like a jerk, but he didn't care. He didn't want to talk about Maggie right now, particularly when he had to figure out how to keep her identity secret while having her do the landscape design. Was that even possible? *No.* He was such an asshole.

"I gotta go," he said, already turning. "I'll see you back here tomorrow morning."

"Can't wait to meet her!" Sara called behind him.

MAGGIE STOOD BACK and surveyed her living room. Wow, she could actually *live* in it. The couch was clean and even had pillows on it, and she'd hooked the television up. There were no pictures on the walls, but she didn't have many of those anyway. Kyle could help her with them later.

Would that be before or after she told him about Natalie Frobish? She dreaded the discussion but knew it had to happen. She just hoped he wouldn't spin out of control. News like this was tough on everyone, but for someone who dealt with addiction and compulsion, it could be catastrophic.

Her phone rang, and she braced herself when she saw it was her mother. She'd already ignored two of her phone calls and decided she'd better pick up this time. "Hi, Mom."

"Magnolia!" Uh-oh, she sounded excited, and not in a good way. "I called you at the clinic earlier, and they said there'd been an attack or something yesterday. Are you all right?"

"It wasn't an attack. One of my patients brought a gun and tried to kill himself. I'm fine, Mom." *Mostly*. She'd done a good job all afternoon of keeping the darkness from taking over her mind and driving her to the Xanax bottle.

"I can't imagine that's possible. You're an emotional person, my tender little flower bud. Maybe now you'll rethink this ridiculous career."

"It's not ridiculous, Mom." It was a lot of things—stressful, depressing, frustrating—but not that.

"It's not for you." She sighed into the phone. "You internalize everything, Magnolia. Treating mentally ill patients is only going to make *you* crazy."

The truth of her words battered at Maggie's tender—yes, tender—emotions. She didn't want to have this conversation. Not today. And maybe never. She heard a car and looked out the window to see Kyle parking in the driveway. "Mom, I need to go."

"You always do." She sounded miffed. "I'll keep badgering you about this."

Maggie knew she would. "Which 'this' are you referring to? My job? My 'tender' sensibilities?"

"All of it."

"Can't wait. Talk to you later, Mom." She ended the call and opened the door to let Kyle in.

He greeted her with a wide smile and a lingering kiss, sweeping her into his arms as he came inside.

The irritation of the phone call washed away in his embrace. She wrapped her arms around his neck and held on, loving the feel of him against her.

When he pulled his head up from hers, he surveyed the living room behind her. "Wow, you've been busy today. Looks great."

She tucked her hair behind her ear. Her insides warmed at his praise. "Thanks. I just need your help to hang the pictures."

"You got it." He cupped her face. "I have the best news."

And she had the worst—or at least really bad news. She was happy to hear him out first. Relieved even. Plus, his enthusiasm was infectious. "Tell me."

He took her hand and led her into the kitchen. "I just came from The Alex, and we're in desperate need of your help."

"*My* help?" She watched him pull two wine glasses down and grab a bottle from the countertop wine rack they'd set up last night.

"The landscape designer has completely vanished from the grid. We have a truckload of plants arriving on Monday and no plan. Please say you'll make it pretty for the wedding."

She shook her head, trying to compute what he was asking. "You want me to design the landscaping at the wedding cottage?"

He opened the bottle and splashed red wine into the glasses. Handing her one, he held his up in a toast. "To our new landscape designer."

"Whoa, hold on." She loved his excitement, felt it herself, but it wasn't that simple. Her brain was a war of anticipation about how to transform the outdoor setting and anxiety over his family's reaction to her. "Have you forgotten who I am?"

He lowered his glass without taking a drink. "No. You're Magnolia, the landscape designer."

She tried not to laugh. "I'm now a uni-monikered person like Madonna or Prince?"

He shrugged. "Sort of. There's no reason to introduce you as anything else. It's not exactly lying…"

No, but it was by omission. Did that matter? "I'm not sure I can do it. Being around your family would be… strange." And difficult. She felt as though she knew them all, at least a little bit, based on things Alex had said.

Lines creased around his eyes. He stepped closer. "Will it? I don't want that. I just thought this was a good solution—we need a designer, and you love doing it. Win-win."

She couldn't argue with him there.

"I know you have to work, but we'll figure it out, and we have the weekend."

"Actually, I don't have to work this week. I'm taking some personal time."

His features softened. "I think that's a great idea. And that's not just me being selfish."

She smiled. "I know. Thank you." When he said things like that, she thought there just might be a future for them, provided they figured out the mess with his family. Could they ever accept her? Could she ever feel comfortable with them? Now wasn't the time to discuss it, not with this landscaping issue and with what she still had to tell him.

"I know we can make this work. It's only for a week. No one will hear your real name, and none of them have ever met you as Alex's therapist. It'll work out, I promise."

He couldn't promise that, but she appreciated his desire to do his best to make it so. "Okay."

"Okay, you'll do it?"

"Yes."

He grinned before dropping a fast kiss on her mouth. "Thank you." He toasted her again, and this time they both drank.

Maggie took two drinks in order to fortify herself for what she had to say next. "I have news, too."

His eyebrows dipped. "That sounds ominous."

"The computer guy e-mailed me—he'd misplaced your information and asked me to forward it."

"Did you? I checked my e-mail earlier but didn't see anything."

"No, I wanted to tell you in person. Let's sit." She went over to her laptop on the table and sat. She set her wineglass down and watched him make his way to the chair next to hers.

He turned it so that he faced her. "You're freaking me out a little bit here."

Her heart raced, and her neck was damp with anxiety. "It's someone you know."

He put his glass down with a clack and slid her computer closer. "Show me." His voice had turned cold.

Maybe that was better than telling him. She opened the laptop and pulled up her e-mail. Finding the message from the computer guy, she clicked on the first attachment.

And watched the reaction play across his face.

Shock, horror, sadness, and finally rage.

He clicked through the rest of the attachments and read through them quickly. "The deceitful bitch. I can't believe she's capable of this." He stared at the screen, but Maggie wondered if he was actually seeing anything. Emotion, thick and harsh, haunted his gaze and inhabited the lines around his mouth. "I mean, obviously she is. But how did none of us know? And how could she do this to our family? To Alex?"

Maggie touched his shoulder, but he jumped up and stalked toward the front door. "Where are you going?" she asked.

He paused, and when he turned, the anguish in his eyes broke her heart. "Somewhere I can dull this pain."

attachment.

Chapter Fourteen

HE WANTED TO run. He needed solace. He craved that
feeling of euphoria that could drive all of his insecurities
and resentments away. That invincibility that only gambling could give him. And which was a total crock.

Maggie came to him and took his hands in hers. She
felt warm and safe. Without words, she led him back to
the table and gently pushed him to sit. She closed the
computer and slid it away. Then her fingers massaged
his shoulders. He shut his eyes and tried to focus on her
instead of the anger and helplessness raging inside of him.

After several minutes, he began to relax. Or at least
the frustration began to dull. He opened his eyes, saw the
computer, and the emotion swept over him again, though
it was less consuming. He exhaled, using the breathing
technique Maggie had taught him.

"I can't tell my Dad it was her. He'll be devastated."
Kyle's insides twisted. Dad was already such a mess over

Alex, but he seemed to be getting better in the last several weeks, even if he hadn't actually confronted his grief. However, learning that one of his most trusted employees had sold Alex the drugs could send him back into the angry spiral he'd been immersed in during the first few months after Alex's suicide—it could very well wreck him. Hell, it was wrecking Kyle.

God, Natalie had actually tried to date him! And he'd flirted with her, at least a little. Nausea roiled in his gut. "How could she do it?" His voice nearly broke, and he wiped his hand over his mouth.

Maggie's hands slid down his chest, and she leaned over to press her lips against his cheek. "I don't know. I'm so sorry. I wish it had been someone else—someone you didn't know and trust."

"Reading those e-mails makes me sick." He laid his hands over Maggie's, seeking comfort from her touch. "I have to get rid of her."

Maggie stiffened. "What do you mean?"

He nearly laughed. Turning his head, he looked back at her and gave her hand a squeeze. "I meant get her out of Archer. I can't have her set foot inside again. She has to resign immediately."

Maggie came around and sat in the chair beside him. "What about prosecution?"

"Definitely." The hurt, which had taken over for a moment, gave way to the anger again. "I'll take these to the police. Can we print copies?"

"Sure. Let me forward you the e-mail, too." She pulled the computer toward her and took care of everything.

"Good thing you set up the printer for me last night." She got up and went to her office.

Kyle's gaze drifted to the open e-mail, but he quickly averted his gaze, not wanting to read it again. Natalie called Alex "sweetie" and signed her e-mails with Xs and Os. It was disgusting. She'd clearly been his crush. Had she played on that to take advantage of him? And how in the hell had someone like her become a drug dealer in the first place?

Anxiety churned through him and drove him to his feet. He paced nervously, wanting to leave. He could be at the casino in thirty or forty minutes.

Maggie came back and set a manila envelope on the table. "They're in here."

He looked at the envelope with distaste, as if it was somehow toxic. With a twitch of his fingers, he plucked it from the table. "Thank you."

Her gaze was strong, earnest, as if she sought to tether him with just a glance. "I want to be here for you. What are you going to tell your dad and the rest of the family?"

He worked to keep from crinkling the envelope in his tense grip. "I don't know. I don't want to tell Dad. I don't want him to have to do anything."

Her brow knitted, making those shouldn't-be-sexy lines over the bridge of her nose. "You want to keep this secret?"

Like he kept her a secret? She hadn't said that, but it was there between them. He thought they both wanted it that way, but maybe she didn't anymore. Hell, he couldn't think about that right now. "No. I just want to wait to tell him until I've talked to her and the police. I want her gone so that he doesn't have to see her again. And I want to know what the police are going to do."

"So long as you have a plan," she said. "You can't hide it from him forever." Just like he couldn't hide her forever. Is that what he wanted?

The envelope bent in his curling fingers. "I know. I just can't do it now. Christ, the wedding's next week, Mom just got back. The timing couldn't be worse. I have to go." He spun on his heel, his mind already halfway to the casino.

She moved fast, stepping in front of him and taking his hand. "Where are you going?"

He didn't look at her. Couldn't. "Let me go." The words were a whisper, a desperate, helpless plea.

Her fingers tightened around his, and her thumb stroked the back of his hand. "I don't want to."

With Herculean effort, he kept himself from giving in to the addiction. She'd thrown him a lifeline, and he grasped it with both hands. "Then don't."

When his eyes found hers, all he saw was understanding and compassion. "We'll figure this out. Tonight we're just going to think it through and keep you from falling into the abyss. Okay?"

The anxiety inside him crumbled and fell away. God, she already knew him so well. Yes, distraction sounded amazing. Necessary. He pulled her close and nuzzled her throat, pressed a kiss to her jugular. "I can think of plenty of ways to do that."

She wound her fingers into his hair. "Good."

And there she went, saving him from himself again. What was he going to do if they didn't stay together?

APPREHENSION TWISTED THROUGH Maggie, leaving knots of tension in its wake. As she walked down the dirt lane toward the wedding cottage, she felt as though she was marching to the executioner, and not even Kyle's presence at her side alleviated the strain.

This was foolish. They had a plan. No one would know she was Maggie Trent, the therapist who'd failed Alex. She was Magnolia, the landscape architect with zero experience and a completely blank résumé. Who was charging them next to nothing.

But she wasn't doing it for the money. She was doing it for herself. For her own peace of mind, to calm the unease in her soul.

As if he could sense her anxiety, Kyle nudged her hand before they reached the cottage. "It's going to be fine."

She nodded, pulling her cap lower over her forehead to shade her eyes from the brilliant sun. It was early still—just after eight—but the day was already bright and warm, well on its way to hot.

Dylan and a young woman who had to be Sara emerged from the cottage. "Hey, Kyle," Dylan said.

Sara came directly toward Maggie, her hand extended. "It's nice to meet you. I'm Sara Archer."

I know. You're the sister everyone coddled but who Alex deeply admired. The unspoken thoughts nearly closed her throat. "Hi," she managed, shaking Sara's hand.

"And you already met Dylan," Kyle said. "Anyone else here yet? I know Tori's plane doesn't get in until almost noon." Kyle had told Maggie that his other sister was returning from San Francisco, where she'd had some work meetings the past few days.

Dylan shook his head. "Derek and Chloe should be here soon, though. They're picking up a dumping trailer that I rented."

Maggie was curious to see the interplay between Derek and Kyle. She wondered how long it would be before they made up and only hoped it wouldn't be forever. According to Alex, ever the observer, their rift had been tough on the whole family, not that either of them had recognized it. "What sort of tools do we have—what did you rent?" Maggie asked.

"Dylan and I brought Dad's tractor." Sara pointed to the smallish vehicle that would be great for clearing the brush.

"Plus a lot of yard tools," Dylan said.

They discussed the equipment and a basic plan for how to tackle the area. Soon, Kyle was busy rototilling while Dylan was driving the tractor. That left Sara and Maggie to trim back shrubbery that wasn't going to be removed.

Sara glanced at the growing pile of clippings. "This is going to be a giant pile of debris."

Maggie nodded. "Smart move renting the dumping trailer so we can move it out. What are they going to do with it?"

Sara shrugged. "I'm not sure."

Maggie had an idea. "Looking forward, it would be great if The Alex had its own vegetable garden and maybe even formal garden with walking paths. A compost pile would be a helpful component to both of those things. If you decided you wanted to do that."

Sara's eyes lit beneath the wide brim of her hat. "I love that! The vegetable garden, the walking garden, the compost—all of it! We might have to hire you as groundskeeper." She laughed.

Maggie smiled, thinking that sounded like an amazing job. But she was already employed. In a job she couldn't currently face.

"How did you get into landscape design?" Sara asked as she snipped branches. "Kyle said you were new to the field."

"Uh, yeah. I've been a bit of a hobbyist until now." Maggie didn't like the thread of unease that wound through her. She wasn't exactly lying, but she wasn't being honest either. And Sara seemed like a genuinely nice person. No, Maggie *knew* she was from everything Alex had said about her. And that made Maggie feel even more uncomfortable—knowing things that Sara had no idea she knew.

Argh.

Sara looked at her askance. "So you and Kyle are just friends?"

And there was the question she'd been at least half-expecting. "Yes." Again, not exactly a lie. They'd never agreed to be anything more than that. The benefits part was personal, right? Not something she needed to confirm or deny.

Thankfully Derek and Chloe arrived then. Maggie noticed that Sara took care of the introductions, while Kyle barely stopped rototilling long enough to wave a greeting. So much for observing interplay. It seemed they were going for all-out mutual avoidance.

"Derek, Magnolia's had the best suggestion for all of this debris. She wants to start a compost area that we can use for future gardening projects. I think it's a great idea—very green of us, too."

"I love it," Chloe said, echoing Sara's earlier reaction. Pretty, with blonde hair that was maybe a shade or two darker than Sara's, she drew on a pair of work gloves. "Where are you going to put the compost?"

"I'm not sure, but I'm thinking over behind the restaurant." Sara glanced at Derek. "There's a clearing we could use for now, until we figure out a plan."

He nodded. "That could work. Let's talk to Tori about the overall design to make sure we aren't screwing anything up. What sort of future gardening projects?"

Sara explained the vegetable and walking garden ideas, both of which seemed to impress Derek and Chloe. Sara finished up by repeating that Maggie ought to be the groundskeeper.

"I never even thought of hiring one," Derek said. "But it's not a bad idea. I really like the idea of a romantic walking garden—goes great with the venue." Chloe slid him a little smile—the sort Maggie might give Kyle.

"And having a vegetable garden will be great for Kyle's restaurant," Sara said.

Derek lowered his eyes, and he didn't respond. The counselor in Maggie longed to drag both men together and make them work things out, but she would never overstep—nor would she reveal who she really was.

At least not today. If she was truly going to do something long-term at The Alex—and who was she kidding, she *so* wasn't—she'd have to come clean. Would that be so bad? These people were nice. She already liked Sara more than she should, and Chloe seemed really nice, too.

What a disaster.

By late morning they were ready to transport the first load of debris to the other side of the property. Kyle climbed into the driver's seat while Maggie joined him in the cab. She was looking forward to a few minutes alone with him until Sara climbed into the backseat.

"I wanted to come along and check out the area. I'm totally jonesing for these gardens. I want to see where we can put them."

During an earlier break, they'd explained the idea to Kyle, who—as Sara had predicted—was especially excited about the vegetable garden. He'd rattled off a bunch of must-have veggies for next summer, and Maggie was beginning to feel a pang of want for a job she had no hope of having.

Maggie turned around in the seat and smiled at Sara, unable to be upset at her joining them—her enthusiasm was too contagious to ignore.

Kyle started the truck and drove along the track.

"So, Magnolia," Sara said, jarring Maggie with the use of her full name, "you should come to the wedding this weekend."

Maggie slipped a look at Kyle, but his gaze was focused straight ahead. "That's awfully nice of you to say, but I barely know any of you."

"*Now*, but after you whip this place into shape, we'll be really close. That's how we Archers work—we suck you into our collective." She laughed, and Maggie joined her as she shot Kyle another glance. No reaction, not even a quirk of his lip. Sara leaned forward in the seat and looked at her brother. "Magnolia can be your date."

That drew a reaction. He clenched the wheel tight, his knuckles whitening. "I don't think I'm going."

"What?" Sara touched his shoulder. "You have to go. Not going isn't an option."

"I doubt Derek would agree with you."

Maggie practically bit her tongue to keep from saying something.

Sara made a sound of disgust. "You two are ridiculous. I can't believe you aren't going to resolve things before Saturday. You're going to regret it. This is Derek's wedding day, for crying out loud. He's been a part of your life—all of our lives—for far too long."

Maggie wanted to applaud but didn't.

Sara turned to Maggie. "I know you both say you aren't his girlfriend, but maybe you can talk some sense into him."

"I can try," Maggie murmured. "I'm not exactly clear on why there's a rift." She knew she was playing with fire but couldn't help herself. It seemed Sara had been right—there was no avoiding being sucked in to the Archer collective.

At last, Kyle glanced in her direction, but the look he sent would've curdled milk. "It's a long story." He gestured out the windshield. "This good?"

"Yeah, I think so," Sara answered.

Kyle pulled the truck around and positioned the trailer to dump the mass of debris. The return trip was made in awkward silence.

Back at the cottage, Sara jumped out of the truck. Before she left, however, she threw her brother a nice, long glare. Maggie stifled a smile as she thought of the countless times she'd looked at her own brother the same way. It was really hard not to like these people. Not that she didn't want to like them, it would just be easier if she didn't. That way when they completely shunned her, she wouldn't feel heartbroken.

Heartbroken? She snuck a look at Kyle and wondered if he could break her heart. She shoved the thought away without fully contemplating the answer.

"Would you mind not ganging up on me with my sister?" He sounded a little pissed, and it reminded her of when they'd first met, when he'd treated her like anathema.

"I didn't mean to. But she has a point. One of the biggest days of Derek's life is next week, and you'd miss it? Forget whatever's keeping you apart, and remember everything before that."

He leaned his head back against the seat. "I do. It's just really complicated."

She turned and shook her head at him. "It doesn't have to be. Ask yourself why you're still holding this grudge. Are you really angry? Are you hurt? Or are you being stubborn?"

When his gaze found hers, his eyes were blazing. "Yeah, I'm angry. And I'm hurt. And you better believe I'm fucking stubborn. I usually appreciate the therapy, but not this time. Keep it to yourself."

He opened the door and got out, slamming it behind him.

She tried to pretend his words didn't sting, but they did. She hadn't been trying to counsel him, she'd been trying to support him. But she knew better than most that you couldn't help those who didn't want to be helped. Or who didn't think they needed any.

Like her.

Though they hadn't been talking about her, she thought of all the times her mother had offered advice or outright told her she was making a mistake. She'd pretty much ignored every single one of her attempts. And taken umbrage. And added the resentment into the pot of disgruntlement she carried about everything to do with the way her parents had raised her.

She understood why Kyle couldn't make up with Derek, even while she understood that he should. It was the same reason she couldn't make things right with her mother.

And maybe she should.

Maggie recoiled and she jumped out of the truck, slamming the door with the force of her distaste.

Once more, the therapist could dole it out but couldn't remotely take it.

KYLE MANAGED TO make it through lunch and into the early afternoon without exchanging more than work-related words with anyone, Maggie included. That certainly lent credence to their assertion that they weren't romantically involved. *Good.* He'd been worried after spending the night with her that their relationship would be obvious, that his feelings would be clear.

Who the hell was he kidding? They were barely clear to him; how could they be to anyone else?

He went back to taking out the patch of blackberries near the start of the lane. They wanted the entire stretch to look good, as guests would be parking in the lot and either walking to the cottage or taking a golf cart. He liked working in this location because it was far away from everyone else.

He could still see them, though. Particularly Maggie and Sara, who were clearing some shrubs just down the track. He watched Maggie work, her arms and back flexing with her movements, showing off her muscle tone. He felt bad about what he'd said earlier, but she'd hit the nail on the head. He *was* stubborn. Like a giant ass. And stubborn asses didn't readily admit their mistakes.

He turned and went back to his task, heedless of the scratches marking his forearms. The tractor could do this, but there was something cathartic about ripping out the thorny shrubs. They might take their swipe at him, but he'd emerge the victor, by God.

It felt good, but not good enough. No, what he really wanted to do was take a piece out of Natalie. He'd lain awake most of last night, Maggie curled against him. Despite her soothing presence, he'd seethed over Natalie's betrayal and longed to take her down. He'd thought about just going over to her house—he knew exactly where she lived. But he'd had to be here today.

He stopped. They'd made a lot of progress. Why couldn't he go now? He and Maggie had driven separately—arriving together wouldn't exactly have supported their "just friends" cover.

He turned and strode toward Maggie. She paused in her work and faced him. "What's up?"

"I need to go." He tugged his work gloves off. "Do you think you'll finish today, or should I plan on coming back tomorrow morning?"

Her little brow pleats emerged. "We'll probably have a little bit of work tomorrow. Then I need to draft the design," *and do a bunch of research to see* how *to even do that,* "so Dylan can get what we need for the sprinkler system. But wait, why are you leaving?"

He cocked his head and tried to send her a nonverbal message—*Natalie.*

Maggie's worry lines only deepened, and he couldn't tell if she understood. "I guess if you have to."

Sara had been out of earshot but now came over. "What's going on?"

"Kyle has to go," Maggie said softly.

Derek took that completely craptastic moment to approach them. He adjusted his baseball hat as he neared.

"Taking a break? I was just going to get some drinks from the fridge in the trailer."

"Actually, Kyle's leaving," Sara said.

Derek's eyes narrowed into a glare. "What the hell? We have at least a few hours' more work here."

"You've got it well under control, and there's something I need to do."

Derek set his hands on his hips. "What? Do tell us what's more important than this."

No way was he telling them about Natalie. Not yet. Not until he'd determined how it was going to pan out. "Nothing."

"Then that means you're staying?"

"No. I have to go. I'll be back in the morning."

Derek shook his head. "Typical. Bail on everyone without explanation."

Kyle's patience was hanging by a razor-thin thread. "I'm pretty sure you knew the reason last time."

"Yeah, I did. And I didn't tell anyone."

Kyle barked a short, hostile laugh. "Only the one person I didn't want you to. Tell me, Derek, how's the view from your moral high ground?"

Sara sucked in a breath. "Kyle."

"Just go," Derek said quietly, his gaze shooting to the ground. He dropped his hands from his hips as he turned and walked away.

"Kyle, say something," Sara urged.

"There's nothing to say. Sorry, Sara-cat, I have to go." He would've turned, but she came toward him, her eyes sparking with anger.

"Just because I'm not pissed at you anymore for leaving four years ago doesn't mean I've forgotten. You still owe me—*all of us*—an explanation. Except for Derek apparently. And someone else. Why do they get to know the truth, but I don't?"

Nothing else she said could've cut him as deeply. He'd never told any of them about his addiction. And even though Dad and Derek knew about it, they didn't really *know* about it. He'd kept it completely hidden. Is that what one did with shame?

He couldn't deal with this right now, not with the Natalie crap hanging over his head. "Sara, can we talk about this later?" He hoped she wouldn't ask when, because he had no idea.

She shook her head. "Listen to Derek and just go." She waved him off and turned back to continue her work.

During the entire encounter, he'd cast surreptitious glances at Maggie. She'd watched everything with unveiled interest, and he could practically hear her mind thinking of how she'd counsel him. But now she looked at him with sadness and disappointment. Maybe even pity.

Well, fuck that right to hell.

He spun on his heel and stalked away as fast as he could without running. God, how he wanted to run.

He jumped into Hayden's SUV and drove toward Natalie's. It was less than ten minutes away, but that was more than enough time for his anger and frustration to boil over into utter fury. When he pulled into her driveway, he was practically shaking with emotion.

Taking deep breaths, he worked to slow his pulse. He needed to get control of himself before he talked to her. He was on a mission. He could do this. For Alex. For Dad. For all of them.

A few minutes later, he knocked on the door of her little rental house. She answered almost right away, and her eyes widened in surprise. "Kyle! What are you doing here?"

He had to work to keep from screaming at her. Every part of him wanted answers and retribution. "Can I come in?"

"Sure." She opened the door wide and gestured for him to come inside. "Can I get you anything? Something to drink?"

He moved into her small living room, taking in the sixty-inch television and the high-end leather couch. It struck him that he'd never wondered how she afforded a new BMW right out of college—he'd assumed she had a trust fund since she'd gone to Williver, where trust funds were run-of-the-mill. Trying to keep a rein on his anger, he turned to spear her with a dark stare. "No, this isn't really a social visit."

"Oh." She nodded once. "I didn't really think so. You were pretty clear about not being interested the other night."

Yes, he had been, and to her credit she'd been really professional about it at work since then. Wait, he was giving her credit for something? *Hell no.* He chose his next words for maximum effect. "I wouldn't be interested in you if you were the last woman on the planet."

Now her eyes narrowed. "Hey, if you came here to be a jerk—"

"I came here to find out why you sold my brother drugs."

The color drained from her face. "I...I—"

"I have the e-mails. You aren't a very smart drug dealer, are you?"

"I'm not a drug dealer!" Her claim was anguished, raw, and so very, very false.

"I have evidence to the contrary." He found a calm he didn't think he could possess in this moment. "This is what you're going to do. You're going to e-mail my father a letter of resignation. I don't care what reason you give, but do not mention the drugs. He'll find out soon enough, but not from you." God, the timing was awful, with Derek's wedding. This should be a happy time, damn it, and no one deserved it more than his family. Thanks to this bitch standing in front of him.

"I don't want to quit." Her eyes filled with tears, one spilling over and tracking down her cheek. "I'm so sorry, Kyle. I didn't know what he was going to do. I just thought...I don't know. It wasn't a big deal."

"Selling narcotics to a man with lung disease isn't a big deal? Did you ever wonder why he had to come to you in the first place? He couldn't get those drugs from a doctor."

She twisted her hands together. "Well, I knew that. But I just figured it was because he didn't need them. Doctors don't prescribe that kind of stuff unless you need it, right?"

"Exactly," he said softly. "Which begs the question—why were you more qualified than a doctor?"

Her tears fell in earnest now. "Please, Kyle. I feel terrible about what happened. Worse than terrible. If you could only imagine the guilt I've felt. But I can't do anything about it now. If I could go back, I would. In a heartbeat. In fact, I stopped selling altogether after…that."

He didn't believe her. "It doesn't matter. The evidence I have will be enough." He hoped so. It had to be. "Tell me how a girl like you winds up selling prescription drugs."

She crossed her arms and hugged herself. She looked pale and fragile, and he couldn't have cared less. "In college, I used to sell ADHD drugs. I needed the money to pay for my room and board. Not all of us have trust funds."

And some of us shouldn't *have trust funds.*

"Then you get a job at Starbucks," he said.

Her answering laugh was dark and hollow. "That doesn't begin to compare with what I pulled in for a handful of Ritalin."

"You're a thoughtless bitch."

She swiped at her wet cheeks. "I'll resign, but that'll be the end of it, right?"

"In your dreams. I'm turning the evidence over to the police. I wouldn't leave town if I were you."

Her features hardened. "How do you think your family will feel once they find out you're dating Alex's therapist?"

He didn't think his animosity could grow any hotter, but it did. "How the hell do you know that?"

"I overheard the two of you talking at the Arch and Vine the other night."

He advanced on her, his patience nearly gone for the second time that afternoon. "Forget what you heard. It's none of your business. Nothing to do with me or my family is any of your business ever again."

"You don't want me to tell them," she taunted.

"No, I don't. But I don't want you to get away with what you've done either. My brother was mentally ill— depressed. You basically handed him a loaded gun."

The tears returned. "I didn't know that he was depressed, and neither did any of you. If you're going to blame me, why not blame his therapist? Why are you dating her of all people?"

He leaned close, sneering in her face. "Do you really think what you did is comparable to what Maggie tried to do? She gave him help, support, a caring shoulder. What did you do? You flirted with him, encouraged his interest in you—all to sell him drugs that killed him. I have no idea if they can charge you with murder, but you better be sure I'm going to ask."

All color drained from her face.

"Consider your employment terminated, effective immediately. And don't bother coming to pack up your desk. I'll have the police do it after they've finished searching it."

Her eyes widened, and for the first time he saw a spark of fear. *Good.*

He turned and left, slamming her front door behind him.

As he drove to the tiny Ribbon Ridge police station, he couldn't stop thinking about what Natalie had said about Maggie and how much that had pissed him off. Why had he ever blamed her? Because they'd all needed someone to be angry at and she'd fit the bill. Because for them to be angry at the person who really deserved it—Alex—had been too hard to contemplate.

Plus, he hadn't known her. Hadn't seen her caring and compassionate nature. Hadn't experienced first-hand the lengths she went to in order to help someone. He didn't blame Maggie. His family shouldn't blame her either. Yet they would, at least right away.

Dad was going to be devastated when he found out about Natalie. What would he be if he learned that Kyle was falling in love with Alex's therapist?

Devastated wouldn't even begin to describe it.

Chapter Fifteen

MAGGIE SET THE last book on the shelf in her office and stood back to survey the results. Another box empty. Another room nearly organized. She picked up her glass of wine from the desk and silently toasted herself as she glanced at the clock on her computer—just after nine. She was surprised she was still going strong after such a long, physical weekend, but she felt great. Better than she had in years.

It might have been the best weekend of her adult life if things with Kyle hadn't imploded. Or whatever they'd done. He'd come back to the cottage this morning and helped out, but by noon they'd finished everything they could without starting the sprinklers, and he'd taken off with everyone else, which had surprised her.

She'd texted him a couple of times, but he hadn't responded. She was dying to know what he'd done regarding Natalie. Had he gone to see her after he'd left yesterday? What about the police? Was he okay?

She set her glass down and picked up her phone. No texts. With a sigh, she went to open another box. A sharp knock on her front door gave her a shock of relief. That had to be Kyle.

Hurrying to the door, she smiled when she saw him, but her happiness quickly turned to apprehension as she took in the tense set of his jaw and the lost look in his eyes.

She gestured for him to enter and closed the door behind him. "I've been trying to reach you."

"I know." He walked farther into the living room.

She sensed his unease but didn't want to scare him off. He'd come to see her, though, which meant he probably wanted to talk. She'd let him take the lead. "How are you?"

He ran his hand through his hair, the number one sign that he was upset. "I'm not sure the police are going to be able to prosecute Natalie."

Outrage bloomed in Maggie's chest and spread angry heat through her body. She went to stand in front of him. "Why not?"

He looked utterly defeated, like every bit of enthusiasm and charm that made him Kyle Archer had been sucked away. "The e-mails alone aren't enough. Ideally, they want to find drugs in her possession or a clear trail of her activities."

Maggie wanted to scream. "But Alex died from drugs she sold him."

"That doesn't mean they're the ones he got from her—it's circumstantial." He sounded frustrated, hopeless.

"That...sucks." It was a wholly inadequate summation, but it was nonetheless true. "You don't think she has any drugs?"

"She says she stopped dealing them after Alex died, but who knows if she's telling the truth." His lip curled. "But by going to see her first, I alerted her to the possibility of the police investigating. If she had any drugs, she had to have gotten rid of them."

Maggie stroked his arm, trying to alleviate some of his pain. "Hey, don't blame yourself. You were upset, angry. You needed to confront her."

"Not at the cost of not being able to prosecute her."

She dropped her hand and twined her fingers with his. "I'm so sorry."

He withdrew from her and walked to the other side of the living room. He stood next to the fireplace and leaned his elbow on the mantle. "I was thinking of gambling, so I came here."

He wanted her to stop him, and she could do that. "I'm glad you did. Can I get you something? A beer or a glass of wine?"

"Sure." His eyes were downcast. "No. I mean, wait." He looked up, and the stark confusion in his gaze pulled at her heart.

This was dangerous. She always reacted to a patient's pain, but this was so much more because of the way she felt about him. She could easily fall in love with him, if she wasn't already. She heard her mother's warning, *you're too emotional*, and tried to keep her head.

"Tell me what you need," she said softly.

He turned from the mantle to face her. "I'm trying to figure out how to make this," he said, gesturing between them, "okay with my family."

His family. And there was the cause of his worry. He might forgive Maggie, but would they? And if they didn't, could he choose to be with her anyway?

This conversation would be so much easier for her to stomach if she could go full therapist. So that's exactly what she did. "You won't know until you talk to them about it, until you open yourself up to them. You have a lot of unresolved issues with your family—and I'm not the primary one." She didn't say it, but she meant his addiction. It was part of him, and some of his family didn't even know about it. And those who did were in the dark because he hadn't discussed it fully with them.

His eyes widened with a flash of ire. "You're saying that you're not the problem here, I am?"

"No. I'm saying I'm not the first thing you need to address with them—your addiction is." There, she'd said it.

His features relaxed. "You're therapizing me again."

Anger sparked in her brain. "Isn't that why you came? You said you wanted to gamble but you came here instead."

"Fuck." He'd whispered the word, but she caught it. He turned to the side, looking toward the front window, which was covered with an outdated set of sheer drapes. "I came here to forget."

Now he was just making her mad. "How? You wanted to screw instead of talk?" She took a deep breath, told herself not to react emotionally. "You want resolution. I know you can't see it, but you do. Contrary to what you might think, *I* can't fix you, I can only suggest how *you* can fix you."

He pivoted, and she started at the coldness of his expression, the absolute ice in his gaze. "This is perfect coming from you. A therapist whose track record of fixing things, including herself, is abysmal."

His words stung, but she reminded herself that she was counseling him and hearing the truth pissed him off. So, she smiled and quoted Amy: "Do as I say, not as I do."

He stared at her a long moment, swore again, then started toward the door.

"Hey, where are you going?" She almost asked if he was running away again, but that would have been his not-quite girlfriend asking, not the therapist. And if she allowed herself to be his not-quite girlfriend right now, she was going to lose it completely.

"Coming here was a bad idea."

She moved toward him, touching his elbow as his hand closed over the door handle. "You have this wound in your life from four years ago. Whatever happened to drive you away—it's going to do it again unless you confront it and resolve it. Just make your peace with your family—with your dad and Derek—and move on."

He didn't turn his head, kept his body positioned toward the door in total flight mode. "You make it sound easy. It's not."

She moved around him and squeezed behind him and the door, pressing her back against the wood. "Tell me why."

"I was in a lot of trouble." He kept his gaze averted from hers. "I owed Shane a shit-ton of money."

"How much is a shit-ton?" It really didn't matter, but the more specific he was, the more honest he would be—with her and with himself.

His gaze flicked to hers. "Thirty grand."

Holy shit. She exhaled and schooled her features to keep from showing a reaction. "What happened?"

"Derek knew I was gambling. He'd met Shane a few times. I was late with payments, and I ended up with a black eye."

She lost the reins on her counseling for a moment as she recalled the beefy build of his former bookie. "From Shane?" How could he remain friendly with a guy who'd beaten him up?

Kyle shook his head. "One of his associates. Shane did everything he could to keep me safe, but it was too much money. Derek figured it out—the bruises, my behavior—and talked to Shane. Then he told my dad, who paid it off."

She didn't have to ask what had happened next. Kyle had been livid with Derek for telling his father. He'd struggled with being the Archer who just wasn't good enough—no college degree, no successful career path, with or without the family company…and then this utter failure. He'd seen no choice but to run as far away as he could.

"You've never discussed this with them," she said softly.

"No." His voice was tight, strained. "I still get so angry."

"Understandably so. Can I ask…what did you do in Florida? Did you get treatment at all?"

He let his hand fall from the doorknob. "I went to Gamblers Anonymous meetings for a while. That whole situation with Shane scared the shit out of me, and I never thought I'd do it again."

"But you did."

His answering nod was almost imperceptible. "When Alex died. I came home for the funeral and for the reading of the trust. Everyone was so sad and angry. It was like the situation I'd escaped had worsened, intensified."

"So you went back to Florida and looked for a way to lighten the load."

He looked at her like he had once before—like she was the only person who truly understood. "Yes."

The relief in his voice made her want to hug him, but not yet. She was getting somewhere, and she wasn't ready to stop. "How much did you lose?"

"I don't know. It was fast—two months and I had to sell most of my stuff and then my car."

"What about your trust fund?" She knew all of the Archer kids had one from their paternal grandfather—except Derek, as he'd joined the family after Benjamin Archer had died.

Kyle's eyes widened briefly, and his nostrils flared. "You know about that?"

Crap. She shouldn't have said anything. She'd gotten too deep into the therapy session. "Forget I asked."

He exhaled sharply. "No, it's fine. We all inherited at twenty-five—but you probably know that. Except me. Dad was the trustee, and he changed the terms of my trust. I get the money whenever he sees fit. Which means never."

She couldn't stand it anymore. She reached up and touched his jaw. "I doubt that. You have to talk to him. Tell him why you gambled, how you struggle with it in terms of your place in the family. Help him understand so that he can support you."

He exhaled. "I don't know if I can. And Derek… I felt so betrayed. I only ever wanted him to apologize, to understand that what he did hurt. We were best friends and brothers—nobody was closer to me. Nobody should've understood me more."

She moved her hand to the side of his neck and then down, lightly massaging his shoulder. "Have you asked yourself what would've happened if he hadn't stuck his nose in?" She purposely used words that Kyle would to characterize the situation—she didn't want to lose him now.

His gaze darkened, and his mouth tightened. "I had a plan. I had the trust fund coming in just over a year. Shane knew he was going to get paid, and he was working on convincing the other guys. I didn't need Derek's 'help.' He completely fucked everything up, especially with my Dad, and he never even said sorry."

"I don't disagree that Derek owes you an apology." At the very least, he could've told Kyle what he'd planned to do instead of going directly to Rob. "However," she said, taking another deep breath, knowing there would be a storm coming, "you also owe him a thank-you. Whether you could've paid that money back isn't the issue. Derek gave you a wake-up call that put a stop to your gambling, and he did it in the face of your denial. That *is* friendship, Kyle. That is family. *That* is love."

He stared at her, his expression inscrutable, and she held her breath.

"You can wait forever for him to apologize, or you can be the one to end this rift."

Finally, emotion entered his gaze, but it was anger. "I should be the one to make things right? Because I'm always the one in the wrong. *I'm* the fuckup. I'm so glad to hear that you're no different than the others. Great therapy session. Thanks, doc."

He pulled the door open, heedless of her having to jump out of the way, and strode through, slamming it behind him.

The vitriol in his tone pricked her skin like tiny razor blades. She was breathing hard, as if she'd run a mile.

His words rang in her brain: *I'm the fuckup.* But she wasn't thinking of him. She was thinking of herself.

She'd endured a horrid relationship and chosen a career that she really didn't like. And for what? Because she was a fuckup? No, because she'd been rebelling. Mom said Mark was awful, so Maggie embraced him harder. Mom said counseling would ruin her, that she'd never withstand the emotional strain, so she'd worked her ass off and graduated a year early.

You can wait forever for her to apologize, or you can be the one to end this rift.

Her advice came back to haunt her. It might not be a rift with her mother, but it was some sort of chasm—a space she kept between them so that Maggie could say she'd never be like her. But why? Maggie had grown up loved and cared for—unconventionally—but she hadn't been abused or physically neglected. So her parents hadn't always been there emotionally. Maggie had turned out all right. Did she want to spend the rest of her life holding a grudge, or did she want to try to find some common ground?

She locked the door and tried not to think of the hurtful things Kyle had said. He was angry, upset, and maybe—maybe—coming to terms with what he needed to do. She'd be here for him when he needed her.

If he still wanted her.

Chapter Sixteen

KYLE SPENT A mostly sleepless night after leaving Maggie's. As he unlocked the door at Archer Enterprises and disabled the alarm, he yawned as if he could swallow the world. Exhausted, he double-timed it up the stairs to make some coffee.

He'd never been in the office this early. What was it, five o'clock? He glanced at the clock near the coffee pot. Just barely.

Once he had the coffee brewing, he turned and looked at Natalie's workstation. He wanted so badly to search every nook and cranny, but the police captain said he preferred for Kyle to leave it alone until they could get here at nine.

Kyle had spent half of yesterday at the police station. They'd called him after obtaining a warrant and searching Natalie's house. Unfortunately, they hadn't found any drug-related evidence and couldn't press charges against

Natalie. They'd impounded her cell phone and laptop, both of which had met with tragic accidents involving water and extreme droppage since Kyle had stupidly visited her. And no, *that* wasn't suspicious.

But given how lazy she'd been regarding her e-mails with Alex, Kyle was certain there had to be something incriminating on the Archer servers. The police agreed.

What the hell was he going to do for the next four fucking hours?

Talk to Dad, for one. He had to tell him why Natalie wouldn't be here today—or ever again—and why the cops were showing up at nine. Was that all he would tell him? Or would he finally breach the topic he'd made forbidden?

Maggie had made a compelling argument last night. He'd been a real jackass about it, too. He'd apologize to her. Later. He could only handle one crisis at a time.

By the time Dad arrived at eight thirty, Kyle had downed two pots of coffee. He'd staved off the exhaustion but now felt as jittery as if he held a full house, aces high, in the World Tournament of Poker. He got up from the couch in Dad's office as Dad came inside.

Dad stopped short in surprise. "Kyle. I didn't know you were in here." He glanced back at Paula, but she shook her head.

"I've been here a while. Can I have a few minutes?"

"Sure." Dad came further into the office and circled around his desk as Kyle closed the door. "Everything all right?"

"No." Why sugarcoat it? Kyle steeled himself. "I've been working on something the last few weeks. Something I thought would help us—you especially—deal with Alex's death."

Dad's face turned a bit gray. "I'd rather not discuss this."

He moved closer to the desk. "I know, but hear me out. I wanted to find out who sold Alex the drugs."

Dad's eyes widened, and his pallor faded even more. He sank into his chair as if he simply couldn't bear his own weight any longer. Kyle wished the worst wasn't yet to come.

"And did you?" His voice sounded like a croak.

Kyle sat in one of the chairs on the other side of the desk, his body tense. "Yes. I wish it had been someone else, but—"

"You're not going to say it was *you*?" Dad went fully white. His hand covered his mouth.

Kyle blinked at him, uncomprehending of what he'd said for a moment. Then it hit him like a fist to the gut. Repeatedly. Over and over, the accusation swung at him like a merciless heavyweight going in for the knockout. "No." The word was barely audible.

Dad slumped in his chair. "Oh, God. I'm sorry, I didn't mean…but your demeanor…You scared the hell out of me."

The pressure in Kyle's chest lessened but didn't completely go away. "Do you really think I'm into drugs too or that I could do that to anyone, let alone my own brother?"

"No, I don't think you could do that, which is why I reacted that way." He looked up at Kyle, his gaze desolate.

"But, Kyle, you don't talk to me. You don't talk to anybody. I have no idea what you're into. Or out of."

Kyle wanted to be angry, but Dad was right. In the absence of information, he'd made up his own. Could Kyle blame him? Yes, but he didn't want to. He was just... tired. "I'm not into drugs, and I never have been. Yes, I'm a gambling addict, but I haven't been doing that either—at least not since I've been home. But listen, we can talk about that...later. I need to tell you who sold him the drugs." He took a deep breath. "It was Natalie."

"*Our* Natalie?"

Kyle nodded, hating that Dad had used the word "our." It made this too personal, but then Kyle had known that was how it would be.

Where Dad had gone pale before, now color rushed to his face until Kyle worried that his head might blow clean off. "Dad?"

"Natalie Frobish. Derek and Hayden's—your—assistant?"

"Yes. I hired a computer forensics specialist to evaluate Alex's computer. He found e-mails."

His tone darkened. "I want to see them."

Kyle picked up the printed e-mails he'd set on the corner of Dad's desk. "Here. But, Dad, I've already confronted her. And fired her."

Dad stared down at the paper, and his hands began to shake. "I can't believe..." His voice trailed into nothingness.

Kyle got up and went to stand beside Dad's chair. "I couldn't believe it either, but she didn't deny it. She couldn't."

"We have to call the police." He reached for the phone on his desk.

Kyle put his hand over his father's. "I've already done that. They searched her house yesterday. Unfortunately, they didn't find any evidence."

Dad's hand tensed, and he drew it back, slamming it on the desk.

Kyle looked down at him. "Dad, they'll find something here at Archer—on our servers or even on her computer. She wasn't very smart about it. Just look at those e-mails." He pointed to the papers on the desk.

Dad was quiet for several minutes as he read. His breathing was audible, sounding like he'd just crested a hill on his bike. Finally, he looked up at Kyle. "You took care of everything."

The grateful look in Dad's eyes was everything Kyle had ever wanted, and it was almost enough to keep him from saying more, but if he was going to make this work, he had to go all in. "I tried to. But if I hadn't gone to see her first, she might not have destroyed whatever evidence she possessed."

Dad stood abruptly, sending his chair skidding backward. "Don't. Son." He put his arms around Kyle and hugged him.

Kyle felt the well of pent-up emotion and self-loathing and angst splinter and fall away. It wasn't gentle or easy; it blew through him like a storm. He grasped at his father and held onto him as an anchor, never imagining how badly he'd needed this comfort.

It was a good, long minute—or ten—before they drew apart. Dad touched the side of Kyle's head. "Son, you did everything I would've done and more. I'm proud of you."

And there it was. The brilliance of his father's approval was as soul-satisfying as he'd imagined, but would he lose it if he said all he'd planned to? It was a risk he had to take.

Kyle backed away. "I'm glad you're proud of me. It's all I ever wanted. But I'm still a gambling addict. I'm still the son you bailed out four years ago. The son whose trust fund you're keeping away from him—and that's fine. You were smarter about that than I was."

Dad's brow furrowed. "I've read about gambling addiction—that it can lead to other addictions, like drugs and alcohol."

"Yeah, that's true. I've been to Gamblers Anonymous with plenty of people who were also members of Alcoholics and Narcotics Anonymous. But so far, that isn't me."

Dad's eyebrows rose. "You go to meetings?"

"I used to, in Florida. Before…Alex. Then I sort of went off the rails."

Dad winced. "How bad?"

"Not like before. Don't get me wrong, it could've gone that way, but I came back here to try to put my life back together—the life I want." He worked to rein in his defensiveness. "I'm not as big of a loser as you all thought."

"I never thought you were a loser." Dad sat back down in his chair and gestured to the seat Kyle had vacated. Dad's complexion turned a bit gray. "Sit, please. I want to tell you something. There's a reason I've been more worried about you than anyone else."

Tensing, Kyle sat, setting his forearms on the armrests of the chair. "Harder on me, you mean?"

He folded his hands together on the desktop. "I didn't mean to be. You were always less focused than your siblings, Alex, Sara, and Evan notwithstanding. Your behavior was always so much larger than life, like you were the star of the family. I worried you were maybe manic."

"Like manic depressive?"

"Yes." Dad's lips thinned, and his hands started to shake again. He laid his palms flat against the desk and then, perhaps thinking better of it, put his hands in his lap. "I've never told anyone this, but mental illness runs in my family. Your grandfather was manic depressive—bipolar."

Apprehension tightened every one of Kyle's muscles. "I had no idea."

"No one did. Your grandmother wanted it that way. He didn't die in a hunting accident." Dad's voice broke. He looked up at the ceiling and blinked furiously. "He wanted it to look that way, but he shot himself." He lowered his head. Tears glistened in his gray eyes.

Kyle had been nine when Granddad died, and he'd vowed never to go hunting. He started to rise. "Dad."

Dad waved him back down. "Let me finish. He committed suicide, and we covered it up. Your mother doesn't even know the truth."

Kyle realized Dad was sharing this with him of all people for a reason, but he couldn't fathom what it might be. "Why are you telling me this?"

"Because I thought you might've inherited his illness. I worried you were going to struggle the way he did. When I found out about your gambling, I wanted to talk to you, ask you to see someone, but then you left and I just…didn't. I didn't want you to end up like him. But I was so focused on you that I completely missed who was really in trouble."

"Alex." The answer hit Kyle harder than anything else he'd heard that morning.

A tear snaked down Dad's cheek. Kyle didn't remember him crying once after Alex died. He wished there was something he could do to take the pain away—wasn't that why he'd gone after the drug dealer in the first place? Now, looking back, why had he thought that would solve anything? There was no bringing Alex back, no erasing what he'd done. "You can't blame yourself, Dad."

"I can, and I do. I should've seen it." He slapped his hand sharply on the desktop as his sad remorse turned to angry regret. "Hell, I'd been looking for it, just in the wrong place. I'd subjected you to unfair criticism all while I should've been seeing the signs in Alex."

Kyle wanted to argue that none of them had seen the signs, but he hadn't even been there. "We all have guilt. I should've been here."

Dad leaned back in his chair, looking utterly defeated. He wiped his hand over his eye. "Yes, we all have guilt."

Seeing Dad like this nearly broke Kyle's heart. "Can I hug you now?"

Dad managed a weak smile. "I'd like that." He stood and met Kyle around the side of the desk.

When they broke apart, Dad cleared his throat. "Can you keep the stuff about Granddad to yourself for now? I need to tell your mother myself."

"Of course." Kyle was glad to hear they were maybe doing better. "How are things with you guys since she got back from France?"

Dad's coloring had returned to normal, but now he frowned. "I won't lie—it's been a little rough. Losing Alex has changed everything for us. I know it has for you too, but we're his parents. It's just different."

"I can imagine." Kyle's heart ached for them, but he knew it was a path they had to travel together—or apart, if that's what they chose. "Your kids will do anything for you, you know."

Dad smiled. "I do. And Kyle, this," he said, gripping Kyle's bicep, "this means more to me than you can know. I've missed you."

"I've missed you too, Dad."

"Do you think you'll be able to talk to Derek? I know he wants to. But the only person I know who's more stubborn than you and Liam is Derek."

Kyle had thought about what he would say to his former best friend. What could he say? Maggie had been dead right. Derek *had* saved his ass, and Kyle had been a total douchebag. None of the other particulars mattered anymore.

"Yeah, I'm going to talk to him. I don't know that I want to burden him during his wedding week."

Dad's eyes narrowed briefly. "That's a cop-out; don't go there. He's busy, yes, and he's taking the week off to prep for the wedding, but he'll always make time for you. Especially now. Nothing is more important to that boy than family."

"You're right. I'll talk to him." Kyle smiled, then glanced at the clock. He was surprised to see that it was nearly nine. "Crap, the police investigator is going to be here any minute. Are you up for seeing him?"

Dad's eyes hardened. "Hell yes. Let's take that bitch down. You and me. Together."

Kyle nodded, feeling better than he had in years. It seemed things were finally falling into place—at least with his family. His mind strayed to Maggie, as it liked to do more and more often. With things going so well, did he dare take their relationship public? Or was that only inviting disaster?

Looking at his dad, feeling the warmth of his love and approval, he wasn't sure he could risk losing it again. Not even for love.

SONNY AND CHER barked happily as Maggie opened the screen door and went into her mother's house on Monday night. She'd spent a long day at the wedding cottage overseeing and assisting with the sprinkler installation and talking to Sara about some additional outdoor decorating ideas—planters, a stone path, and a water feature. They wouldn't have time to implement them all before Saturday, but Sara was excited about every one of them. Maggie doubted she'd be around to see the execution, but she tried not to dwell on that.

She'd also spent all day thinking about how she wished she could spend every day like that. How she'd never felt more at ease, more challenged, and more excited about work. It hadn't even *felt* like work. And when she thought about going back to her real job, she froze up, her entire body going rigid with anxiety and loathing.

Yeah, she pretty much hated her job at this point. She struggled to remember why she'd chosen it and recalled that she used to like it, if not love it. Helping people had seemed a noble cause. That she'd chosen something her mother thought was a bad idea had only increased her drive, but now that she'd decided to let the past go, it was time to admit her career was a mistake and let that go, too.

Mom padded into the living room from the kitchen at the back of the house, her bare feet slapping against the hardwood floors. She wore ratty denim cut-offs and a cap-sleeve cotton shirt that was cinched just below her breasts, providing at least a modicum of support for her girls, which swung bra-free. It was precisely the kind of outfit that had made Maggie flush ten shades of red when she'd been fifteen and they'd gone grocery shopping. And normally it would make her uncomfortable now, but she was going to try not to let it.

"Hi, Mom."

"Magnolia! You didn't tell me you were stopping by."

Sonny and Cher ran back to Mom. They'd stopped yipping, but they were still dancing around excitedly.

Now that she was here, Maggie wasn't sure how to start. "Uh, I wanted to talk to you."

Nice and vague. Great opening.

Mom smiled. "That's nice. Surprising, but nice. I was going to call you. I'm thinking of getting dreadlocks. What do you think?"

To say she'd look ridiculous with dreadlocks as a late-middle-aged Caucasian woman would be an understatement. Again, Maggie considered her reaction. "Uh, I think I'm not the right person to ask. What do your friends think?"

Mom blinked at her. "What, no admonishment? Not even an exasperated sigh?"

Maggie laughed softly. "Sorry to disappoint you." She sobered. "But, Mom, are you *trying* to provoke a reaction from me?"

Mom's mouth turned down. "I guess maybe I was. My bad, flower bud. It's just that you're always so disapproving."

"I know." Here was the perfect opening. Could she take it? She'd driven over an hour so she might as well… no, this had been well more than an hour in the making. It had been years. "Can we sit, Mom?"

Mom's gaze turned dubious. "Sure."

Maggie offered a warm smile. "I didn't come to argue." She'd planned to ask her mother if she'd ever really mattered or if she and Rowan had simply been afterthoughts, but she realized she already knew the answer. If she and Rowan were truly insignificant, then Mom wouldn't be the opinionated and caring busybody she knew and loved—yes, loved. It was better to let old hurts go and embrace the future. Wasn't that why she'd really come? "I wanted to…apologize."

Mom sat down and immediately turned to Maggie, who'd perched beside her. "What for?"

Maggie shrugged, feeling strangely uncomfortable. This all felt so personal, and she'd kept her mother at arm's length for so long... "I've made a point of shunning your advice, of tuning you out. If I hadn't, maybe I wouldn't have made some pretty catastrophic mistakes."

The gentle touch of Mom's hand on her knee soothed her nerves. For the first time in ages, she thought of happy memories of Mom tending her scrapes from a bike accident and holding her while she cried after a "friend" had embarrassed her at school. "You haven't either."

"Mark wasn't a mistake?"

Mom patted her knee. "Well, yes, of course *he* was. And I knew that you thought so, too. You don't have to say things for a mother to hear them, you know. Or maybe you don't know. You will when you have children of your own."

Maggie wondered if she ever would—have children of her own—but didn't want to think about that right now. "My job has also been a total failure. I've decided to quit counseling." It was like a burden had been lifted. She felt...liberated.

Mom hugged her. "I'm so glad!" She pulled back. "What are you going to do?"

"I've actually been doing some landscape design. Just one job, actually, but it's a good one and I think it could lead to more." Having the Archers recommend her would go a long way—but first she had to come clean about who she really was. And to do that, she needed Kyle on board.

On second thought, she could be one and done with this gig. She shoved that disquieting thought away.

"That's great, Maggie. That's exactly what you should be doing. It's your calling—and you know, most people don't have a calling."

She'd told her that so many times before, but it was the first time Maggie really listened. And she felt very lucky—a word she never would've used to describe herself. "You called me Maggie. You never call me that."

"Don't I?"

Maggie shook her head, recognizing that her mom was giving her something in return—using the name Maggie preferred for once. "Thanks."

"Should we go get a beer at the Sasquatch?" The neighborhood bar just down the street was Mom's favorite place to grab a drink.

"Sure, but are you going to wear a bra?"

Mom laughed, and the sound was as loud and unruly as Maggie's entire childhood. "No. I am who I am, and you either accept it or you don't."

"I can accept it—I *guess*. But, Mom, I don't have to love it. Your lifestyle is just…crazy. Cray-*zee*."

"I know, dear. And I know it isn't who you are, much to my chagrin." She exhaled and stood up. "I think I've decided to pass on the dreadlocks."

Maggie got to her feet. "Why?"

Mom shrugged. "Too much work."

Maggie suppressed a smile. She couldn't know for sure, but she thought that maybe just this once, Mom had opted to be a little more mainstream. "Good choice."

"Let me grab my purse." Mom disappeared into the kitchen for a moment and came back with her hobo bag slung over her shoulder. She kept her shoes in a basket by the door and dug out a pair of orange Birkenstocks. "Now that you're going to have your dream job, we need to find your dream man."

Maggie arched a brow at her as she slipped her feet into her shoes. "Just one?"

Mom laughed again. "I said you weren't like me, unless you've changed your mind. Monogamy is so overrated."

"No, I haven't changed my mind. One man is plenty." Especially if that man were Kyle Archer. He was funny, caring, thoughtful, and he made her feel like she could do anything. "I'm actually sort of seeing someone."

Mom opened the door for her. "Kyle Archer, right?"

Maggie stepped outside and turned around as Mom locked the front door. "How'd you know?"

"The way he looked at you. Hungry. Possessive. Very sexy."

Gooseflesh raced across Maggie's arms and neck, and her stomach did flips. "Really?"

"Oh, yeah. Well done, flower bud. He's hot."

Maggie shook her head. "Mom!"

She hooked her arm through Maggie's and walked her to the sidewalk. "I call it like I see it."

Hungry. Possessive.

The words rang in Maggie's mind during the entire walk to the bar and resonated until she lay down to go to sleep that night. He'd wanted her. Did he still, or was the compulsion over for him?

She wanted to call him but didn't. Part of that was fear, and part of it was just wanting to give him the space he needed to come around. His plate wasn't just full, it was overflowing. And she had to accept that there just might not be any room for her.

Chapter Seventeen

IT WAS A rare overcast afternoon as August bloomed, but it was still warm. Maggie patted dirt around the batch of perennials she'd just put into the ground. She sat back on her heels and watched workers from Dylan's construction team putting the final touches on the pergola that overlooked the breathtaking vista of the rolling hills of Willamette Valley. It was going to be a stunning place for Derek and Chloe to be married on Saturday evening, and Maggie almost wished she could see it.

No, not almost. She wanted to come. And not just to see how beautifully it was all going to come together. She wanted to come because she liked these people, who also seemed to like her in return, particularly since several of them had now invited her—just about everyone but the person who mattered most: Kyle.

While she'd kept busy with the landscaping, her mind strayed to him almost constantly. She'd pushed him too hard, had played the counselor too well. He'd also said some pretty obnoxious things. She wished she knew where things stood—she hadn't heard from him since he'd stormed out two days ago, and she hadn't seen him here either. Everyone else had been around—Derek, Chloe, Sara, Tori, even Emily Archer, who was now coming toward her, a wide-brimmed hat shading her face.

"I think I'm going to take off, Magnolia," Emily said, stopping next to Maggie. Emily had spent the afternoon helping to plant.

Maggie brushed her gloved hands on her apron and looked up at her. "Thank you so much for your help today. I think we'll actually get everything done, thanks to you."

Emily shook her head. "No, no. Thanks to *you*. It's our good fortune that Kyle hired you."

"And mine that I've had the opportunity to do this," Maggie said quickly, always working to avoid having to answer the inevitable question, which, shockingly, no one had yet asked: *how did you and Kyle meet?*

Emily smiled, and it reminded Maggie so much of Sara—they were clearly mother and daughter. "Well, you're quite good at it. I may have to hire you to do some redesign in our backyard. I've been inspired by several gardens in France. I'd love to get together and talk through some ideas."

Maggie tried not to choke. Every moment she spent with this kind woman made her feel like a massive fraud. She was the sort of mother Maggie would've liked to have had growing up, and when she thought of the pain Alex had caused her...well, Maggie tried not to think of that.

"That would be fun," Maggie said, knowing it would never come to fruition. The moment Emily and the rest of them learned she was Maggie Trent, they wouldn't want anything to do with her ever again. And Maggie couldn't continue this "Magnolia" deception indefinitely—she couldn't betray these nice people.

"Don't work too hard," Emily said. "See you tomorrow?"

Maggie smiled up at her. "I'll be here."

With a wave, Emily turned and went to her car at the edge of the narrow road, where they were in the process of carving out a handful of handicap parking spaces. As she drove away, Maggie told herself to stop obsessing over the situation. There was nothing she could do but get through it.

Going back to her work, she focused on the bright spot, which was the relief she felt about quitting her counseling career. She'd tendered her resignation in person that morning and had already started the arduous task of letting her clients know that she was no longer practicing. Her boss and colleagues had understood and insisted on throwing a "retirement" party in a couple of weeks. Maggie smiled to herself, still amused by the idea of retiring.

"You look happy."

She snapped her head up to see Kyle standing just a few feet away. She hadn't heard him approach, hadn't even seen him from the corner of her eye. Her heart thudded, both from the surprise and just from seeing him. He wore a dark blue polo and khakis, and his blond hair was mussed from the breeze. Or maybe he'd been raking his hand through it again. Was seeing her causing him angst?

Don't get ahead of yourself, Maggie.

"I am happy. I resigned from my job today." *And you showing up just totally made my week.* God, she hadn't even realized how badly she'd missed him. But now that he was here, a palpable ache settled in her chest, and she longed to touch him, to hold him.

He smiled. "You did? That's great. And totally explains your look. I don't think I've ever seen you so relaxed."

A rush of warmth swept over her at his easy tone. It was the way he used to talk to her, when they'd been flirty and playful. When he wasn't looking for therapy and she wasn't trying to "cure" him of his compulsions.

She stood, and it felt good to stretch her legs. "Thanks. I've been wondering how you're doing."

"Since I stalked off the other night?" He winced, lines fanning around his eyes. "It wasn't my finest move. I was a total dick, actually. I'm sorry."

She warmed to his attention, glad to hear he'd been as bothered by their discussion as she'd been. "It was understandable. I was...pushy."

He stepped toward her and tucked a flyaway curl behind her ear. "You're cute when you're pushy."

His nearness sparked a fire in her belly, and the look in his eyes sent the flame lower. She moved closer until they were just a few inches apart. "Did you come by for a reason?"

He ran his fingertips down her bare arm. "To see how things were coming."

"Running into me was just an accident?"

"A happy one." He kissed her, and the familiar tide of want and need that he always provoked crested over her. She clutched his shoulders and pressed against him.

His tongue met hers as he palmed the back of her head. It was a thorough, bone-melting kiss. "Missed you so much," he murmured against her lips.

"Me, too. So much. The bed was delivered to the cottage today," she said. "But I suppose it would be rude to use it this close to the wedding. Besides, I'm kind of dirty and sweaty and gross."

He licked at her neck. "You're delicious. But you're probably right that it might be in bad taste. I like where your head's at, though."

She laughed as his mouth dipped lower toward the V-neck of her T-shirt. "Stop, please. I *am* dirty and gross. Let me go home and shower. You can come over later. If you want."

He lifted his head with a resigned sigh. "Okay. I wanted to tell you that I talked to my dad yesterday morning."

"You did?" She quashed an urge to smack him. "You could have led with that information! That's great. I'm so proud of you. How did it go?"

He smiled, looking more at ease than she'd ever seen him. "Good. He was devastated about Natalie, which I expected, but the police found evidence on her work computer yesterday. She's been told not to leave the state, but she hightailed it out of Ribbon Ridge. The investigator said she's staying with her mom in Hillsboro."

Maggie couldn't stop grinning. She was so happy for him. "You must feel so relieved. Will they arrest her soon?"

"I think so. They also found some pills and residue in a few baggies stashed in a compartment in her desk. We're waiting on lab results to see what they are."

"That's so incredible."

"I also talked to my dad about the gambling." He cracked a half-smile and shook his head. "Don't look so surprised."

She flinched. "Sorry. I really am proud of you."

Wow, he was really doing it—listening to her. Patients rarely did that, at least not fully. They did bits and pieces of what she suggested, but Kyle seemed to be committed to what he needed: resolution. She was sort of speechless. Until she wasn't. He wasn't the only one who was making progress in the fix-yourself business.

"It's thanks to you," he said. "I knew deep down I had to do it, but you convinced me that I could trust my family, that they do want to help and support me. I knew that deep down too, but sometimes I'm a stubborn prick."

She laughed. "So I noticed. You aren't the only one who's stubborn and making amends. I talked to my mom last night. I realized I needed to take my own advice. She's tried to be a good mother, butting in even when I didn't want her to. If I'd only listened to her instead of keeping her at arm's length because of our differences, I might not have made some of the colossal mistakes I have. She's a good mom, even if she shirks a bra and thinks monogamy is for swans."

He arched a brow. "Swans?"

"They typically mate for life. When I was sixteen, I went through a phase where I had swan everything—T-shirts, posters, knickknacks. I even had a swan necklace that I wore every day. It drove my mother insane."

His eyes narrowed, but with appreciation. "I didn't realize you could be so conniving. Very hot."

"Ha! That's what my mom said about you when I told her we were dating."

The flirtation leached from his expression. "You did what? Shouldn't we discuss taking this public?"

Oh, shit. That had been the wrong thing to say. She hadn't meant to tell him about that, but then she hadn't meant to keep it secret either. She was really tired of secrets. "I admitted I was seeing you. She figured it out anyway." Ugh, that made her sound like a little girl with a weak defense when she really didn't need to defend herself at all.

"Seems like something we should've decided together."

She wanted to find joy in his words—*we, together*—but he was obviously annoyed. "You mean like couples do? Are we a couple, or aren't we?"

He turned from her and looked out over the valley. "If we are, you would've talked to me."

Ouch. "I should've talked to you first. I got a little carried away. What can I say? I was feeling good. I'm happy. You make me happy." Another lock of her hair fluttered in the wind, and she swiped it behind her ear.

He looked at her for a long moment, and then his mouth opened. But she would never hear what he'd been about to say.

"Kyle!" Derek's call made them both turn toward the dirt track.

As Derek approached, Maggie knew their talk was over, as was any hope for a sexy, happy interlude. She bent and picked up her spade and the stack of empty flowerpots.

"Maybe I'll see you later?" She peered over at Kyle, unsure of where things were now.

He nodded, but she saw the motion for what it was—noncommittal. She turned to go, waving her spade at Derek in greeting and then hurrying to the parking lot as fast as she could.

She'd messed up. Again. Only this time, she wasn't sure it could be fixed.

KYLE WAS TORN between going after Maggie and staying to talk to Derek. Both options made him somewhat uncomfortable, but for wholly different reasons. With Derek, he had to face a past hurt. With Maggie, he had to try to predict the future and see if the hurt was to come.

Derek came to stand next to him at the edge of the hillside. "It's a gorgeous view. And Magnolia's done a beautiful job on the flowers. I admit I was wrong—you completely saved the day by hiring her."

Kyle appreciated the olive branch and knew it was his turn. As hard as it had been to come clean with Dad, this was even harder. "You got my message?" Kyle had left a voicemail for him earlier in the day. Yesterday had passed in a flash, between the police search and he and his father assisting with the investigation.

Derek nodded as he slipped his hands into the pockets of his shorts. "I stopped by the office, but Rob said you were here. He told me about Natalie. I...I can't believe it. I'm so fucking pissed off."

A surge of adrenaline coursed through him. It felt good to be on the same side as Derek again. "I know. I am, too."

"*You* didn't hire her." Derek said the words with such vehemence that it sounded like a curse. It was definitely a self-recrimination. "I should've hired the woman who cracked gum throughout the interview; then Natalie never would have entered our lives and Alex might still be here."

Kyle turned toward the man he used to consider closer to him than any of his brothers. "Don't do that. There's no point to the 'if only' game. How many times did your mom tell you that when you'd say, 'If only Dad hadn't taken that extra shift'?" Derek's father, a cop, had been killed in the line of duty when Derek was just nine. They'd moved from Tacoma to Ribbon Ridge, and he'd been an introverted sad sack, a project Kyle had eventually taken on, but only after they'd butted heads for a while.

Derek blew out a breath. "I'd forgotten I used to do that about my Dad. I couldn't when Mom died. There had been no 'if only.' The cancer came, and there was nothing we could've done." He looked at Kyle, and the sadness in his gaze was deep and painful. "I miss them both so much this week."

It was like the last four years had never happened. Kyle clapped his hand against Derek's bicep. He coughed to clear the emotion from his throat. "I get it. I miss your mom, too."

They were quiet a long moment. The air around them was filled with the buzz of bees, bird calls, a gentle breeze, and the warm companionship that only existed between two people who had known each other a very long time.

"So why did you call?" Derek asked.

Suddenly there was no anxiety, no resentment, just a lingering ache of regret. "To apologize for holding a grudge."

Derek surprised him by laughing. "Is that what this was?"

Kyle shrugged. "That and you being a dick."

"Yeah, I was a dick. I'm sorry, too. Really. I just wanted to help." His gaze was steady, intense. "You know that, right?"

"I didn't for a long time, but I do now."

"Is it really that easy?" Derek asked. "We just go from 'I fucking hate you' to 'I love you, bro'?"

"We're dudes. Once we're over it, we're over it, right?"

"That sounds about right." Derek leaned his head back and smiled up at the sky. "Just in time, too. Now you can be my best man." He looked at Kyle expectantly.

Kyle hadn't realized how badly he'd wanted to be until that moment. But there was a consideration. "What about Hayden?"

"He won't care. He knew he was second choice."

"I'd feel bad for him, but he's spending a year in France living a dream."

Derek let out a short laugh. "Yeah, don't bother. Emily said he's got French babes crawling all over him."

Kyle grinned. "Loser."

"So, there's one more thing," Derek said, sounding cautious. "There's another reason I came up here to see you."

"Sounds ominous."

Derek pulled a folded envelope from his back pocket. "Sorry about the crease."

The handwriting coaxed a visceral reaction from Kyle—it was Alex's. A tremor rattled his frame as he took the envelope. "Why do you have my letter?"

"I stopped by Aubrey Tallinger's office and got it. She told me months ago that when you resolved things with Dad—and with me—that it would be time for you to get your letter and asked if I would let her know when it happened."

Why had Derek gotten some sort of special task? "She *told* you?"

"Per Alex's instructions. The only way she could know if things got worked out is if she talked to one of us, and she chose me, I guess."

Kyle understood why. Dad had been pretty unapproachable in the weeks after Alex's death, and he hadn't been too friendly to Aubrey in particular because of the role she'd played in setting up the trust. "But *we* hadn't resolved anything—I only talked with Dad."

Derek lifted a shoulder. "I figured it was close enough. And like you, I was going to apologize anyway. Life's too short. I preach that to all of you enough, you'd think that I would've listened to my own advice."

That reminded him of Maggie—counseling him and then turning it back on herself. He felt a pang of regret for how their conversation had gone. He wasn't really mad that she'd told her mom, more like surprised. He should make sure she understood that.

He stared at the letter in his hand and knew that he had to read it with her. She'd been close to Alex too, and she wasn't going to get a letter.

"Yeah, you do preach that," Kyle said, "but a friend told me recently, 'Do as I say, not as I do.'"

Derek smiled. He nodded toward the letter in Kyle's hand. "You going to read that?"

"Later."

Derek went to one of the rose bushes Maggie had planted—she insisted a wedding garden in northwestern Oregon needed roses—and leaned over to smell one of the flowers. "I get it. I couldn't read mine immediately either."

"Did he say why you got your letter right away?"

"Sort of." Derek straightened. "He told me he hoped I would support everyone—that I was the lone voice of reason in a sea of crazy. I guess he wanted me to keep the peace." He looked askance at Kyle. "He also reamed me out for the way I handled things with you."

Kyle snorted. "How did he even know?"

"Because he knew everything. Did you ever notice that? No secrets with him."

That was so true. Alex picked up on everything. The consummate observer. "Yeah, but he certainly kept some from us."

Derek looked down at the ground. "That he did."

They were quiet for a moment. Finally, Derek said. "I'm going inside, I heard the bed was delivered."

Kyle turned and looked up the lane. "Is Chloe meeting you?"

Derek smirked at him. "Ha-ha, very funny. Actually, I'm hiding a present under her pillow." He pulled a box from his pocket and opened it.

Kyle recognized the star-shaped pendant. "That was your mom's."

"Yeah. She gave it to me to give to my future wife."

Memories flooded Kyle's brain, and he regretted losing the last four years. "I remember. You said you weren't ever getting married."

Derek closed the box. "I did. You pledged the same thing."

Kyle remembered that, too. "I win." He flashed a victorious grin.

Derek lifted a shoulder. "Or you lose, depending on how you look at it. I'm so crazy about Chloe. I can't imagine my life without her. I hope you find someone, some*thing* like that."

For a fleeting moment, Kyle wondered if he already had.

Chapter Eighteen

ALEX'S LETTER SAT beside him in the car, almost as if his brother were there in the flesh. It was silly to think of it that way, but that's the only way Kyle could characterize the eerie feeling he had—that his brother was with him.

He parked in Maggie's driveway and wondered if this was a bad idea. He had no inkling of what the letter might say. Would there be anything she ought not know? Anything that should be kept secret? Nothing Kyle could think of.

Clenching his jaw, he picked up the letter and got out of the car. He knocked on her door and waited only a moment before she came to open it.

She'd showered. Her hair hung in damp curls, and he could smell her shampoo—a citrus and spice scent. She didn't wear any makeup, not that she ever needed any. Her skin glowed from her days spent outside, and her lush peach-hued lips beckoned him.

Her gaze flickered with doubt. "I wasn't sure you'd come."

"I said I would."

She still looked uncertain. "You were pretty upset about me telling my mom about us. Things seemed…unsettled."

Yeah, they did. They'd both discussed the need for secrecy, especially during this landscaping project. He wasn't sure when he could come clean about her, but it definitely wasn't going to be this week with the wedding and all the Natalie bullshit. "I'm sorry about that. I was just surprised that you told your mom. Can I come in?"

"Sure." She held the door, and he moved over the threshold. "What's that?" Her gaze dipped to the envelope in his hand as she closed the door.

"It's the reason I came." He walked into the living room and turned to face her. "Also, I made up with Derek."

Her features, so tense since he'd arrived, softened. "That's great."

"He brought me Alex's letter—he wrote one to each of us before he died and posthumously instructed his attorney on when we should get them."

Her jaw tightened, and her aura of anxiety returned. "He planned everything down to the minutiae, didn't he?"

Kyle was a bit surprised by the bitterness in her tone, but why should he be? He and his siblings, particularly Sara, had discussed Alex's careful planning several times. It was downright macabre to think of all he'd done to pull it off. And without any of them knowing. It was equal parts brilliant and demented.

"I wanted to read it with you," he said. "If that's okay."

Her eyes widened briefly. "Are you sure?"

He nodded as he sat on her couch. "Sit with me?"

She came and sank down beside him.

"I'll just read through it first." Kyle opened the seal and pulled out the letter—a single page. He felt a surreal calm as he opened the paper.

> *Dear Kyle,*
>
> *You are my hero.*

Maggie's touch on his shoulder made him realize the sound he'd just heard in his head had been his audible reaction—part exhalation and part anguished cry. His throat burned.

> *You're either laughing or crying right now. Why are you my hero? Because you're fearless. You do everything one hundred and fifty percent. And it's different from Tori or Liam and their drive. You have this joy and lust for life that's infectious. You're the whole package—charming, charismatic, funny, smart, creative, and ridiculously good looking. Girls always followed you around, and everyone wanted to be your best friend. If Kyle Archer smiled at you, you were cool. If he talked to you, you were in. If you were in his inner circle, you were a prince of the world—not the king, because that was Kyle. But being one of your princes was enough. Thank you for making sure that I was a member of the court. You made life almost bearable.*

Kyle felt wetness on his cheeks, but he didn't wipe it away.

> *But do not for a second think that means my life became unbearable when you left. No guilt allowed! My life was always a breath—pun intended—away from utter desolation, but you were often what kept that breath in check.*
>
> *If you're reading this, you've come back home and you've made up with Dad and Derek, and you've apologized to Sara for ditching her (that was a douche move, but I won't bust your balls about it since I'm pretty sure she did a good job of that).*

"Yes, she did," Kyle murmured, thinking of the weeks he'd been home before Sara would listen to his apology. They'd been close, and his abrupt departure had hit her the hardest—and he'd known it. Yeah, it had been the douchiest of douche moves.

> *It's about goddamn time, don't you think? You are one stubborn son of a bitch, but then I suppose that's an Archer trait we all share in varying degrees.*
>
> *Are you cooking? If you aren't, it's a damn shame and I hope you'll fix that. I hope you'll create a world-class restaurant at the monastery and blow everyone's mind. You have the talent and the drive—but do you believe in yourself enough? That's your biggest flaw, dude. Always thinking you're behind or a loser or the*

flake. Newsflash: no one thinks that but you. Okay,
maybe Liam, but he's a dick.

Kyle laughed. Liam *was* a dick, and the only person
who could possibly think that more than Kyle was Alex.
Kyle might have felt overshadowed by Liam's drive and
success, but at least they didn't share the same looks and
that mystical twin bond that simultaneously drew Liam
and Alex together and drove them apart.

So you're a gambling addict. Yeah, I knew about
that, but maybe you figured that out already. It doesn't
make you a failure, and neither does losing thirty grand.
You fucked up. We all fuck up. I'm going out on a limb
and predicting your fuckup will pale in comparison with
mine. I failed at life. You couldn't if you tried. Your spirit
and your attitude are just too relentless. Do not make
my mistake. Don't hide who you are, what you've done,
and what you feel. Our family is full of bullshit, but it's
also full of love, and there will always be someone—
multiple someones—to lend you a hand when you need
it. Don't ever be afraid to ask. If there's one thing you
take from me, take that, please.

I love you, Kyle. I'm sorry I had to go, but I just
did. I hope that Mom and Dad aren't suffering too
much. Help them find laughter and joy, and make
them a lot of comfort food.

The scrawl of his name was so familiar and yet so
strange at the same time. Kyle ran his fingers over the

letters as if touching them was somehow touching his brother.

He didn't know how long he sat like that, but at length, Maggie's fingers caressed his forearm. "You okay?"

His eyes still felt a little wet. He brushed his hand over them. "Yeah. Here, you read it." He looked at her, saw the compassion burning in her gaze.

He leaned back against the couch while she read.

Silence reigned for several long minutes. He didn't watch her, just stared at the ceiling and thought about what Alex had written. He had no idea Alex had... *what, idolized him?*

She refolded the letter. "Wow."

He sat up and faced her.

Blinking back tears, she tried to smile. "I always knew he was an excellent observer, but he really nailed you, didn't he?"

"To the wall."

She handed the letter back to him. "You're all so lucky. I had a sense of your family from Alex, but watching some of you together the past several days and now, reading this... it's such a rare thing."

He was entranced by her words. "Why?"

"The camaraderie, the ferocity with which you fight and support each other, the love. If I'd never known Alex, I might feel like I did after reading that." She pressed a finger beneath her eye to catch a tear before it fell. "I could hear his voice, as if he were sitting here reading the letter to me."

"Me, too." He liked that this woman had known his brother because no one ever would again.

"Are you going to take his advice?"

He slipped the letter back in the envelope and clutched it in his hand. "Cook my parents comfort food?"

Her lips lifted in the hint of a smile. "No. He told you not to repeat his mistake, to not hide who you are and what you're feeling."

"I sort of already did. I mean, I talked to Dad. And Derek."

"Yes, but what about the rest of your family? What about Sara? Doesn't she deserve to know about your addiction?"

"Deserve?" He grimaced. "I don't know if I like that word."

"Why not? Don't *you* deserve their love and support? That's what you'll get if you share your struggles with them. That's what Alex was trying to say."

Kyle pushed up from the couch and walked to the front window. "I know what he was trying to say."

"You're hiding your addiction. Just like you're hiding me." Her words pierced his back like little daggers. He turned to look at her. She still sat on the couch, her dark eyes wide, her expression frank.

He'd been a fool to think they wouldn't end up talking about this. "I have good reasons for hiding both of those things—reasons you are more than aware of."

"Yes, I'm aware, but there's no good reason to keep your addiction from them. As for me, well, I understand why you don't want to say anything. What's to tell, any-way? We had a nice time together the past few weeks, but that's all it is." She looked away.

No, that wasn't all it was. He cared about her. More than he'd cared about anyone. She challenged him, she soothed him, she gave as good as she got. "We're good together."

She smiled at him, but it was sad. "We were, yes. But it's time for you to choose, and I want you to choose your family. I'm in a good place, the best place I've been in for a long time—maybe ever. I don't really want the stress of dealing with your family's outrage or aggression or whatever they'd end up feeling when they learned who I really am."

Was she breaking up with him? Could they even break up in this sort of situation?

Of course they could. They might not have classified themselves as boyfriend and girlfriend, but parting ways, not seeing each other anymore, definitely constituted a breakup. "What are you saying?"

"That you should focus on your family and rebuilding what you have there. I need to focus on me and my new direction. Maybe you could give me a letter of recommendation since The Alex is my only landscaping experience." She stood up from the couch and walked toward the door.

Damn, she was escorting him out. Yeah, she was definitely breaking up with him. He held up his hand. "Wait. I can't quite process this. With everything going on this week and Alex's letter…"

She looked resolute. "It's for the best. We both knew this didn't have legs. Even if your family miraculously accepted me, I'm probably always going to therapize you, and you're always going to have a compulsive personality, which is problematic enough, but for someone who has trouble owning their addiction, it can be disastrous."

"But I…" He what? Was he in love with her? He didn't know. He'd never been in love before. He had no idea what that should feel like. What he did know is that he'd never felt the way he did about her about anyone else. Despite that, her words resonated in his battered mind. His shoulders bunched with tension. "I don't have trouble owning my addiction. Did I ever try to hide it from you?"

"No, but that's because you wanted me to help you with it. You've never gotten straight-up counseling until you met me. I think you should find someone to talk to. If you want a recommendation—"

Suddenly it was all too much—the letter, this entire conversation. His patience snapped. "Save it. You're right, I don't want you therapizing me anymore." He opened the door. "Thanks for everything, Maggie. Take care of yourself." He barely kept himself from slamming the door to release some of the emotion raging through him—anger, frustration, sadness.

He went to his car and climbed inside, automatically starting in with the breathing Maggie had taught him and realizing she'd left her mark. Given the vague nausea swirling in his gut and the sharp pang of loss, he suspected her impact was deeper and would be far more lasting than either of them imagined.

Chapter Nineteen

"SOUNDS LIKE YOU'VE had quite a week," Amy said near the end of their appointment on Friday. "First your mom, then deciding to leave counseling." She shook her head. "I can't say I'm not disappointed. You're a good therapist, Maggie."

Maggie wasn't sure she agreed but didn't say so. She ran her hand along the smooth arm of the couch. "Thank you. I think I'll be a better landscape designer."

"If that's going to give you joy and fulfill your life, then I wholeheartedly support you. In fact, I've been interested in doing an English garden in my backyard. Maybe you can help me out." She smiled warmly.

"I'd be happy to—but you can't pay me. You'll be doing me a favor by giving me a project for my portfolio."

Amy looked as though she might argue, but she winked instead. "We can discuss the specifics later. I'd say at your next appointment, but I'm not sure you need one. Unless you want to talk more about Ryan Dillinger and what happened."

They'd spent close to half the session discussing his failed suicide attempt and its effect on Maggie. "I feel surprisingly good, but that doesn't mean that won't change after I e-mail him back." He'd been released from the psych ward and had e-mailed her to apologize. She hadn't yet responded but planned to—with Amy's encouragement—in order to close that chapter in her life. "Can I touch base with you in a week or so?"

"Please do. If there's anything I can do for you, I hope you'll let me know. You're my patient, but you've also been a colleague, and I hope we can be friends."

"I'd like that." Everyone had been so supportive of her decision to leave. Sure, Dr. Innes had tried to talk her out of it, but he'd ultimately understood. The clinic was doing a great job helping her patients to transition.

"When are you going to be done at the clinic?" Amy asked.

"I sort of already am. I'm meeting with a few patients next week, but I'm going in tomorrow to start cleaning out my office."

"How have your patients been taking your departure?"

"Overall, they've been fairly positive, but a few were pretty upset." She'd had to navigate two or three very uncomfortable phone calls.

Amy scratched a note on her pad. "That doesn't seem to be affecting you too much—you're not internalizing their emotion."

Maggie had noticed that too, and it felt good. "Yeah. I take it as confirmation that this is the right decision."

"I'd say that's a good assessment." Amy slid the pen behind her ear. "I sense there might be something else, but then I often feel that way with you. You have many layers." She chuckled.

"And you're very astute. I've actually been thinking a lot about Mark lately."

Amy cocked her head to the side. "Really, why?"

"I think it's because this feels like after we broke up—when I reset my life. I moved to a new town, launched a new career, set my life in a whole new direction. This seems like the same thing, minus the new town, but it feels different somehow. It feels better."

"And why do you think that is?"

Maggie should've expected the question. She shrugged. "Maybe because of the conversation I had with my mom. Or maybe it's because of the career shift—this time it feels like I'm making the right decisions instead of running away."

Or maybe it was because she was in love.

She wanted to say the thought had come out of nowhere, but it hadn't. It had been growing, slowly taking root and spreading until it had overtaken her.

Telling Kyle to choose his family had been the hardest thing she'd ever done. She wanted to fight for him, to find a way to make it all work, but she'd known it was a losing battle. Maybe if they'd met at a different time, when Alex's death wasn't still so fresh. She'd considered waiting it out, but now that she'd turned a corner, she didn't want to put things on hold. She needed to move forward, and if that meant doing so without Kyle, then that's what she'd have to do. Her experience with Mark had taught her to never plan her life around a man again.

"Are you sure it isn't something else?" Amy asked. She really was an excellent therapist. It was as if she had a sixth sense about suppressed thoughts and feelings.

"Maybe, but nothing I want—or need—to talk about." When Amy's gaze turned doubtful, Maggie added, "Truly. I'm fine."

The skepticism in Amy's expression only intensified. "Well, when you figure out what happens with Kyle Archer, I hope you'll let me know."

Maggie narrowed her eyes and then laughed softly. "You are too keen for your own good." She stood. "Thanks, Amy. I'll be in touch soon."

They exchanged a warm hug, and then Maggie drove up to the wedding cottage to do a final review before the rehearsal, which was due to start in a couple of hours. She parked in one of the handicap spots they'd made and was pleased to see that nobody was there yet. She'd only be a few minutes.

Armed with pruners and a small bucket, she made a quick circuit to ensure everything looked fresh and beautiful. Not quick enough, however, as the sound of a car coming down the track drew her to turn. Damn, she was really hoping to get out of here before anyone arrived.

She recognized the little Honda because it had been up here at least once a day all week. Chloe English—almost Sumner—got out of the car and waved. There was no avoiding her unless Maggie wanted to be rude. And she didn't; she liked Chloe.

Maggie walked over to her car. "Happy almost wedding day."

Chloe smiled—the kind of smile that couldn't be contained, the kind that lit up the sky with its joy. "Hi, Magnolia! I know I keep saying this, but you've done such an amazing job. I can't believe how you've transformed this space over the past week. It's just perfect."

Everything was trimmed, flowers bloomed in the beds, climbing roses twined up the sides of the new the pergola. Several large pots, overflowing with plants in the wedding colors of lavender, blueberry, and sage, surrounded the covered outdoor area that would be the dancefloor.

"I'm glad you like it," Maggie said. "I was just finishing up. The sprinklers are all set, and the pots have drip systems." Dylan and his crew had been instrumental in pulling this off. Without their help moving dirt, installing the sprinkler system, and building the pergola, this would all still be an idea on paper.

Chloe touched Maggie's hand. "Thank you."

Maggie smiled warmly. "It was my pleasure. Congratulations. I hope tomorrow is everything you dreamed it would be."

"You can see for yourself."

"Oh, I won't be here tomorrow. My work is done."

"Not to work. I invited you to come, remember?" Chloe reached into her car and pulled out a small duffel bag.

"I know, and thank you for including me. I hope you understand, but I'm exhausted after this week. I also have a prior commitment." Not that she'd spend tomorrow evening cleaning out her office—she'd likely be done before the wedding—but she still wasn't coming.

Chloe frowned briefly. "That's too bad. Well, if you get done early and aren't too tired, I hope you'll stop by. I'm sure the party will be going late, and there's enough Archer beer to float a fleet of ships."

Maggie laughed softly. "I'm sure. Take care."

"Don't be a stranger," Chloe said. "Sara and I thought it would be fun to go out sometime. I'll get your number from Kyle."

For a brief second, Maggie panicked, wondering why Chloe would think she could get her number from Kyle of all people, but then she realized it was because he'd been the one to hire her. *Duh.* Maggie only nodded in response, not wanting to encourage her. Anyway, she doubted very much that Kyle would give them her number. Her chest constricted as she thought about a future in which she didn't see or talk to him.

Maggie waved before she turned and walked to her car. As she put the bucket, her pruners, and her gloves in the backseat, she watched Chloe unlock the cottage and go inside with her bag.

She didn't know if she'd be back up here ever again. While she'd suggested other landscaping elements—some pathways, a water feature—they hadn't hired her to do anything. And if they contacted her, she didn't know what she would say. She didn't want to hide behind

"Magnolia" anymore. She was Maggie Trent, former therapist to their beloved Alex. If she couldn't be honest about that, she'd have to walk away. And so that's what she was prepared to do.

Determined, she got into the car and put the key in the ignition. She supposed she might come up here some day after the hotel and restaurant were open. It was going to be quite the hot spot in the valley. But could she come and eat in Kyle's restaurant? She leaned her forehead against the steering wheel and closed her eyes. That sounded like torture.

Get a hold of yourself, Maggie!

She sat up, shook her head, and started the car. Time to put this behind her. Time to break free and embrace the future.

"HIT ME," HAYDEN said, holding out his wineglass. They'd finished the wedding rehearsal about twenty minutes ago and had made a few toasts. Soon they would head over to the dinner being held at the winery where Dylan's brother, Cameron, worked. Sara had worked with him to organize the event.

Kyle refilled Hayden's glass with the garnet-red wine. "Not too much of a French wine snob now to drink our local pinot?"

"Hell no. If anything, it's made me love it even more. France is great, but the wine we make here is unparalleled." He toasted Kyle before taking a drink.

Kyle splashed more wine into his glass—he needed a buzz to power through this joy-fest, which was at complete odds with his black mood. So far he'd done a good job of putting on a happy face the past few days, but he didn't know how much longer he could last. A wedding was just about the worst place to try to get over a breakup. He mentally shook himself: *pull your head out, Archer; she said it was for the best, and she was right.*

He pushed thoughts of Maggie to the back of his mind but knew they wouldn't stay that way. "Thanks for not being pissed about the best-man thing."

"No sweat. It was always your gig." Hayden glanced around the interior of the wedding cottage. "It's good to see everyone here for something happy."

It was, even if some of them weren't exactly on the best terms. Liam and Tori were over near the windows chatting, probably plotting their next steps toward world domination. Evan was standing nearby with Sara and Dylan. Chloe and Derek were with her family—her parents, brother, sister, and three grandparents—as well as Mom and Dad, plus an old friend of Chloe's from Pennsylvania who was in the wedding party. Mom and Dad seemed to be getting along pretty well. It wasn't yet the happy warmth he recalled from his childhood or even from four years ago, but the air was less stilted. He only hoped the joy of this occasion would linger for a while. Too bad it wasn't doing shit for his state of mind.

The spectre of Maggie rose once more, as did the weight of his gambling addiction and when he planned to spill the beans. He'd found a GA group and attended a meeting yesterday, which had helped. At least on that front. As for the Maggie problem, it had only reminded him of her—the way she cared about him. The way no one had ever cared about him before and maybe never would again.

"Dude, you look way too serious. What's up?"

Hayden's question prompted Kyle to come up with a reasonable explanation for his air of gloom. No way was he revealing the real reason. "I was just thinking about Natalie. I'm glad they arrested her this morning. Makes tonight even more of a celebration." The drugs from her desk had been OxyContin. Upon investigating her medical records, the police found a pattern of drug-seeking behavior. She was obtaining drugs and then selling them—and she'd lied about stopping after Alex died.

Hayden raised his glass in a toast. "Right on. I'm still shocked it was her. And so pissed. I hope she goes to jail for a nice long time."

That would depend on a lot of factors, but the prosecutor planned to swing for the fences, despite her lack of a criminal record. She'd certainly have to pay penalties, and Dad was considering a civil suit for negligence. None of it made up for anything, just as Maggie had said it wouldn't, but it did offer a small bit of closure.

Sipping his wine, Hayden scrutinized Kyle. "I get the sense there's more to your mood, but I won't bother asking since you'd just change the subject. Tell me about this year's Oktoberfest plans."

Relieved to turn the conversation to something that wasn't about him and would distract him from thoughts of Maggie, Kyle gladly launched into an overview of the annual fall festival hosted by Archer Enterprises in downtown Ribbon Ridge.

After a few minutes, Dad interrupted everyone with a gentle clink on his glass. "Time for us to get to the winery. Sara's put together a great dinner." He lifted his glass toward Derek and Chloe. "One more toast for the bride and groom."

Cheers sounded around the room as glasses clinked. All eyes were on Derek and Chloe as he pressed a kiss to her lips. They both smiled, love shining in their eyes and practically blinding everyone around them with its brilliance. Or maybe that was just how Kyle felt. He turned away and set his glass on a tray, then went around collecting glasses, preferring to be a worker instead of a participant.

Tray full, he took the glasses into the kitchen and carefully loaded them into one of the dishwashers.

Sara peeked her head in. "Need any help?"

"Nah, thanks."

She flashed him a smile. " 'K. See you over there."

"Yep." Even as he said it, he thought about how he could simply not go. He'd done his best-man duties at the rehearsal; did he really need to go to a dinner and pretend to be happy?

He could hear Maggie telling him he had to go, that he'd be sorry if he didn't. Maybe he would be. He was more sorry that she wasn't here with him. Was there a chance she might want to be? He'd thought so, but then the other night she'd told him to choose his family over her. Maybe she didn't feel the same way about him as he felt about her. Maybe she'd been ready to let him go.

Damn, that hurt even worse.

He set the dishwasher to run and hesitated in the kitchen. He'd just gotten paid, and his Archer paychecks were more than enough to pay the bills on Hayden's house, take care of his own expenses, and still have plenty left to stash away. Or gamble…

He didn't know how long he stood there staring at the wall, but Derek's cough startled him. "Kyle? You ready?"

Kyle shook his head. "Yeah. You go on ahead. I'll meet you there."

Derek came further into the kitchen, frowning. "What's going on with you? You've been miles away all day. The last few days, actually. It's not Alex's letter, is it?"

"No. It was good." He offered a weak smile. "Just contemplating things, I guess."

Derek rested his hip against the counter and crossed his arms. "What things?"

"Nothing. Come on, let's go." Kyle moved toward the door to the main room, anxious to evade this interrogation. That made two nosy inquiries so far tonight, and if he went to the dinner, it would just get worse. He could either suffer through it—but fuck, he was tired of doing that—or bail.

Derek snagged his forearm and drew Kyle to stop. "Let's not. Spill. I'm not leaving until you do, and then you can have the wrath of my bride on your head. You don't want to piss Chloe off."

Kyle turned, anger flaring in his chest. "Let it go, will you? This is your day. Weekend. Whatever."

"So? Life happens. And if life is happening to you *right now*, let's talk about it. Waiting until after my honeymoon might be too late."

"God, I hate when you're logical."

Derek shrugged. "It's a gift."

"More like a menace. Fine. I'm miserable."

Derek resumed his arm-crossed stance against the counter. "Why? You want to gamble? I see that weird glint in your eye."

"Christ, you can look at me and see when I want to gamble by the look in my eye? Remind me to wear sunglasses from now on."

Derek's mouth quirked up briefly. "Not really, I just took a guess. Maybe I'm wrong?"

Kyle turned and leaned his backside against the opposite counter. "You're not wrong. I was just calculating how much I could wager tonight."

Derek nodded, pivoting so they faced each other across the small space. "Your paychecks are pretty good, so I'm guessing that was a dangerous amount."

Self-loathing itched up Kyle's spine. "Any amount is a dangerous amount."

"I hadn't thought of it like that, but yeah, I guess so." He winced. "Sorry."

Some of the tension left Kyle's muscles. He was actually relieved that Derek had interrupted him. "Don't apologize. I need to do a better job of explaining this to you. Of helping you understand my addiction."

"I'd like that. What about everyone else?"

Kyle ran his hand through his hair and exhaled sharply. "I need to talk to them. I just...I don't know how. When I think of telling Sara, my stomach twists in knots. And when I think of telling Liam, my teeth grind."

"I can understand that. But I'll be there for you every step of the way." He looked at Kyle with concern and compassion. "You know they'll support you, right? Even Liam. His bedside manner may not be the best, but maybe this will help him, too."

"Help him feel superior," Kyle muttered.

Derek laughed. "You guys are so competitive."

"Ha. It's hard to compete with someone who routinely kicks your ass in life."

"Not true. Liam is nowhere near as genial as you."

Kyle snapped his gaze to Derek's and arched a brow. "*Genial*? What am I, ninety?"

Derek laughed again. "You know what I mean. He's always so focused and uptight. He practically broods."

"Good description."

"Anyway, if he's a jerk about it, screw him. No one else will do that."

Derek was right. They would all be supportive, especially Sara. And with a team behind him, maybe he *could* make it...

But he realized there was someone missing from that team. The person he wanted most on his side. The person he constantly thought of and went to the very moment he felt wobbly. "I don't want to hide who I am anymore."

"That's good."

Kyle looked over at Derek, feeling tentative but determined. "Alex's letter…he called me on that. But it's more than the addiction. There's someone who's important to me, someone you're all going to be inclined to hate."

Derek's brow furrowed. "I can't imagine why."

"Just trust me. I was inclined to hate her too, but then I got to know her, and she's smart and funny and caring and pretty much the best person I know." He threw Derek a sheepish smile. "No offense."

"None taken. Sounds like you're in love with her."

"Completely." The admission soared through his chest and banished all of the darkness and weight he'd been carrying. He couldn't stop from smiling.

Derek smiled back. "Awesome." He reached over and briefly clapped Kyle on the shoulder. "I'm so happy for you. Can I ask, is it Magnolia?"

"Yeah, but that's not really her name. It *is*, but…never mind."

"Why didn't you bring her tonight if you guys are together?"

"Because we aren't together." A shadow fell over him as he remembered where they'd left things.

Derek put his hands on the counter on either side of him, bracing himself. "Why the hell not? You're in love with her. She's probably in love with you."

"I don't know that, actually. She broke up with me a couple of days ago."

"What the hell for?" The outrage in his voice gave Kyle comfort—damn, it was good to have Derek with him again.

"It's complicated. You'll understand when you meet her."

Derek looked confused. "I *have* met her."

Kyle shook his head. "I'm not doing a good job explaining, and I can't right now." He suddenly had to see her, had to know if she truly didn't want him or if she'd just been doing the most amazing thing anyone had ever done for him. "Would it be okay if I went and got her and brought her to the dinner?"

Derek pushed away from the counter. "I was just going to insist that you do."

"It's going to take me a bit—she lives in Newberg." He hoped she was home.

"Take as long as you need, but, bro, if something happens"—he wasn't specific, but the implication was if things went south, either with Maggie or with wanting to gamble—"call me."

Kyle nodded, already moving toward the door.

"I mean it," Derek said loudly, following him.

Kyle turned and gave him a little shove in the shoulder. "I promise. Now fuck off."

Derek grinned. "You first."

Kyle practically ran up the road to the parking lot, where Hayden was waiting for him. Shit, he'd forgotten all about Hayden.

Hayden leaned his head out the car window. "Where've you been? I was about to put out an APB."

"Listen, can you catch a ride with Derek and Chloe to the winery? I need your car."

Confusion clouded Hayden's eyes. "Uh, I guess?"

Kyle opened the door for him, anxious to be on his way. He resisted the urge to pull Hayden out of the car, jump inside, and tear out of the lot like he was commandeering his vehicle and taking off on a hot pursuit.

Derek pulled into the lot—he'd parked down by the cottage—and rolled down his window. "You're coming with us, Hayden."

Kyle sent Derek a silent thank-you and a wave.

Hayden finally got out of the car, leaving the door open. "Where are you going?"

"See you in a bit." Kyle jumped into the car and fired it up, then sped out of the lot only slightly less chaotically than he'd envisioned.

Apprehension, excitement, anticipation—all of it bubbled inside of him. He likened the feeling to when he went to the racetrack or the casino or a poker game, but it was so much better. Maggie was an addiction he didn't want to fight, and he hoped she felt the same way about him.

Chapter Twenty

As MAGGIE FINISHED watering her garden, she softly apologized to the plants for neglecting them a little this week. "But don't worry. I'm done with those hectic hours." She ran a finger over one of the ripening tomatoes and felt a pang of sadness over the loss of Kyle's salsa.

"Will they be ready in another week maybe?"

Kyle's voice seemed to come from somewhere inside of her. Had she been thinking about him so hard and for so long that she now imagined she heard him?

"Eh, maybe closer to ten days."

This time she swung around.

Kyle held up his hands. "Are you going to drench me again? Please don't, I spent a lot of time on this outfit."

And he looked gorgeous. He wore a black button-down with the sleeves rolled up and a pair of dark blue jeans that hugged his thighs in just the right way. But on his feet were one of his many pairs of flip-flops. You could take the man off the beach, but you apparently couldn't take his shoes.

She felt plain and disheveled, though she'd showered when she got home. After that, she'd wound her hair up on top of her head, donned a pair of cut-off shorts that looked like they could be in her mother's closet, and she hadn't stopped there—she'd put on a tank top *without a bra*. And she realized it wasn't the first time as she recalled the night after the accident at the clinic.

She lowered the hose. "Sorry. You look really nice. Why aren't you at the rehearsal dinner?"

"I'm on my way."

She frowned. "This is not remotely on your way."

He chuckled as he moved toward her. "Ah, Maggie, I will never get tired of looking at these little worry lines." He smoothed his thumb between her eyes and drew it up over her forehead. Then his touch was gone, and she had to keep herself from swaying toward him.

She shook herself. "Why are you here?"

"Because I can't stop thinking about you. Wanting you. Loving you." He lightly touched her upper arms. "I pick my family *and* you."

Had he said loving? She couldn't form words and just stood there staring at him like an idiot.

He wrapped his hands around her biceps and stroked her warm skin. "It was never about you. It seemed like it was—to both of us. But I was worried they would hate me, not you. I would never let them hate you. Not when I love you so very much."

She let out a sound that was somewhere between a sob and an inhalation of disbelief, but she quickly clapped her hand over her mouth.

He moved closer until he was all she could see and smell and touch—if she wanted to. And oh, how she wanted to. But she didn't. Not yet. She was too afraid this was all a dream.

"I...I love you, too."

He exhaled with what sounded like relief. His lips curved up. "Thank God. Derek said you probably did, but you broke up with me, so I wasn't sure."

She looked up at him and allowed herself to fall into his gaze. "I thought it was the right thing to do. You're dealing with a lot."

His hands stilled against her flesh. "So, you didn't really want to break up?"

She shook her head. "No. Like I said, I was just trying to do the right thing."

His arms came around her, and he snatched her up against his chest. "You are the most amazing woman. I am completely yours—to have, to hold, to do whatever you want with." His lips covered hers in a searing kiss.

She clutched him tightly, her body awash with sensation and longing and a joy she'd never known. They kissed like it was the first time or maybe the last. God no, she hoped it wouldn't be the last. No, she *knew* it wouldn't.

She broke away, gasping. "I don't understand how this is going to work. What about your family?"

"What about them? I'm not hiding anymore—not who I am and not who I love. I came to take you to the rehearsal dinner with me."

She pushed away from him. "No, no. I can't do that."

"Yes, you can."

She waved her hand at him and then bent to pick up the spray nozzle. "No." She walked the hose back to the spigot on the house. "I love that you want to take me public, but not at the rehearsal dinner."

He walked behind her. "Why not? It's a joyous occasion. They're inclined to be in a good mood."

She wound the hose around its hook. "Which is why it's a terrible idea. I don't want to ruin Derek and Chloe's moment."

"Derek knows you're coming."

She snapped her head up to look at him in surprise. "He does?"

Kyle nodded. "He might not know exactly who you are, but I prepped him…a little. He'll support me. And so will everyone else."

She finished winding the hose. "Including your parents?"

He took her hands in his. "Maggie, trust me. It's going to work out."

She shook her head. "I do trust you, but I can't do this tonight. Look at me. I am so not ready for a dinner."

"So go upstairs and change. I'll help." His gaze dropped to her breasts. "Although, I enjoy this look. Very, very sexy."

Heat pooled in her core. "Stop it. You're not helping."

"I'm not?" He sidled closer to her and kissed her jaw, bringing his hand up to cup her breast. His thumb and finger teased her nipple until it was rock hard. "Oh yeah, I could get used to this access."

She skipped away from him toward the house. "You need to go. You're the best man now. You can't miss the rehearsal dinner."

He followed her inside. "I'm not going to. And I'm sure as hell not going without my date."

She scooped up the glass of chardonnay she'd poured earlier and took a hearty, bolstering swallow. "What exactly do you plan to do? Just waltz in and introduce me as Alex's therapist?"

"No. I'm going to introduce you as my girlfriend, Maggie Trent, aka Magnolia the Amazing Landscape Designer Who Totally Saved Our Bacon."

She couldn't resist a smile at that. "I didn't do it to score points."

"I know you didn't, and I'll make sure they'll know it, too." He came toward her, his heart in his eyes. "Tell me what I have to do to get you to come. I'll do whatever it takes. I'll scream your name from the mountaintops and tell everyone who cares—and even those who don't—how much I love you and how I can't live without you."

She sucked in a breath, her heart feeling as though it were fifteen sizes too large for her chest. "You can't live without me?"

He shook his head. "I tried. For three miserable days. I can't do it."

He'd been miserable? So had she. But misery could do things to him that it wouldn't necessarily do to her. "Did you gamble?"

"No, but I thought about it. A lot. I even went to a GA meeting."

"You did? That's great." She held up her hand. "Wait. Here we go again. I can't be your counselor."

He cupped her face. "You can't help who you are, and that's an extraordinarily caring person who tends to react emotionally. That I get to be at the center of that is incredibly humbling and makes me feel like the luckiest person on earth. You aren't my therapist. You're my partner. At least that's how I see you. The question is whether you can get that out of your head. Can you see me as just a man and not a project in need of fixing? Can you see past my compulsion, my addiction, and all of my other imperfections?"

Partner. She'd never had one of those before. She liked that. "No, *I'm* the luckiest person on earth. You aren't perfect, but who is? Certainly not me, and yet you make me feel like I'm Wonder Woman. Without the golden lasso."

He grinned. "I'd sure like to see you in a Wonder Woman outfit. Think we can make that happen?"

She laughed, the sound building from her chest and warming every part of her. "I'm not sure I'd fill it out the same way."

He ran his hands under the hem of her tank, skimming them up her rib cage until he'd pushed the fabric to her breasts. "I beg to differ. You'd fill it out just fine." He stroked his thumbs over her nipples, sending shocks of desire ricocheting through her.

She looked at him through narrowed eyes. "We are never going to make it to the rehearsal dinner if you don't stop that."

His hands stilled. "Does that mean you're coming?"

She arched a brow at his choice of words, and he responded with a wicked smile.

He drew the tank over her head. "Upstairs. *Now*."

She spun on her heel and dashed to the stairs. "I need to get dressed. You stay here."

"Not a chance." He chased her up to the bedroom and tackled her to the bed.

She already had her shorts undone and was wriggling out of them as he kicked his shoes off. She tore at the buttons of his shirt, but his fingers knocked hers away. "Careful," he said, "I need to put this back on. Don't even think about sabotaging tonight."

"Then you better shut up and make this quick if you want to get there."

His mouth crushed down on hers in the hottest kiss she'd ever received. She helped him push his shirt off and giggled as he took extra care to lay it gently on the floor. He wasn't so meticulous with his jeans, thank goodness. He pulled them off as fast as possible, taking his boxer briefs with them. But before he dropped them, he snagged a condom from the pocket.

She reached between them and stroked his cock as he worked to get the condom on.

"Will you stop?" he said. "Now who's not helping?"

She giggled. "Sorry, it's been a few days."

"More than that." He stroked her folds. "God, you are so wet."

She pushed up into him, losing all semblance of humor as desire pulsed through her core. "Kyle," she breathed, needing him.

He plunged into her, sheathing himself to the hilt for a long, delicious moment before he began to move. His fingers continued their maddening work, focused intently on her clit, driving her so fast to the brink of orgasm. It was good they had to be fast, as she didn't want to prolong this. She wanted satisfaction, and she wanted it *now*.

He pummeled her with swift, almost brutal strokes, but she wanted every single one of them with a ferocity that might've scared her if she hadn't had the emotion to match her lust.

She pulled his head down. "I love you so much." She kissed him, drawing his tongue into her mouth as surely as she was drawing his cock into her body, her heels pressing against his ass. Her orgasm shattered through her as he gripped her hip and drove into her hard and deep.

He pulled back from her kiss and shouted his own release, his muscles clenching. They rode the storm until sanity seemed to finally reenter the room. He rolled away from her and flung his arm over his forehead. "Damn, Maggie."

She was already bounding out of the bed and heading toward her closet. "What should I wear? You're in jeans... but it's at least semidressy? Sundress?"

"Whatever. I can't move."

She laughed. "You better, because I'm not going alone." In her partially organized closet, she hesitated. What was she thinking? Just because she and Kyle were good—way better than good—could she really intrude on their family event right now?

She ran her fingers over a few dresses but didn't pull anything out. A few minutes later, Kyle came in fully dressed.

"Hey," he said, "can't decide?"

She shot him a timid look. "Lost my courage."

"No, no, no." He gathered her into his arms. "You have plenty of courage, and if you don't, you can have some of mine. Everything is going to be fine. Worst-case scenario, they throw me out of the family and it's their loss. I have a family right here." He tipped her chin up and looked into her eyes. "Right?"

She'd never loved anyone more than in that moment. "Right."

"I love you, Maggie Trent, and tonight everyone is going to know it."

Chapter Twenty-One

THE PERSON WHO met them at the entry of the winery informed them that dinner was already being served. Now their entrance was going to be especially conspicuous, not that Kyle wanted to sneak in. Okay, maybe he wanted to sneak in, but wasn't it better to just rip the Band-Aid off?

He squeezed Maggie's hand. "Ready?"

"No."

He pressed a quick kiss on her cheek. "We'll be fine."

He led her up the stairs to the event space and paused when they reached the top. The room was large, with a massive stone hearth and windows on two walls that offered a panoramic view of the vineyard and the sun sinking behind the hills in glorious reds, oranges, and purple. Two long, rectangular tables took up more than half the space.

Derek, seated at the head of one table, caught sight of him and smiled. He gestured for them to join him—there were two empty seats on his left, while Chloe was on his right.

Kyle took in the array of people—Archers, Chloe's friend and family, and a handful of other people, including George, an old family friend and the bartender at The Arch and Vine. Maybe thirty people in total. Way more of an audience than he wanted for announcing the identity of his new girlfriend. He didn't want to hide her, but he also didn't want to create a spectacle if his family reacted poorly.

He guided Maggie to the table and leaned down to whisper. "I'll introduce you after, when it's just my family. If that's okay."

She nodded quickly, and he guessed she would've been happy to put it off indefinitely. But they both knew that wasn't an option. The longer they waited, the harder it would be and the more unfair it was to his family to be kept in the dark.

Chloe smiled at them as they took their seats. "Magnolia, I'm so glad you came."

"Please, call me Maggie," she said, tossing Kyle a glance.

He nodded imperceptibly. They *should* get to know her as Maggie.

Sara was on the other side of Chloe. "Does this mean you're 'official' now?" She looked between Maggie and Kyle with a sly smile.

"Yes," Kyle said. "Maggie and I have been seeing each other for a few weeks." Was that all it had been? It felt so much longer. In fact, he had trouble imagining what life felt like without her in it. That wasn't precisely true—he'd gotten a good look at that the past few days, and he'd hated it.

Sara grinned. "Awesome." She held up her glass of white wine in a toast.

Derek poured red wine for Kyle and Maggie. "Cameron opened the library for tonight—this is a three-hundred-dollar bottle of wine."

"Is that all?" Kyle asked, taking a sip. The pinot noir was delicious, and more importantly, it took the edge off his nerves. He took a deeper drink.

A server brought them salads. "I'll catch you up to the entrée, no rush." She smiled. "Cracked pepper?"

"Please," Kyle said, as Maggie shook her head.

"So, how'd you guys meet?" Derek asked.

Shit. He exchanged worried glances with Maggie. "Uh, it's a good story. I'll tell you later. When there are less people."

Derek arched a brow. "Sounds interesting. Or maybe R-rated."

Maggie let out a laugh that drew a few heads to turn. She blushed. "Uh, no. But that was funny." She looked down and attacked her salad.

They managed to make it through dinner and keep the conversation light, deflecting incriminating questions with humor and in some cases outright evasion. Derek watched them with curiosity but didn't press for information.

During dessert, people made toasts and told stories about Derek and Chloe. Kyle shared the infamous story of their tenth birthday party, which had been filmed for the reality show. In it, the Archers' backyard had been turned into a mini-carnival, complete with pony rides. Derek had been one of several guests, but he'd stolen the show when he'd freaked out while riding a pony—which he'd only done after Kyle had bet him a hundred dollars. That was before they'd become friends. Derek had fallen off the pony into the swimming pool in spectacular fashion.

"It wouldn't have been such a dramatic display if you hadn't pretended you couldn't swim," Kyle said.

Derek laughed. "I had to get back at you somehow, right? You were supposed to get in trouble."

"I did! Plus, I had to pay you a hundred bucks." Kyle hadn't realized it, but apparently he'd always had a penchant for gambling, even at ten years old.

"Which I then had to donate to the local animal shelter—my mom wasn't too happy with me either."

"But it made for awesome TV," Hayden said, laughing.

After a while, people began to make their departures. Kyle stood up and tapped a spoon against his glass. "Could the Archer folks hang out for a few minutes?"

Sara looked at him with wide eyes. "Are you making an announcement?" Her gaze flicked to Maggie.

Kyle got her meaning and laughed. "Yes, but not *that* one."

"Oh." Sara looked somewhere between relieved and disappointed.

As people left, Kyle drew Sara over to the windows. "I'm about to become the least popular that I've ever been. I hope you won't hate me—"

Sara crossed her arms and squeezed her muscles in a sensory response. "You're freaking me out."

"Don't. It's not the end of the world—in fact, it's the start of a whole new one. For me."

She exhaled. "Okay. I can't imagine why anyone would hate you for being happy."

Put like that, Kyle wondered how that could happen, too. But then again, they'd vilified him for moving to Florida and enjoying a life there, so he really thought that anything could happen.

At last, they were alone—just the Archers, plus Chloe and Dylan.

Dad came over to the windows, where they'd all gathered close to Kyle and Sara, though Evan hung back a little, which wasn't surprising. "What's this about, son?"

Maggie had been chatting with Tori and now made her way to Kyle. He took her hand and gave her a reassuring smile.

"I wanted to officially introduce you all to my girlfriend. You met her as Magnolia, but she prefers to go by Maggie. Maggie Trent."

Kyle scanned their faces and could instantly see who recognized her name: Sara, Derek, Tori, and Mom, who'd gone completely pale. Thankfully, Sara was next to her, and she took her hand in a firm grip.

The room was silent for a moment. Liam was the first to speak. "Why was that a bombshell? I feel like the only one on the outside of the joke."

"There's no joke," Hayden said darkly, apparently remembering the name at last. "Maggie Trent was Alex's therapist."

Dad's inhalation sounded like a gunshot. "Kyle. What are you doing?"

Kyle felt Maggie tense and squeezed her hand. "I went to Maggie for help in finding who had sold Alex the drugs he took. She was very helpful, actually." He glanced at her, hating the uncertainty and fear in her eyes, but pressed onward. "I'll admit I wasn't predisposed to like her, but life has a funny sense of humor, and not only did I like her, I fell in love with her."

Mom covered her mouth with her hand and shook her head. Sara put her arm around her shoulders and drew her close. She gave Kyle a stern look but quickly softened it. "You didn't mean to."

Kyle frowned, his hackles rising. "And I'm not sorry for it, either."

Liam held up his hand. "Let me get this straight, you fell for Alex's therapist and now you want us all to congratulate you and welcome her into the fold?"

Kyle wasn't sure if Liam was asking a legitimate question or being a smart-ass. He would've assumed the latter, but his tone was practically genuine. "I'm introducing my girlfriend. I get that you all need time to get used to the idea of who she is, but it shouldn't matter. She isn't to blame for Alex's death. None of us are."

"Wow, this is a new level of jackassery, even for you." Liam shook his head.

Derek glared at Liam. "Shut it." He looked at Kyle, and there was sympathy in his gaze. "It's a bit of a shock, but you're right. She isn't to blame for Alex's death."

"Thank you." Maggie sounded small and scared. She cleared her throat. "For what it's worth, I cared a great deal for Alex, and if I could go back in time, I would. I had no idea he was suicidal."

"And why was that?" Dad said angrily. "You're a god-damned professional."

Kyle pulled Maggie closer to his side. "Dad, Alex hid what he was planning from everyone. Not even Aubrey knew what he was doing, and she set up the trust."

"He's right," Hayden said, clasping Dad's shoulder. "I know we want someone to blame, but that's solely on Alex. And since he's not here, it's been easy to direct our anger and hurt at the people who are. Some of us were pretty awful to Aubrey at first." He threw an accusing look at Liam, who'd been the most vocal about question-ing what Aubrey knew before Alex's death.

"Hey, I wasn't the only one," Liam said.

"So you…knew him," Tori said softly, drawing every-one to look at her. She and Maggie had something in common, Kyle realized. Tori tended to react emotionally, just like Maggie did. "But you probably can't share any-thing with us." Of all of them, Tori seemed the most hurt by Alex's actions. But then, she was a one-woman fix-it machine. There was no problem too big to handle, no crisis that couldn't be managed. That Alex would choose death over life absolutely confounded her.

"Yes, and I liked him a lot. I was shocked when he died. Utterly shocked." The sadness and regret in Mag-gie's tone were unmistakable.

Kyle hoped they could see that she'd been as affected as they had. "I'm not sure it's possible to feel as guilty as Maggie did. She had a breakdown and had to quit practicing for a few months."

Mom made a sound in her throat. She narrowed her eyes. "Forgive us if we don't feel sorry for her."

"I didn't tell you that to encourage your pity," Kyle said, trying not to become frustrated, especially in the face of his mother's anger. Her opinion meant everything to him, and if she couldn't accept Maggie...he didn't want to contemplate that. "I wanted you to maybe understand her perspective."

"It's going to take time, Kyle," Hayden said. "You get that, right?"

"I do."

"Why'd you have to do this now?" Liam asked. "Great timing with the wedding. You couldn't have waited until next week?"

Kyle flexed his free hand in an effort to expel his growing irritation. He speared Liam with a frank glare. "When you've gone back to Denver so you wouldn't have to deal with it?"

Liam gave a little shrug, clearly communicating his unspoken answer: *Yeah, that would've suited me fine.*

Telling himself to ignore Liam, Kyle squeezed Maggie's hand again, this time for himself. He looked around at all of them. "I wanted to talk to you about more than this. I'm through hiding who I am, and that means introducing you to the woman I love and telling you that

I'm"—he took a deep breath to try to calm his suddenly racing heart—"a gambling addict."

MAGGIE WAS SURE you could've heard a pin drop. Two bombshells in one night seemed excessive, but she understood why he'd done it. He wanted to own who he was, and she couldn't have been prouder of him.

"I need a chair," Kyle's mom said, looking nearly as pale as when Kyle had said Maggie's full name.

Evan, who was closest to the table, grabbed a chair and helped Emily sit.

Derek leaned toward Kyle and whispered, "Don't you think *that* could've waited?"

"It had to be done," Kyle responded in a low tone. "I don't mean to shock you, Mom, or anyone else, but I wanted to say this to all of you, and I don't know when we'll be together again. And tomorrow is Chloe and Derek's day."

"I'd argue right now is still their day," Liam said. Maggie had never met him, but when she recalled what she knew of him from Alex and his behavior tonight, she sort of wanted to kick him in the balls.

"Liam, you'd argue about the color of the sky." Rob's angry comment drew everyone's attention. "Give your brother some respect here."

Emily looked up at her husband. "Did you know?"

Rob nodded, his face tensing. "I did."

"My goodness, Rob, I wonder what else you're keeping from me." She glared at him before turning to look at Kyle. "Is that why you left before?"

"Yes. I got into some trouble. But I've sought some help, and I'm doing better now."

Hayden rubbed his eyes. "I can't even get my head around this. Maybe it's the jet lag." He blinked several times. "So is Maggie your therapist or something?"

Maggie nearly choked on the air she'd just inhaled.

"No, she's no longer practicing. As you saw, she's a fantastic landscape architect." He flashed her a warm smile that helped ease her raging nerves.

"Who else knew?" Sara's question was tentative. Dylan had his arm around her while she fidgeted with a bracelet. Maggie knew about her sensory processing disorder and from her own professional training recognized that she was having trouble regulating.

"Just Dad and Derek. I didn't want to upset you, Sara-cat."

Maggie heard the anguish in Kyle's voice and put her other hand over the back of his, holding him between her palms.

"I could've handled it," Sara said. "I wish you would've trusted me."

"It's not about you," Maggie said, unable to keep from both defending the man she loved and giving her professional input. "It's about Kyle's inability to be honest with himself and with you."

"She's right," Kyle said. "I left because Derek found out and told Dad. I was pissed and hurt and most of all, embarrassed. The only thing I had left was my pride, and even that had taken a massive hit. The only thing I could think to do was leave."

Derek set his hand on Kyle's shoulder. "We get it. At least, *I* get it. The others will, too." He looked at everyone else. "He needs our support, not our criticism or judgment. We're a family, and we look out for each other—in good times and especially in bad."

Sara took a deep breath. "You're right." She wiped a finger over her eye and blinked. "I'm here for you, Kyle. Whatever you need." She went to him and gave him a hug.

Kyle let go of Maggie and hugged Sara back. Maggie was glad for this positive reaction, but without his touch, she felt alone and threatened, like a boat stranded among a sea of sharks.

Sara and Kyle broke apart, and she turned to Maggie. "I'm so glad you're with my brother. I can already see you've had a good influence."

Maggie was flummoxed by Sara's kindness. As much as they might talk about there not being blame, she still struggled with guilt over Alex's death, and maybe she always would. "Thanks." She looked around at all of them. "I just want you to know that I love Kyle so very much. In a way, it feels to me like maybe Alex brought us together. That maybe our finding each other through him was fate. I'm incredibly grateful to him for bringing Kyle into my life."

Kyle turned to look at her, love shining in his blue-green eyes. "I hadn't even thought of it that way, but you're absolutely right."

A peace settled over Maggie, and she knew in that moment that whatever happened, she'd be okay. "I know it's going to take time for all of you to adjust and accept me—but I hope you will. I'll wait as long as it takes."

Kyle put his arm around her. "I may not be quite so patient. As you can see, I'm pretty anxious to get on with my life."

"Clearly," Hayden said, half-smiling for a brief moment before becoming serious again. "What about the gambling? What do you need us to do?"

"Just understand and support me. I'll be going to Gamblers Anonymous meetings—which I did in Florida. And I'm going to find a therapist who isn't Maggie."

"Good call," Derek said. "And I don't mean offense by that," he rushed to add. "Just that you being a couple and all, seems like you're already playing the role of therapist."

Chloe smacked him on the arm. "Are you saying that's our job as women?"

Derek laughed, rubbing his bicep. "Ouch, no. Kyle's just a handful." He winked at Kyle. "All right, people, I need to get my bride home—to the Archer house, I guess—so she can get the beauty sleep she doesn't really need." He hugged Kyle and then surprised Maggie by hugging her, too. "Welcome to the family."

Everyone slowly began filtering out, even Liam, who—to his credit—came over and spent a few minutes talking to her while Kyle was speaking with his parents. "I suppose you know all sorts of nasty secrets about us," he said.

"Not as many as you might think." *And mostly about you.*

"What…what was he like?" The question threw her off guard. He asked it with an intensity and a vulnerability that rattled her.

"Funny—he had a very dry sense of humor. Smart, thoughtful, though I know that must sound bizarre given his actions. He spoke very highly of his family."

Liam's expression turned skeptical. "I doubt that included me. He wasn't angry?"

Maggie considered whether she should answer that. She'd already shared more than she ought, but did it really matter? She wasn't a practicing counselor anymore, and Alex was dead. If she meant to have a relationship with Kyle and his family—and she did—couldn't she share certain things? *Not everything*, she thought, especially with Liam. "Yes, he was. He hated his condition. He struggled with anger management and depression. I thought we were making progress." The familiar wave of emotion crept over her, but she swallowed it back. "I was wrong."

"For what it's worth, I don't think it mattered," he said flatly. "I'm sure you did your best. Alex had a plan, and he was going to execute it no matter what. I know that like I know myself."

He was absolutely correct. Alex had possessed a singular drive, but so many of the things he'd wanted to accomplish were physical and therefore beyond his reach. In this, he was able to dream big—establish this trust, draw his family home again, and provide a legacy that would last a lifetime and beyond.

"Will you ever come back—permanently?" she asked, knowing that had been one of the most important things to Alex, even though he'd never said so.

"I doubt it. Not to live, anyway. But I pop up all the time. I'll be back in a few weeks to run Hood to Coast, and then I'll head up to Washington for the Dave Matthews Band shows." He smiled. "That's my annual end-of-summer Northwest jaunt."

"So I'll see you then?"

"You'll see me tomorrow." He shook her hand and left, leaving her to reflect on the fact that Liam Archer was a very complicated person—so much like Alex.

Maggie joined Kyle with his parents. Both of them eyed her dubiously. They'd met earlier in the week, but now that they knew who she really was, Maggie was suffused with anxiety.

His mom spoke first. "I'm happy you have a girlfriend, Kyle. I don't remember you ever having a real girlfriend before."

Kyle slid his arm around Maggie's waist, giving her some much-needed comfort. "Because I haven't." He looked at her. "Never had a reason to until now."

His mother's features softened. "I want to be upset about this, but I just can't be. I've spent too many months in darkness, and I don't want to go back. We'll figure this out, Maggie." She took Maggie's hand between hers and gave it a gentle squeeze. Then she turned and left, leaving them alone with Rob.

"Is she going without you?" Kyle asked.

His dad nodded, looking weary. "She's pretty mad at me right now. I told her about your granddad the other day, and now this. She thinks I'm keeping secrets and is wondering about our entire marriage—what else I've kept from her." He shook his head. "Never mind, that's our problem. I'm glad you came clean tonight, son."

"Thanks. You encouraged me to do it—about the gambling and Maggie. You have to know, Dad, I was so worried about how you would take this. It's important to me that you're okay with it, but at the end of the day, I'm going to choose her. I love her."

Maggie's heart swelled, but she also held her breath.

Dad pressed his lips together. "You never knew this, but my folks weren't always a huge fan of your mother's. And no, that's not a secret. She's well aware of that. Your mother broke up with someone in order to date me, and the way it went down...well, this is a small town; people talk. My parents came around eventually—I didn't give them any choice. So I can't fault you. I won't." Rob's eyes crinkled at the corners as his face relaxed into an almost smile. "I can already see that she's good for you." He looked at Maggie. "Keep him in line, no matter what."

She tucked her hand around Kyle's waist. "I will."

Rob and Kyle hugged, and then Rob left. The tension whooshed out of her like a balloon going flat. Kyle took her hand. "That wasn't so bad, was it?"

"Better than a firing squad."

He laughed. "That's not a good comparison. What were you and Liam talking about? Was he being a dick?"

"Actually, no. We were talking about Alex. There are a lot of unresolved issues there."

"Yeah, I suspected there would be. They always had this weird twin thing—very push-pull. The six of us sort of had our pairings—me and Sara, Tori and Evan, and then Alex and Liam. Except it wasn't the same. It was a love-hate relationship, if you really want to know."

"I know I'm not supposed to reveal things, but I can tell you, right? You're my boyfriend."

A sexy smile spread over his face, lighting his eyes. "Absolutely. Of course you can tell me things. And my lips are sealed." He zipped his fingers over his mouth.

"Alex talked about all of you, but it was the conversations about Liam that stuck with me the most—the competition he felt, the inadequacy, the utter depression he struggled with over not being like Liam."

"Wow." Kyle's eyes darkened. "You can't ever tell him that."

"I know—and you can't either."

"In the vault." He pulled her against him and stroked her back. "I want you to tell me anything and everything. I don't want any secrets like my parents."

She tipped her head back and looked up at him. "That's going to take effort. You're a guy who likes to keep things close."

"Not as close as I like to keep you." He brushed a kiss against her forehead before notching her chin up and claiming her mouth.

She sighed into him, twining her arms around his neck and kissing him back. When they broke apart, she gazed up at him with love and joy, so ready for the future awaiting them. "Keep me as close as you like—in fact, don't ever let me go."

Epilogue

KYLE COULDN'T REMEMBER a better day. The wedding reception was in full swing. The placed looked fantastic, especially the exterior lighting design Maggie had insisted they add. It allowed the guests to wander out to the garden and just enjoy the spectacular summer night. In fact, he saw Dylan and Sara doing just that.

Maggie came up behind him and slid her hands around his waist for a quick squeeze. "What are you looking at?"

He watched them curiously, a bead of apprehension wending down his spine. "My sister and her boyfriend. Out there at the pergola."

Maggie moved around him to look and gasped. "He's down on his knee."

"I see that." He smiled as he turned and gave Maggie a quick, fierce kiss. "Let's go congratulate them."

"Wait! Is she going to say yes?"

He stared at her like she'd grown a second head. "You've seen them together, right?"

She laughed. "Yes. Just give them a few minutes. Oh my goodness. He's putting a ring on it!" She clasped Kyle's arm and tried to turn him around. "We should give them privacy."

He resisted, his eyes glued to the romantic scene before him. "It's forty yards away. In the middle of a wedding reception. If he wanted privacy, he should've taken her to the underground tunnels."

"Good point." Maggie sidled up to him. "Maybe we should get popcorn."

Tori joined them, smoothing the skirt of her purple bridesmaid dress. "What are you guys staring at?"

Kyle's eyes misted. "I think our baby sister just got engaged. I have to say, I'm a little choked up. I guess she'll be the first of us Archer kids to get married."

Tori started coughing. She brought her hand to her mouth and tried to recover, but it became a full-blown fit.

Kyle patted her back. "You okay?"

"I'll get you some water," Maggie offered, disappearing.

"I'm fine," Tori wheezed. "Just inhaled a bug. Happens all the time when I run."

Kyle laughed as Maggie came back with a glass of water. "Here."

Tori took several gulps. "Thanks."

Kyle turned back toward the pergola in time to see Sara and Dylan coming toward them, both of them wearing the biggest shit-eating grins he'd ever seen. "Something you want to tell us?"

Sara's blue eyes rounded. "Did you see?"

"We did. It was quite a show." He wiped a finger under his eye and affected a mock-anguished voice. "You almost had me in tears, right, Tor?" He glanced back at his other sister, but she wasn't there. He looked at Maggie, who only shrugged in response.

"Was Tori here?" Sara asked. "Don't mind her. She's been in a mood all day. It's like she took an antilove pill this morning."

"Congratulations to both of you," Maggie said. "Can I hug you?"

"Of course!" Sara hugged her, laughing. "I don't know why I'm laughing. Just have to let the happiness out, I guess."

Kyle shook Dylan's hand. "Well done. I hope you asked Dad first."

Dylan chuckled. "I'm not stupid."

"Let me see the ring." Maggie grasped Sara's hand and held it up. "Oooh, so sparkly."

Kyle peered over at it and exhaled. "How are any of us going to live up to that?"

Dylan shrugged. "Not my problem." He put his arm around Sara. "We should go tell your mom."

She looked up at Dylan, her eyes practically glowing with love. "Yes, we should. See you guys!"

"Hey." Kyle stopped her with a quick, fierce hug. "I'm so happy for you, Sara-cat."

"Thanks."

Maggie twined her hand in his. "What do you think is up with Tori?"

"I don't know." He looked at her in question. "Have you talked to her?" He'd noticed that for the most part his family had been very welcoming to Maggie today, and he couldn't be more grateful.

"Not about anything important. I think I make her a little tentative. She has a lot of questions about Alex, and I think she's afraid to ask."

"Would you answer them?"

Late last night, after going back to her house, they'd discussed whether she ought to talk about Alex with the family. He understood there were things she didn't want to disclose, especially to Liam, but if she felt comfortable sharing information, he had no problem with it.

"I'm not sure. It depends on what they are, I suppose. I just sense that she's seeking some closure." She shook her head and looked down at the ground for a moment. "Sorry. I promise I'll stop therapizing someday. Hard habit to break. I need more landscape jobs to get my brain rewired."

He led her farther out into the garden, to a shadowed area, and drew her into his arms. "You're a caring, intuitive person, Maggie. Don't confuse that with being a therapist. And please don't rewire your brain. I love it just the way it is. I'm the one who needs fixing, remember?"

She slid her hands up his shirtfront. He'd long ago shucked his jacket, and now she was fiddling with his tie, which ignited his insatiable desire for her. "No, you don't. You're hilarious and thoughtful and sexy and perfect. For me. And I'm the only one who matters."

"Now *that* is very true. You told me once that I maybe didn't like myself very much, and you were right. But you taught me how to do that again, how to accept who I am and be comfortable—something I'm still working on."

"We're all still working on that," she said quietly but with infinite warmth. "We're all just works in progress, and we're lucky enough to have found each other for the journey."

His gaze connected with hers and held. As they stood on the edge of the hillside, the stars sprinkled above them in the ink-black sky, he thought of how miraculous it was that two beings could even find each other. From the corner of his eye, he saw a shooting star. He sucked in a breath. "Did you see that?"

"I did," she breathed, her head turned toward the sky where the streak had already faded.

"I was just thinking how lucky we are to have found each other. And I can't help but think that was Alex."

She said his name at the same moment he did. They faced each other, smiling.

"Thanks, bro," Kyle said just before his lips met Maggie's.

Don't miss the next Ribbon Ridge novel from
USA Today best-selling author
DARCY BURKE

The secret Tori Archer is running from
just might catch up with her in…

WHEN LOVE HAPPENS

Coming May 26 from Avon Impulse!

Acknowledgments

I KNOW so many people who have battled and continue to suffer from depression. This book is for you, and this is a fight you can win. Whether it's a temporary bout or a lifelong challenge, you are never alone. Help, support, understanding…it's all within reach, even from where you least expect it.

Thank you to my agent, Jim McCarthy, and my editor, Nicole Fischer, for loving this story. It was my first time jumping without a net, and I can't think of two better people to catch me.

I so appreciate my writing peeps, who also happen to be my very dear friends: Erica Ridley, Rachel Grant, Elisabeth Naughton, and Joan Swan. Thank you for the endless support. Special thanks to the lovely Kristina McMorris for our amazing weekend on Mt. Hood. It really jumpstarted this book and put me on a roll that thankfully didn't stop until I typed The End.

Hugs to my family for enduring a very stringent writing schedule. But hey, I managed to make dinner most weeknights (thank you for cooking on weekends, honey!) *and* help at school. I'll try to duplicate whatever I did that made this book work so well…wish me luck on that.

Thank You!

Thank you for reading *Yours to Hold*! I hope you're enjoying the Archer family as much as I am, and I hope you'll come back to Ribbon Ridge for Tori's story, *When Love Happens*.

Ribbon Ridge is a fictional town based on several cities and towns dotting the Willamette Valley between Portland and the Oregon Coast. It's pinot noir wine country, very beautiful and picturesque—and a short drive from where I live. My brother actually dwells right in the heart of it in a tiny town with no grocery store or traffic light. There is, however, an amazing antique mall in a historic schoolhouse.

Reviews help readers find books that are right for them. I hope you'll consider leaving an honest one on your preferred social media or review site.

Be sure to visit my Facebook page (http://www.facebook.com/DarcyBurkeFans) for the latest information, follow me on Twitter (@darcyburke), check out images of the northern Willamette Valley and other things that inspired this series on Pinterest (http://www.pinterest.com/darcyburkewrite), and sign up for my newsletter (http://www.darcyburke.com/newsletter/) so you'll know exactly when my next book is available.

Thank you again for reading and for your support!

About the Author

DARCY BURKE IS the *USA Today* best-selling author of hot, action-packed historical and sexy, emotional, contemporary romance. Darcy wrote her first book at age eleven, a happily ever after about a swan addicted to magic and the female swan that loved him, with exceedingly poor illustrations.

A native Oregonian, Darcy lives on the edge of wine country with her guitar-strumming husband, their two hilarious kids who seem to have inherited the writing gene, and two Bengal cats. In her "spare" time Darcy is a serial volunteer enrolled in a twelve-step program where one learns to say "no," but she keeps having to start over. She's also a fair-weather runner, and her happy places are Disneyland and Labor Day weekend at the Gorge.

Discover great authors, exclusive offers, and more at hc.com.

Give in to your impulses . . .
Read on for a sneak peek at six brand-new
e-book original tales of romance
from HarperCollins.
Available now wherever e-books are sold.

WHEN GOOD EARLS GO BAD
A Victorian Valentine's Day Novella
By Megan Frampton

THE WEDDING BAND
A Save the Date Novel
By Cara Connelly

RIOT
By Jamie Shaw

ONLY IN MY DREAMS
Ribbon Ridge Book One
By Darcy Burke

SINFUL REWARDS 1
A BILLIONAIRES AND BIKERS NOVELLA
By Cynthia Sax

TEMPT THE NIGHT
A TRUST NO ONE NOVEL
By Dixie Lee Brown

An Excerpt from

WHEN GOOD EARLS GO BAD
A Victorian Valentine's Day Novella
by Megan Frampton

Megan Frampton's *Dukes Behaving Badly* series
continues, but this time it's an earl who's meeting
his match in a delightfully fun and sexy novella!

"While it's not precisely true that nobody is here, because I am, in fact, here, the truth is that there is no one here who can accommodate the request."

The man standing in the main area of the Quality Employment Agency didn't leave. She'd have to keep on, then.

"If I weren't here, then it would be even more in question, since you wouldn't know the answer to the question one way or the other, would you? So I am here, but I am not the proper person for what you need."

The man fidgeted with the hat he held in his hand. But still did not take her hint. She would have to persevere.

"I suggest you leave the information, and we will endeavor to fill the position when there is someone here who is not me." Annabelle gave a short nod of her head as she finished speaking, knowing she had been absolutely clear in what she'd said. If repetitive. So it was a surprise that the man to whom she was speaking was staring back at her, his mouth slightly opened, his eyes blinking behind his owlish spectacles. His hat now held very tightly in his hand.

Perhaps she should speak more slowly.

"We do not have a housekeeper for hire," she said, pausing

between each word. "I am the owner, not one of the employees for hire."

Now the man's mouth had closed, but it still seemed as though he did not understand.

"I do not understand," he said, confirming her very suspicion. "This is an employment agency, and I have an employer who wishes to find an employee. And if I do not find a suitable person within . . ." and at this he withdrew a pocket watch from his waistcoat and frowned at it, as though it was its fault it was already past tea time, and *goodness, wasn't she hungry and had Caroline left any milk in the jug? Because if not, well,* "twenty-four hours, my employer, the Earl of Selkirk, will be most displeased, and we will ensure your agency will no longer receive our patronage."

That last part drew her attention away from the issue of the milk and whether or not there was any.

"The Earl of . . . ?" she said, feeling that flutter in her stomach that signaled there was nobility present or being mentioned—or she wished there were, at least. Rather like the milk, actually.

"Selkirk," the man replied in a firm tone. He had no comment on the milk. And why would he? He didn't even know it was a possibility that they didn't have any, and if she did have to serve him tea, what would she say? Besides which, she had no clue to the man's name; he had just come in and been all brusque and demanded a housekeeper when there was none.

"Selkirk," Annabelle repeated, her mind rifling through all the nobles she'd ever heard mentioned.

"A Scottish earl," the man said.

Annabelle beamed and clapped her hands. "Oh, Scottish! Small wonder I did not recognize the title, I've only ever been in London and once to the seaside when I was five years old, but I wouldn't have known if that was Scotland, but I am fairly certain it was not because it would have been cold and it was quite warm in the water. Unless the weather was unseasonable, I can safely say I have never been to Scotland, nor do I know of any Scottish earls."

An Excerpt from

THE WEDDING BAND
A Save the Date Novel
by Cara Connelly

In the latest *Save the Date* novel from Cara
Connelly, journalist Christina Case crashes a
celebrity wedding, and sparks fly when she comes
face-to-face with A-list movie star Dakota Rain . . .

Dakota Rain took a good hard look in the bathroom mirror and inventoried the assets.

Piercing blue eyes? Check.

Sexy stubble? Check.

Sun-streaked blond hair? Check.

Movie-star smile?

Uh-oh.

In the doorway, his assistant rolled her eyes and hit speed dial. "Emily Fazzone here," she said. "Mr. Rain needs to see Dr. Spade this morning. Another cap." She listened a moment, then snorted a laugh. "You're telling me. Might as well cap them all and be done with it."

In the mirror Dakota gave her his hit man squint. "No extra caps."

"Weenie," she said, pocketing her phone. "You don't have time today, anyway. Spade's squeezing you in, as usual. Then you're due at the studio at eleven for the voice-over. It'll be tight, so step on it."

Deliberately, Dakota turned to his reflection again. Tilted his head. Pulled at his cheeks like he was contemplating a shave.

Emily did another eye roll. Muttering something that

might have been either "Get to work" or "What a jerk," she disappeared into his closet, emerging a minute later with jeans, T-shirt, and boxer briefs. She stacked them on the granite vanity, then pulled out her phone again and scrolled through the calendar.

"You've got a twelve o'clock with Peter at his office about the Levi's endorsement, then a one-thirty fitting for your tux. Mercer's coming here at two-thirty to talk about security for the wedding . . ."

Dakota tuned her out. His schedule didn't worry him. Emily would get him where he needed to be. If he ran a little late and a few people had to cool their heels, well, they were used to dealing with movie stars. Hell, they'd be disappointed if he behaved like regular folk.

Taking his sweet time, he shucked yesterday's briefs and meandered naked to the shower without thinking twice. He knew Emily wouldn't bat an eye. After ten years nursing him through injuries and illness, puking and pain, she'd seen all there was to see. Broad shoulders? Tight buns? She was immune.

And besides, she was gay.

Jacking the water temp to scalding, he stuck his head under the spray, wincing when it found the goose egg on the back of his skull. He measured it with his fingers, two inches around.

The same right hook that had chipped his tooth had bounced his head off a concrete wall.

Emily rapped on the glass. He rubbed a clear spot in the steam and gave her the hard eye for pestering him in the shower.

She was immune to that too. "I asked you if we're looking at a lawsuit."

"Damn straight." He was all indignation. "We're suing The Combat Zone. Tubby busted my tooth and gave me a concussion to boot."

She sighed. "I meant, are *we* getting sued? Tubby's a good bouncer. If he popped you, you gave him a reason."

Dakota put a world of aggrievement into his Western drawl. "Why do you always take everybody else's side? You weren't there. You don't know what happened."

"Sure I do. It's October, isn't it? The month you start howling at the moon and throwing punches at bystanders. It's an annual event. The lawyers are on standby. I just want to know if I should call them."

He did the snarl that sent villains and virgins running for their mamas.

An Excerpt from

RIOT

by Jamie Shaw

Jamie Shaw's rock stars are back, and this time
wild, unpredictable Dee and sexy, mohawked
guitarist Joel have explosive chemistry—but will
jealousy and painful memories keep them apart?

"**K**iss me," I order the luckiest guy in Mayhem tonight. When he sat next to me at the bar earlier with his "Leave It to Beaver" haircut, I made sure to avoid eye contact and cross my legs in the opposite direction. I didn't think I'd end up making out with him, but now I have no choice.

A dumb expression washes over his face. He might be cute if he didn't look so. freaking. dumb. "Huh?"

"Oh for God's sake."

I curl my fingers behind his neck and yank him to my mouth, tilting my head to the side and hoping he's a quick learner. My lips part, my tongue comes out to play, and after a moment, he finally catches on. His greedy fingers bury themselves in my chocolate brown curls—which I spent *hours* on this morning.

Peeking out of the corner of my eye, I spot Joel Gibbon stroll past me, a bleach-blonde groupie tucked under his arm. He's too busy whispering in her ear to notice me, and my fingers itch to punch him in the back of his stupid mohawked head to get his attention.

I'm preparing to push Leave It to Beaver off me when Joel's gaze finally lifts to meet mine. I bite Beaver's bottom lip between my teeth and give it a little tug, and the corner of

Joel's mouth lifts up into an infuriating smirk that is *so* not the reaction I wanted. He continues walking, and when he's finally out of sight, I break my lips from Beaver's and nudge him back toward his own stool, immediately spinning in the opposite direction to scowl at my giggling best friend.

"I can't BELIEVE him!" I shout at a far-too-amused-looking Rowan. How does she not recognize the gravity of this situation?!

I'm about to shake some sense into her when Beaver taps me on the shoulder. "Um—"

"You're welcome," I say with a flick of my wrist, not wanting to waste another minute on a guy who can't appreciate how long it took me to get my hair to curl like this—or at least make messing it up worth my while.

Rowan gives him an apologetic half smile, and I let out a deep sigh.

I don't feel bad about Beaver. I feel bad about the dickhead bass guitarist for the Last Ones to Know.

"That boy is making me insane," I growl.

Rowan turns a bright smile on me, her blue eyes sparkling with humor. "You were already insane."

"He's making me homicidal," I clarify, and she laughs.

"Why don't you just tell him you like him?" She twirls two tiny straws in her cocktail, her eyes periodically flitting up to the stage. She's waiting for Adam, and I'd probably be jealous of her if those two weren't so disgustingly perfect for each other.

Last semester, I nearly got kicked out of my dorm when I let Rowan move in with me and my roommate. But Rowan's asshole live-in boyfriend had cheated on her, and she had nowhere to go, and she's been my *best* friend since kindergarten. I ignored the written warnings from my RA, and Rowan ultimately ended up moving in with Adam before I got kicked out. Fast forward to one too many "overnight visitors" later, I still ended up getting reported, and Rowan and I got a two-bedroom in an apartment complex near campus. Her name is on the lease right next to mine, but really, the apartment is just a decoy she uses to avoid telling her parents that she's actually living with three ungodly hot rock stars. She sleeps in Adam's bed, his bandmate Shawn is in the second bedroom, and Joel sleeps on their couch most nights because he's a hot, stupid, infuriating freaking nomad.

"Because I *don't* like him," I answer. When I realize my drink is gone, I steal Rowan's, down the last of it, and flag the bartender.

"Then why is he making you insane?"

"Because *he* doesn't like *me*."

Rowan lifts a sandy blonde eyebrow at me, but I don't expect her to understand. Hell, *I* don't understand. I've never wanted a boy to like me so badly in my entire life.

An Excerpt from

ONLY IN MY DREAMS
Ribbon Ridge Book One
by Darcy Burke

From a *USA Today* bestselling author
comes the first installment in a sexy and
emotional family saga about seven siblings
who reunite in a small Oregon town to
fulfill their brother's dying wish . . .

Sara Archer took a deep breath and dialed her assistant and close friend, Craig Walker. He was going to laugh his butt off when she told him why she was calling, which almost made her hang up, but she forced herself to go through with it.

"Sara! Your call can only mean one thing: you're totally doing it."

She envisioned his blue eyes alight with laughter, his dimples creasing, and rolled her eyes. "I guess so."

He whooped into the phone, causing Sara to pull it back from her ear. "Awesome! You won't regret it. It's been waaaaay too long since you got out there. What, four years?"

"You're exaggerating." More like three. She hadn't been out with a guy since Jude. Easy, breezy, coffee barista Jude. He'd been a welcome breath of fresh air after her cheating college boyfriend. Come to think of it, she'd taken three years to get back in the game then too.

"Am I? I've known you for almost three years, and you've never had even a casual date in all that time."

Because after she and Jude had ended their fling, she'd decided to focus on her business, and she'd hired Craig a couple of months later. "Enough with the history lesson. Let's talk about tonight before I lose my nerve."

"Got it. I'm really proud of you for doing this. You need a social life beyond our rom-com movie nights."

Sara suspected he was pushing her to go out because he'd started dating someone. They seemed serious even though it had been only a couple of weeks, and when you fell in love, you wanted the whole world to fall in love too. Not that Sara planned on doing that again—if she could even count her college boyfriend as falling in love. She really didn't know anymore.

"I was thinking I might go line dancing." She glanced through her clothing, pondering what to wear.

"Line dancing?" Craig's tone made it sound as if he were asking whether she was going to the garbage dump. He wouldn't have been caught dead in a country-western bar. "If you want to get your groove on, Taylor and I will come get you and take you downtown. Much better scene."

No, the nearby suburban country-western bar would suit her needs just fine. She wouldn't be comfortable at a chic Portland club—totally out of her league. "I'll stick with Sidewinders, thanks."

"We wouldn't take you to a gay bar," Craig said with a touch of exasperation that made her smile.

"I know. I just don't want company. You'd try to set me up with every guy in the place."

"I'm not that bad! Taylor keeps me in line."

Yeah, she'd noticed. She'd been out with them once and was surprised at the difference in Craig. He was still his energetic self, but it was like everything he had was focused on his new boyfriend. She supposed that was natural when a relationship was shiny and new. "Well, I'm good going by myself. I'm just going to dance a little, maybe sip a lemon drop, see what happens."

Craig made a noise of disgust. "Don't ass out, Sara. You need to get laid."

An Excerpt from

SINFUL REWARDS 1
A Billionaires and Bikers Novella
by Cynthia Sax

Belinda "Bee" Carter is a good girl; at least, that's
what she tells herself. And a good girl deserves
a nice guy—just like the gorgeous and moody
billionaire Nicolas Rainer. Or so she thinks,
until she takes a look through her telescope
and sees a naked, tattooed man on the balcony
across the courtyard. He has been watching
her, and that makes him all the more enticing.
But when a mysterious and anonymous text
message dares her to do something bad, she
must decide if she is really the good girl she has
always claimed to be, or if she's willing to risk
everything for her secret fantasy of being watched.

An Avon Red Impulse Novella

I'd told Cyndi I'd never use it, that it was an instrument purchased by perverts to spy on their neighbors. She'd laughed and called me a prude, not knowing that I was one of those perverts, that I secretly yearned to watch and be watched, to care and be cared for.

If I'm cautious, and I'm always cautious, she'll never realize I used her telescope this morning. I swing the tube toward the bench and adjust the knob, bringing the mysterious object into focus.

It's a phone. Nicolas's phone. I bounce on the balls of my feet. This is a sign, another declaration from fate that we belong together. I'll return Nicolas's much-needed device to him. As a thank you, he'll invite me to dinner. We'll talk. He'll realize how perfect I am for him, fall in love with me, marry me.

Cyndi will find a fiancé also—everyone loves her—and we'll have a double wedding, as sisters of the heart often do. It'll be the first wedding my family has had in generations.

Everyone will watch us as we walk down the aisle. I'll wear a strapless white Vera Wang mermaid gown with organza and lace details, crystal and pearl embroidery accents, the bodice fitted, and the skirt hemmed for my shorter height. My hair will be swept up. My shoes—

Voices murmur outside the condo's door, the sound piercing my delightful daydream. I swing the telescope upward, not wanting to be caught using it. The snippets of conversation drift away.

I don't relax. If the telescope isn't positioned in the same way as it was last night, Cyndi will realize I've been using it. She'll tease me about being a fellow pervert, sharing the story, embellished for dramatic effect, with her stern, serious dad—or, worse, with Angel, that snobby friend of hers.

I'll die. It'll be worse than being the butt of jokes in high school because that ridicule was about my clothes and this will center on the part of my soul I've always kept hidden. It'll also be the truth, and I won't be able to deny it. I am a pervert.

I have to return the telescope to its original position. This is the only acceptable solution. I tap the metal tube.

Last night, my man-crazy roommate was giggling over the new guy in three-eleven north. The previous occupant was a gray-haired, bowtie-wearing tax auditor, his luxurious accommodations supplied by Nicolas. The most exciting thing he ever did was drink his tea on the balcony.

According to Cyndi, the new occupant is a delicious piece of man candy—tattooed, buff, and head-to-toe lickable. He was completing armcurls outside, and she enthusiastically counted his reps, oohing and aahing over his bulging biceps, calling to me to take a look.

I resisted that temptation, focusing on making macaroni and cheese for the two of us, the recipe snagged from the diner my mom works in. After we scarfed down dinner, Cyndi licking her plate clean, she left for the club and hasn't returned.

Three-eleven north is the mirror condo to ours. I straighten the telescope. That position looks about right, but then, the imitation UGGs I bought in my second year of college looked about right also. The first time I wore the boots in the rain, the sheepskin fell apart, leaving me barefoot in Economics 201.

Unwilling to risk Cyndi's friendship on "about right," I gaze through the eyepiece. The view consists of rippling golden planes, almost like . . .

Tanned skin pulled over defined abs.

I blink. It can't be. I take another look. A perfect pearl of perspiration clings to a puckered scar. The drop elongates more and more, stretching, snapping. It trickles downward, navigating the swells and valleys of a man's honed torso.

No. I straighten. This is wrong. I shouldn't watch our sexy neighbor as he stands on his balcony. If anyone catches me . . .

Parts 1 – 8 available now!

An Excerpt from

TEMPT THE NIGHT
A Save the Date Novel
by *Dixie Lee Brown*

Dixie Lee Brown concludes her thrilling
Trust No One series with the fast-paced
tale of a damaged hero and the sexy
fugitive he can't help falling for.

She pursed her lips and studied him. "That's deep, Brady." A crooked grin gradually appeared, erasing the worry wrinkles from her forehead. Then, without any encouragement from him, Mac took a step closer and leaned into his chest, sliding her arms around his waist.

He hesitated only a second before wrapping her in his arms and pulling her close. A groan escaped him.

She shifted her head to glance up. "Do you mind?"

A soft chuckle vibrated through him. "Sugar, I'll hold you anytime, anywhere."

Mac snuggled closer, and he tipped her head with his fingers, slowly covering her mouth with his, giving her plenty of time to change her mind. When she didn't, he drank of her sweetness like a man dying of thirst. Again and again he kissed her, his tongue pushing into her mouth, swirling and dancing with hers. He couldn't get enough of her full, soft lips, her sweet taste, and the bold way she pressed against him.

Brady couldn't say which of the day's events was responsible for her change in temperature where he was concerned, but it wasn't important. They were taking steps in the right direction, and he wasn't going to do anything to screw that up. He wanted her warm and willing in his hands, but he also wanted her there for the right reasons. The decision was hers to make.

When he lifted his head, there were tears on her eyelashes, but her smile made his heart grab an extra beat. He let his fingers trail across the satin skin of her cheek as he kissed her neck tenderly and breathed in her sweet scent.

"God, you smell good." He kissed each of her closed eyes, then leaned his forehead on hers and took a deep breath. "I'd love for this to go on all night. Unfortunately, Joe wants us to meet with Maria." He steadied her as she straightened and took a step back.

Mac's gaze was uncertain. "We could meet later . . . if you want to . . ."

"Aw, sugar. If *I* want to? That's like asking if I want to keep breathing." He threaded his fingers through her hair and brushed his lips over hers. "I've wanted you since the first time you lied to me." Brady chuckled as her eyes lit up.

She punched his chest with a fisted hand. "Hey! That was the only time I lied, and I had a darn good reason. Some big galoot knocks me down, pounces on me, and then expects me to be truthful. Nuh uh. I don't think so." Her eyes sparkled with challenge.

"*Galoot*, huh? No more John Wayne movies for you, sugar."

She sucked in a big breath, and he could tell by the mischief in her eyes that she was getting ready to let him have it. He touched his fingers to her lips to silence her. "Let me say this, okay? There's a good chance we'll go in and meet with Maria, and sometime before, after, or during, you'll think about us—about me—and decide we're not a good idea. I want you to know two things. First . . . it's the best idea I've had in a long time. Second . . . if you decide it's a mistake or that you're not ready to get any closer, that's okay. No pressure."

He stepped back and gave her some room. It struck him that he'd just lied to her. What he said would have been true for any other woman he'd ever known, but he damn sure wasn't going to give up on Mac that easily.

A grin made the sparkle in her eyes dance as she slipped her hand into his. "Obviously you're confusing me with some other woman, because I don't usually change my mind once it's made up, and I'm a big girl, so you can stop worrying that your charm, good looks, and sex appeal will bowl me over. As for thinking about you—yeah." She stepped closer and lowered her voice to a silky whisper. "You might cross my mind once or twice . . . so let's get this meeting over with."

"You got it, sugar." Brady couldn't remember when he'd been so contented—or when he'd ever used that word to describe himself before. Whether or not tonight ended with him in bed with this amazingly beautiful and brave woman didn't really matter. The last few minutes had made it clear that his interest in her went way beyond just the prospect of sex. He wanted everything she had to give. *Shit!* She'd turned him upside down and inside out until he doubted his own ability to walk away . . . or even if he wanted to.